"Your parents' death was not your fault . . .

...But if you make yourself more than just a man...

...if you devote yourself to an ideal...

". . . then you become something else entirely."

"Which is?"

"A legend, Mr. Wayne."

THE ART AND

BATMAN BEGINS
Screenplay by Christopher Nolan and David S. Goyer
Story by David S. Goyer
Based upon Characters Appearing in Comic Books Published by DC Comics

THE DARK
Screenplay by Jonathan Nolan
Story by Christopher
Based upon Characters Appearing in

IGHT TRILOGY

Jody Duncan Jesser & Janine Pourroy
ABRAMS | NEW YORK

KNIGHT
and Christopher Nolan
Nolan & David S. Goyer
Comic Books Published by DC Comics
by Bob Kane

THE DARK KNIGHT RISES
Screenplay by Jonathan Nolan and Christopher Nolan
Story by Christopher Nolan & David S. Goyer
Based upon Characters Appearing in Comic Books Published by DC Comics
Batman created by Bob Kane

Art direction and design by CHIP KIDD

Alfred. Gordon. Lucius. Bruce... Wayne. Names that have come to mean so much to me. Today, I'm three weeks from saying a final good-bye to these characters and their world. It's my son's ninth birthday. He was born as the Tumbler was being glued together in my garage from random parts of model kits. Much time, many changes. A shift from sets where some gunplay or a helicopter were extraordinary events to working days where crowds of extras, building demolitions, or mayhem thousands of feet in the air have become familiar.

People ask if we'd always planned a trilogy. This is like being asked whether you had planned on growing up, getting married, having kids. The answer is complicated. When David and I first started cracking open Bruce's story, we flirted with what might come after, then backed away, not wanting to look too deep into the future. I didn't want to know everything that Bruce couldn't; I wanted to live it with him. I told David and Jonah to put everything they knew into each film as we made it. The entire cast and crew put all they had into the first film. Nothing held back. Nothing saved for next time. They built an entire city. Then Christian and Michael and Gary and Morgan and Liam and Cillian started living in it. Christian bit off a big chunk of Bruce Wayne's life and made it utterly compelling. He took us into a pop icon's mind and never let us notice for an instant the fanciful nature of Bruce's methods.

I never thought we'd do a second—how many good sequels are there? Why roll those dice? But once I knew where it would take Bruce, and when I started to see glimpses of the antagonist, it became essential. We reassembled the team and went back to Gotham. It had changed in three years. Bigger. More real. More modern. And a new force of chaos was coming to the

fore. The ultimate scary clown, as brought to terrifying life by Heath. We'd held nothing back, but there were things we hadn't been able to do the first time out—a Batsuit with a flexible neck, shooting on IMAX®. And things we'd chickened out on—destroying the Batmobile, burning up the villain's blood money to show a complete disregard for conventional motivation. We took the supposed security of a sequel as license to throw caution to the wind and headed for the darkest corners of Gotham.

I never thought we'd do a third—are there any great *second* sequels? But I kept wondering about the end of Bruce's journey, and once David and I discovered it, I had to see it for myself. We had come back to what we had barely dared whisper about in those first days in my garage. We had been making a trilogy. I called everyone back together for another tour of Gotham. Four years later, it was still there. It even seemed a little cleaner, a little more polished. Wayne Manor had been rebuilt. Familiar faces were back—a little older, a little wiser . . . but not all was as it seemed.

Gotham was rotting away at its foundations. A new evil bubbling up from beneath. Bruce had thought Batman was not needed any more, but Bruce was wrong, just as I had been wrong. The Batman had to come back. I suppose he always will.

Michael, Morgan, Gary, Cillian, Liam, Heath, Christian... Bale. Names that have come to mean so much to me. My time in Gotham, looking after one of the greatest and most enduring figures in pop culture, has been the most challenging and rewarding experience a filmmaker could hope for. I will miss the Batman. I like to think that he'll miss me, but he's never been particularly sentimental.

BY MICHAEL CAINE

One Sunday morning, the phone rang. It was Christopher Nolan. I said, "I am a big fan of yours," having seen two of his films, *Memento* and *Insomnia*—both very good small-production thrillers. I got very excited, as these are the types of productions I love best. He came to my house and gave me a script to read (though he took it away with him after I read it—Christopher is known to be very secretive about his work). The script wasn't the small-budget thriller I was expecting: It was *Batman Begins*. He asked me to play the butler, Alfred. I was then off on an adventure in a picture that would become the start of one of the biggest moneymaking series in movie history.

Working on a movie is all about people and how talented they are. On The Dark Knight Trilogy, we had an enormous team, everyone a professional.

Having worked with him on five movies, I can say that Christopher Nolan is a multitalented director on a par with Alfred Hitchcock, David Lean, and John Huston. Many years ago, I asked three directors "What is the art of directing?" David Lean said, "Being a great editor," which Christopher is superb at—he cuts in his head as he shoots. John Huston said, "Casting." Nolan's casting is perfect—just look at the cast list of the three Batman films. The third, Joe Mankiewicz, said "It's The Script, The Script, The Script." Christopher cowrote all of the brilliant scripts for The Dark Knight Trilogy. I think, because of these talents, you have the reason for the great success for this great

Christopher also belongs to an elite group of directors who can direct both action *and* actors. Here you have a director who can do both, which is very rare. And if you want to see the wide range of Nolan's talent, look at the incredible opening action sequence of *The Dark Knight*, and then watch the opening and closing speeches of Heath Ledger, who won an Oscar for his role as the Joker.

Christopher also works very closely with his wife, Emma Thomas, who has been a producer and coproducer on all his movies. (She has also produced his four children.) The atmosphere they create on their movies, apart from being brilliantly professional, is one of great relaxation, which is very important for me—I can't work from tension. Their on-set interaction with actors is quiet and knowledgeable; Christopher's handling of massive action sequences is extraordinary, but he is also a great Director of Actors.

One of the greatest things about this Batman series is that, in an age when fantastic computer and digital technology is available and used in most action movies, the stunts in The Dark Knight Trilogy are done by stuntmen, who give the effects a special appeal above most other big-production movies. It is all real action, not computer technology—except, of course, when we needed six million bats. Those were computer-generated. Christopher's strong preference for practical effects is why these films have a realism most

The camera crew, with my brilliant friend Wally Pfister, the stunt crew, and the special effects team must be among the best in the world. Add to this the spectacular design teams, sound and editing, and the extraordinary composers Hans Zimmer and James Newton Howard—Christopher and Emma brought all these extraordinary people together.

As you can see, I love working on these movies, and so did everyone else lucky enough to be involved.

The people who recognize me in the streets are now very young people who have seen The Dark Knight Trilogy. I used to be stopped for autographs by young girls wanting autographs for their mothers, but now, because of Batman, I am stopped by mothers wanting autographs for their children. At last, I've found some respect: I started off as "Alfie"—now, I'm known as "Alfred."

The Dark Knight wound up being the third highest-grossing picture of all time, and I had one of the greatest journeys of my life—not bad for a Sunday morning phone call.

I hope you enjoy our last effort in this series, *The Dark Knight Rises*.

A lifelong lover and aficionado of comic books, screenwriter David S. Goyer was a regular visitor to the comic book store situated not far from his home in Los Angeles. It was not a remarkable circumstance, then, when the store's manager noticed Goyer browsing the racks of the shop one day in early summer 2003. When he picked up more than the usual number of Batman graphic novels and comic books, however, the manager—with whom Goyer had a friendly relationship—became suspicious and began grilling him about his sudden renewed interest in the Caped Crusader. Goyer shrugged off the questions, but the store manager continued to press him. "Something's up," he said. "You're writing a new Batman movie, aren't you?" Goyer insisted that he was *not* writing a new Batman movie, quickly paid for his comics, and left the store.

In Hollywood, some lies are inevitable—and necessary.

In truth, Goyer had been meeting with filmmaker Christopher Nolan in a makeshift office in the director's garage for weeks, helping him to craft the story line for *Batman Begins*, a reboot of the Warner Bros. Batman franchise.

At the time that Nolan initiated talks with Warner Bros. about writing and directing a new Batman movie, the studio had completed a series of four big-budget Batman films—the first two directed by Tim Burton, and the second pair by Joel Schumacher—a scant five years before. It might have seemed a little soon to dip back into the Batman well, if not for the fact that Nolan, known for startlingly original films like *Memento* (2000), had a bold new vision for the franchise—a vision that he explored with David Goyer in his garage.

It was a humble beginning for The Dark Knight Trilogy, an epic series of films that would bring in billions of box-office dollars while thoroughly reenergizing and reimagining the super hero genre. The garage office was small and had the requisite pile of junk in one corner. It had no heating or air-conditioning. A washer and dryer stood at one side, and Nolan's cleaning lady would occasionally interrupt the creative process to throw in a load or two of laundry. The only piece of office furniture was an old partners desk at which the writers sat, facing each other as they argued over the developing story.

When they needed a break, Nolan and Goyer would take a walk, often strolling to the site of the Batcave from the '60s *Batman* television series—where Adam West and Burt Ward had been filmed racing out in the Batmobile—which was located just a few blocks from Nolan's home. The pair would eat lunch at a nearby diner, where their quiet but intense brainstorming fueled Internet speculation that a new Batman movie was in the works.

To protect against leaks, Nolan gave the project a fake title utterly unrelated to Batman—*The Intimidation Game*—that appeared on every document associated with the project, including each successive draft of the screenplay, which Nolan wrote in the months following Goyer's departure from the garage, with final-stage help from his brother Jonathan.

When the screenplay was finally completed, no photocopies were made—not even for executives at Warner Bros. Rather, those executives, acquiescing to the secretive director's wishes, came to his home and read the script in his cluttered garage.

Surroundings were soon forgotten, as what the executives found in that screenplay was a compelling story that was more classical drama than super hero fluff. Devoid of high-camp villains wearing ludicrous and inexplicable costumes, this story took its characters and their predicaments seriously. This Batman wasn't a one-dimensional comic book hero in black tights, cape, and bat ears, but rather a complex, multidimensional human being, a real man struggling to overcome life's tragedies and his own inner demons.

It was an inventive and audacious vision of a super hero movie, one that existed only on the printed pages of the carefully guarded screenplay in that summer of 2003—but Christopher Nolan's Batman had begun.

"Oh, my God—this is not your father's Batman film . . . "

CHAPTER 1

From the beginning, even as he first began to toy with the notion of writing and directing a new Batman movie, Christopher Nolan suspected that Bruce Wayne's story was bigger than what could be told in a single film; in the back of his mind, he considered ideas about where that story could go if he were to make not just one film, but a series of films. "We never sat down and specifically plotted out a trilogy," Nolan said, "but we had a notion of what the shape of Bruce Wayne's story would be were we to make three films—even from the first one. Just to come up with the first film, we had to have some idea of what Bruce Wayne's life story would be."

And that would have suited Nolan just fine. Having come from the world of independent film, with its modest budgets and guerilla filmmaking techniques, the young director—only thirty-three years old at the time—had no burning desire to make a series of "big Hollywood" blockbusters. Rather, what compelled him as he began developing the story for *Batman Begins* was the tantalizing prospect of taking the "comic" out of the comic book movie.

"From the beginning," said Nolan, "my interest was in taking on a super hero story but grounding it in reality, never looking at it as a comic book movie, but rather as any other action/adventure film. I was interested in removing the frame of the comic, if you will, the two-dimensional reality of what a comic book looks like. It would be a darker, more human Batman—and the opportunity to approach this great iconic character in a new way was *very* exciting to me."

The movie's narrative framework, as Nolan saw it, would be Batman's origins, the events that led billionaire Bruce Wayne to don a Batsuit and fight crime in Gotham City. Surprisingly, it was a story that had never been told in its entirety, in the comics *or* on film. "There hadn't been a single definitive account of the journey of Bruce Wayne into Batman," Nolan stated, "which meant that there were fascinating gaps in the mythology to be played with. I wanted to tell that origin story with a certain degree of gravity, and in a more grounded way than what had been done before, giving the story and the characters a more realistic spin."

That was the initial pitch Nolan made to Warner Bros. executives, and they responded to it enthusiastically, giving the project an immediate green light. "It wasn't a difficult sell at all," admitted Jeff Robinov, president, Warner Bros. Pictures Group, "even though there was no screenplay—nothing but Chris's vision about the type of film he could deliver. At the risk of giving away too much, there's very little that I wouldn't say yes to Chris Nolan on because I think he is the filmmaker of his generation. His body of work, the way he's been received critically, and how he raises his own bar each time he makes a movie all make him an incredibly impressive person."

Having reached an agreement with the studio, Nolan sought out David S. Goyer—writer of the Blade series of

Laying a foundation for a trilogy wasn't foremost in Nolan's mind as he embarked on creating *Batman Begins*, however. For one thing, he'd always had an aversion to what he called "sequel bait," narrative threads that anticipate and rely on a sequel. For another, there was considerable risk in what Nolan was proposing to do with *Batman Begins*—essentially turning the super hero genre on its head—and neither he nor Warner Bros. knew if his unusual take would succeed or fail. If it failed, there would be no sequel, and certainly no trilogy.

PAGE 30: Early concept art for *Batman Begins* reveals a silhouetted Batman descending into the Narrows, Gotham City's isolated "slum of slums" located on an island in the middle of Gotham River. This striking image would echo throughout The Dark Knight Trilogy—both within each film and in poster designs for each film's marketing campaign.

ABOVE: Director Christopher Nolan saw *Batman Begins* as more "classical drama" than comic book fantasy, and built *his* hero's journey within a gritty, reality-based vision of Gotham.

films and something of an authority on Batman and other comic book icons—to help him work out a story and write the first draft of the screenplay.

"Even though I've always been a fan of Batman," said Nolan, "I am by no means a comic book expert, and so I didn't feel capable of doing a first draft and coming up with that story myself. I needed a writer on the project who knew the character inside and out, and knew the comic world. Everything we did in translating the character's comic story to film would have to be extremely reverential to the mythology of Batman."

At the time, Goyer was heavily into pre-production on *Blade: Trinity*, his first feature-film directing assignment. When he was contacted by Nolan's agent, he cited the scheduling conflict and passed on the offer to cowrite the story—reluctantly. "I'd always wanted to write a Batman movie," Goyer insisted. "I remember telling my mother when I was a kid that I was going to go to Hollywood one day and do a Batman film. So, in a way, I had been waiting my whole life for this call. But, at the time, I was so busy I didn't think I could do it. About a week later, Chris Nolan called and said that he'd really like me to do it, and again, I had to say that I didn't have the time. 'But if I *was* going to write it,' I said, 'this is what I would do'—and then I talked for about an hour."

What Goyer related in that phone conversation was his conviction that in order to reengage an audience's interest in Batman, the story line had to either jump forward to the future—which had been explored in the animated *Batman Beyond*—or go back to the beginning, to Batman's origin story. Goyer's take dovetailed perfectly with Nolan's, and the director called Goyer yet again, a few days after their initial conversation. "Chris said, 'You have to do this,'" Goyer recalled. "'You *have* to.' And we worked it out. I would work on *Batman Begins* from seven in the morning until noon, and then I would go to the production office on the other film until ten at night. It almost killed me, but it all worked out in the end."

To craft the story, Nolan and Goyer—meeting in Nolan's garage—began by envisioning the film's first teaser trailer. Rather than flashes of a dark figure in a bat costume swooping over the rooftops of Gotham City, the image that

captured their imaginations was the famous photograph of a very young John F. Kennedy Jr. at his father's graveside. "That photograph, which showed this little child trying to look stoic and brave, triggered something for us," Goyer revealed. "We thought it would be great if the first trailer showed Bruce Wayne as an eight-year-old boy, after his parents had been killed. We referred to him as the loneliest boy in the world because he becomes heir to this multibillion-dollar company, Wayne Enterprises, but he can't run it for another twenty years. We viewed him as a prince regent

Writer David S. Goyer—a lifelong comic book aficionado—was lured in by Nolan's compelling take on the Batman story, despite a previous commitment to direct *Blade: Trinity*, his first feature-film directing assignment.

being groomed to one day become king—and the common- ers can't touch him."

Another evocative image that came to the writers was that of Bruce's childhood friend, Rachel Dawes, the daugh- ter of one of Wayne Manor's maids, looking up and waving at his forlorn visage in an upper-story window of the Manor after his parents' funeral.

"She would look up and see this lonely little boy waving back at her," said Goyer, "as if he was a prisoner of Wayne Manor." This post-funeral scene was one of the gaps in the Batman mythology that Nolan had been eager to explore, as very little of Bruce Wayne's boyhood had ever been depicted in the comic books. "All you ever saw of him as a little boy was the brief flash of him coming out of the movies with his parents, and then the bad guy shooting

them—and that was it. We didn't know anything about the parents, or what happened to Bruce after their deaths. This was our 'in' into the psychology of Bruce Wayne—that he grew up as the loneliest boy in the world, sheltered and secluded, a very tragic figure."

The writers conceived another significant event in Bruce's childhood, one that would provide a psychological rationale for his choice of disguise when he embarks on his crime-fighting career as an adult: While playing on the grounds of Wayne Manor with Rachel, young Bruce falls into an abandoned well and is swarmed by bats emerging from adjacent caverns. "In the previous films," said Goyer, "and even in the comic books, you would see Bruce's parents killed, and then they would jump forward twenty years to Bruce in his study, in an evening jacket, reading or smoking

The image of an orphaned Bruce Wayne standing alone at the window of Wayne Manor filled a gap in the Batman mythology for Nolan and Goyer.

The indelible impression of three-year-old John F. Kennedy Jr. saluting his father's casket informed the writers' characterization of the young Bruce Wayne, whom they viewed as "the loneliest boy in the world" after his parents are murdered, leaving him heir to multibillion dollar Wayne Enterprises. Shown here, John F. Kennedy Jr. in Washington on November 25, 1963, three days after the president was assassinated in Dallas. Widow Jacqueline Kennedy, center, and daughter Caroline Kennedy are accompanied by the late president's brothers, Senator Edward Kennedy, left, and Attorney General Robert Kennedy. (AP Photo/File)

The murder of Bruce Wayne's parents was pulled straight from the pages of DC Comics, as recounted here in a detail of David Mazzucchelli's cover art from *Batman: Year One*, written by Frank Miller and illustrated by Mazzucchelli. *Batman: Year One* was originally serialized in DC Comics's *Batman* nos. 404–408, 1987.

Young Bruce Wayne (Gus Lewis) and his parents (Linus Roache and Sara Stewart) are confronted by stickup man Joe Chill in an alley behind Gotham's opera house in *Batman Begins*.

a pipe. And then a bat would crash through the window, and in the next panel, he would be in a bat costume, on a rooftop in Gotham. So a bat crashes through a window, and suddenly: 'I know! I'll turn into a bat!'

"We thought that was too facile a way of explaining that transformation. So we came up with this traumatic experience that happens to Bruce when he's eight years old, being trapped at the bottom of this well for hours, and then having millions of bats pour out, getting caught in his hair and scratching him. It would be a terrifying experience for anyone, but especially for a little boy, and it becomes a formative experience for Bruce Wayne."

The one traumatic event of Bruce Wayne's childhood that *had* been chronicled in the *Batman* comics—if only superficially—was his witnessing of his parents' murders in an alleyway. While remaining true to that well-known element of Batman mythology, Nolan and Goyer gave it a spin that added another layer of complexity to Bruce Wayne's psychological makeup. "In the comics," Nolan explained, "they are going to see a movie, *The Mask of Zorro*, but I felt that an opera would be a grander, richer source of Bruce Wayne's fear. So we changed it to an opera house, where he's watching *Mefistofele*, which has these batlike creatures very elaborately presented onstage.

"It reminds him of his trauma—this terrible experience with the bats—and he asks his parents if they can leave, and it's in leaving the opera that they encounter the mugger who kills them. We wanted to tie together Bruce Wayne's feeling of guilt over his parents' death with his fear of bats. We wanted his parents' murder to be forever associated with the idea of the bat, which is why that symbol becomes so significant in his life."

In *Batman Begins*, all of these events form a backstory that explains the highly complex, dark, and troubled nature of Bruce Wayne. As the writers structured their screenplay, Bruce Wayne—not Batman—would be the story's central character, with Batman not making an appearance until a full forty minutes into the movie. "Bruce Wayne had to be just as interesting to the audience as Batman," Nolan commented. "To me, what was even more interesting than the duality between Batman and Bruce Wayne was the duality *within* Bruce Wayne. There was his public face as a

dilettante and playboy, the last person anyone in Gotham would suspect of being Batman. And then there was the private Bruce Wayne—and that's the figure that our film had to bring to life."

Jumping from the present to the past, the first act of *Batman Begins* follows Bruce as a lost and angry young man, with flashbacks to the traumas of his childhood. Unable to sate his hunger for revenge, he leaves Gotham to travel the world. Bruce Wayne's journey and his ultimate return to Gotham had been first chronicled in "The Man Who Falls," a 1989 comic book story written by Dennis O'Neil and Dick Giordano.

"That story suggests various points in the development of Bruce Wayne into Batman," said Nolan, "including the idea that he disappears for seven years and travels the world, learning all of the skills that eventually become important to being Batman. That was the jumping-off point for our story."

By taking Bruce Wayne outside Gotham city limits, Nolan and Goyer were making a significant departure from previous Batman films, all of which had been set entirely within the city. Both to open up the film and to reinforce Bruce Wayne as the central character, the writers dramatized Bruce's seven-year absence from his point of view, not from the perspectives of those left back in Gotham, thus revealing Bruce's experiences in the outside world.

The movie opens, in fact, with Bruce in a prison in Bhutan. "The first time you see the adult Bruce Wayne, he's in this prison, beating the crap out of somebody," related Goyer. "This prison is a hellhole, something right out of *Midnight Express*, and as soon as the audience sees that, they realize, 'Oh, my God—this is not your father's Batman film.'"

"When we pick him up in the story," elaborated Nolan, "Bruce is in terrible shape. He has endured the horrific experience of his parents' deaths, and he carries within him this very powerful sense of rage against the world. We wanted to start our story showing the true depths of despair that Bruce Wayne would be reduced to in his search for how to use that rage."

A mysterious figure, Henri Ducard, arrives at the prison to offer Bruce an outlet for his rage, inviting him to join the

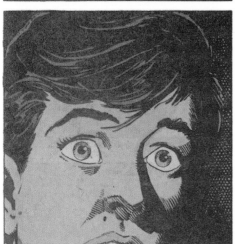

TOP: As Nolan and Goyer developed their story, they embraced both logical and traditional aspects of the tale, but eschewed easy answers to Batman's obsession with bats, such as Bruce Wayne's traumatization by the winged creature breaking through the window of his study. Shown here, panels from page 20 of "The Man Who Falls," a short story written by Dennis O'Neil and illustrated by Dick Giordano, originally published by DC Comics in *Secret Origins*, 1990.

BOTTOM: The back-alley murders of Thomas and Martha Wayne—the time-honored source of Bruce Wayne's darker nature and the impetus for his transformation into a fighter of crime—were carefully woven into the *Batman Begins* screenplay by Nolan and Goyer. Shown here, details from page 11 of "The Man Who Falls," written by Dennis O'Neil and illustrated by Dick Giordano.

League of Shadows, an ancient order of assassins committed to "fighting injustice"—but, as Ducard later reveals to Bruce, their method of doing so is to destroy what they deem to be corrupt and decayed civilizations. "As the most human of the super heroes," noted Nolan, "Bruce Wayne is always poised on this knife-edge between taking the right path and taking the wrong path. Ducard and the League of Shadows offer him one way to deal with criminality, which involves many positive things. He learns combat skills, theatricality, and deception, all things that will play into the Batman persona. But, ultimately, the path they offer is questionable, and Bruce must decide whether to follow it or go his own way."

Bruce chooses the latter, rejecting the League of Shadows and returning to Gotham. Nolan and Goyer found key story elements for Bruce Wayne's return in the narrative arc of 1987's *Batman: Year One*, by Frank Miller and David Mazzucchelli.

The tone of Miller and Mazzucchelli's comic book story was particularly appealing to the writers, as it struck the hard-nosed, gritty, realistic chords they sought. "*Batman: Year One* was very tough and no-nonsense," said Goyer. "Also, Frank Miller had developed a great relationship between Batman and Gordon—who is not yet Commissioner Gordon—and I think Miller was the first to suggest that the police force in Gotham City was corrupt. That was important, because it left an opening for Batman. If the police were doing their job, there wouldn't be a *need* for Batman." Yet another narrative influence was *The Long Halloween*, a series of Batman stories by Jeph Loeb that introduced mob boss Carmine Falcone.

Upon his return to Gotham, Bruce Wayne conceives the idea of fighting crime, not as a man, but as a symbol that will strike fear into the city's criminals and inspire hope in its citizens. Crucial to Nolan's take on the story was depicting Bruce Wayne's transformation into Batman in a way that wouldn't require major suspensions of disbelief in the audience. *Why* Bruce Wayne decides to fight crime, *why* he chooses a bat as his symbol, and *how* he creates the accouterments of that persona were all questions that demanded rational, plausible answers.

The most elemental question to be answered was "why?" Instead of living the comfortable, pleasurable life his riches

could afford him, why does Bruce Wayne go out into the mean streets of Gotham every night to confront the criminal element, risking his life and often returning home with all manner of injuries?

"The core of Bruce Wayne's drive to become Batman," explained Nolan, "is his frustration with the corruption of Gotham City, and his inability to reconcile his desire for revenge through conventional police work or within a legal framework. Driven by this tremendous engine of unresolved anger, he devotes himself to fighting crime, to righting the type of wrongs that have been done to him." It was important that, as the film's hero, Batman be seen as controlling that rage, however. Batman couldn't be reduced to a common vigilante. "It is the point of the story, in a sense,

ABOVE: "The Man Who Falls," which chronicles Bruce Wayne's seven-year disappearance from Gotham, provided a jumping-off point for the writers. Shown here, details from page 7 of "The Man Who Falls," written by Dennis O'Neil and illustrated by Dick Giordano.

OPPOSITE: Frank Miller's darkly toned *Batman: Year One* offered ways to bring Bruce Wayne back to Gotham—and provided a model for the film's no-nonsense realism. Shown here, the first trade paperback edition cover of *Batman: Year One*, written by Miller and illustrated by David Mazzucchelli.

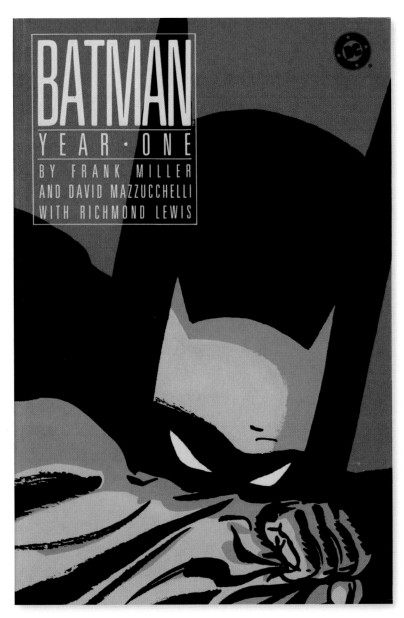

this tension between the desire for revenge and the desire to do good. He's driven by very dark, negative impulses, but by using those impulses, he makes Gotham a better place. It was important to get that part of his character across in the story."

The second crucial question was: Why a bat? Why not just go out and fight crime as Bruce Wayne, or, if his identity had to be hidden, why not wear a simple mask or hood? In other words, why the getup? "We started to examine why Bruce Wayne would dress up as this very theatrical figure," said Nolan. "The best explanation offered by the comics, and the one that was the most interesting to me, was the notion of him using fear against those who would use fear themselves. It was the idea of becoming a symbol, and not

just a man. A flesh-and-blood man can be destroyed. A symbol is much more frightening and intimidating. And so he looks for the most intimidating symbol that he can think of, and he naturally gravitates toward the thing that has frightened him most since he was a child—bats."

The final question to be answered was "how?"—the specifics of how Bruce Wayne, a mere mortal, transforms himself into a powerful figure with seemingly superhuman capabilities. "We wanted the audience to experience the process of becoming Batman through Bruce Wayne's eyes," said Nolan, "to really get inside this guy's head and go on that journey with him." To do that, the writers imagined real-world sources for Batman's tools of the trade. "We got into the detail of his gadgetry and how that hardware came to be. How would you put together the tools to be Batman? We thought of things like Bruce spray-painting his equipment a matte black, or using a grinder to form his own metal Batarangs. It was a homemade approach, because that's how Batman would have to start. He couldn't jump in as a branded figure with these beautifully designed gadgets. It was important that we start with more crude tools, and show where they came from and how they were put together."

Lucius Fox, head of Wayne Enterprises' all but defunct Applied Sciences Division, introduces Bruce Wayne to the high-tech tools that enable him to "fly" from Gotham rooftops, climb vertical walls, and race through city streets at ultrahigh speeds in the Tumbler, a state-of-the-art military vehicle. Bruce's transformation is also aided and abetted by Alfred, the longtime Wayne family butler who becomes a father figure to the orphaned boy. "The main theme in the movie is how fear regulates our lives," said David Goyer. "But the other important theme is about fathers, and living up to the legacies and expectations of fathers."

Another father figure is Henri Ducard, the mentor who trains Bruce in martial arts in a Bhutanese monastery early in the film. Later, Ducard is revealed to be Rā's al Ghūl, leader of the League of Shadows and one of the film's two main villains. Previous Batman films had put their villains front and center, devoting more screen time to their backstories and character development than to Batman or Bruce Wayne. Though Nolan and Goyer rejected

OVERLEAF: Early production art for *Batman Begins* drew upon comic book traditions while steering Gotham in a new visual direction.

41

that villain-centric approach, they recognized the need to pit their central character against formidable and well-rounded foes.

They were determined, as well, to feature villains that would be new to Batman movie audiences, and felt strongly that they should avoid using any of the villains that had been seen in previous films. Already introducing audience members to a different kind of Batman, they didn't want to further confuse them with a reinvention of the Joker or Penguin.

It was a tough standard to meet, however, as most of the high-profile villains in Batman's rogues' gallery had already seen screen time. "Chris and I had a long discussion about the various rogues that were left," recalled Goyer, "and I knew them all. He asked me: 'Okay, who's left? Who can we use?' So I told him, 'Well, there's the Calendar Man.' 'What does he do?' 'He kills people based on holiday themes.' Chris said: 'No way. Who else?' 'Well, there's the Mad Hatter.' Gone. 'There's Killer Croc, this half-human, half-crocodile that lives in the sewers.' Gone. 'There's Clay Face, the human mud heap.' That wasn't going to work, either.

"And then I told Chris that among the villains that hadn't been seen in features yet was one of my favorites—Rā's al Ghūl. Chris asked, 'Who's Rā's al Ghūl?' And I said, 'Funny you should ask,' because we'd been talking about coming up with a villain who was older and could function as Bruce's mentor, and then go bad and be the villain. Rā's was perfect for that because, in the comics, he is older and has a paternalistic quality. He's also the only villain to figure out Batman's secret identity. We loved the idea of Rā's teaching Bruce the fighting skills that he would use as Batman, and since Rā's is the one who teaches Bruce those techniques, he recognizes them in what Batman does—and that's how he knows that Batman is Bruce Wayne. That makes him a very formidable villain."

Another villain yet to be featured in a Batman film was the Scarecrow, the alter ego of Dr. Jonathan Crane. Crane, the administrator of Arkham Asylum—a key institution in Batman mythology—becomes involved in the development and distribution of a fear gas that produces intense phobic reactions. "He's a psychiatrist who is driven by the idea of manipulating people through fear," said Nolan, "and we felt

that had an interesting relationship to what Bruce Wayne was embarking on with the Batman persona. So, Dr. Crane assumes a high degree of importance, both as himself and as the Scarecrow."

One characteristic of the Scarecrow that Nolan disliked initially was his mask, for which there appeared to be no logical purpose. "Chris insisted that every thing and every character have a sense of verisimilitude," said Goyer, "and so he asked if the Scarecrow had to use a mask; as the 'protector' of the comic book lore, I said, yes. He said, 'But I don't like the mask.' And I said, 'The Scarecrow has to use a mask—he *has* to.' He said, 'Fine,' but we had to come up with a good reason for the Scarecrow to wear a mask. There had to be a 'why,' and it had to be real.

"That was Chris's mantra the whole time we were working on the script—'it has to be real, it has to be real.' For example, we were looking at a comic book one day and Chris noticed that there are bars on Batman's gauntlets. So he asked: 'What are those things? What do they do?' I had no idea. 'They have to do something, Goyer. Figure it out.' He was like that with every little thing. 'Why are the bat ears so tall? There has to be a reason for that!' He was very exacting, and there were times when that drove me completely crazy—but it was also great. You want someone to push you, and you're willing to be pushed by Chris because he's so good and he cares so much."

Ultimately, Nolan and Goyer decided the "why" for the Scarecrow's mask was that it acted as a gas mask, protecting him from the effects of the fear toxin. One of the victims of Crane's hallucinogen is Rachel Dawes, Bruce's friend since childhood and an assistant D.A. whose tenacity in going against the city's mob bosses puts her life at risk. "It was important for us to have a person who was close to Bruce from childhood," said Nolan, "who knew him before everything went wrong."

As Bruce's love interest, Rachel represents the normal life he might have had if not for his role as Batman. The poignancy of what might have been is underscored in a quiet scene between Bruce and Rachel at the film's end. "She essentially tells him, 'You need to be Batman,'" said Goyer, "'but I can't be with you while you're Batman, because it's too heartbreaking.'"

In addition to such touching, character-revealing scenes, the screenplay would boast moments of dry humor, with Alfred, especially, delivering a number of droll one-liners. But this was a Batman movie, and the writers met audience expectations by scripting dynamic action sequences, such as a breathtaking chase through Gotham's streets, an explosive finale involving a runaway monorail train, and the burning of Wayne Manor.

This literal torching of Bruce Wayne's past was a somewhat shocking turn, and the screenwriters were aware even as they wrote it that they might be pushing narrative boundaries beyond what Batman fans or DC Comics

would accept. "Frankly," Goyer admitted, "I was amazed that DC Comics let us do it. But it seemed like the best thing to have happen at that point. We had this company that Bruce's father had helped build, and we had this manor that had been in the family for generations—and we thought, 'Wouldn't it be great to literally see all of it crumble, to have Bruce feel as if he's utterly failed his father?'"

During May and June, Goyer incorporated many of these ideas and characters into his draft of the screenplay before turning it over to Nolan. Nolan continued to refine the screenplay as he scouted locations and set up the production in London, ultimately finding his way through a total of seven drafts. Eventually, he invited his brother Jonathan—called "Jonah" by friends and family—to accompany him.

"I came onto *Batman Begins* late in the day," Jonathan Nolan related, "just to spitball ideas with Chris and be an extra brain for him on the script as he went into prep. I flew around with him for many, many months, all around the world, and then spent more nights than I care to remember in and around London trying to think up dastardly scenarios and misadventures for Bruce Wayne."

There was a kind of symmetry to the collaboration, as Christopher Nolan had given his younger brother a copy of *Batman: Year One* for Jonathan's thirteenth birthday. "I grew up not reading a lot of comic books," Jonathan Nolan said, "but *Batman: Year One* just blew my mind. It was such an evocative, exciting, and real take on this character that it stuck with me. So the opportunity to come back and work on that character, which is the only comic book character that I found terribly appealing when I was a kid, was wonderful."

Included in the final *Batman Begins* screenplay was a moment in the third act in which a joker is left as an apparent calling card at a crime scene. Christopher Nolan had written, and subsequently shot, the joker card reveal not knowing if *Batman Begins* would be successful enough to warrant a sequel, or if he even *wanted* to embark on a second film. "We wanted to suggest possibilities for how the story would continue," Nolan explained, "not because we knew we were going to make a sequel, but because that

As the writers searched for villains not yet featured in Batman films, Goyer suggested the Scarecrow, the alter ego of Arkham Asylum administrator Dr. Jonathan Crane. Nolan was intrigued by the character, but put off by his mask—until a logical reason for it could be justified in the script. Shown here, page 213 of *Batman: The Long Halloween*, written by Jeph Loeb and illustrated by Tim Sale. *Batman: The Long Halloween* was originally serialized by DC Comics from 1996–1997.

With its release on June 15, 2005, the movie performed very well, indeed. Audiences "got" what Nolan had tried to do in his reimagining of the Batman legend, and they thoroughly embraced it, evidenced by the movie's $49 million take in its opening weekend and its final gross of close to $400 million. The overwhelmingly positive response to *Batman Begins* made the prospect of a sequel not only possible but, from Warner Bros.' perspective, at least, highly desirable.

Even so, Nolan and his creative colleagues didn't jump into a Batman sequel; rather, they moved from *Batman Begins* to *The Prestige*, a tale of rival magicians set in nineteenth-century London, which Nolan cowrote with his brother.

After completing *The Prestige*, Nolan remained unsure as to what form a Batman sequel might take—even though, throughout the course of their *Batman Begins* collaboration, he and David Goyer had worked out *general* parameters for where a second story, and even a third, could go. "It wasn't until *Batman Begins* was completely finished," recalled Nolan, "and we'd taken some time off that we got the chance to sit down, and think, 'Okay, what exactly are we going to do with this?'"

One idea that intrigued the writer/director as he considered a sequel was how he might interpret the Joker in the hyperreal world of *Batman Begins*, and how the Joker might act as the catalyst for Bruce Wayne's becoming more entrenched in his Batman mission. "We'd laid down the idea in *Batman Begins* that Bruce Wayne's plan in becoming Batman was to do what he could for a finite period of time," said Nolan. "He had something like a five-year plan, a set amount of time he would spend setting Gotham straight, and then he would go off and do something else with his life, because, like anybody else, he wanted a life other than one of vigilantism and subterfuge."

To borrow from an old aphorism: Men make plans, and the Joker laughs.

"With the reveal of the joker card at the end of *Batman Begins*," said Nolan, "we created the sense that it wasn't going to be as simple as Bruce doing what he could for five years and then getting out. And then, in *The Dark Knight*, we would see Bruce getting deeper and deeper into his

was the *feeling* we wanted the audience to leave the theater with. The ending of *Batman Begins* was specifically aimed at spinning off that element of the mythology in the audience's mind so that they could imagine what the Joker would be in that world."

Even executives at Warner Bros. were unsure as to how to read the joker reveal. "Chris is a very singular filmmaker," observed Jeff Robinov. "It's difficult to get him to talk about anything while he's making a movie because he's completely in his own world, and in the world that he's creating. So, the joker card at the end of *Batman Begins* was, frankly, a surprise to me. It was a very elegant and delicate moment that *allowed* a sequel, but didn't promise one. Until we saw how *Batman Begins* performed, a sequel remained an open question."

Writer Jonathan Nolan—known as "Jonah" to friends and family—began contributing to the *Batman Begins* script while scouting locations for the movie with his brother. He would continue as screenwriter for all three films in The Dark Knight Trilogy.

role as Batman. Batman's extraordinary response to crime would evoke a similar response from the criminal world. In a way, Batman himself would raise the extremity of behavior in Gotham, and would give rise to the Joker."

Created by Jerry Robinson, Bill Finger, and Bob Kane, the Joker first appeared on the pages of DC Comics in *Batman* no. 1 during the spring of 1940. The character was initially conceived as a homicidal maniac, his appearance modeled after a joker playing card. Over the years, however, the Joker emerged as more prankster than malevolent clown—an option Nolan firmly eschewed—until finally returning as an evil genius bent on mayhem.

For *The Dark Knight,* Nolan and Goyer embraced the idea of introducing a Joker who was a flesh-and-blood psychopath, a very different villain from the more cerebral Rā's al Ghūl and Scarecrow of *Batman Begins*. The anarchic character would also be the catalyst for pushing Bruce Wayne to his limits and determining, once and for all, just how far Bruce Wayne was prepared to go as Batman. "The Joker is not a logical criminal," Nolan noted. "He's devoid

of sense, devoid of logic. This makes him an extraordinary adversary for Batman, because Batman relies on tapping into criminals' fears and playing those fears against them. But the Joker is not responsive to that."

"We always talked about the Joker as being like the shark in *Jaws*," added Goyer, "this force of nature that is unknowable. That's why he has a kind of 'choose your own' origin story. We never wanted to explain his origin, which had become another lame convention of these types of movies. With each successive film, it was 'What's the origin of the new villain?' That had become a real cliché, and so we decided to subvert that by not showing his origin at all, which we thought would make him much scarier. The Joker had never been scary in previous film depictions, but we were determined to make him *very* scary in *The Dark Knight*."

In addition to the Joker, Nolan and Goyer were intrigued by a character DC Comics had also introduced in the '40s: Gotham City District Attorney Harvey Dent. "The real story of Harvey Dent," commented Nolan, "the origin story

Revealed at the end of *Batman Begins*, the joker card had been written into the script as a suggestion—not a guarantee—of how the story might continue.

of who he is and what he represents about Gotham, is a very grand-scale tragedy that hadn't been done on film. I thought he was an incredible character to explore."

As written by Nolan and Goyer, Dent—and not Bruce Wayne—would be *The Dark Knight*'s tragic hero. "Bruce Wayne was the protagonist of the first film," explained Goyer, "but we decided early on that he would *not* be the protagonist of the second film—that, in fact, Harvey Dent would be." One of the defining characteristics of a protagonist is that he changes in the course of a story. Having determined that Bruce Wayne would not be the protagonist of *The Dark Knight*, the writers purposely constructed a story line in which the character remains *un*changed. "The character that changes is Harvey Dent. He goes from being a White Knight to a horrifically scarred and tragic figure."

The battle for that tragic figure's soul became the story's thematic thru-line. "We had Batman/Bruce on one side, saying that Harvey Dent represents a good vision of what the city can become," said Goyer, "and then we had the Joker on the other side, saying that *any* man can be corrupted and turned into a villain if you push him hard enough. And the Joker is kind of right, which is why we wrote an ending in which Batman and Gordon conspire to hide that truth from Gotham. They protect the image of Harvey Dent, and Batman sacrifices himself. That makes the ending of *The Dark Knight* very tragic."

As the film's hero, it is District Attorney Harvey Dent—and not Batman—who leads the charge against crime and corruption in Gotham City. In developing that narrative thread, Nolan and Goyer began to recognize that the story was taking on a very different tone than the one established in *Batman Begins*. Whereas the first film was a classic hero's journey, the second shared many of the elements of an urban crime drama.

"We talked about antecedents going into each film," Goyer commented. "For *Batman Begins*, we talked about *Lawrence of Arabia*, *The Man Who Would Be King*—movies about epic figures searching for themselves. And then, for *The Dark Knight*, we talked about *The Godfather* and other movies about crime. *The Dark Knight* was also about escalation and terror, because terror is the weapon that the Joker employs to fight Batman."

Batman, too, employs a kind of terrorism in fighting Gotham's criminal element, using dubious tactics of which Harvey Dent approves. "Harvey doesn't question Batman as much as Gordon does," said Nolan, "and therein lie the seeds of his ultimate trouble, because what Batman does *is* questionable. There are some disturbing ramifications to the way Batman chooses to fight crime, but Harvey Dent is in favor of Batman's approach, and avails himself of the advantage it gives him in fighting criminals—which immediately raises the question: How far will Harvey Dent go?"

That question is answered, disturbingly, when a fire horribly disfigures one side of Dent's handsome face—and also poisons his soul, transforming him into the villainous Two-Face. Once a staunch supporter of Batman, Harvey Dent succumbs to insanity and rage and becomes the Dark Knight's archenemy.

DC Comics first introduced the Joker in *Batman* no. 1 during the spring of 1940; shown here is page 33 of the graphic novel, *Batman: The Killing Joke*, written by Alan Moore and illustrated by Brian Bolland. Published by DC Comics, 1988.

After Christopher Nolan and David Goyer had developed the essential characters and plot points of the new story, Jonathan Nolan came on board to craft the first-draft screenplay. For him, the essence of *The Dark Knight*'s story was captured in a line added late in the development of the script. "The idea that you either die a hero or you live long enough to see yourself become the villain is really the theme of the movie for me," he said. "And Batman lives long enough to see himself become the villain, or to allow himself to be *mistaken* for the villain. That was the idea coming out of the story that David and Chris had put together that most excited me."

The younger Nolan was also excited by the story's poignant ending: the image of a disgraced and disavowed Batman, chased by Gotham police, disappearing into the night. "Chris is very driven by endings," Nolan observed, "and he likes to pare down endings to an image. In early drafts of the script, that image was of Batman on foot, being chased from rooftop to rooftop. In the final version of the script, we had him on his amazing Bat-Pod, but it was the same essential image—Batman being pursued by the people he's just helped to save. There was something very tragic about that."

*T*he Dark Knight*'s release was met with much fanfare and big box-office numbers, grossing $158 million its first weekend—more than three times the opening take for *Batman Begins*—and eventually earning $1 billion worldwide. Critical acclaim was also immediate and enduring, and the film garnered numerous honors, including eight Academy Award® nominations—two of which would be won, by the late Heath Ledger for his performance as the Joker and by Richard King for sound design.

However, even after the phenomenal success of *The Dark Knight*, Christopher Nolan had no sense of certitude that he would do a third Batman movie. "I think Chris was initially reluctant because he felt that it would be hard for the team to top itself," explained David Goyer. "Also, historically, there have been very few good third iterations of movies. We didn't want to let the audience down, we didn't want to let the other actors down, and we didn't want to let ourselves down. The first two films could have stood alone—there didn't *need* to be a third film. So, we did a lot of soul-searching about what to do after *The Dark Knight*."

The decision as to whether or not to do a third Batman movie rested, more than anything else, on whether there was a third and final story worth telling. Nolan didn't want to work backward—making the decision to do a third film, and then trying to find a story for it. Rather, he wanted to conceive a story so compelling that it not only suggested another Batman movie, it *demanded* it.

"When we started the process of talking about a third film," Goyer recalled, "we had no idea if we were going to find that story. As we had for the first two movies, we wanted whatever story we came up with to be driven by theme and character. Everything had to be born out of that. So we began by asking ourselves some basic questions: What did we want to say about Bruce Wayne and Batman?

Gotham District Attorney Harvey Dent's transmutation into Two-Face is chronicled in *Batman: The Long Halloween*, a comic book limited series written by Jeph Loeb and illustrated by Tim Sale. Shown here, page 347 of *Absolute Batman: The Long Halloween*, published by DC Comics, 2007.

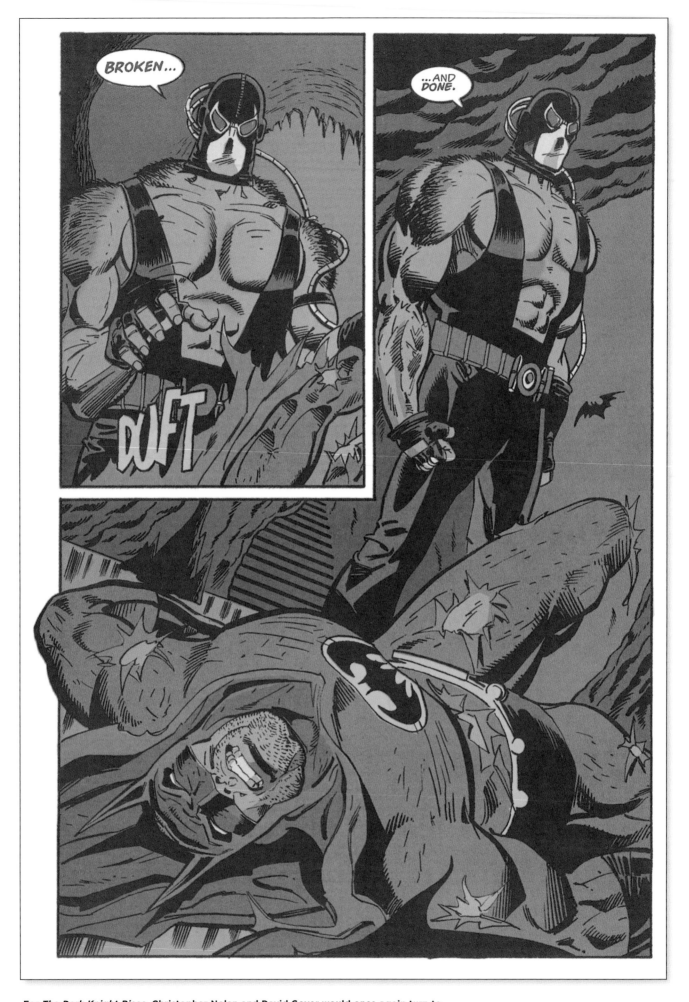

For *The Dark Knight Rises,* Christopher Nolan and David Goyer would once again turn to
Batman's comic book roots in search of an antihero, this time landing on Bane, a lesser-
known villain when compared to the Penguin or Riddler, but the perfect archetype
for the severity—and extremity—of the third film's plot. Here, Bane breaks Batman's
back on page 22 of *Batman* no. 497 by Doug Moench, with illustrations by Jim Aparo.
Published by DC Comics, 1993.

How did we want this story to end? Chris said, 'If we can't answer those questions, we shouldn't do a third movie.'"

From the earliest days of developing the story for *Batman Begins*, Nolan and Goyer had talked, in general terms, about the arc of Bruce Wayne's life. The first film would be about his becoming Batman—but only temporarily, as an extreme but short-term means of setting Gotham on a better path. The second film would be about his being drawn deeper into the life of his alter ego. The third film, if it came to pass, would have to resolve that dilemma and close the Batman chapter of Bruce Wayne's life.

As always, Christopher Nolan started at the end. "Endings are very important," Nolan observed. "I don't embark on a project if I don't have a very strong sense of how things are going to end. That's been the case with all three films, and very much so with *The Dark Knight Rises*—because the entire story arc is ending with this film. And so, even as we started to develop the story, we had a very strong sense of what the ending of the movie would be. We came up with it several years ago, in fact, and everything had been building toward that conclusion."

Nolan and Goyer returned to the garage to hash out story ideas for *The Dark Knight Rises*, writing plot points and character notes on index cards and soliciting input from Jonathan Nolan. "I roped Jonah in at various stages to comment on and add to what we were doing," Nolan said, "and that input from him was very valuable, even though he wasn't sitting in the room with us. I always bounced ideas off of him as we were developing the story."

Just as he had for *The Dark Knight*, Jonathan Nolan wrote the first draft of the screenplay for *The Dark Knight Rises*. "That first draft is the most important draft," Christopher Nolan stated, "because it is where all of these loosely structured story ideas on index cards have to come together. To incorporate those ideas into an actual screenplay is, I think, one of the hardest parts of the process." With his younger brother busy on other projects, Nolan wrote the subsequent drafts of the screenplay himself.

The story the writers crafted picks up eight years after the events of *The Dark Knight*. The conspiratorial pact between Gordon and Batman that ended the second film—which had Batman taking the fall for the late Harvey Dent's misdeeds so that Dent could remain a hero in the minds of Gotham's citizens—has had its intended impact. Gotham, inspired by Dent's supposed heroism, has cleaned up its act and is now a shining example of urban functionality—on the surface. But there is something rotten at the city's core, an undercurrent of criminality and suffering. The narrative of *The Dark Knight Rises* is the eruption of that underworld, which surfaces with all the violence of a volcanic explosion, pushing Bruce Wayne to the limits of his strength and endurance.

"What was important in *The Dark Knight Rises*," said Christopher Nolan, "and what David and Jonah and I talked a lot about, was the idea that the victory at the end of *The Dark Knight* is based on a lie, and therefore, over time, they are just papering over the cracks. The underlying theme of *The Dark Knight Rises* is 'Truth will out,' the idea that though things seem better in Gotham, there is an evil beneath the surface that is going to bubble up. At some point—at Jonah's suggestion—we decided to literalize that metaphor and actually have a villain that is tunneling up from within the sewers of the city."

The third film's emerging themes and story lines suggested yet another genre shift: neither hero's journey nor crime drama, *The Dark Knight Rises* would encompass the tone and wide-scale destruction of an epic disaster movie or war film. "What was exciting to me about doing this trilogy," noted Jonathan Nolan, "was that we weren't repeating ourselves. We took these characters on a journey through three different genres, each time raising the stakes. The challenge coming out of *The Dark Knight* was, 'What do we do next? How do we raise the stakes of *that* film?' To me, the answer was making it bigger and darker—just going for it. And that created a genre shift into an epic disaster movie, hopefully without losing any of the emotional heart."

"Going for it" meant conceiving action sequences that would be exponentially larger in scale and would consume considerably more screen time than did those in *Batman Begins* or *The Dark Knight*.

In scripting the film, however, Nolan and his cowriters didn't invent action sequences for their own sake; rather, the action grew, organically, out of the story. "In putting

The story for the third film of The Dark Knight Trilogy—*The Dark Knight Rises*—recalls the epic scale of *Batman Begins*, while also exploring new themes. Shown here, concept art depicting an underground prison that figures prominently in the narrative.

together the story for *Batman Begins,*" said Christopher Nolan, "and then moving on to *The Dark Knight,* David and I had plotted out exactly how many action beats we would need, where they would be in the film, and so forth. When we came to *The Dark Knight Rises,* it was very important to me that we not engage in that process at all. It had worked very well for us in the first two films, but for this one, I wanted to throw that away and just write the story that needed to be there for the characters—and then we would create whatever action arose from that story naturally.

"The danger of going into a third action film is that you inflate the action components as a way to meet audience expectations. Most third films are very disappointing to people for exactly that reason: 'Yes, it's bigger and louder, but it doesn't interest me.' So I wanted to go with the characters and their stories, first, and trust that the action would arise out of that approach."

"We absolutely resisted the idea of making *The Dark Knight Rises* bigger just because it was a third movie," affirmed David Goyer. "We didn't go *into* it saying that we were going to make an epic war movie, and then develop the story from that idea. It was decidedly the opposite of that. In fact, again, the first thing we came up with was the ending, which was very personal, and we wrote a beginning that also had Bruce Wayne in a very personal place. That's what we had when we started. It wasn't until a month or two into the writing process that things got very big and destructive in the middle."

The key character driving the destruction is Bane, a Batman villain depicted in comic books wearing wrestling gear and a mask. Unlike the Joker, Scarecrow, and Two-Face, all of whom dated back to *Batman* comics of the '40s, Bane hadn't appeared until 1993, created by Chuck Dixon, Doug Moench, and Graham Nolan (no relation to the filmmakers).

Just as the action evolved out of the story, so too did the choice of Bane as the main villain for *The Dark Knight Rises.* "I think that often in comic book films," noted Goyer, "as they get to the second and third iterations, the filmmakers will decide ahead of time 'We're going to use this villain,' and then they'll develop their story from that decision. I think the studio and others assumed that after *The Dark Knight* we would perhaps use the Riddler or the

Penguin—one of the other canonical villains. But that's just not how we approach things. Our approach has always been: 'What's our theme? What story do we want to tell about our character? Okay, given that, which villain makes the most sense to have in this story?' That's how we chose Bane for *The Dark Knight Rises*."

On the surface, Bane seemed an odd choice, especially for the edgy Batman world that Nolan and his collaborators had created. Design-wise, there was an almost silly aspect to the character as he'd been rendered in the comics—a hulk in a brightly colored *luchador* (Mexican wrestling) mask. And his only "promotion" to the film world was a brief appearance as a mindless brute in 1997's *Batman and Robin*. But as Nolan and Goyer considered their story line and its themes, Bane seemed perfectly suited to *The Dark Knight Rises*. "For the story we were attempting to tell," said Goyer, "I think Bane was the *only* choice we could have made for our villain."

What Bane brought to the equation was an archetypal villain that fit the extremity and severity of the events in *The Dark Knight Rises*, raising the stakes for both the audience and Batman. Bane would also be as physically strong and intimidating, if not more so, as Batman—something neither of the first two films' villains had been. "We'd never had a physical monster as our villain," said Nolan. "Bane is a very well-conceived, physical villain in the comics, but someone who has an incredible mind as well. And whereas the Joker's backstory was very obscure, Bane's is epic. We wanted to go the opposite way this time, using a villain with a very rich origin story."

Bane's backstory—that of an orphaned boy thrown into a hellish prison by his father—was, in many respects, the diametric flip side of Batman's origin story. "We thought it would be interesting to explore those parallels," said David Goyer. "We also thought his name was interesting for our story. The definition of the word 'bane' is 'source of harm or ruin; a curse,' and he functions as all of those things in the movie."

The writers scripted an opening prologue sequence that would introduce Bane in a dramatic fashion, and prove him to be a most formidable "source of harm or ruin." The prologue—a stand-alone sequence, much as the bank heist prologue in *The Dark Knight* had been—starts with unidentified armed men delivering nuclear physicist Dr. Leonid Pavel and some hooded mercenaries to a waiting CIA turboprop plane on an eastern European airstrip. Once airborne, a CIA agent begins to interrogate the hooded men about Bane—only to find Bane himself beneath one of the hoods.

Suddenly, a much larger C-130 Hercules transport plane appears above the turboprop, and skydivers repel out the back, land on the wings of the CIA plane, and attach a cable to its tail—causing it to dangle beneath the C-130, nose-down, like a fish on a line, when the transport plane ascends. Inside the turboprop, the mercenaries kill the CIA and Special Forces agents and transfuse Pavel's blood into the body of a dead man as part of a plot to fake Pavel's death. They then attach Bane and Pavel to a cable, and detonate charges that release the fuselage, leaving the pair hanging from the C-130. The sequence ends with a shot of the uncabled turboprop falling to earth.

The prologue sequence, as written, would reveal much about Bane's intelligence and ruthlessness, but his full history—including his childhood years as an orphan—wouldn't unfold until later in the story.

Orphans, and an orphanage for boys, would figure prominently in the screenplay, creating a narrative link between Bruce Wayne, Bane, and John Blake, a young cop—also orphaned as a child—whom Commissioner Gordon takes under his wing. "Blake has a literal connection to Bruce Wayne, who, having been an orphan himself, is involved with boys' homes in the city," explained Nolan. "Orphans are the most vulnerable members of a society, among those who would be the most affected by the consequences of a rotting society. It was something my brother introduced in his draft, and I ran with it in the rewrites."

Another character central to *The Dark Knight Rises*'s screenplay was Selina Kyle—Catwoman—a cat burglar and grifter seeking a fresh start and a way out of her criminal life. Early on, Jonathan Nolan was alone among the three writers in his enthusiasm for including Catwoman in *The Dark Knight Rises*. "I was a big advocate of that character," he said. "It seemed to me that if we were trying to create

had questions about how we were going to justify her cat-suit, but Chris just pushed that question aside until later."

"I wasn't sure how to illustrate that character in our world," Christopher Nolan added, "but it was an interesting challenge. And, for me, what clinched it was abandoning the idea of her costume persona. We said: 'Let's look at her as a cat burglar, a grifter, a con woman, and a real-life character. Let's write that character, put her in the story, and trust that the theatrical elements of what makes her specifically Cat-woman as opposed to any other cat burglar would evolve.'"

Though there is sexual tension between Selina and Batman in the story, Bruce Wayne's real love interest is Miranda Tate, a passionate advocate of Wayne Enterprises' now-defunct fusion energy program. Like Rachel Dawes, Miranda was a character drawn not from the comics but from the imaginations of the screenwriters. "We looked at the various romantic entanglements that Bruce Wayne has had in the comic books," said Nolan, "and none of those characters quite seemed to fit what we were looking for. We wanted a kind of jet-set, international figure who was from outside Gotham, but part of Gotham society. Miranda's character helped us to get across the idea of Gotham as the hub of a global culture."

For Christopher Nolan, finalizing the screenplay was only the first step in bringing *The Dark Knight Rises* to the big screen, and it was followed by an intense eighteen months of production and post-production. But for David Goyer and Jonathan Nolan, the completed screenplay signified the end of their involvement in the film, in the trilogy, and—by all accounts—in the world of Batman. They had written their last wry and witty line of dialogue for Alfred, their last action sequence showcasing a Bat-inspired vehicle moving at breakneck speed, their last fight sequence, and their last scene between Batman and Commissioner Gordon.

"It was a little sad to have it be over," Jonathan Nolan admitted, looking back over the experience, "because writing for this character was a source of endless fun for me. But, I also think ending with this third film was absolutely the right thing to do. We told a complete story, and then we walked away."

a complete arc for Batman, we couldn't do it without Cat-woman, and without that relationship between Catwoman and Batman."

But both Nolan and Goyer feared the potential for high camp to which the character lent itself, and, given the Cat-woman characterizations of the television show and previous movies, it didn't seem that she would fit easily within the hyperrealistic world they'd created.

"We kept thinking about Eartha Kitt in the role," Goyer admitted, "which was not of the Christopher Nolan Batman universe *at all*. But we talked it through and found a way into the character that we thought was interesting. We still

In the graphic novel, *Catwoman: The Dark End of the Street*, written by Ed Brubaker and illustrated by Darwyn Cooke, Selina Kyle's alter ego pulls a Batman-like move from one of Gotham's taller buildings. Originally serialized by DC Comics in *Catwoman* (vol. 3) nos. 1–4, 2002.

"It crossed our minds to throw out everything and try something new . . ."

CHAPTER 2

With each and every sojourn into the makeshift office to hash out the story line for a film in The Dark Knight Trilogy, Christopher Nolan and David Goyer had been assaulted—at one point or another—by the fumes of model glue wafting from an adjacent room, olfactory evidence of a separate but parallel creative process unfolding in that garage.

In the earliest stages of conceiving the story line for *Batman Begins*, Nolan had invited production designer Nathan Crowley—a friend and colleague with whom he had worked on *Insomnia* (2002)— to join his at-home sessions with Goyer and create concept art and models that would inform and inspire the screenplay. What Nolan wanted, first and foremost, was a scale model of the Batmobile.

To Nolan's mind, the Batmobile was *the* iconic piece of Batman hardware that would illustrate exactly what he was trying to do with his film. "Our entire approach to telling Batman's story could be found in the look and feel of that vehicle," explained Nolan. "We were looking to present Batman as a functional figure, somebody concerned with utility, and so his vehicle would have features that were functional as well, rather than features whose only purpose was to look good. I felt that if we could crack that design and produce a model, it would give us a simple and clear expression of the tone of the piece, which was going to be a combination of heightened reality and utilitarianism."

Nolan envisioned the vehicle as having the armor and weight of a tank, and yet the low profile—and speed—of a Lamborghini. Prior to Crowley's involvement, Nolan had illustrated the concept for David Goyer by shaping a ball of clay in his hands. "He said, 'I think it should look something like this,'" Goyer recalled, "and he showed me this

very crude clay—and damned if that isn't what the Batmobile ended up looking like!"

That crude but illustrative shape served as reference for Crowley when he set about building the initial Batmobile model, which would be followed by more refined iterations in the weeks to come. Throughout that period, Crowley also produced drawings and Photoshop renderings of sets and Batman-related weapons and gadgetry.

All of these visual concepts would impact the story, just as the emerging story would impact Crowley's designs. "While we were working up the story," Nolan recalled of the period, "Nathan and I started putting together the initial visual elements that would form the basis of that story. Nathan and David and myself were able to develop a lot of the ideas that became important in the film, *before* we had to explain ourselves to too many people. We didn't know yet what the limitations were going to be in actually making the film, and so we were free to design and dream on the grandest scale imaginable."

PAGE 56: The colors and lines of production designer Nathan Crowley's early view of Gotham, above, began emerging during the first few weeks of pre-production.

ABOVE: Nathan Crowley and Christopher Nolan in Nolan's garage, which served as a secret art department during the earliest stages of *Batman Begins*.

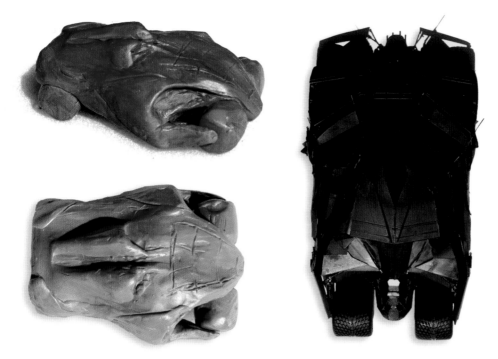

Reinventing the Batmobile was the first order of business. To convey his initial concept to Crowley, Nolan fashioned a crude Tumbler out of clay, which Crowley then extrapolated into more refined versions, using model kit-bashing techniques and computer-based sketches before arriving at the final rendition.

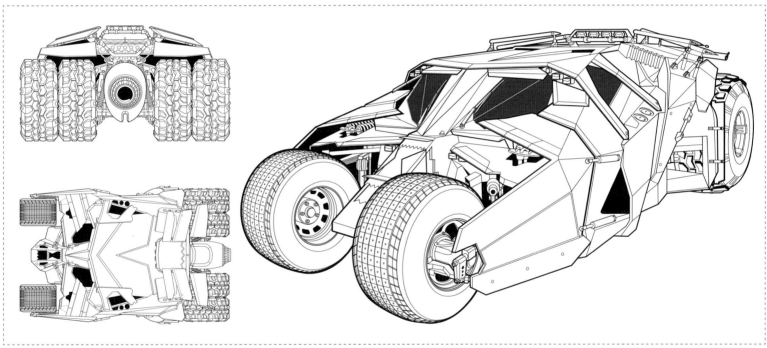

"It was very much a film-school atmosphere," David Goyer agreed, "and I loved that. It was all about the work—three or four people that really cared about what we were doing, just working in Chris's backyard, basically."

"The garage was fantastic," offered Nolan's wife and producing partner, Emma Thomas. "It was just brilliant having David Goyer in one room working on the script, while Nathan was in another coming up with the look of the film. There was a synergy in having them both in the same place, with Chris flitting between the two. It advanced our process considerably. It felt very normal for us, as well, because that's the way we'd always worked. Our first feature film was shot with friends over weekends, in our flat or in Chris's parents' house. So this felt like a very organic, natural thing for us. The only difference was that instead of a low-budget, independent film, we were doing *Batman*."

Starting with the all-important Batmobile, Crowley pulled bits and pieces from a variety of car and airplane model kits and assembled them into a first-stage model. "I started 'kit bashing,'" Crowley recalled. "From time to time, Chris would take a break from writing the script and find me covered in glue and car concepts."

Assimilating input from Nolan, Crowley built a series of kit-bashed Batmobile models until he arrived at a final design, which Nolan then presented to executives at Warner Bros. Nolan's hope was that this single model would clearly communicate to them his broader vision for *Batman Begins*—and it did. Studio executives responded enthusiastically to the Batmobile model and the utilitarian vision that it represented—so enthusiastically, in fact, that they financed the building of a full-size, functional Batmobile prototype.

Nolan's plan was to shoot *Batman Begins*'s high-speed Batmobile chase scenes using a series of real vehicles. Previous Batman productions had never attempted such a thing, instead opting to photograph essentially cosmetic Batmobiles that could do little more than slowly accelerate for a few feet and then roll to a stop on set. Typically, Batmobile action sequences had relied heavily on visual effects, with models or computer generated effects providing the vehicle's prowess and speed.

"There have been some magnificently designed Batmobiles in the films of the past," Nolan offered, "but there had never been a Batmobile that could handle a chase along the lines of that in *The French Connection*, which is what I had in mind for *Batman Begins*. I was determined not to use a digital Batmobile. I wanted a real car out on real streets."

In the six months prior to the *Batman Begins* shoot, special effects supervisor Chris Corbould worked with mechanical engineers Andy Smith and Kevin Heard and

fabrication expert Richard Gregory to build that real Bat-mobile in full-scale, reproducing Nathan Crowley's kit-bashed model.

"We took that model to England to show them," recalled Nolan, "and the first thing they asked when they saw it was: 'How is this going to steer? It has no front axle.' And Nathan and I kind of looked at each other, and shrugged—because we'd never thought about anything as mundane as *steering* when we built this thing! So I said, 'Well, I guess we could put in a front axle and then paint it out through visual effects.'"

The car builders suggested that Nolan hold off on mak-ing that compromise and give them some time to solve the steering problem. "They said, 'Let us sit with it for a few weeks, and we'll try and figure out a way to make it steer properly,'" said Nolan. "And they did. Within about six months they'd designed and built from scratch five of these things that could really do all of the things that the Batmo-bile had to do in the film."

The list of things the Batmobile "had to do" in the film was long. It had to be able to travel at speeds of up to one hundred miles per hour, and to accelerate from zero to sixty in only five seconds. The car would also have to be dura-ble enough to withstand a sixty-foot jump and subsequent hard landing.

On top of those structural and mechanical require-ments, the design mandated that the Batmobile crew build a custom chassis, as no existing chassis would accommo-date the car's extra-long and extra-wide dimensions. "We've customized cars for various films through the years," noted Chris Corbould, "but this was the first time we'd built one from scratch. We used existing engines and shock absorb-ers and wheels and that sort of thing, of course, but every piece of the body was custom-built."

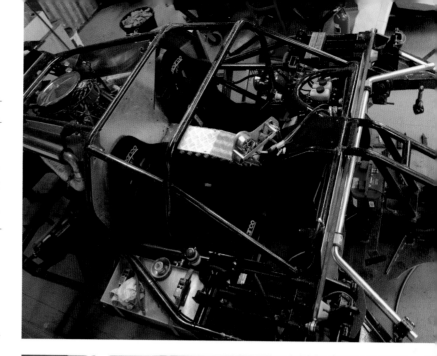

OPPOSITE: Nathan Crowley in the garage. His initial design concepts were mounted above the washer and dryer.

TOP: Because Nolan wanted the Batmobile to be a "real car out on real streets"—rather than a computer generated one, as realized in previous Batman movies—the special effects team, working with a crew of custom car builders, had to translate the Tumbler/Batmobile design into a practical vehicle. Shown here, the skeletal framework of the prototype Tumbler's cabin, chassis, and rear-mounted engine.

MIDDLE: The earliest stages of the Tumbler's interior reveal the humble beginnings of its steering wheel and dashboard, both of which would evolve considerably in design—and utility—throughout the vehicle's development.

BOTTOM: In *Batman Begins*, the Tumbler is built by Lucius Fox and the Applied Sciences Division as a prototype vehicle intended for military bridge laying, shown here with its original camouflage exterior.

Construction started with Crowley's art department carving the form of the vehicle out of a large block of Styrofoam, by hand. The Styrofoam shape measured nine feet, four inches long and was utterly faithful to the original kit-bashed model, reproducing it down to the smallest detail. "The full-size mockup even had the wrong-scale pieces and globs of glue that were on the original model," Nolan recalled.

From that foam model, the Batmobile crew made wooden molds for the car's sixty-five separate body panels, which would be mounted to a steel frame. The automakers built a test frame first, which enabled them to develop the engine, suspension, and braking systems before committing to the costly final vehicle.

The steering issue, for example, was worked out on the test model, with extra brakes mounted to the two rear wheels that would enable the stunt driver to turn sharply to the left or right by manipulating hand levers on either side of him. The crew also used the test frame to conduct jump tests, driving up a five-foot-long ramp at fifty miles per hour and launching the vehicle into the air. The first jump test resulted in the entire front end collapsing, requiring that a new test unit be rebuilt from scratch.

After working out all of the bugs, the crew built the first prototype, which sported a 5.7-liter Chevy V-8 350-horsepower engine and truck transmission within its steel frame, and had a body composed of sixty-five carbon-fiber panels. The vehicle was also fitted with off-the-shelf, extra-wide mud tires in the rear and Hoosier racing tires in the front. Safety for the stunt driver was assured with the installation of automatic fire extinguishers and a roll cage.

The unveiling of the prototype for Warner Bros. executives was a day of some anxiety and trepidation, as their response to the practical Batmobile would determine whether or not the studio was willing to invest in building the five vehicles Nolan had decided would be necessary for the production. It was no small sum of money, as each practical Batmobile would cost £250,000, or nearly half a million U.S. dollars.

The unveiling turned out to be an unmitigated success. Studio executives were bowled over by the slick, powerful, matte black vehicle displayed before them. "It was a very exciting day for us," Corbould recalled, "and at the end of that day, when everyone went away with smiles on their faces, Chris Nolan brought us a few bottles of champagne. We all had the feeling of, 'Yes, we've got a winner here.'"

Encouraged by the studio's response to their initial Batmobile model and the prototype, Nolan and Crowley applied that same utilitarian aesthetic to the design of other elements of Batman's world, such as the unusual, custom-made tools he employs to fight crime. "Batman has no superpowers except for his extraordinary wealth," commented Nolan, "and so, we wanted to address the story from this point of view: If you had limitless financial resources, how could you focus them on creating some very useful crime-fighting tools? And what would those gadgets look like if they were based on science and real-world logic?"

While playing with ideas for Batman's tools, Crowley also focused his attention on the design of Gotham, which Nolan had always envisioned as a hyperreal New York City. "It was an exaggerated idea of New York," Nolan said, "New York on steroids, if you will. Since we were going to be seeing Gotham from outside Gotham for the first time, we wanted to frame it as one of the great cities of the world, like London or Los Angeles or Paris."

Crowley began by mixing and matching architectural features from metropolitan areas around the globe—inserting, for example, an elevated freeway from Tokyo into a New York street via Photoshop. "We expanded on the idea of freeways running down the main streets," Crowley explained, "as if Gotham were a city gone crazy. I also made interpretations of buildings that I liked, such as Grand Central Station and the Grand Hyatt in New York."

A focus of the early stages of designing Gotham was the Narrows, the decayed, criminal-infested underbelly of the city. "We wanted the Narrows to represent the slum of all slums," Nolan noted. The Narrows would stand in stark juxtaposition to the glittering, hopeful Gotham of Bruce Wayne's childhood, the Gotham with clean streets and a sleek, high-tech monorail elevated above it all. If Gotham's best were above, its worst would be below, a cancer eating into the city's infrastructure.

RIGHT, TOP: As ideas evolved, even familiar images—such as Batman over Gotham, shown here—began to transform into something fresh and different.

RIGHT, BOTTOM: Imagined as an island in Gotham River, the Narrows connect to the main city by a series of bridges. The Narrows model included the Gotham monorail—a critical story element—rising above the slums.

Seeking reference for the Narrows, Crowley looked at the Walled City of Kowloon—a largely ungoverned, densely populated area of Hong Kong—and then built an elaborate model of a walled slum growing like a fungus around monorail track supports. Crowley and Nolan further emphasized the isolation of the Narrows by placing it on an island surrounded by a river—much as Roosevelt Island sits within New York City's East River—linked to Gotham proper by a series of bridges.

During the three-month-long conceptual free-for-all in the garage, Crowley and Nolan developed the foundational visual elements for *Batman Begins*—elements that, ultimately, would establish the tone and look of the entire trilogy. "It was a joy to be allowed to design *Batman Begins* while Chris and David wrote the script," Crowley stated. "The input and feedback were magical, and the bones of everything we did in that garage were applied to the film."

As *Batman Begins* went into official pre-production, Crowley set up his production art department at Shepperton Studios in London, where supervising art director Simon Lamont, art directors Peter Francis, Paul Kirby, Dominic Masters, Alan Tomkins, and Susan Whitaker, and a team of thirty artists fleshed out the models and computer concepts Crowley had generated in Nolan's garage.

Translating those concepts into final designs meant striking a balance between iconic Batman imagery and Nolan's fresh vision of that world. "We wanted to change things up," said Crowley, "but we still had to be true to the long history of Batman as he had appeared in DC Comics. So we launched into the film knowing that some of the designs would have to have that familiar Gothic feel, for example. It would have been too much of a push to completely change it, even though it crossed our minds to throw out everything and try something new."

In designing Wayne Manor interiors, for example, Crowley and his art directors rejected the clichés of wood paneling and suits of armor, and emphasized a more modern vision of wealth that still evoked a sense of the Wayne Family dynasty. "I actually ignored the design of Wayne Manor for a while," admitted Crowley, "because I was trying to think of a new way of looking at it. In the

end, we imagined it as an American East Coast house built of stone—but we avoided designing dark, gloomy rooms because we would already be spending a lot of the film outside at night."

The designers also conceived a new take on the Batcave—a man-made construct in all of its previous incarnations. Nolan, looking for a more realistic spin, imagined the Batcave as an actual *cave*, part of a natural system of caverns beneath the foundations of Wayne Manor. "Instead of the Batcave being this very elaborately and somewhat

improbably constructed place," said Nolan, "we designed it as this real cavern that was damp and filthy and full of real bats. And then we showed Bruce Wayne moving in equipment and stringing lights to make the cavern more 'livable.'"

Under Crowley's direction, construction crews translated production designs into small interiors built on Shepperton's soundstages or—more ambitiously—expansive sets housed within an abandoned and cavernous World War I–era dirigible hangar, one of the Cardington Sheds in Bedfordshire, a rural area of England. There, the *Batman*

Early concept art for *Batman Begins*: Gotham as viewed from the Wayne Enterprises boardroom.

Begins art department erected many fully realized Gotham City blocks, with paved streets, multistory buildings, streetlights, and signage.

The second-largest interior space in all of Europe, only Cardington proved big enough to accommodate the full-scale Gotham City that Nolan and Crowley had envisioned. "The scale of the film was *huge*," explained Crowley. "We not only needed to construct large, full-scale buildings, we also needed room for all of our large-scale effects work and stunts. We were going to be doing a lot of high wirework for

shots of Batman leaping off Gotham rooftops and the like, and that required a lot of height and space."

Even the most spacious studio soundstage didn't have the ceiling height to accommodate such stunt work. The solution favored by most productions with large-scale stunts and effects was to build sets outdoors on studio backlots, but Nolan wanted to avoid shooting on a backlot, if possible, as it would have subjected the production to the vagaries of weather—and not sunny Hollywood weather, but rainy, foggy, bone-chilling London weather.

The fact that Batman was a nocturnal creature posed another problem in shooting outdoors, as it would mean many, many weeks of night shoots, which are notoriously exhausting for cast and crew. "Chris wanted to avoid having to do all those night shoots," said Crowley. "For all of these reasons, what we needed was a huge indoor space, a space much, much bigger than any known soundstage—but we didn't know where we were going to find it. And then, one day, Emma said, 'There's this place where I grew up that looks pretty big…'"

Emma Thomas had grown up not far from Bedfordshire, situated about forty-five miles from London, and had regularly driven past the Cardington Sheds. The filmmakers drove out to investigate, and found two empty hangars—one beyond repair, but the second structurally sound enough to be transformed into a soundstage. The hangar measured a whopping 800 feet long, 400 feet wide, and 160 feet from floor to ceiling. "Since Cardington was originally an airship hangar," said Nolan, "it had been built on a much larger scale than any existing soundstage. You could fit *ten* of the larger stages at any of the film studios in the space that Cardington occupies. When you're on a stage set, you've got about 45 feet of height, whereas this space had 160 feet!"

With sixteen stories of fly space, the hangar could easily accommodate even the most extensive stunt rigging. Furthermore, the production would be able to simulate a controlled nighttime environment by blackening the windows, eliminating the need for night shoots. "It was essentially an indoor backlot," said Nolan, "which would allow us to portray Gotham in a more realistic manner than what we could have achieved on a normal soundstage. We wouldn't feel set-bound, because we were building it on such a large scale. We could have a stuntman jump five stories out of a building—and we could do that *inside*, without having to worry about weather conditions, and without doing it at night."

The Cardington hangar offered another unexpected bonus: It housed three substantial buildings—the tallest being eleven stories high—which would give the construction crews existing structures on which to mount facades and other set pieces. The buildings had been built by the local fire department to use as training facilities for exercises involving multistory firefighting and rescues, and Crowley integrated those structures into his Gotham City set designs.

Cardington was by no means film-ready, however. A dirigible hangar is not a soundstage, and production teams had to do a tremendous amount of refurbishing before they could even start building sets. "It took us ten months from the moment we took over that place to get it ready to shoot," said Emma Thomas. "They had to make all sorts of health and safety modifications to it before we ever got to building sets."

"After securing the site, making it safe, and putting in all the infrastructure, we needed to make the space usable," added *Batman Begins* producer Chuck Roven. "It only took four to five months to build that entire Gotham set—and by the time they were done building that set, it was like being in a major city. It was vast."

While production crews prepared Cardington for the shoot, the filmmakers also secured and prepped the film's many location sites. One of the defining features of previous Batman movies had been their confinement to Gotham stage sets, but Nolan and his cowriters had opened up Batman's world to include expansive settings *outside*

Gotham—and Nolan intended to shoot them at real and equally expansive locations.

Among them were glacial sites in Iceland that would stand in for the film's early Himalayan environments. To simulate the high altitudes, the filmmakers needed a location that was mountainous and above the tree line, but also accessible to the production's cast, crew, and equipment. "It's hard to find glaciers below 3,000 feet," noted Nathan Crowley, "but our location in Iceland was at sea level. It had a glacier, it had mountains, and it had absolutely no trees, which was fantastic. It *felt* like the Himalayas."

"We were very fortunate to find a spot that gave us so many options," said *Batman Begins* producer Larry Franco. "If you looked one way, you could see ocean, and when you turned around 180 degrees, it looked as if you were at twenty thousand feet. That was key for us, because it meant we could drive right into this area that looked like we were high up in the mountains. We knew it was still going to be difficult, because we were going to be there in

the winter, and there was going to be snow and rain—but it was a great location."

Crowley's team of designers, builders, and artists arrived at the glacier site in Iceland many weeks ahead of the film crew to build both the village Bruce Wayne passes during his Himalayan climb and the exterior facade of the Bhutanese monastery where he trains with Henri Ducard. "It was amazing," Crowley recalled. "The glacier creaked and moved about four feet each week, but we built an entire village there, with the front doors of the monastery just around the corner. It was tough going, though, because this was in January. There was almost no light, and we had a lot of storms and rain."

At some of the more rugged Iceland sites, crews first had to build roads on which to transport their construction materials, and then, later, camera and lighting equipment, cast, and crew. "Logistically," noted Emma Thomas, "it was an absolute nightmare. The crew had to carry all of that stuff up that hill, and then basically live there for months on end. It was all very nice for us, of course, sitting back

OPPOSITE: To add a sense of reality, the Batcave set included a running stream, weeping walls, and a waterfall.

ABOVE: One of the two Cardington Sheds—long disused airship hangars not far from London—was transformed into a working soundstage, and offered an impressive sixteen stories of fly space.

in our offices in England and just turning up to that location on the day!"

The filmmakers had found photogenic—and less logistically challenging—locations around England, as well, for interior and exterior shoots of key settings such as Arkham Asylum, the prison in Bhutan, and Wayne Manor. After looking at about twenty manor houses, the filmmakers chose Mentmore Towers in Buckinghamshire, about an hour and a half north of London, as their Wayne Manor.

In part, what appealed to them about Mentmore—a grand house built in the 1850s by the Rothschild family—was that it had a white interior, which provided a stark contrast to the film's otherwise dark color palette. To create the look of a mausoleum in the scene in which Bruce Wayne returns to Wayne Manor from college, set dressers shrouded all of the furniture in white as well, and laid down white marble floors, making it look as if the Manor had been leeched of all life and color in the absence of its master.

To dress the Mentmore grounds for the happier times of Bruce Wayne's childhood, crews built conservatories and formal gardens, which were later distressed to suggest the disintegration of the estate over time. "It was actually

a complicated set," said Nathan Crowley. "It wasn't just a matter of going on location. We had to show Wayne Manor in four stages: when Bruce's parents were alive, when he returned home from college, and after he brought it back to life as an adult. Then, at the end of the film, we had to show it as having been burned down. There was a lot to do at that location."

Advance crews also prepped locations in Chicago, where production would capture Gotham exteriors for establishing shots and action sequences. Specifically, the filmmakers planned to shoot the majority of the film's dynamic high-speed car chase, a centerpiece action sequence, on a stretch of underground road known as Lower Wacker.

All of the Chicago locations would expand Gotham, giving the fictional city a real-world scope and scale. "We built up a world of Gotham through the use of these real locations, as much as possible," said Christopher Nolan, "and then we mixed those locations with the wonderful sets that Nathan Crowley designed and built in Cardington."

To a large degree, the production design for *Batman Begins* had been constrained by the need to retain classic Batman iconography. In dramatizing an origin

ABOVE: An Icelandic glacier stood in for the Himalayas, where Bruce Wayne's journey to becoming Batman begins.

TOP: Conservatories and formal gardens were built at Mentmore Towers for *Batman Begins*, as was the set for the Wayne Manor ruins revealed at the end of the film (shown under construction here).

BOTTOM: Built by the Rothschilds in the 1850s, Mentmore Towers served as both interior and exterior for Wayne Manor.

tale, Christopher Nolan and his designers had felt bound to the well-established physical world of Batman. Furthermore, Nolan had recognized that his reality-based take on the Batman legend was already pushing the boundaries of what fans and DC Comics might find acceptable, and neither he nor Nathan Crowley had dared break all ties to the visual elements that had evolved over the character's seventy-year history.

"On *Batman Begins*," noted Crowley, "we'd had to tread carefully, because we were entering a world that people had a lot of passion for, and we hadn't wanted to ruin that for them. We'd had to find a way to fulfill their expectations while still giving them something new."

The shackles of the "old" Batman came off, however, as they approached the design of *The Dark Knight*. Rather than an established origin tale, the sequel was an entirely new story, unique to Christopher Nolan's Batman. The filmmakers also felt liberated by the fact that they had laid the foundation for edgier, more utilitarian, and hyperreal visuals in *Batman Begins*—and no one had demanded their heads on plates. In fact, rather than provoking widespread outrage among fans or undue anxiety at DC Comics, the design aesthetic so artfully wrought in *Batman Begins* had been enthusiastically lauded.

With confidence born of that response, Nolan and Crowley embarked on the design of *The Dark Knight*, concentrating early efforts on a new vehicle that would be introduced in the film: the Bat-Pod. "We didn't want to rely on simply bringing the Tumbler back," explained Nolan. "And so the idea of a two-wheeled vehicle came about. I hesitate to call it a motorcycle because its design was much more exotic and powerful-looking than a traditional motorcycle—yet it was connected to the world of motorcycles the way the Tumbler was connected to the world of cars."

As he had for the original Batmobile, Nathan Cowley designed the vehicle through trial and error, building a series of kit-bashed models in Nolan's garage. "I ended up sketching elements for the Bat-Pod, as well," Crowley said. "Then, because it was more like a motorbike than a car, we decided to build a full-size prototype out of bits and pieces of hardware—drainpipes and such. Most of the parts came from Home Depot."

With steering aparatus and engine still absent, this initial Bat-Pod prototype was more about form than function—and, in fact, at that stage, neither Crowley nor Nolan knew if the unusual design ever *could* be made to function. Seeking an answer to that essential question, Nolan flew Chris Corbould—who had overseen the building of the Batmobile for *Batman Begins*—from London to Los Angeles to look at the prototype model.

"When I got to L.A.," Corbould recalled of his introduction to the Bat-Pod, "I went out to Chris's garage and there was this 'article' in the middle of the room. Chris said, 'Well, what do you think?' And I said, 'You've got to be joking.' It was the weirdest, most bizarre-looking thing ever. Chris is a great one for developing ideas nobody else would ever think of, and he certainly achieved it this time. But it was clear that neither Chris nor Nathan had ever ridden a motorbike in their lives! In retrospect, that was probably a good thing, because if they'd had that experience, they most likely would have been swayed in the design of the Bat-Pod."

Corbould's primary concern as he studied the Bat-Pod was its maneuverability—or lack thereof. Conceived as forming out of the Batmobile, the Bat-Pod featured very fat tires—the Batmobile's tires, reconfigured to align with a two-wheeled, rather than four-wheeled vehicle. In Corbould's estimation, such extra-wide tires would make the Bat-Pod very difficult to steer.

"When I was in Los Angeles," said Corbould, "I told them: 'I don't know if we're going to be able to steer that thing. It'll probably do great in straight lines, but I don't see how we can get it to turn corners.' And Chris just gave me that look of his that says: 'You'll sort it out.'"

Once back in England, Corbould gathered his team and began kicking around ideas for solving the various maneuverability issues presented by the Bat-Pod's unusual design. "I set a couple of my lead guys, who happened to be motorbike fanatics, on the problem," he said. "They quickly pulled together a very basic prototype, and we progressed from there."

Within four weeks, the Bat-Pod team had built a rough, running prototype based on engineering principles straight out of Applied Sciences. The section of the vehicle on which

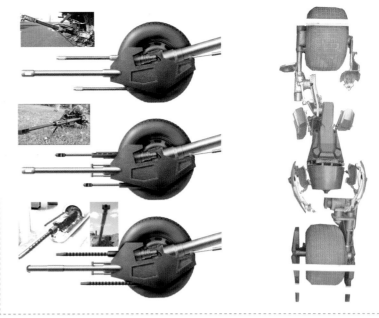

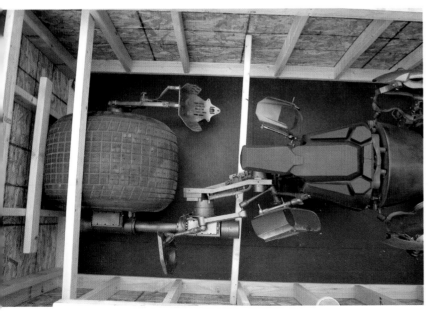

TOP, LEFT: An early sketch of the Bat-Pod taped to a door in Nolan's art department-garage, which was expanded for *The Dark Knight* and would serve as the filmmakers' conceptual home base throughout The Dark Knight Trilogy. For the second film, the filmmakers didn't want to rely on simply bringing the Tumbler back, which led to the idea of creating a two-wheeled vehicle. Though vaguely similar to a traditional motorcycle, it had to be much more powerful—and clearly connected to Batman's world.

TOP, RIGHT: Like the Tumbler, the Bat-Pod's design incorporated the latest Applied Sciences technology, including state-of-the-art weaponry, as illustrated here.

MIDDLE, LEFT: This tabletop version of the Bat-Pod reveals Nathan Crowley's "model kit-bashing" process of design.

MIDDLE, RIGHT: Nolan and Thomas's son, Rory, and nanny Monika Sury contemplate the full-scale Bat-Pod model, displayed on Nolan's patio.

BOTTOM: Upon viewing the Bat-Pod for the first time, special effects supervisor Chris Corbould felt immediate concern for the vehicle's complete lack of maneuverability. The full-scale model, shown here, was shipped to England where Corbould and his team built a rough, running prototype that included a gyrostabilized gimbal that enabled it to stay upright and angled tires that made it slightly easier to steer.

the driver would lie nearly flat, known as the "tower," was on a gyro-stabilized gimbal that enabled it to stay upright even if the Bat-Pod turned over or crashed. The effects team cleverly concealed the engine within the body, and built the exhaust system into the chassis, with radiators disguised as footpads. Large wheel wells contained the enormous, extra-wide tires, which were angled outward to make the surface area that actually touched the road considerably narrower—and the Bat-Pod slightly easier to steer.

While Corbould and his crew wrestled with the problem of how to translate the Bat-Pod design into a functional vehicle (see pages 177–178), Crowley and Nolan turned their attention to designing the various sets and environments that would be featured in *The Dark Knight*.

To depict the epic "hero's journey" aspects of the first film, Nolan and Crowley had set much of *Batman Begins* in natural, scenic settings. The film had featured slow pans across splendid Himalayan landscapes, pullbacks on the lush gardens, trees, and rolling lawns of the Wayne estate, and wide shots of natural—not man-made—caverns beneath the Manor's foundations, alive with rushing streams and waterfalls.

In contrast, what *The Dark Knight*'s story line suggested to the filmmakers was a much more architectural, industrial, and modernist aesthetic. "We had this chaotic Joker character who was trying to destroy the city that Batman has cleaned up and put to order," explained Crowley. "To portray that orderly Gotham, we wanted it to have hard lines and clean streets. We started asking, 'What if Gotham City Hall was like a modernist Mies van der Rohe building?' And we continued in that direction, deciding that we would create this very structured, ordered environment, and then the Joker would introduce anarchy into that environment."

The new direction would also reflect Bruce Wayne's state of being in the film. "In *The Dark Knight*, he's living an extraordinarily lonely and bleak existence," Christopher Nolan suggested, "which was reflected in the design. Through the design of his surroundings, we wanted to draw the audience's attention to the starkness of his new reality."

Top: The designers envisioned a new Gotham for *The Dark Knight*, based on modernist architecture.

Bottom: The Bat-Bunker served both form and function—and gave Bruce Wayne a convenient place to park the Tumbler while Wayne Manor was being rebuilt.

PRODUCTION DESIGN

Though not written with that specific intention, the burning of Wayne Manor at the end of *Batman Begins* provided the filmmakers with the ideal rationale for a change in Bruce Wayne's living environment, as well. "Bruce Wayne says that he's going to rebuild Wayne Manor brick by brick," said Nolan, "and so we thought it was unrealistic to have him moved back into the manor by the start of the second movie. Also, there was a period in the comics when he lived downtown, which we took as a jumping-off point to escape from Wayne Manor and get into the city. *The Dark Knight* is very much a city story that deals with all the different people in Gotham and how they interact, and it felt important to put Bruce Wayne right in the middle of that." To that end, the screenwriters moved Bruce Wayne into a modern penthouse apartment atop a Wayne Enterprises skyscraper.

The Dark Knight's urban setting suggested to Nolan and Crowley a different approach to creating the world of the film than they'd taken on *Batman Begins*. "We thought: 'Let's move away from set builds, which make a film look theatrical,'" recalled Crowley. "'Let's completely change it up, make it more raw.' If we were going to tell a second story, we wanted to treat it as a separate film with its own set of ideas, without hanging on to what we'd done in *Batman Begins*. It made sense, because in *The Dark Knight*, Batman *himself* has changed."

Nolan and Crowley would create a new Gotham not through the construction of massive sets, but rather by shooting a real city with real modernist architectural features. Location filming would support the urban-crime-drama vibe they'd envisioned for *The Dark Knight,* and would also serve to open up the film, visually. "The geography of *The Dark Knight* is actually smaller than that of *Batman Begins*," Nolan commented, "because—except for the Hong Kong sequence—the entire film is set within the city of Gotham. But by shooting most of it on location, instead of on stage sets, it would *feel* bigger."

After scouting locations in numerous U.S. cities, the filmmakers chose Chicago as their new Gotham and began making plans to shoot there. Set construction was still required for some interiors, however, such as the Bat-Bunker that would serve as Bruce Wayne's Batcave in the city. "We needed a space for Batman to have a workshop and operate from while he was repairing the Batcave," noted Nathan Crowley, "but we first had to figure out where this place *was*. We wondered if Bruce Wayne could just build it in the basement of his penthouse, but that solution seemed too easy and, at the same time, too hard—because how would he get the Batmobile in and out of the basement of a building right in the middle of the city without being detected?"

A panoramic view of Gotham City, as conceptualized for *The Dark Knight*.

To solve this logical problem, the filmmakers set the Bat-Bunker in an underground location somewhere on the outskirts of Gotham. Bruce would gain entrance to the Bat-Bunker by way of a freight container that descended into the inner sanctum—conceived as a cold concrete room that befit the film's overall modernist aesthetic. "We based the look of the Bat-Bunker on some of the sixties buildings we'd been looking at in Chicago," said Crowley. "We designed it to have a long, low ceiling, which created enormous perspective, and then we brought it to life by adding the workshop and equipment Bruce Wayne uses to make his Batman weapons."

The Bat-Bunker also gave Bruce Wayne a handy place to store his Batsuit. "The idea was that because it was a temporary space, everything went into the floor," explained Crowley. "That meant everything was on pistons: the suit, all the tables, the equipment—they all cleared out, and the Bat-Bunker became an empty box."

With the start of official pre-production on *The Dark Knight*, the art department oversaw the construction of the Bat-Bunker and other sets at Cardington and Pinewood Studios. Members of the art department also prepped locations in the United Kingdom and Chicago, many of which were familiar to them, as the production would be returning to a number of sites that had served it well on *Batman Begins*.

The production design process for *The Dark Knight Rises* closely followed the methodology that had been established for *Batman Begins* and continued with *The Dark Knight*. "As usual, Chris brought me in very early to design the film while he was writing," said Nathan Crowley. "I came on around the time that he had a first draft of the script; while he and Jonathan [Nolan] were doing a rewrite, I was plugging in visuals, putting together a visual version of the script, basically, which would then feed back into their writing. The result—as on the previous films—was that the final script really reflected those visuals."

The method of working was the same, but the setting had changed considerably since the inception of The Dark Knight Trilogy in the summer of 2003. Where once there had been only a cramped space with an old partners desk in a small writing area, linked by a single door to an even smaller model-building area, now there was a fully equipped screening room, a real office, and a separate building that housed the art department.

"For *The Dark Knight*," said Crowley, "Chris had fixed up the garage and turned it into real offices and a screening room, which folded up and became the art room. But after *The Dark Knight* he decided that he liked the screening room so much, he didn't want it to be the art room as well, and so he bought the house behind him, knocked

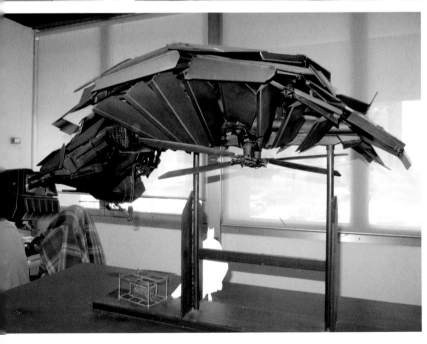

through a wall, and we started using the garage from the new house as the art room, with a linking door back into Chris's office. By the time we got to *The Dark Knight Rises*, we had a whole model-making department and art room equipped with tools and workbenches and drawing tables—everything we needed."

Crowley started, as always, with the design of the new vehicle that would be introduced in the film—this time, the Bat, a flying craft with all the dynamics and aesthetic appeal of Batman's previous rides. The initial challenge was designing a Bat that was based on real-world technology. "On both *Batman Begins* and *The Dark Knight*," Crowley said, "we had said that we wouldn't do anything that wasn't believable. For example, the Bat-Pod—even though it was a very hard thing to realize—was based on some pretty sound logic. It wasn't whimsical.

"So when Chris said, 'We're going to do a flying machine for *The Dark Knight Rises*,' my response was: 'Okay, but we said we'd never do a flying machine. How do we make that believable for the audience? And does this mean we're going to have to do it with CGI?' CGI has improved tenfold since *Batman Begins*, and so there was no question that they'd be able to do a CGI Bat that looked real—but we still had to give it a foundation that would make the audience believe it *was* real, rather than us just making it *look* real. So my first job in the garage for *The Dark Knight Rises* was designing the Bat, and figuring out how something like that would exist in our world."

As it happened, something like that *did* exist in the real world—more or less. "The Bat is based on various vertical-takeoff-and-landing craft that are used for urban fighting right now," explained David Goyer, who, working with Christopher Nolan, had introduced the flying craft into the film's story line. "It's a way to get troops into urban centers because, increasingly, that's the type of fighting that the army is doing. So the defense industry is experimenting with a bunch of these types of vehicles."

The narrative groundwork for where Bruce Wayne might obtain such a flying craft had been laid in *Batman Begins*. "We already know from the earlier film that the Bat is the type of thing he might find in Lucius Fox's Applied Sciences," said Nathan Crowley. "That had been all set up in *Batman*

TOP: The Bat, a third-generation Applied Sciences vehicle, was created for *The Dark Knight Rises* as Batman's newest mode of transportation.

MIDDLE: The designers initially imagined the Bat as a Harrier jet combined with a helicopter.

BOTTOM: The Bat, in "flying bug" profile.

Begins, and it is even more believable in *The Dark Knight Rises* because, unlike then, the Applied Sciences Division is fully functioning now that Lucius is the head of Wayne Enterprises. So there was logic in *where* he would get it—but we still had to make it believable, and make it look like it was part of the same military tradition as the Batmobile."

Crowley started by building Bat models inspired by helicopters and Harrier jets, much as the features of a Hummer and a Lamborghini had inspired the design of the Batmobile. The vertical takeoff capabilities of the Harrier, in particular, made perfect sense within the context of the story. "Obviously," said Crowley, "there is no runway out of the Batcave, and so we needed a vehicle that could lift off and hover like a Harrier. But for the action in the streets, we wanted something that would move like a helicopter. So we had this idea of the Harrier jet combined with the helicopter, and we began to design these aerodynamically whimsical vehicles."

As the screenplay evolved, story points emerged that suggested the Bat would have to be much bigger than originally envisioned—big enough to carry the Batmobile inside it. "At that point, we realized that we had to make it much bigger and more armored," said Crowley, "like an Osprey—a big military flying machine. It had to be much more aggressive, as well, just because of the action in the script. So the design grew from there, and it wound up looking like a flying bug. It was faceted and paneled like the Batmobile, but much more organic, with jump jets on the front and underslung choppers."

Throughout the Bat's modeling phase, Christopher Nolan watched Crowley's work and made suggestions. "Chris would be standing over my shoulder," Crowley said, "as he always does when we build these vehicles, saying: 'What about this? What about that?' We're kind of in it together in that way, and what I've learned after all these years of working with Chris is that it always takes about five designs before we get it right. And that was true of the Bat, as well." In keeping with a tradition between the two men, Crowley took home the fourth-stage Bat model—the Mach 4—and Nolan kept the final Mach 5 as his own. The other three Bat designs remained on display in the garage.

Once again, Chris Corbould accepted the challenge of translating Nolan and Crowley's ambitious design—illustrated in an eighteen-inch model—into two practical, full-scale versions of the aircraft. The practical Bat wouldn't be capable of flight, obviously, but it would be mounted atop a tow truck by way of a hydraulic column—also engineered by Corbould's team—that would raise and lower the craft as it was driven through city streets at high speeds. "That one also had working parts," said Corbould, "such as flaps that moved and a cockpit that opened. And then we built a second one that was a lot lighter so we could fly it underneath a helicopter or on zip lines."

Crowley next moved on to designing key sets suggested in the screenplay, integrating and fusing the natural landscapes of *Batman Begins* with the modernist architecture of *The Dark Knight*. "By the time we got to *The Dark Knight Rises*," said Crowley, "we said: 'Let's go one step further now and mix landscapes and architecture.' We'd describe the emotional journey of Batman being an outcast in large, remote landscapes, but we'd also use architectural elements to present the idea of Gotham as a place that had been living a lie since the death of Harvey Dent, a place that isn't as good as it once was. Mixing the two seemed like the best way to achieve this movie."

"In design and visual terms, *The Dark Knight Rises* is very much a fusion of the first two films," Christopher Nolan elaborated. "We used elements from both films, because both are relevant to the story. Bruce Wayne's story in *Batman Begins* isn't just relevant to Gotham—it's a global story. And we return to that idea in *The Dark Knight Rises*. Bane's story, too, is a global one. He's a threat that comes from outside of Gotham, whereas the Joker really sprang from *inside* Gotham."

Perhaps no set in *The Dark Knight Rises* better exemplifies the fusion of the design philosophies from the first two films than the new Batcave, which has modernist cubes rising from a running spring within a natural cavern. "We spent a full four weeks in the garage trying to figure out how to mix the Bat-Bunker from *The Dark Knight*—which turned out to be my favorite set ever—with the Batcave from *Batman Begins*," Crowley recalled. "How do you mix the idea of this natural cave with the modernism and power of the Bat-Bunker? We finally came up with the idea of

Concept art for *The Dark Knight Rises*.

having these cubes rise up out of the water in the Batcave." Crowley's art department would build the new Batcave set at Sony Studios in Culver City, enabling Nolan to shoot scenes there during the production's tenure in Los Angeles.

Given that New York had always been the model for Gotham—not only in Nolan's film, but also in the *Batman* comics and graphic novels—the city was a major influence on the design of Gotham as it would appear in *The Dark Knight Rises.* New York provided inspiration for the underworld over which Bane presides, as well. "I live half the time in New York now," Crowley explained, "and so I've spent a lot of time wandering around the subways of New York, thinking: 'Oh my God, this is phenomenal. We should shoot down here!' There's huge history there, and some of the older stations have all of this Victoriana and tile work.

"I'd played with that a bit for the monorail stations in *Batman Begins*; and we didn't need it for *The Dark Knight*—but on this film, it all came back into play because Bane had to go through the subway to get to the sewer system. So New York's subway stations gave me an immediate underground network, and my thought was that if we filmed in some of those subway stations, we'd have half of Bane's world right there, without having to build all of it."

Initially, the filmmakers had also considered shooting *The Dark Knight Rises*'s sewer scenes in actual sewer systems, and they explored some of those systems while scouting locations. "We looked at every sewer system in the world," said Crowley, "and that was going to determine where we were going to shoot. But, in the end, we decided to build a lot of it. The idea was to mix large-scale sewer sets with some great subway systems in various cities, as well as some water and sewer systems we found in Los Angeles."

It was in scouting subway stations and sewers that Crowley realized that the mixing and matching of different locations and sets would be an eminently workable approach. "From looking at all of these real-world underground sites, I learned that you could connect any one look with any other. You can have a sort of Victoriana subway that leads into a modernist sewer system—and it doesn't matter, because it's underground. I believed that as long as we had enough space and we had water,

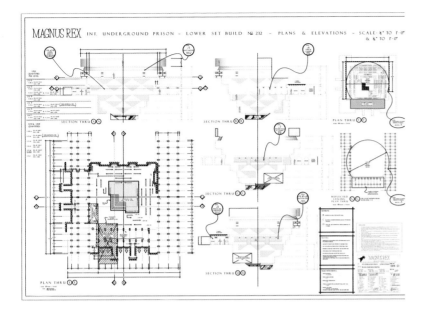

TOP: Plans and elevations for the *Magnus Rex* pit prison. As with the first two films in The Dark Knight Trilogy, *The Dark Knight Rises* was given a code name based on one of director Christopher Nolan and producer Emma Thomas's children—in this case, their son Magnus. Though originally entitled *The Intimidation Game*, the code title for *Batman Begins* was changed to *Flora's Wedding*, while *Rory's First Kiss* stood in for *The Dark Knight*.

BOTTOM: The prison's design was inspired by the Indian stepwells of Rajasthan.

OPPOSITE: The new Batcave mixed the modernist cubes of *The Dark Knight* with grottolike elements from *Batman Begins*.

OVERLEAF: Director Christopher Nolan on the Batcave set for *The Dark Knight Rises*.

we could make Bane's underground world feel real and appropriately confusing."

In fact, the designers came to appreciate that the more looks they shot and built for Bane's underworld, the better it would serve the story. "It would create the feeling of a maze," said Crowley, "and it would lend credibility to the idea that Bane could live under there undetected. So we created that sense of confusion in the designs of everything leading to Bane's lair, and then, Bane's lair itself had a simple, modernist feeling. So there was chaos leading down to his lair, but the lair itself was this perfectly geometric, simple space. It was important to keep that space simple because a big fight takes place there and we wanted the eye to focus on the fight rather than on the architecture around it."

Another underground set that figures prominently in the story is the 500-foot-deep pit prison. "When Chris first mentioned that he wanted an underground prison," Crowley recalled, "I asked him if he'd ever seen Indian stepwells, which are these crazy, geometric steps leading down to water that ancient cultures in India built. Originally, we thought maybe we could shoot one of these stepwells as a prison, and so we went out to Rajasthan [India] and drove across it, looking at these stepwells.

"We came to the conclusion that it was so remote an area that we wouldn't be able to bring a whole crew out there for the amount of shooting we had to do in that prison. So we decided to build our own stepwell as a set, but we still wanted to use that area of India as the place Bruce Wayne comes out of when he escapes the prison. So we ended up building the underground prison in Cardington, and then we shot the exterior in India."

At the end of production on *The Dark Knight Rises*, Nathan Crowley reflected on the experience of designing all three films in The Dark Knight Trilogy, and on the satisfaction of seeing the project through from beginning to end. "I got to complete a journey," Crowley said, "and it was much more satisfying than it would have been if I'd only done one of the films. The most satisfying part of it was that I got to explore—and that not only changed the way I design film, but it also helped me to discover what kind of designer I am. I've definitely changed my ideas about design over the course of these three films."

"At the end of the day, Bruce Wayne is just a guy who does a lot of push-ups..."

CHAPTER 3

When Christopher Nolan initiated the *Batman Begins* project, he knew that the single most critical decision he would make would be his choice of actor to play Bruce Wayne and his alter ego, Batman. Nolan was looking for an actor with range enough to portray the many nuances and dualities that he and David Goyer had written into the character, but who also possessed a Batman-size physical strength and intensity.

The first actor Nolan met with was none other than Christian Bale, who had expressed interest in playing Batman after being introduced to the darker manifestations of the character as portrayed in graphic novels. His interest level rose when, in 2003, he learned that Christopher Nolan—

In addition to packing on weight, Bale had prepared for the screen test by engaging Nolan in a number of in-depth conversations about his take on the character and the story. "I picked his brains as much as he would let me," recalled Bale, "and found out as much as I could so that I could be confident going into the screen test. I said to Chris: 'I don't want to waste time here. If we're going to do a screen test, I don't want to guess.' I had to know if we were on the same wavelength."

As clear on Nolan's vision for the character as he could be without having had access to the script, Bale gave the screen test all he had, wondering as he did so if he was giving too much. "I really went for it," Bale said. "I knew it might be more extreme than they would like, that they might look at me, and think: 'What the hell is he doing? There's no way he's going to be in our big-budget movie doing *that*!'"

"That" had been a feral, frightening, and almost freakish take on Batman, an interpretation that had Bale speaking in an animalistic growl—and it was precisely what Nolan was after.

"When Christian was playing Batman," Nolan recalled of the performance, "he communicated a lot of intensity just through his eyes and mouth. He was also very controlled and specific in how he portrayed the aggression of this character, the animal-like quality. He talked a lot about Batman crouching in the shadows, on railings or sides of buildings—very much the way he does in the comics.

"Then, when he was playing Bruce Wayne, he had that same intensity, a fire in the eyes that made you believe that this was an ordinary man who could make himself extraordinary, simply through self-discipline—because, at the end of the day, Bruce Wayne is just a guy who does a lot of push-ups."

Nolan cast Bale soon after, with the understanding that the actor would continue to build his body to Batman size in the months leading up to the start of principal photography. "I impressed upon Christian that for Bruce Wayne to really fill the suit, he was going to have to be very, very large," Nolan said.

Bale took Nolan's dictum to heart, but though his efforts yielded extra pounds, his muscle mass remained seriously

a filmmaker he admired—was planning to direct a reimagined Batman. Just what that reimagining would be, however, remained a mystery. "When I first met with Chris, he was very secretive about the script," recalled Bale, "but he did tell me enough about the story line and the way he wanted to film it that it intrigued me."

Equally intrigued with Bale, Nolan suggested a screen test. It was more than a small leap of faith as, at the time of that first meeting, the thirty-year-old actor was extremely thin, having lost nearly seventy pounds for his role as chronic insomniac Trevor Reznik in 2004's *The Machinist*. Bale assured the director that he could regain the weight in time for the screen test, scheduled a mere eight weeks later, and sure enough, when he arrived for the test, his gaunt appearance had radically changed. "I had assumed that Christian would be rake-thin still," Nolan recalled, "and that Warner Bros. and DC Comics would have to make a big conceptual leap to imagine him as Batman. But by the time he came back in, he'd regained the seventy pounds—and more."

PAGE 84: Christian Bale surveys the scene as Batman in *Batman Begins.*

ABOVE: Cast in the most essential role of The Dark Knight Trilogy, actor Christian Bale would play both Batman and the multidimensional Bruce Wayne in all three films.

OPPOSITE: Bale immediately understood the extreme nature of Batman, but he also realized that in playing Bruce Wayne, it would be necessary to inhabit the character's private and public personas as well as his super hero alter ego.

OVERLEAF: Christian Bale as Bruce Wayne in the Bat-Bunker, Batman's modernist lair, as reimagined for *The Dark Knight.*

diminished. "It was all pudgy fat," Bale admitted. "I was up to my regular weight, but there was no muscle at all. I couldn't run properly and my cholesterol was through the roof. I was not in good shape, and when I first arrived in England, I could see the look on Chris's face: 'Oh Christ. What has this guy done?' I looked like a bear, all heavy and hefty, not at all muscled and ripped. The crew looked at me like, 'Bloody hell, Chris, what are we doing here: Batman or Fatman?' I had a lot of work ahead of me before I could put on the Batsuit."

With characteristic self-discipline, Bale transformed his physique through an aggressive training and diet regimen, which he maintained throughout the shoot, eating little other than high-protein foods. "He was religious about it," producer Larry Franco recalled. "He didn't really start eating normally until the end of the shoot when he knew he wasn't going to have to take his shirt off again!"

Every bit as important as the size of Bale's body was the size of his persona—the presence he would bring to the role of Batman. "It takes somebody very special to put on Batman's costume and not be dominated by it," noted Christopher Nolan. "Christian had the ability to wear the suit, rather than let it wear him."

"The first time I saw Christian in the suit, I knew he was meant to play Batman," Emma Thomas agreed. "He took on a completely different presence. He got a different look in his eye. Christian's a fantastic guy, but when he put on the suit he became very intimidating, and in exactly the way Batman is meant to be."

Bale delivered a remarkable performance as Bruce Wayne and Batman from the moment cameras first rolled on *Batman Begins*, and his performances only strengthened as he plumbed deeper into the character in *The Dark Knight* and *The Dark Knight Rises*. Through all three productions, Bale exhibited a work ethic that matched Bruce Wayne's. "It was truly effortless to work with Christian on the first film," Nolan reflected, "although for him, it certainly was a *lot* of effort. He had to get himself in incredible shape, learn all kinds of different skills—the way Batman fights and moves, the wirework. There was a great deal for him to do, but Christian had the intensity and self-discipline to do it. Of course, these are the very qualities that Bruce Wayne brings to bear in changing himself from an ordinary man into this extraordinary crime-fighting figure, and Christian presented that very credibly and comprehensibly."

Faced with the prospect of reprising the role for *The Dark Knight*, Bale explored the ways in which Bruce Wayne and his alter ego had changed since the events of the first film. "In *Batman Begins*, Bruce Wayne was an angry young man seeking purpose with some degree of naïveté,"

Bale noted. "He imagined his role as Batman as being finite and believed he'd be able to leave this character he's created behind.

"In *The Dark Knight,* however, he realizes the burden of responsibility that goes with it. He suffers because of this Joker character he's unleashed—and who he's unable to rein in—and he still has so much anger that it's easy for him to tap into negative emotions. He's the angriest super hero I know of."

The Dark Knight Rises would demand that Bale dig deeper still into the character, as the Bruce Wayne introduced in the third film is as broken and dispirited a man as any the actor has played in his Oscar-winning career.

"In the first film, you see the tragedy and pain that motivate this young man who is searching for a path," he observed. "He's dying to be useful and to find out who he is and what he can become. In the second, you can see that he's found it. He has discovered his path; he is useful. He's doing what he imagines to be the best thing he can do with his life.

"But equally, we wanted to show the consequences of what Bruce Wayne does. He doesn't get to go out and have these adventures at night without coming home with a few broken ribs. In *The Dark Knight Rises,* we can see it all catching up with him, and not just physically, but mentally. How much longer can he allow this pain—and all that has happened in his life—to control what he does? At what point does it start to become completely self-destructive? That's where we got to in the final movie: What's his choice going to be?"

Taking a cue from director Richard Donner's 1978 *Superman,* Christopher Nolan—along with casting director John Papsidera—sought to surround Bale with high-caliber actors in all three films. "One of the things that made *Superman* so epic was the great casting," Nolan remarked. "You had Marlon Brando, Gene Hackman, Ned Beatty, and Glenn Ford—all these great actors around Christopher Reeve. I felt that Batman deserved a similarly epic treatment, and so we decided to go for the best actors possible, even to play the smallest roles."

That mindset led to the casting of Sir Michael Caine as Alfred Pennyworth, Bruce Wayne's mentor, butler, and friend. "It was a very different casting choice for Alfred than what we'd seen in other Batman films," commented Emma Thomas, "because Alfred was a very different character in our film, a more rounded character. He was also the emotional core of the film. We needed an actor who could do Alfred's great one-liners, but could play the heart of the role, as well. Michael Caine was perfect."

When Nolan drove out to Caine's home near London to offer him the role, Caine—known for his work in more character-driven films—was intrigued, but also surprised. "I had never done one of these great productions," Caine remarked, "but then, neither had he. Chris had never done great car crashes and explosions and things like that. So we sort of went into it together, and he made a wonderful job of it. He was brilliant."

For Caine, the appeal of playing Alfred was that, as written by Nolan and Goyer, he was a real, multidimensional *character* rather than a caricature of the classic English butler. "Usually in these big special-effects films," observed Caine, "the characters are ciphers. But these characters aren't ciphers. Alfred, in particular, was written as a very human character. Rather than a 'Dinner is served' kind of butler, he is Bruce Wayne's guide and mentor. He's also his family, all he's got left. He's the one person in Bruce's life who never gives up on him." Caine also saw Alfred as a kind of Everyman, the person in the Batman saga to whom the audience could most relate. "Alfred is *us* in this incredible world. You can't really identify with Batman or the villains. But Alfred is our spokesman. He reacts like a human being."

After working with Nolan on *Batman Begins* and *The Prestige,* Caine returned to the Batman chronicle for *The Dark Knight,* in which Alfred continues to act as Bruce Wayne's protector and friend, the one who worries about him and tends his wounds after his nocturnal exploits as Batman. "Bruce Wayne goes running around in a Batsuit and usually comes home punched in the nose, or all cut up—and Alfred sews him up," said Caine. "Alfred's good at that kind of thing. He's the human touch amongst all this—and Bruce Wayne keeps going back to him to see if he's done wrong this time. I think Alfred understands that if Batman turned dishonest, he would be a terrible villain. He'd be worse than the Joker."

By the time Caine returned for *The Dark Knight Rises,* Christopher Nolan and Emma Thomas had worked with

OPPOSITE, TOP: Sir Michael Caine portrayed Bruce Wayne's loyal servant, friend, and mentor, Alfred Pennyworth, throughout The Dark Knight Trilogy.

OPPOSITE, BOTTOM: Morgan Freeman as Lucius Fox, head of Wayne Enterprises' Applied Sciences Division in *Batman Begins*—and Wayne Enterprises CEO for the remainder of the series.

the actor on four previous films and had dubbed him their "lucky charm." "It's actually the opposite," noted Caine. "They are *my* good luck charms. I've now done five movies with them, and they've all been fabulous for me." With so much "Nolan time" under his belt, Caine had come to appreciate how adept the young director was at working with his actors. "He's quiet on the set, and he'll just come up to you very quietly to make a suggestion. The sign of a great director—and this happens with Chris—is that when he makes a suggestion, you go, 'Why didn't *I* think of that?'

"He's also always right there with you, watching you. A lot of directors watch everything from the video in the back, but Chris is like the old directors who would be right there with the camera, looking at you. He watches the real scene, right in front of him, and the real you."

It was with some degree of sadness that Michael Caine ended his tenure in Batman's world with the wrap of filming for *The Dark Knight Rises*, but he had a treasured memento to remind him of the experience that had encompassed eight years of his long and distinguished career and had introduced him to a new generation of filmgoers. "During the filming of *Batman Begins*," Caine recalled, "I'd remarked to Chris Nolan that, as Alfred, I'd never once had to say 'Dinner is served.' That Christmas, I received a gift from him—a butler's gong engraved with DINNER IS SERVED."

Another venerable addition to the cast was Morgan Freeman, drafted to play Lucius Fox. Unlike so many others associated with the production, Freeman came to *Batman Begins* as a fully formed comic book fan. "I was one of those kids, like millions of other kids, who read all the comic books," he said, "*The Spirit* and *Batman* and *Captain Marvel*. If there was a comic book, I read it."

Freeman never recalled seeing the character of Lucius Fox in those old *Batman* comics, however. "I didn't even know Lucius was in the comic books," he noted. "He must have been in the later ones because, when I was a kid, there wasn't anybody black in Batman. Later on, in the seventies, they started being more socially inclusive—all the comic books did."

Having made Lucius his own in *Batman Begins*, Freeman re-created the character for *The Dark Knight*—but it was a different Lucius this time around. Having been kicked down to the basement office of the Applied Sciences Division at the beginning of *Batman Begins*, Lucius was now occupying the top floor as CEO of Wayne Enterprises.

Lucius also stepped up to serve as Bruce Wayne's conscience in *The Dark Knight*—illustrated in a scene in which Batman asks Lucius to help him find hostages by eavesdropping on all the citizens of Gotham via a high-tech monitoring device. "Lucius doesn't want to do it," Freeman said, "because there is a lot of power in doing that, and he sees the potential for the misuse of that power. So he's very gratified when his boss destroys that equipment. It's like, 'Yeah, *that's* the man I work for.' And he becomes much more entrenched with Bruce and Wayne Enterprises, as a result."

Freeman was happy to return for *The Dark Knight Rises*—and wasn't at all surprised when he learned that Nolan was going to do a third Batman film. "When we finished *The Dark Knight*," Freeman recalled, "I remember saying to Christopher: 'You know, you're going to have to come back with a third one.' And he said, 'Yeah, I know—I just haven't figured it out yet.' And I said, 'Well, you will.' After that, I waited and waited—and then I got the call. Yes!"

The filmmakers turned audience expectations on their heads by casting Gary Oldman—known for portraying dark and troubled characters such as Sid Vicious, Joe Orton, Lee Harvey Oswald, Dracula, and Harry Potter's Sirius Black—as the altogether decent family man and incorruptible cop, Jim Gordon.

"I don't think Gary Oldman had ever played such a wholesome character," observed Christopher Nolan. "But he inhabited the role of Gordon. He took on his essence, his goodness, and the weariness he feels. Gary is such a chameleon, he even took on the appearance of the character from *Batman: Year One*."

Oldman returned to *The Dark Knight* as the beleaguered public servant—now promoted to lieutenant—and then to *The Dark Knight Rises* as Commissioner Gordon. Oldman's commitment to the Batman films was, in good measure, due to his admiration for Christopher Nolan. "He's a very unusual and unique filmmaker," Oldman noted. "He always delivers, so you never feel as if you've been cheated. At the end of the day, it's talent. He has great instincts and makes great choices."

TOP, LEFT: A panel featuring Jim Gordon from page 5 of *Batman: Year One*, written by
Frank Miller and illustrated by David Mazzucchelli.

TOP, RIGHT: Gary Oldman effectively took on the appearance—and essence—of the comic
book character throughout The Dark Knight Trilogy.

BOTTOM: As Gotham Police officer Jim Gordon, actor Gary Oldman first meets young
Bruce Wayne (Gus Lewis) shortly after the boy's parents are murdered.

After playing Jim Gordon in three films, Oldman was sensitive to the ways in which his character had evolved since *Batman Begins*. "When we first met him," Oldman said, "he was weary from trying to clean up a city, and then this strange guy that runs around looking like a bat became his ally in that. In *The Dark Knight*, the Harvey Dent episode injured him, spiritually, and he's had to live with the cancer of that ever since. By the end of *The Dark Knight Rises*, he is restored. I think that a lot of paper-pushing in the intervening years dampened his spirits, but on this, he's out in the field again, like a soldier at the front line, right next to Batman. The old Gordon is back."

Actors returning to play recurring roles would prove to be a hallmark of The Dark Knight Trilogy, and in the course of making the three films, there was only one cast change—the role of Rachel Dawes, Bruce Wayne's friend since childhood.

The character, which had originated in the imaginations of the screenwriters rather than on the pages of *Batman* comic books, was written as a young woman who could be both tough and idealistic in her job, and both loving and demanding in her relationship with Bruce Wayne.

When a scheduling conflict prevented Katie Holmes from reprising the role in *The Dark Knight*, Maggie Gyllenhaal stepped in and made the character her own. "Maggie was just wonderful as Rachel because she brought such warmth, intelligence, and spunk to the character," said producer Chuck Roven. "She delivered a great performance that combined the reality we were looking for with tremendous depth."

Gyllenhaal agreed to the project based on Christopher Nolan's reputation as a filmmaker and the high-caliber cast he'd already put into place. Batman didn't figure into the equation. "When Chris approached me about the film, it was almost incidental that it was about Batman," she admitted. "I was lured into becoming intrigued by the character through the process of making the movie. From the very beginning, Chris was so interesting and engaging—and so interested in me and my ideas about Rachel—that I wanted to be a part of it."

ABOVE, LEFT: Katie Holmes portrayed Bruce Wayne's childhood friend Rachel Dawes in *Batman Begins*.

ABOVE, RIGHT: Maggie Gyllenhaal stepped in as Rachel Dawes—now promoted to assistant district attorney—for *The Dark Knight*.

While characters such as Alfred, Lucius, and Rachel would provide emotional support to Bruce Wayne, the trilogy's villains would each test Batman in turn.

Liam Neeson set the standard for The Dark Knight Trilogy's villains in his portrayal of Henri Ducard/Rā's al Ghūl in *Batman Begins*. "The great thing about Liam is the authority and presence he has," said Chuck Roven. "When he talks to Bruce about having 'the will to act,' you know that this is a guy who *has* the will to act. He's not telling Bruce to do anything that he can't do himself."

"Liam's got such integrity about him," Emma Thomas added, "which was something we really wanted for this role." Neeson's history of playing noble film characters also helped to safeguard *Batman Begins*'s third-act revelation of Ducard as the real Rā's al Ghūl. "We were able to turn Liam's history of playing good guys on its head when it's revealed later in the film that he's not who he seems to be."

The third-act surprise was just one element of the screenplay that appealed to Neeson. "I thought the writing was superb," Neeson recalled of his introduction to the *Batman Begins* screenplay. "To have a script with those kinds of character dynamics made it truly appealing." Neeson was also eager to work with Christopher Nolan. "I thought he was quite extraordinary for someone so young. He's such a wonderfully complex man—I actually stole little bits of him for my character."

For the dual role of Dr. Jonathan Crane and the Scarecrow, Nolan cast Cillian Murphy, a relatively fresh face at the time. "I can't claim to have discovered Cillian Murphy," said Nolan, "because he'd done plenty of other great films, including Danny Boyle's *28 Days Later*. But he wasn't immediately familiar to American audiences, and that helped to invest the character with a degree of mystery. Cillian has an extraordinary screen presence, as well."

Ken Watanabe also brought great presence to the role of the ninja master first introduced to Bruce Wayne as Rā's al Ghūl, while distinguished English actor Tom Wilkinson brought a street-bred ruthlessness—and accent—to the role

Liam Neeson appeared as Bruce Wayne's mysterious mentor, Henri Ducard, who was later revealed to be Rā's al Ghūl. Shown here, the character is stopped by Bruce Wayne's sword in *Batman Begins*.

TOP: Nolan cast Cillian Murphy in the dual role of Dr. Jonathan Crane and the Scarecrow, while Tom Wilkinson played Carmine Falcone, Gotham's head gangster in *Batman Begins*.

BOTTOM, LEFT: Ken Watanabe appeared as the initial embodiment of Rā's al Ghūl.

BOTTOM, RIGHT: Aaron Eckhart portrayed Gotham District Attorney Harvey Dent, a complex character reborn as the villain Two-Face after tragedy drives him insane.

of mob boss Carmine Falcone. Even the relatively minor role of Wayne Enterprises CEO Bill Earle was filled by the renowned Rutger Hauer.

The filmmakers struck gold in the casting of Heath Ledger—who had been nominated for an Academy Award the previous year for his sensitive portrayal of Ennis del Mar in *Brokeback Mountain*—as the Joker in *The Dark Knight.*

"In casting the Joker, the main quality we were looking for was fearlessness," explained Nolan. "We were looking for an actor not afraid of comparisons with previous actors, and not afraid of taking on such an iconic role. We needed someone with a strong point of view on how they'd approach that—and Heath Ledger had those qualities in spades. That, and his extraordinary talent and skill as an actor, made an ideal combination. We had a sense of what he was going to do with the role going in, and it turned out to be stunning."

In fact, casting Heath Ledger as the Joker helped Nolan finish shaping the story he'd started with David Goyer and Jonathan Nolan. "Heath answered a lot of questions in terms of where that character would go and how he would appear relative to the other elements we'd first reinvented for *Batman Begins*," Nolan said. "To me, it was about creating a psychologically credible anarchist, a purposeless criminal, a psychopath. The most frightening enemy is the one who has no rules, who's not out for anything, who can't be understood.

"Heath immediately related to that. He understood that this character could be extraordinarily frightening and fresh and different from anything that had been done before."

With Ledger in place as villain-in-chief, the filmmakers quickly began seeing new ways for the character to upset the balance in Gotham. The writing continued in concert with Ledger's own development of the character, during which he invented original ways of speaking, laughing, and moving. "When Heath came over to do makeup tests and costume development," Nolan recalled, "he would try things on and you could see him start to develop a feel of this character just by moving around the room. It was extraordinarily exciting to watch."

As Nolan considered the casting of *The Dark Knight*'s other villain—Batman's ally-turned-adversary, Harvey Dent—he recalled Aaron Eckhart, whom he had met a few years earlier. Nolan admired Eckhart's talent and presence, and thought he embodied the all-American charm he was seeking for Gotham's much-needed "Hero with a Face."

"We wanted somebody who had that heroic presence, with an almost Robert Redford sort of aura," said Nolan. "But he also had to have an edge, an undercurrent of anger and darkness to him, so that when Harvey Dent needs to go there in the story, it isn't a cheat. After he was established as a very attractive heroic figure at the beginning of the movie, it had to be believable that this was a guy who would go to lengths that were questionable. Aaron embodied those qualities very, very well."

Nolan sent the script over to Eckhart with an assistant, who waited discreetly outside the room as the actor read. Impressed by the well-crafted story and fully realized characters, Eckhart didn't think twice about accepting the part. "It was a no-brainer, really," Eckhart said. "I'm a huge fan of Chris Nolan's, as well as of Batman in general. Batman's really the MacGyver of super heroes, transforming rudimentary things to suit his needs. There's also something fascinating about the way he lives a dual life. He has everything, and yet he comes from a place of great tragedy. That same duality exists in Harvey Dent. The yin and the yang, the night and day—all those opposites—make good drama. Like Batman, Harvey's conflicted, and acts out of a deep rage over an injustice that changes his life."

In terms of sheer formidability, neither Harvey Dent, as Two-Face, nor the Joker would test Batman to the extent that Bane would in *The Dark Knight Rises.* The mysterious and masked villain not only matched Batman in raw intelligence, IQ point for IQ point, but in pure physical strength.

In casting the character, Nolan and the producers looked for an actor who could convey both a physical threat and an agile mind—even from behind the mask that would cover most of his face. "It's very difficult to act through a mask," Nolan said. "In the opening of *The Dark Knight*, Heath was introduced as the Joker wearing a mask. All you can see of him are his movements, and he managed to convey a character in every gesture and every movement. So to me,

OVERLEAF: For *The Dark Knight*, actor Heath Ledger was cast as Batman's nemesis, the Joker. Ledger's portrayal so personified the anarchic villain that his take on the character helped the writers finish crafting the screenplay.

97

that answered the question of whether we needed a great actor to portray this muscle-bound, physical monster—yes, absolutely, we did."

Knowing that whoever portrayed Bane would be limited to body language and voice, Nolan immediately thought of Tom Hardy. "I had worked with him on *Inception* and found him to be one of those actors who can draw on every aspect of his instrument, if you will," Nolan said. "He has the ability to use every finger and toe and every eye blink to create a character. He is so physical in his approach to performance, I thought he might be interested in the challenge of playing a character of great importance to the film from behind a mask."

Hardy was in Vancouver, working on another film, when he received Nolan's initial call regarding *The Dark Knight Rises.* "Chris phoned out of the blue," Hardy recalled, "and said: 'Tom, I'm doing another *Dark Knight*, and there's a character you might be quite good for, but it's going to demand that you wear a mask… for six months.' And I said: 'Let me get this straight. You want me to work with you around the world and have the use of the entire stunt team and as many weapons as I want for six months, and all I have to do is wear a mask? I'm in—absolutely!' "

Only later would Hardy learn more about the pivotal character he was to play in the film, and it would be later still before he entirely grasped Bane's ruthlessness and determination to bring about complete destruction and chaos in Gotham. "I think it was Alfred who, talking about the Joker in *The Dark Knight,* said, 'Some people want to watch the world burn,' " Hardy noted. "Well, Bane is going to *make* it burn. He's come to pull the pin on the grenade and hold it close." In discussing the character with Hardy, Nolan referenced silverback gorillas and great white sharks. "Colonel Kurtz from *Apocalypse Now* was another figure that we liked for Bane," said Hardy.

With his facial expressions hidden behind the mask, Bane's voice would be particularly crucial in conveying the character, and Hardy took inspiration from Richard Burton and bare-knuckle boxer Bartley Gorman—the "king of the gypsies"—in creating Bane's vocal quality. "Bane is in tremendous pain all of the time," Hardy explained, "and so we wanted him to have an older voice. He is a slightly florid character, as well. Normally, a man of that size and weight has very few words to say. But Bane is as florid as Shakespeare!"

Bane may have been a talker, but above all else, he was a fighter. To portray a character that was Batman's physical equal, Hardy began training immediately after agreeing to take the role, even as he continued work on his current film, *Lawless.* The physical training resulted in Hardy's gaining considerable body mass, which he hid from that film's cameras by wearing an oversize cardigan. "As my back grew," Hardy recalled, "the cardigans had to get bigger and bigger."

Having built up so much muscle, Hardy felt exceedingly confident about his first screen test with Christian Bale. "I remember seeing Christian in the makeup chair, and he looked reedy," Hardy said. "I thought to myself: 'Oh, I can handle *him.* That's not a problem.' So I got changed into my Bane costume and went out and started flexing my muscles—and then Batman turned up. Suddenly, my arms felt really small, and I felt like I was about three feet tall. He just didn't look like Christian Bale anymore, and he was looking at me like, 'Oh *yeah*, I'm Batman.' And I was like: 'Yes, you are. I underestimated you.' "

In signing on to play Selina Kyle/Catwoman, Anne Hathaway was stepping into shoes previously filled by Eartha Kitt, Julie Newmar, Michelle Pfeiffer, and Halle Berry. But the character as written for *The Dark Knight Rises* was more nuanced than its predecessors, and Nolan felt Hathaway had the right combination of talents to bring a more complex Selina to life on the big screen.

"Anne's an absolutely extraordinary actress," he said, "and when we tested her, she knew exactly how to play that character. She is an incredibly naturalistic actress on film, but she's also a very talented theatrical performer who can fill an auditorium with her presence and persona. This character required both of those things—the naturalistic quality and the theatrical quality—because she is a real person, but she deals with the world in a way that is very theatrical, adopting a series of guises. Anne was able to present both the underlying reality of the character and the persona she presents to the world."

A deep admiration for Nolan spurred Hathaway to eagerly accept a meeting with the director—although

British actor Tom Hardy was cast as the ruthless villain Bane in *The Dark Knight Rises.* Hardy's interpretation of Bane required both verbosity and body mass; he began a rigorous training regimen as soon as he got the part.

she had no idea when she met with him which role they might be discussing. "Everybody was guessing," Hathaway recalled. "I thought: 'Okay, it's not going to be Catwoman because Michelle Pfeiffer just did that with Tim Burton not too long ago… I know! It's Harley Quinn!' And so I went into the meeting sort of dressed up as Harley Quinn—wearing a colorful top and balloon pants—and with a little bit of manic energy. After about an hour of us talking, Chris said, 'So, the role is Catwoman.' I misread the whole thing! And then I tried to go from being a manic court jester to a cat.

"I was thrilled to find out that it was Catwoman, but it didn't really matter. If you can be Cop Number Two in a Chris Nolan movie, you know that he's going to lead you to do some of the most exciting work that you've ever done. It wasn't just that I was excited about doing Catwoman—one of the most famous, if not *the* most famous comic book character for a woman—it was that it was Catwoman in *this* franchise. I'm a huge fan of Chris Nolan's, and a huge fan of the first two films."

To prepare for the role, Hathaway made a point to avoid studying previous Catwoman performances. "The most important thing," she commented, "was to fit into Chris's Gotham City. And so, as wonderful as Eartha Kitt and all the other Catwomen have been, it wouldn't have made sense for me to study or imitate them. My Catwoman had to be Chris Nolan's Catwoman. I did look at a lot of the comics, though. I got the archival ones and read through them. I read a lot about what Bob Kane was thinking when he created the original Catwoman, and I found out that he based her partially on Hedy Lamarr.

"So then I went back and watched a lot of Hedy Lamarr films to see if I could pick up any traits that might have interested him. I saw a film she made called *Ecstasy*, and I noticed the way she breathed in that film, which was very controlled. That was something I tried to bring to this character. Selina has learned to control her emotions and her adrenaline to the point where nothing really rocks her that much—at least, not in a way that you would notice externally. She feels things very deeply, but she keeps a lid on it."

For the role of idealistic young cop John Blake, the filmmakers cast Joseph Gordon-Levitt, with whom Nolan had worked on *Inception*. "For Blake, we were looking for an actor who embodied a youthful idealism," said Nolan, "and Joe had that energy and focus. He's an extraordinarily talented actor. We needed a strong presence, someone who could play with Gary Oldman."

Anne Hathaway appeared as Selina Kyle, the cat burglar/con-artist who takes on a "catwoman" persona through her costume and tools of the burglary trade. Christopher Nolan recognized both naturalistic and theatrical qualities in Hathaway—qualities shared by Selina Kyle. Hathaway based her Catwoman portrayal, in part, on actress Hedy Lamarr.

Prior to finishing the screenplay, Nolan related the story line of *The Dark Knight Rises* to the actor. "I'd loved Batman long before Chris started making Batman movies," admitted Gordon-Levitt. "I think pretty much everybody has. But Chris approaches these movies differently from the typical super hero genre where the heroes are simply good guys and villains are simply bad guys. That's not how it works in the real world, and that's not how it works in Chris's movies. John Blake's a good guy, but he has some flaws. He makes some mistakes. He's really passionate and he sometimes gets hotheaded. But he's young. He's growing."

French actress Marion Cotillard was cast in the role of Miranda Tate, Bruce Wayne's love interest in the film, and the first woman to capture his heart since the death of Rachel Dawes in *The Dark Knight*. "Miranda was always going to be non-American," said Nolan, "whoever played her. And we were very lucky to have Marion Cotillard take the role, because she was perfect. She brought just the right international quality I'd wanted in the character."

Like Rachel Dawes, Miranda Tate emerged from the pages of a Chris Nolan screenplay, rather than being pulled from comic book origins. "She was created by Chris," said Cottillard, "and to develop the character together was very interesting. He is a very special director. He writes scripts, which is unusual, and he turns these big action movies into something very intimate and emotional. In French, we have this term: film d'auteur. Chris Nolan is an author of film."

All the actors who contributed their talents to The Dark Knight Trilogy approached their roles with the same serious consideration they would have brought to portrayals in the most thoughtful drama. The actors never thought of The Dark Knight Trilogy as a series of "comic book" movies; rather, they saw the world of Christopher Nolan's Batman, and the characters within that world as real, complex, and multidimensional.

When asked in a TimesTalks interview if he feared not being taken seriously as an actor after having played Batman, Christian Bale provided an answer that reflected the attitude of the entire cast: "Luckily, I met with Chris and he's really shown that what they call a 'tentpole,' 'blockbuster' movie can also be intelligent and thought-provoking, and doesn't have to be dumb… As for being taken seriously, that's not really up to me anyway. That's other people's opinions, and if they don't take me so seriously, so be it. I'm still doing something that I believe has merit."

ABOVE, LEFT: **Marion Cotillard was cast as Miranda Tate, Bruce Wayne's new love interest, in *The Dark Knight Rises*.**

ABOVE, RIGHT: **Joseph Gordon-Levitt appeared as the idealistic Gotham cop John Blake.**

Christopher Nolan on the various sets of The Dark Knight Trilogy, interacting with his leading actors. The actors appreciated Nolan's "up close and personal" style of directing, which had him situated very near them, next to the camera, rather than sitting at a distance, watching scenes on video monitors. Top row from *Batman Begins*, middle row from *The Dark Knight*, and bottom row from *The Dark Knight Rises*.

"No one on earth wants to wear a Batsuit . . ."

CHAPTER 4

Just as Nathan Crowley anchored his production designs in a hardcore reality that was unprecedented in the super hero film genre, so too did costume designer Lindy Hemming reject the overt theatricality of past Batman incarnations as she clothed the characters in all three films of The Dark Knight Trilogy.

Hemming focused her early work for *Batman Begins* on the central character of Bruce Wayne and his alter ego, Batman. To support Bruce's public "performance" as a billionaire playboy, Hemming chose wardrobe pieces that would look as expensive—but subtly so—as possible. "I wanted him to look like a modern man in a suit," said Hemming, "rather than a stuffy rich guy. Part of that came from Christian's poise and the way he wore the suits—because Christian has a really good body."

Suit 4

2 Piece

Jacket:
Single Breasted
1 Button
Peak Lapel
No pocket flaps
NO Vent

Trousers:
1 pleat (PC09)
No Turn up

Shirt:
Collar B
Double Cuff

PAGE 104: Bruce Wayne's full Batsuit regalia for *Batman Begins*.

TOP: *Batman Begins* costume designer Lindy Hemming dressed Christian Bale in bulky, oversize clothing to create the illusion of youth and disguise his bulked-up Batman physique.

BOTTOM: For billionaire playboy Bruce Wayne, Hemming opted for "modern man in a suit" rather than "stuffy rich guy."

That body went through many changes, however, between Bale's first fitting and the start of the *Batman Begins* shoot. "Many actors *say* they're going to lose weight for a part," said Christopher Nolan, "and the wardrobe people will just roll their eyes. But I had to warn them that Christian was actually going to do what he said. There aren't many actors with his kind of self-discipline."

"The hardest part fell on the poor tailor, who nearly had a nervous breakdown," Hemming recalled. "As Christian kept losing weight and working out, he'd have to keep taking in the waist of his pants. Every time Christian tried them on, he'd need new alterations."

The single most critical costume was the Batsuit, introduced in the story as an impenetrable military combat suit, one of the high-tech treasures in Lucius Fox's Applied Sciences Division. To design the suit, Christopher Nolan and the design team studied *Batman* comic books and graphic novels, looking for the essential features of the Batsuit as it had been rendered through the years. "Those elements that had stuck would be important to the new design," said Nolan, "but we also wanted to give it a more contemporary hardware quality. I wanted to combine functionality with the more operatic, graceful elements of the costume I'd seen in the comics since the seventies, particularly the way the cape was used in many of the later graphic novels. There are wonderful illustrations of Batman in iconic poses with the cape flowing, and we felt that it was important to get that aspect into our portrayal of the character. Overall, we wanted to get some of the drama of the costume onto the screen."

Nolan advised Hemming against studying designs from the previous Batman films and, instead, to take her cues from the comic book illustrations and the *Batman Begins* screenplay. Hemming and her team first designed the prototype combat suit. From there, they imagined what modifications Bruce Wayne might make to arrive at the Batsuit—such as painting the original charcoal color a deep matte black that would help him disappear into the night. "We learned from the army that there actually is a spray-on black latex paint that removes the heat signature," noted Hemming, "so a heat-seeking camera would be unable to see the person wearing such a suit."

Hemming designed the head-covering mask and neck of the costume—collectively forming the "cowl"—to be slightly more flexible than previous versions, reasoning that for optimal visibility, Batman would have to be able to turn his head without completely turning his upper body. The mask portion was designed to be especially thin and formfitting as well, so Christian Bale's expressions would be readable beneath it.

Creating a more flexible cowl was among the challenges taken up by costume effects supervisor Graham Churchyard, a veteran of Tim Burton's *Batman.* "You don't need to have worked on a Batman movie to know that Batman used to do the 'Bat turn,'" Churchyard commented. "He had to turn his whole body to move because he couldn't turn his neck. Back in the '90s, the cowl was literally bolted down to the suit, which restricted any movement whatsoever."

Working over a life cast of Christian Bale, artist Julian Murray sculpted the Batsuit, including the cowl. "We tried to sculpt what we thought would give Christian the maximum amount of movement," Churchyard explained, "but would still give him the look you see in the poster image of *Batman Begins*, where he has his head down, and you see this huge neck that flows into the cape shape. Batman needed that big kind of bulldog neck to really sell the silhouette, but to get that look meant that there were two and a half inches of foam on either side of his neck." To allow more flexibility, the crew trimmed the foam piece to create something resembling foam vertebrae. "We hollowed out parts of it, creating a kind of honeycomb system within the foam to allow for more movement."

Churchyard continued to develop the particulars as he and his crew built multiple suits in a workspace dubbed the Bat-Shop, but referred to as "the Kitchen" by Christian Bale due to the materials, chemicals, and solutions cooked up there in the course of the Batsuit fabrication process. Suits were assembled out of combinations of silicone, rubber, and wet-suit neoprene—just as earlier Batsuits had been. "The fear we all had about re-creating a suit using that same technology," noted Churchyard, "was that the neoprene muscles created rather stiff movement. Fortunately, neoprenes had moved on since the nineties, and we were able to use a super-stretchy version for our Batsuit."

THE INTIMIDATION GAME | TITLE: BATMAN BATSUIT | DWG NO.
DRAWN BY: SIMON MCGUIRE | DATE: | REVISED:

DESIGN: LINDY HEMMING

DESIGN: LINDY HEMMING

THE INTIMIDATION GAME | TITLE: BATMAN BATSUIT | DWG NO.
DRAWN BY: SIMON MCGUIRE | DATE: | REVISED:

COSTUMES & MAKEUP

110

The design and construction of the *Batman Begins* Batsuit—which required the involvement of approximately twenty people—resulted in a costume comprised of fourteen separate pieces, each of which was fitted onto Christian Bale every time he appeared on set as Batman.

Batman's iconic cape was designed to both flow and stiffen—a goal accomplished through parachute nylon, electrostatic flocking, and Department of Defense technology.

THE INTIMIDATION GAME	TITLE:	BATMAN BATSUIT
DRAWN BY:	SIMON MCGUIRE	DATE:

experimenting with now. It's very soft and supple, but when an electrical current is applied to it, it takes on a rigid shape. I thought that was something Bruce could utilize for his cape. It would flow when he was walking, but when he jumped off a building and applied current, it would take on the shape of a glider."

The final cape was made out of the finest parachute nylon. "In previous Batman movies," said Graham Churchyard, "they backed the cape with latex to give it a very sculptural look. But Chris wanted something that would move in a very light breeze, and so we made the cape out of a light material that would fly up with very little wind."

In the end, the costume department made about a dozen different versions of the cape, each customized for a particular purpose. A shorter cape accommodated scenes in which Batman was inside the Batmobile, for example, to alleviate the performer's having to sit on six yards of material inside the small space. "Another one we called the 'action cape,'" said Churchyard, "which hit the ankle bone, so he wouldn't trip over a long train. There was a longer walking cape that just touched the ground, and an even longer one that trailed behind him."

Yet another cape was built specifically for scenes in which Batman activated the electrical charge that transformed it into its hang-glider form. Costumers sewed tubing into that version of the cape, which would be filled with air by an air compressor rig devised by special effects supervisor Chris Corbould and his crew. Mounted to the back of the suit, the rig allowed Christian Bale (or his stunt double, Buster Reeves) to walk through a scene with the cape flowing, and then make the cape stiffen with a flick of a switch.

The final *Batman Begins* Batsuit was composed of fourteen separate pieces, each of which had to be fitted onto Christian Bale each and every day he went on set as Batman. "By the end," said Churchyard, "we had at least twenty people who had their hands on that suit. A tremendous amount of labor went into it."

Batman's cape was also challenging, as the screenwriters had introduced the idea that it was made of a special fabric with dual properties.

"We were determined that the cape have a very supple quality to it," said David Goyer, "so it would flow like it did in the comics, but we also liked comic book images where the cape looked more like rigid wings, allowing Batman to use it like a hang glider. So, early on, I did some research with the Department of Defense and found that there's something called 'memory fabric' that they're

The Batsuit was subjected to a complete redesign for *The Dark Knight*, with Hemming joining Nolan and Crowley in the garage office early in the film's development to contribute ideas for the suit's new look. "I became an honorary member of 'the garage gang,'" Hemming quipped, "and I loved it. Normally, you start working on a production twelve weeks before filming begins, but by that point, everybody's already too busy to sit down and develop ideas. It was wonderful to have those early months before it

Batman's cowl—the head-covering mask and neck of the costume—required intensive redesign efforts to enhance facial mobility and diminish the stiff, whole-body "Bat turn" of previous films.

actually kicked into high gear, and it made a big difference in the long run. Later, when Chris was preoccupied with other things, I could still keep working on ideas I'd gleaned during that development time. Even if things changed later, I still had that basic 'I remember what we talked about' from the garage, which was underneath everything."

Because of time and budgetary constraints on *Batman Begins*, Hemming had relied on a manufacturing process for the Batsuit similar to that used in previous Batman films. For *The Dark Knight*, however, both she and Christopher Nolan were ready to look at the suit from an entirely new angle and to solve some of its inherent problems.

Most of those problems involved comfort and flexibility. Made of rubberized materials, the suits were extremely hot and caused the actor to perspire heavily, which only added to his overall discomfort and introduced the secondary issue of body chemistry damaging the suit. Also, the Batsuit's unyielding structure made it nearly impossible for the actor to sit comfortably, making the physically demanding role—and long days on the set—all the more exhausting.

Christian Bale's need to move his head and neck was yet another fundamental issue. "Poor Christian," said Hemming. "On the first film, one of our major preoccupations was to try and make the neck more moveable for him, but we didn't quite pull it off."

Although eager for the suit redesign, Nolan didn't want to thrust a new Batsuit on moviegoers without some justification for it in the film. "We were looking for story reasons for redesigning the suit," said Nolan, "and then it occurred to me: Use the real reason. Batman wants to move faster and be more flexible. It was really very simple. And so, in the film, there's a brief scene in which Bruce Wayne asks Lucius Fox to make the suit lighter, faster, and more agile."

Hemming went straight to work on the redesign, and—with the help of concept artist Jamie Rama—rendered over twenty different concepts for the new Batsuit, ultimately arriving at the high-performance, streamlined design seen in *The Dark Knight*. The final design included smaller plates of armor with open spaces between them, which would allow the performer in the suit more flexibility than the former single-piece armor plate.

The design team then set its sights on finding a new material to replace the foam latex panels and neoprene used for the first suit. "Foam latex is not durable at all," explained Graham Churchyard. "In fact, we had to handle it with gloves in *Batman Begins* because it was so easy to damage the surface. As we looked for a better material, we settled on urethane, which is used for everyday things like car components and cell phones."

To replace the neoprene, Churchyard discovered a mesh material, woven in Britain, which was used both medically and in sportswear. The mesh would not only be lighter and more flexible than neoprene, it would vastly improve the ventilation in the suit, reducing the temperature inside.

While the design of the ear-portioned upper cowl was the same as in *Batman Begins*, the costume crew redesigned the stiff neck portion. "Chris Nolan worked with us very

The Dark Knight's suit called for the molding and casting of more than one hundred individual sections—compared to the simpler silicone and neoprene Batsuit from the first film.

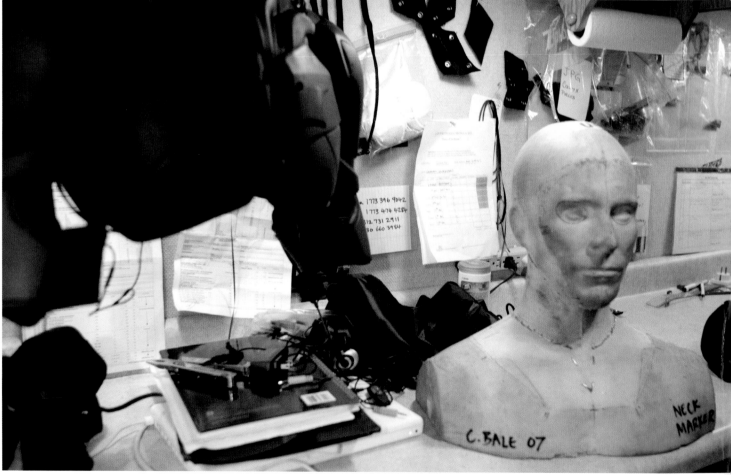

The Batsuit was redesigned for *The Dark Knight* based on real-life body armor and constructed atop an underlayer of mesh that made it more flexible and breathable than the original version.

closely on every aspect of the costume," said Churchyard, "but particularly on the neck. We came up with all kinds of prototypes, but he persevered with the idea of armored panels with crumple zones between them. It was quite simple in the end, but we did go through a lot of grief getting there."

This simple solution involved separating the head portion of the cowl from the neck, but with a counterintuitive twist. Instead of the cowl and neck extending *down* into the suit, as it had originally, the neckpiece would be part of the suit and come *up* to meet the cowl. To blend the scaled-down neck with the bottom of the cowl, the designers scaled down the size of the jaw area as well.

Whereas the *Batman Begins* suit was essentially one large piece of molded latex, *The Dark Knight* suit called for the molding and casting of more than one hundred individual pieces. To create the components, Julian Murray sculpted each of the small sections in clay; these clay pieces were then computer-milled as molds from which the final urethane pieces were cast.

"The urethane molded precisely and gave a beautiful factory finish," said Churchyard. "It was a very industrial look. As it turned out, it also acted as built-in stunt armor with a high level of protection."

In the end, the new Batsuit made good on two out of the three requests Bruce Wayne makes of Lucius Fox when asking for a new suit: It was faster, and it allowed for more flexibility—but it wasn't lighter than the *Batman Begins* suit had been. "All those panels added up!" said Lindy Hemming. "But it *was* easier to wear, and perhaps Christian wasn't quite so hot in it. And being able to take the hard part of the cowl off made his life a little better, too, I hope. No one on earth wants to wear a Batsuit, but if you have to, then I think this was the one to wear."

The reconfigured Batsuit was so successful—both practically and aesthetically—that it remained essentially unchanged for *The Dark Knight Rises.* "The only changes to the Batsuit involve the things that happen to Batman when he is wearing it," said Hemming. "Other than that, it's the same suit as last time."

Batman's cape had remained more or less the same since *Batman Begins*, as had the design of the utility belt and boots. "We've maintained those things throughout all

three films," asserted Graham Churchyard. "Even the cowl is very much the same. It was trimmed down dramatically for *The Dark Knight* to allow him better movement—but it still has the expression that Julian Murray sculpted into it for *Batman Begins.*"

Throughout the many months of filming The Dark Knight Trilogy—which, when laid end to end, consumed a full twenty-one months of his life—Bale never ceased to appreciate being the one chosen to wear the costume. "It never stopped being surreal," he reflected. "Standing in the Batsuit never stopped giving me goose bumps. There were times I had a love-hate relationship with it, of course, but I always recognized the honor of playing this icon. Just little old me, inside the suit."

The new high-performance, streamlined Batsuit offered Christian Bale enhanced flexibility—and provided real protection during fight scenes.

The trilogy's villains presented the costume department with the opportunity to create an array of costumes every bit as interesting, unusual, and challenging as the Batsuit, and the disparity in those villains' backstories, goals, and methods of wreaking havoc translated to a wide range of costume styles.

Liam Neeson's role as Henri Ducard/Rā's al Ghūl in *Batman Begins*, for example, called for a monastic influence in his garb, but the costume design team took pains to ensure he would not resemble Jedi Master Qui-Gon Jinn, Neeson's role in *Star Wars* Episode 1: *The Phantom Menace*.

In costuming the film's other main villain, Dr. Jonathan Crane/Scarecrow, Hemming incorporated features into the psychiatrist's suits aimed at making the naturally handsome and appealing Cillian Murphy look a little strange. Crane's suits were made purposely too small for the actor, for example, with sleeves that were too short, making his hands look oversize and his arms appear ungainly. The costumers also made the suits' shoulders too small, which—when paired with a small shirt collar and thin necktie—created the illusion that Crane's head was disproportionately large, like that of a scarecrow. The costumers also placed the button of his jacket slightly askew, altering the balance of the actor's body.

The costume designers expended considerable energy conceptualizing the Scarecrow's mask, producing more than one hundred sketches and twenty different prototypes before arriving at the final version. "Everyone had a hand in the look of the mask," said Hemming, "and we came up with some very strange designs. In the end, we pulled back toward the mask of the Scarecrow in the comics, just making it a bit less cartoonish. It came off really spooky, but it was terribly simple."

In approaching the costume design for *The Dark Knight*'s Joker, Hemming started by considering what audience expectations for the character would be, with Jack Nicholson's memorable Joker coming immediately to mind. Though Hemming appreciated designs from the 1989 Tim Burton film, she wanted to avoid the kind of retro-dressing concepts that would look nonsensical in the realistic world Christopher Nolan had created. "I wanted this Joker, especially as he was going to be played by a young and very trendy guy, to have a quality young people could look at

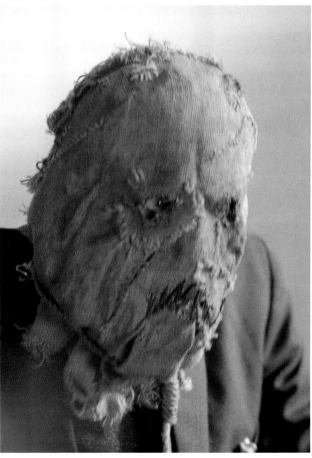

Attention to detail was present in every design decision for each of the hundreds of characters throughout The Dark Knight Trilogy, including such particulars as the button placement and sleeve length on Dr. Jonathan Crane's suit, shown here.

The Scarecrow's mask went through twenty different prototypes before arriving at this simple, but spooky, design.

and identify with," said Hemming. "I wanted to be able to rationalize why he dressed that way. We had to make our Joker believable."

To inspire ideas for the Joker's wardrobe, Hemming started collecting images from Vivienne Westwood—the British fashion designer famous for bright colors, radical lines, and geometric prints—as well as pictures of Johnny Rotten, Iggy Pop, and Pete Doherty. As another point of reference, Christopher Nolan asked Hemming and the design team to look at Francis Bacon's *Study After Velàzquez's Portrait of Pope Innocent X* (1953), more familiarly known as *The Screaming Pope*, which, to him, communicated the Joker's edgy, unsettling essence. "That's what made me believe it was alright for him to wear purple," Hemming said.

Nolan and Hemming made the decision to create one clearly defined costume for the Joker—a purple coat and emerald green vest—with additional disguises and masks that would be worn at various points throughout the film. To accommodate the long and action-heavy shoot, the team made twenty Joker coats and vests, as well as multiples of the character's shirt, which was based on an antique shirt Hemming had found.

For the Joker's tie, Heath Ledger suggested a thin, 1960s style. Hemming turned to Turnbull & Asser, the company responsible for creating James Bond's shirts and ties. "I asked to see their old tie fabric books," said Hemming, "and they actually wove us the fabric so we could custom-make his ties. It's the weirdest tie that Turnbull & Asser ever made, I think."

The designers searched for logical explanations for the Joker's colorful hair and makeup, originally rendered in the comics in the 1940s. "We came to the conclusion that his scars were always on his face," said Hemming, "as though someone attacked him at some point in his life. Then, as he went crazier and crazier, he began painting the scars, eventually ending up with an overall makeup. His green hair, we decided, was a bleach job that had gone terribly, terribly wrong."

Prosthetics makeup supervisor Conor O'Sullivan was tasked with creating the realistic scars that make the Joker's face look as if it is drawn up into a permanent smile.

As a fifteen-year prosthetic makeup veteran, he knew that different types of skin and wounds result in very different types of scars. "The skin has a nap," he said, "just

DESIGN: LINDY HEMMING

In designing the Henri Ducard/Rā's al Ghūl costume for Liam Neeson in *Batman Begins*, Lindy Hemming wanted to suggest a monastic influence, while avoiding any resemblance to Jedi Master Qui-Gon Jinn, the actor's role in *The Phantom Menace*.

117

ABOVE: For Police Commissioner Loeb's funeral procession in *The Dark Knight*, Heath Ledger appeared in disguise as a police officer while wearing full prosthetic scar makeup—but without the identifying clown makeup he typically wore as the Joker. The Joker's permanent grimace was based on the nap and healing patterns of scarred human skin.

OPPOSITE: Prosthetics makeup supervisor Conor O'Sullivan adjusts Ledger's prosthetic scars on location in Chicago.

like fabric does. If you cut it one way, there will be minimal scarring. If you cut it another way, the scarring is very difficult to heal, and can be excessive, which was clearly the case for the Joker."

Basing his design on these fundamentals—and Lindy Hemming's Joker concept art—O'Sullivan created three sculptures and brought them to Christopher Nolan, who assured him that he was on the right track. From there, O'Sullivan created a new sculpture, an amalgam of the three versions, and began the process of molding and producing Joker prosthetics for application on the set.

Traditionally, such prosthetics would have impeded the actor's facial performance. For the Joker makeup, however, O'Sullivan implemented an innovative prosthetic transfer technique he'd first stumbled upon while filming *The Last Samurai* in 2003. By the time *The Dark Knight* went into production three years later, O'Sullivan had refined the process, which involved producing molds made of a silicone product. The prosthetic pieces that came out of those molds were unusually supple and skinlike, and could be applied directly to the skin while still inside the mold. "That way, they always went on in the right place," said O'Sullivan. "All the edges, all the blending—everything—was done when you took away the mold. It was a lot harder to produce these molds, but it only took twenty-five minutes to apply them—and the results were a hundred times better. The resulting skin texture was incredibly realistic and refined."

To design and execute the clown makeup that would go over the prosthetic scars, Christopher Nolan called in makeup artist John Caglione, with whom he had worked on *Insomnia*. "I'd been Al Pacino's makeup artist ever since *Dick Tracy*," Caglione said, "and I did some scars and other things for Al on *Insomnia*—which is when I met Chris and Emma. I think that's why Chris thought of me for *The Dark Knight*."

After receiving Nolan's call, Caglione sketched eight clown makeup concepts and created them as overlays on photographs of Heath Ledger at his shop in New York. Caglione then flew to London to meet with Nolan and Ledger and do some preliminary makeup tests. "When I first went to London," he recalled, "one of Chris Nolan's notes was that he wanted the makeup to look organic. He didn't want a clean, pristine clown makeup. He wanted it to

look broken down and smeared. Partly, that had to do with the Joker's inner state—this is a guy who is breaking down internally and falling apart. But the messy look was also what would happen with a makeup that he wore for days and slept in night after night. His wardrobe never changes in the movie, so you get the idea that he's stinky and smelly and broken down. So that was the concept—to make it look like this guy lives in this makeup."

In addition to *Study after Velázquez's Portrait of Pope Innocent X*, other Bacon paintings—contained within a book brought in as reference by Nolan—proved tremendously inspirational in the development of the Joker makeup. "The images in that book became like our bible," Caglione recalled. "We all had an 'aha' moment when we saw those paintings. They were our springboard."

With the concept clarified, Caglione proceeded to apply test makeups to Ledger's face, creating a broken-down and worn look by implementing an old theater makeup technique that he recalled. "I had Heath wrinkle up his face—raise his eyebrows and crinkle his crow's feet—and then I

painted over those areas while he was contorting his face," said Caglione. "Then, when his face went back to its normal position, it created these very creepy cracks everywhere and added a lot of texture to it. Once we got into applying it on the set, every morning Heath would go through this series of facial expressions that we'd worked out—almost like a dance routine—and I'd paint layers of white and gray over those expressions. And that created all these great cracks and expressive details."

To ensure the makeup would last throughout the long shooting day under hot lights, Caglione used a dry face paint activated with alcohol. "You spray alcohol on it," he explained, "and then it dries very quickly and stays on all day." After painting a base coat of gray and white, Caglione applied Kryolan Aquacolor black makeup paint around Ledger's eyes, and then smudged it. "Once we had it smudged the way we wanted, I would spray Evian water over it, and Heath would shake his head and move his face to create little drips around his eyes."

The last step in the makeup application was smearing red lipstick over Ledger's mouth—an almost ritualistic act that the actor performed himself each and every day of the shoot. "I would do the whole makeup," said Caglione, "and then Heath would put on the red lipstick as the final touch. He felt that he needed to do that, as part of the character. The Joker would make himself up, and Heath wanted to make himself up—even though he couldn't do the base paint and all the other stuff I was doing. So we would always finish with Heath smearing the red lipstick on his mouth."

On the set, Conor O'Sullivan and his assistant, Robert Trenton, would first apply the prosthetic scars, and then Caglione would apply the clown makeup, a process that took about fifteen to twenty minutes. Rather than apply the makeup exactly the same every day, Caglione and Ledger would consider what scene was being shot on any given day, and how the Joker's makeup might be impacted by the context of what was happening in the story. "In the bank heist, for example," Caglione explained, "he's sweating under a hot mask through the whole thing; and so, when he pulls off the mask, the makeup had to look very smeared and messy, as if he'd sweated some of it off. But

TOP: To find a common language for defining the Joker, Nolan turned to Francis Bacon's *Study After Velàzquez's Portrait of Pope Innocent X* (1953) as a reference point. [Used by permission. Purchased with funds from the Coffin Fine Arts Trust; Nathan Emory Coffin Collection of the Des Moines Art Center, 1980.1.]

BOTTOM: In considering the Joker, Lindy Hemming wanted to avoid retro-dressing the villain and, instead, to portray him as a "young and very trendy guy," in keeping with Christopher Nolan's realistic vision for the film.

then, when he was going to shoot the scene where the Joker is meeting with all the mob bosses, Heath's idea was that the Joker would want to spruce himself up for that meeting. I remember he said: 'John! This is the scene where he's meeting all the kingpin guys and he wants to make a good impression—so let's make the makeup look especially good!' Heath called those shots on a day-to-day basis, depending on the scene. I'd get him in the makeup chair, and he was so intimate with the character, he'd have ideas for what was going to be shot that day."

A kind of magic transpired when Heath Ledger appeared on set in full makeup and costume. "The first time I saw Heath at the wardrobe test, complete with his makeup and green hair, my jaw dropped," Chuck Roven recalled. "You couldn't stop looking at him. And then to hear him talk, with that vocal quality Heath gave the character—it just blew me away. It wasn't what I expected, which was the beauty of it. He completely made it his own, from every physical nuance to every vocal turn of phrase. He immersed himself in the character to the point where he was no longer recognizable."

In costuming Aaron Eckhart, the designers had to achieve the look of the successful, debonair Harvey Dent, and then determine how that look would evolve into the disfigured Two-Face. "We dressed Aaron as Harvey as impeccably as we could," said Lindy Hemming, "in custom-made Zegna suits. From there, Chris wanted to find a way for him to become Two-Face without wearing two different costumes."

Hemming worked backward from the scene in which the left side of Dent's face is burned off in a calamitous explosion. "Knowing that his face would be all red and black from the burns," said Hemming, "we decided to dress him in a gray suit with red lining. Our thinking was that when his clothing burned, it could fuse together and become plastic-y and horrible. Because of the way he lay in the petrol, half of his body would go toward the red and black, while the other half stayed the way he was as Harvey Dent."

Although a fully refined Two-Face concept would not be finalized until post-production—at which time the visual effects team would design the look and execute it digitally—a preliminary maquette, or scale model, was

developed by Batsuit sculptor Julian Murray, who based his sculpture on conversations with Nolan and what he gleaned about the character from the DC Comics. "Chris talked about the various looks of the character," said Murray, "and we studied the original cartoon concepts and isolated the things that were essential—the exposure of the teeth, the big eye, the grimace, the crazed look. We had to find a balance between a look that would turn people completely off and one that was simply gruesome, in a horror movie sense. In truth, realistic burns of that kind would have been far too upsetting for an audience to look at."

Villains for *The Dark Knight Rises* would present Lindy Hemming with a fresh set of challenges, but by the time she began designing the costume for Bane, *The Dark Knight Rises*'s villain, she was fully steeped in Nolan's method of working, which entailed one-on-one collaboration in the very earliest stages of the film's development, even before a final screenplay had been written. "I love how we work on these films," Hemming said, "the fact that we actually work together with Chris in pre-production and spend time talking about the characters. We'd developed that approach on the other films, and I looked forward to continuing it on this one."

The key to designing Bane's costume, as for those of all the characters in the trilogy, was first determining the *function* it served. That held especially true for his mask. In

ABOVE, LEFT: To help envision the Two-Face makeup—which would not be finalized until post-production—a maquette was developed by Batsuit sculptor Julian Murray, who based his sculpture on comic book art and lengthy conversations with Christopher Nolan.

ABOVE, RIGHT: Lindy Hemming's concept art for Aaron Eckhart's Two-Face character.

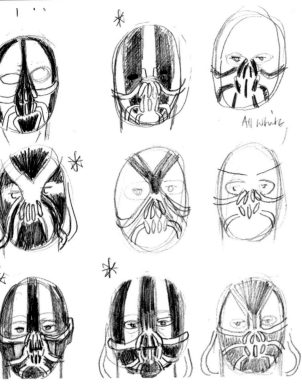

ABOVE, LEFT: Lindy Hemming and the design team went through dozens of possible mask options for Bane before arriving at the final look of the mask (below).

ABOVE, RIGHT: The Bane mask was sculpted onto a life cast of Tom Hardy, which was then cyber-scanned. Here, Mario Torres Jr. adds detail to the mask sculpture. (Photo credit: Mario Torres Jr.)

LEFT: *The Dark Knight Rises*'s Bane posed the challenge to the costume crew of designing and building an industrial looking facemask that continually pumps anesthetic into Bane's system to alleviate his chronic pain.

BELOW: The principal Bane "hero" mask worn by Hardy during closer shots of the actor.

OPPOSITE: Lindy Hemming and Christopher Nolan, with Tom Hardy in full Bane costume.

the comics, Bane had worn the colorful, full-head mask of a *luchador*—a Mexican-style wrestler—but in *The Dark Knight Rises*, the mask would require a more industrial look, as it served a practical purpose: pumping a continuous dose of anesthetic into Bane's system to help alleviate his chronic pain.

After drawing many, many iterations of the mask on photographs of bald actors such as Marlon Brando and Terence Stamp, Nolan and the designers came to the realization that for purposes of clarity, Bane's mask would have to create a very different silhouette than Batman's. "A lot of the film was going to take place in the dark, with Bane and Batman fighting," Hemming explained, "and we couldn't have one black lump of a head fighting another black lump of a head. And so, to make sure they would be easily identifiable, we had to make those two silhouettes—Batman's and Bane's—look completely different."

The search for a distinctive silhouette for Bane led to the designers removing pieces of the full-head mask to create a more streamlined, minimalist look. "I'd been playing with all kinds of elaborate tubing and devices for the mask," said Hemming, "but all of that had to be streamlined, because as we made the mask smaller, there was no place to put it all. So the mask was just reduced and reduced. I also wanted the mask to look animalistic, like something that might bite you, and so I referenced a lot of gorillas and spiders and the like."

Once Tom Hardy was cast in the role, sculptors sculpted the mask onto a plaster form of the actor's head, created from cyber-scanning, a technique in which laser beams are bounced off a subject to create a computer-generated 3-D representation of the subject. "A cyber-scan is like a photograph in the computer," said Graham Churchyard, "and then that photograph is re-created as a three-dimensional head form that you can sculpt on in clay."

The approved clay design was then re-sculpted in the computer and fit, piece by piece, over a digital rendering of Tom Hardy's head. When that digital mask was generated as a prototype prop, it fit so tightly that it restricted Hardy's breathing. "We always knew the breathing was going to be a problem," said Churchyard, "but we had to start with that finished mask before we could begin hollowing out the

tubes to help him to breathe. Tom hated it the first time we put it on him."

"It really gripped his head like a vise," Hemming affirmed, "but Tom was amazingly patient about that. We designed it with magnets underneath the front panel, so it could be removed easily. The layer below that was rubber to create a kind of gasketlike seal. The gasket pressed into his skin by tension, so it created the feeling of a very hard-pressed, tightly sealed thing. It was a big challenge for an actor to have to perform behind that thing, to not have his mouth on view. Tom put up with it really well."

As he grew accustomed to wearing the appliance, Hardy discovered that the mask did not impede his performance—in fact, it became integral to his portrayal of Bane. "As an actor," Hardy said, "as soon as you put on a mask, you adopt a character. It's like Halloween—you put on a mask and you can be absolutely anybody. So I didn't feel limited by the mask. The only problem I had with it, initially, was the claustrophobia, and the panic of not being able to get out of something that's close to your face. But that passed very quickly."

"By the end, Tom didn't even take off the mask to talk to Chris when they cut the camera," Graham Churchyard recalled. "He just wore it all the time. I think he almost liked wearing it."

The real-world foundation for the remainder of Bane's costume was his quasi-military, mercenary background. "Bane had to wear things that looked like they came from different armies all over the world," said Lindy Hemming. "So we had to make his costume from fabrics that looked as if they could have come from many different places." The most militaristic feature of the costume was the chest armor, which the costumers made of cut-up military tents and leather. "The armor couldn't be made of solid plates because of all the fighting Bane does, so even the panels that look metallic were actually leather with foam inside them," said Hemming.

Based on a Swedish Army coat, Bane's coat was also made of heavy leather. The team made about a dozen duplicates of the coat, each of which had to be distressed identically. "It was so big and heavy, I actually hid the first day we had to give Tom Hardy that coat to wear in the middle of summer in Pittsburgh!" Hemming admitted. "But it worked great. When we first saw the football stadium scene, Chris made the comment that Bane looked like a silverback gorilla in that thing."

The Dark Knight Rises's other "villain" was Selina Kyle. Wanting to avoid the high-camp, kitten-with-a-whip aspects of the Catwoman character as she'd been portrayed in the past, Nolan worked long and hard with the costume designers to conceive a plausible basis for her cat costume.

Selina's exploits as a cat burglar provided much of the rationale. "The suit enables her to disappear into the

The Catwoman suit was designed to emphasize Anne Hathaway's body, without actually revealing it.

darkness," said Lindy Hemming. "And so it is a very simple, action-oriented suit. It's also not a sexual catsuit. It emphasizes the shape of her body, but it doesn't *reveal* her body—and that's a big difference between this Catwoman and the last Catwoman." For her part, Anne Hathaway was delighted with the formfitting Catwoman costume, dubbing it Julie Newmar 2.0.

Similarly, Nolan and the designers developed a practical foundation for Selina's cat ears, incorporating them into goggles she wears as part of her utilitarian cat burglar uniform. "Chris wanted the goggles themselves to have a very high-tech military look," said Graham Churchyard, "as if they'd been made by the police or the army for night-vision surveillance. That made sense: She's a cat burglar, and so she needs this magnifying jeweler's loupe in the goggles and a built-in light to do her job. And then, they were designed in such a way that when she flipped them up on her head, the goggles would create a cat-ear shape.

They would be kind of 'accidental' cat ears, and everyone was very inspired by that idea."

Eventually, the concept evolved so that the goggles were part of an entire mask, developed in drawings and cardboard cutouts. The crew then fit digital renderings of the concept to a cyber-scan of Anne Hathaway's head. The data drove a 3-D rapid-prototype printer, which "grew" the mask in three dimensions based on Hathaway's head measurements and proportions.

As they had for the previous films, the costumers had to dress not only the protagonists and antagonists of *The Dark Knight Rises* but also the citizens of Gotham. The difference, this time round, was a matter of volume: The third film in the trilogy would feature an unprecedented number of citizens, police officers, and mercenaries in its epic fight sequences, requiring Hemming's crew to costume thousands of extras.

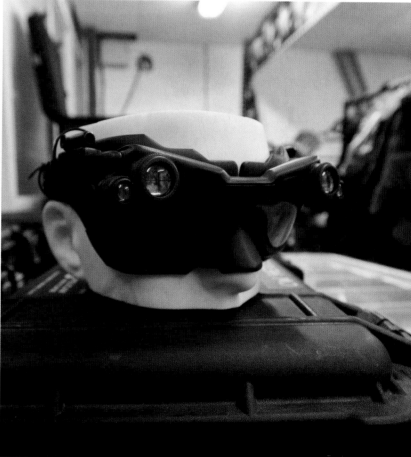

ABOVE, LEFT: As with every decision throughout The Dark Knight Trilogy, Selina Kyle's cat ears and goggles had to respond a real-life, practical situation, in this case: What kind of night goggles might a cat burglar use? As a solution, the goggles were designed to form the shape of "inadvertent" cat ears when pulled up to her head.

ABOVE, RIGHT: The final rendition of Catwoman's night-vision goggles reveals design elements consistent with other technology in Batman's world.

"It was an intimidating task to dress all of those people," key costume supervisor Dan Grace commented, "and it's rarely done anymore. You could shoot a battle like that with fifty people, and then fill in the rest with CGI people, but Chris would never do it that way. His brief to us from the beginning was that if the script said there were going to be thousands of people fighting on the streets, there were *really* going to be thousands of people."

In terms of sheer numbers of people, no sequence topped the football stadium scene in which a Gotham Rogues game is interrupted by violence and the appearance of Bane. Rather than create a digital crowd in the stands, production arranged for twelve thousand extras to fill the

LEFT: The Gotham Rogues football uniform. One of *The Dark Knight Rises*'s design challenges was to create costumes for two football teams, a number of coaches, and twelve thousand extras.

stadium's seats—and many of those had to be dressed in the Gotham Rogues' colors.

The sequence also required the costumers to design and build the Rogues' football uniforms. Before costumes and logos could be designed, the filmmakers had to decide on a name for the team. Coproducer Jordan Goldberg and Christopher Nolan, in particular, gave much thought to naming Gotham's football team, finally settling on the Gotham Rogues—a nod to the *Batman* comics' Rogues Gallery. "We actually had to invent an entire football team for Gotham," said Grace, "with uniforms that looked completely authentic and believable. We were very proud, in the end, to have created costumes for an entire football team, coaches, and twelve thousand extras!"

Despite its thousands of extras and epic-scale action sequences, *The Dark Knight Rises* was still, in large part, the saga of one man, Bruce Wayne. "For me," said Lindy Hemming as she came to the end of her tenure on The Dark Knight Trilogy, "*The Dark Knight Rises* related more to the first movie, emotionally, than it did the second one, because it was much more about the character of Bruce Wayne. There is a lot more information about Bruce Wayne in this movie, and in that way, it reminds me more of the first film.

"But in all three films, you had to believe in Gotham, and you had to believe in these characters as real people. There's a definite humanity to all of these characters, and we worked very hard to make them more than just people in Lycra suits."

ABOVE: One of the vast and extremely well-organized dressing rooms used for *The Dark Knight Rises*.

OVERLEAF: Plenty of spare Batsuit parts were kept on hand by The Dark Knight Trilogy's wardrobe department.

"When it comes right down to it,
it's just me behind the camera, Chris
sitting next to me, and the actor..."

Principal photography for *Batman Begins* commenced in February 2004,

the start of what would be a 129-day shoot—unusually long, even for a

large-scale film. The main reason for the extralong schedule was that

Christopher Nolan intended to shoot the entire film—even those scenes

heavy with stunts and special effects—as part of his main unit, rather than

have a second unit shooting action sequences simultaneously.

"Early on," recalled director of photography Wally Pfister, "Chris told

me that he thought that we could, and *should*, shoot the entire picture

ourselves. And so Chris and myself and the rest of the first unit became the

second unit, and except for a couple of days of background photography in England, and some of the visual effects plates photographed in Chicago, we shot the entire film ourselves. That was very unusual for a big action picture in Hollywood."

Not just unusual—it was nearly unheard of on a big-budget, large-scale action movie; but Nolan would maintain the approach throughout the production of all three films in The Dark Knight Trilogy.

"It's a clever way to work," noted special effects supervisor Chris Corbould, "because by shooting all of the action himself, Chris only shoots what is in his head. Second units often shoot a lot of extra footage, just to make sure they're covered, but Chris only shoots exactly what he wants and needs. It is a very frugal and economical way to shoot action sequences."

Nolan also bucked standard operating procedure by having Wally Pfister operate the camera himself throughout the shoot. "I like to operate the camera when I'm working with Chris," Pfister said, "and he prefers it, as well—in fact, he insists on it! It brings a huge-scale film down to a very simple, approachable level. We can have hundreds of people around us, but when it comes right down to it, it's just me behind the camera, Chris sitting next to me, and the actor." Much of the movie would be shot using hand-held cameras, with Pfister and Nolan right in the middle of the action. "I love to put the camera on my shoulder and jump into a scene. I can't see working any other way with Chris."

Originally, principal photography on *Batman Begins* had been scheduled to start in March, in Iceland, but when weather reports suggested that the Icelandic locations were

PAGE 130: Stunt performer Buster Reeves hangs off the edge of an Icelandic cliff in *Batman Begins*.

ABOVE: Christopher Nolan and director of photography Wally Pfister on location in Iceland at the start of principal photography on *Batman Begins*.

warming up, threatening to melt the icy landscape, the schedule was moved up a month. Even in February, the special effects crew had to dress locations with barrels of fake snow. "I took two containers of snow out there," recalled Chris Corbould, "expecting that we'd never even open them. And then we got to Iceland and there wasn't a bit of snow there! So we spent about four days covering the whole landscape with fake snow."

First up on the shooting schedule was the sword fight between Bruce Wayne and Henri Ducard on the frozen lake, shot at the edge of a massive glacier. "It was quite amazing," recalled Neeson of the experience. "I'd never seen a glacier before, and certainly not up close. To film at the foot of this glacier that was moving about a meter every week was a remarkable way to jump in. Every so often, between setups, we'd see ice crumbling away at the head of the

glacier, reminding us that this was a big, living force moving toward us. It was beautifully dangerous and strange to be in a section of the world where there wasn't a tree or bird anywhere. It was like a gorgeous Beckett wasteland."

Cast members arrived on a Saturday, and production had scheduled Sunday as a rest day before the start of filming on Monday. But when local experts warned that the ice on the lake was rapidly thinning, Nolan became concerned. "They couldn't guarantee there'd be any ice there on Monday," Nolan recalled. "In fact, they told us that the lake could be melted by the next day, and so we made the decision to jump right into filming on Sunday."

Liam Neeson and Christian Bale knew the sword fight moves well and had practiced them on ice rinks prior to the start of principal photography—which was fortunate, since the sudden rush to shoot the fight before the ice melted left

Christian Bale and Liam Neeson do battle on a frozen—though quickly melting—Icelandic lake.

TOP: Christopher Nolan and Christian Bale on the monastery exterior set.

BOTTOM: Rising temperatures caused much snow to melt at the start of production in Iceland, while high winds and heavy rainfall both complicated the shoot and enhanced the cinematography later on.

OPPOSITE: Christian Bale and Liam Neeson on the set of the monastery interior, which was built at Shepperton Studios, near London.

no time for on-site rehearsals. "We suddenly got the call," Christian Bale recalled. "'No time, no free day, just get to the lake right now!'"

On the lake, the sound of cracking ice unnerved everyone on the crew, and local authorities dictated that no more than ten people were to stand on the frozen surface at a time, as a safety precaution. As a result, Nolan worked with as small a crew as possible to shoot the scene. "It was essentially a guerilla filmmaking unit out there on the frozen lake," Nolan said, "and we were able to get something like thirty-three setups in one day. In that way, it was very similar to the smaller films I'd made in the past. It was a pretty extreme way to start, but the cast and the crew came through with flying colors."

Though stunt performers stood in for the actors in wide shots, Neeson and Bale performed most of the fight on the ice themselves, working throughout a shoot day made tense by the instability of the lake conditions.

"As we started banging about and hitting each other and smashing into the ice," recalled Bale of shooting the fight, "we'd occasionally hear the sound of a big crack, and we'd all stand dead still and wait. Someone would say, 'Get off.' Then they'd test the ice, and say, 'Okay, I think you're good for one more take.' Thankfully, we got the whole sequence

in that day, because by the next day, there was no ice whatsoever. It had become a lake again."

For the shot of Bruce Wayne falling through the ice, the special effects crew built a tank at the side of the lake and covered its surface with a sheet of wax to simulate ice. The waxy surface was rigged to break on cue and send Bale's stunt double, Buster Reeves, into the icy water.

Production remained at the glacier for two more days, shooting monastery exteriors, and then moved to a second location for shots of Bruce Wayne making his trek up the mountainside. By this point, the warming trend had changed, and shots were complicated by seventy-mile-an-hour winds and heavy rainfall.

"The weather conditions were really rough," said Wally Pfister. "Chris and I had talked about making Christian Bale's walk up the hill a crane shot, but partly because of the weather, I just threw the camera on my shoulder and walked up the hill with him, in the wind and rain, getting as much as I could before we had to pull the plug and get out of there."

"You can see in the movie that there's a huge storm going on in those scenes," added Chuck Roven. "Crew people were literally blown off their feet by the winds. But with Chris, you never stop shooting."

The remaining days in Iceland had the crew filming Ducard's and Bruce Wayne's slide down an icy slope after Bruce has rescued his mentor from the monastery fire. Nolan shot part of the slide at a location that had a real cliff at the bottom of a slope, photographing the action from a camera that was mounted to a Technocrane.

The Technocrane had been Nolan's second choice as a means of shooting the stunt. Wanting the most dynamic shot possible, Nolan's first instinct was to have Pfister operate a handheld camera as he slid down the hill along with the performers. "I said that if there was a way to do it safely, I'd do it," Pfister said, "but, physically, I didn't know if we could get over the edge as fast as he wanted it. So I tested a lot of ideas to find some way of doing that."

Among Pfister's tests was mounting the camera to a harnessed Technocrane, and sending it down and over the edge of a slope set piece built by the stunt department at Shepperton Studios. The results weren't promising. "I showed Chris that test," Pfister said, "and he laughed because it was so slow. He kept pushing for me to slide off the edge myself, holding the camera, but it wasn't feasible to do that and get the shot he wanted. So we wound up bringing the Technocrane up to that location in Iceland, and they made it move as fast as they could."

Just getting the fifty-foot Technocrane up to the location was a monumental feat, let alone controlling its slide down the mountain. "It had to be chained down," said Pfister, "because if this thing fell off the cliff, not only were they out a couple of million dollars, it could have done enormous damage on its way down. As it turned out, we were able to get a number of good shots with it. We never achieved the speed that Chris wanted, but we got a lot of dynamic shots from the side, sliding along with the characters."

For tighter shots on the sliding characters, the crew moved to a different slope—one without a 200-foot drop at the end—where Pfister aimed a handheld camera on the actors and slid down the hill with them. "I squished myself onto a small bit of plastic and slid down the hill as fast as possible," said Pfister, "keeping the camera on the action. We got some good stuff on location, and then we shot it

With walls of simulated rock and visible foundations of Wayne Manor, the cathedral-like Batcave set was constructed on the largest soundstage at Shepperton.

again about six months later, in seventy-degree weather, on a large set piece with fake snow on it that we built at Cardington."

The production crew moved from Iceland to Shepperton Studios, where Nathan Crowley and his team had built a number of smaller sets, such as the monastery interior. After those scenes were shot, Chris Corbould's crew took chainsaws to the support structures in the solid-timber set and laced them with explosives for shots of the monastery erupting in a fiery explosion, ignited when Bruce Wayne engages Ducard and his ninjas in battle and inadvertently sets off kegs of gunpowder. The explosion, filmed by eight cameras stationed around the set, reduced the monastery interior to millions of matchstick-size pieces of wood.

Shepperton housed a Wayne Manor interior set, as well—a corridor and a couple of manor rooms built specifically for shots of Bruce and Alfred escaping the inferno after Rā's al Ghūl sets fire to the mansion. "That was a big fire day," recalled stunt coordinator Paul Jennings, "and

we actually had Christian underneath the fire for the shot where a piece of burning ceiling falls on Bruce Wayne. I talked to Christian about whether he'd be willing to do it, and, of course, he was more than happy to do it—he was always up for doing these things! So we had burning logs and debris on release wires that special effects rigged up. We rehearsed it with a stunt double first, made sure it was all controllable, and then on the day, we actually dropped all of these burnings logs on Christian."

The largest set built at Shepperton was the cathedral-like Batcave. With walls of simulated rock and Wayne Manor foundations reaching a height of sixty feet, the Batcave set filled every square inch of the studio's largest soundstage. Construction crews plumbed the set, enabling water to be pumped in to create a running stream, weeping rock walls, and a waterfall. "The water really brought the Batcave to life," said Chris Corbould, whose team engineered the water effects, "because it gave us all of these reflections and twinkles on the set. It was a very dark set, but the water made it a living cave."

Wally Pfister mounted a camera on a fifty-foot Technocrane to capture shots of Bruce Wayne and Henri Ducard going off a Himalayan cliff, pictured here with harnessed stuntmen in Iceland.

The cast and crew of *Batman Begins* on the monastery set during the climactic
conclusion to Bruce Wayne's battle with Henri Ducard and his ninjas. After all monastery
scenes were shot, the set's intricate interior was carefully chain-sawed, then laced with
explosives to collapse on cue.

The Batcave is first revealed in a shot in which Bruce Wayne slides down a rock face and ignites a torch to explore the caverns beneath the manor.

"It's the widest shot we ever see in the Batcave," noted Wally Pfister. "The day before we shot that, I spent an entire day tweaking out that set, lighting it exactly the way I wanted to, with very little compromise. I think we achieved the look of a real cave, which is what Chris wanted."

Another scene set in the Batcave has Batman administering the antidote to Crane's fear toxin to Rachel after he rescues her from Arkham Asylum. The scene marked one of Christian Bale's early on-set appearances in the Batsuit.

Wally Pfister had conducted lighting tests on the Batman costume while it was still in development, determining how the cape and cowl materials photographed under different lighting conditions. "The materials would look a certain way in person," said Pfister, "and then look very different once we put them on film and saw them in dailies. So testing was critically important."

One of Pfister's concerns, from the beginning, was the suit's matte black color. "It completely absorbed the light," he explained. "You could put a light right on it, and it would still be black. I was always conscious of the fact that if the cape was falling against something very dark, we weren't going to see it. That just meant I had to do things like silhouette it, rather than fully light it. Ultimately, lighting Batman was a matter of focusing on the face and the cowl."

While challenging for Pfister, the Batsuit had a profound effect on the entire cast and crew throughout the shoot. "Everybody on set felt quite a charge when Christian walked in wearing the Batman costume," recalled Christopher Nolan. "It was this iconic presence, and you felt it in your bones. To have Batman walk across the room and speak to you was quite shocking, and we tried to capture that on film."

"When you saw Christian in the suit," Katie Holmes commented, "he *was* Batman. His physicality and movements

OPPOSITE: Christian Bale embodied the essence of Batman while wearing the Batsuit, alternately dazzling and intimidating the cast and crew whenever he appeared on set in character.

ABOVE: Wally Pfister's murky lighting infused Batman's dark world with mystery—while veiling the idiosyncrasies of the neoprene Batsuit.

At Shepperton, two forty-foot monorail carriages—with windows draped in green screen—were mounted to gimbals to simulate train movement for early scenes of Bruce Wayne riding with his parents, as well as the climactic encounter between Batman and Rā's al Ghūl.

were spot-on. It was surreal to be rescued by Batman and carried around by him. I felt kind of thrilled by it."

For his part, Christian Bale appreciated the stature and presence the Batsuit afforded the character. "Everybody knows the amount of dork that they have within them," Bale offered, "which just doesn't fit with being such an iconic character. So, at first, I loved putting on the suit, just to get that sense."

As the long shoot continued, however, the burden of wearing the suit wore on the actor, and he suffered from headaches caused by the restriction of the cowl. "After months of filming, there was, naturally, a love-hate relationship with the thing," Bale admitted. "But I didn't want to say: 'I can't deal with it anymore. Take it off.' So I'd say to myself: 'Don't whinge about it. Use it. The headache is making you feel fierce, and this guy's fierce.' My head would be throbbing, but I loved wearing it, just the same." In a show of solidarity with the actor, the costume crew wore T-shirts they'd had silk-screened with Bale's oft-repeated assessment of the suit: "It's hot, it's sweaty, and it's giving me a headache."

Bale performed in full Batman regalia for his part of the finale fight with Rā's al Ghūl inside the monorail cars, also shot at Shepperton on two 40-foot carriages mounted to gimbals to simulate the movement of the train. Nolan had conceived the train fight, the final match between the two ninja masters, as the ultimate confrontation—bigger than previous fights, but also down-and-dirtier. "Their confrontation at the end is almost a street fight," said Nolan, "with a lot of butting heads and throwing elbows and kicking. It's also very grubby in that it takes place in this interior covered in graffiti. So even though we were using the spectacular environment of the city and this speeding monorail as the backdrop, the actual conflict between the two men was done in as realistic a way as possible."

To enhance the fight's gritty realism, Wally Pfister illuminated the carriage set with the interior fluorescent lighting common in real trains, using a flickering effect to add a chaotic element. "In addition to that," said Pfister, "I had a series of thirty or forty tracking lights with different colored gels on them just outside the windows of the train. They were on a chaser board, so the lights would go on

and off one at a time. The effect was a flickering light on the actors' faces that looked like the train was moving past city lights. Between the flickering fluorescent lights and the chasing lights outside the windows, we created a wonderful bit of interactive lighting on the actors as they fought."

After being stage-bound at Shepperton for a few weeks, the crew was happy to get out into London and surrounding areas for a series of location shoots. The first of these was Mentmore Towers for the filming of Wayne Manor interiors and exteriors. Because Mentmore was a historical site, the crew took great pains to protect the property. "There's a Rubens fireplace there that's worth more than the house," joked Nathan Crowley, "which we

Christopher Nolan, in harness, takes a trial run in preparation for shooting Batman's Arkham Asylum stairway "flight" (shown on pages 12–13).

had to completely cover to avoid damage. We also protected the wood floors before covering them with white marble."

The abandoned Midland Grand Hotel represented some Arkham Asylum interiors, with St. Pancras Chambers' elaborate Gothic stairwell chosen for the grand stairway in the lobby, the site of an aerial stunt in which Batman jumps from the landing, opens his wings and lands at the bottom of the stairs, all in one shot.

Space within the stairwell was tight, barely wide enough to accommodate the Batman stunt rigging—let alone Wally Pfister on yet another wire rig, operating the handheld camera. "Chris was keen to get shots of Batman with the camera traveling up and down with him," stunt coordinator Paul Jennings explained, "and so, we put Wally in a harness and wire so he could travel up and down exactly as Batman was doing. Wally did it great, and the shots look fantastic, but it was a pretty funny thing to see at the time—Wally in this harness, holding the camera, going up and down this stairwell."

Other U.K. locations included the Event Hall at the ExCel Centre, an exhibition and conference center in the London borough of Newham, where Nolan shot the scene in which Lucius Fox demonstrates the camouflaged Tumbler

for Bruce Wayne. "That location was a last-minute find," recalled Wally Pfister, "after our original plan to shoot in the Millennium Dome in Greenwich [London] fell through. It turned out to be a great location."

Opening scenes at the Bhutanese prison—such as Bruce Wayne's jail cell meeting with Henri Ducard and his fight against eight attackers in the prison yard—were shot at the Victorian-era Coalhouse Fort, on the banks of the Thames in Essex.

Moving from the muddy prison yard to the height of Gotham City elegance, production crews next shot the opera house scene at the Garrick Theatre on Charing Cross Road, in the heart of London's West End.

The Gotham docks, where Batman makes his first appearance in the film, was actually the Tilbury Docks in Essex; the Farmiloe Building—a Victorian-era warehouse that would become a favorite and oft-used location throughout the making of the trilogy—served as Gotham City's police headquarters. The Gotham courthouse lobby, where Joe Chill—the murderer of Bruce Wayne's parents—is gunned down, was shot at Senate House, University College London, and the university's Rockefeller Building was the site for the scene in which Bruce Wayne struggles to control

Bruce Wayne (Christian Bale) and his Bhutanese prison cellmate (Vincent Wong) in *Batman Begins*.

TOP: Christian Bale is marched through Coalhouse Fort, a Victorian-era facility that served as a Bhutanese prison yard for *Batman Begins*.

BOTTOM: Christian Bale's intensity was evident in every aspect of his performance as Batman and Bruce Wayne, pictured here with Larry Holden (as Gotham District Attorney Carl Finch) and Katie Holmes during the trial of Joe Chill.

his rage as he attends Chill's parole hearing. "I very clearly remember shooting that," said Christopher Nolan. "It was extraordinarily exciting to watch a great performer put across so much just through his eyes, without saying anything. Shooting that close-up on Christian was very intense."

After weeks of location work, production crews moved to the Gotham City sets at Cardington to shoot night exteriors—mostly scenes involving Batman's nocturnal exploits. Due to the "indoor backlot" that Cardington provided, Nolan and his crew were able to shoot all of the nighttime scenes during the day.

Shooting inside the massive hangar also provided Wally Pfister with a degree of control he'd never had shooting nights on location or on a backlot. "There were tons of buildings inside this hangar," said Pfister, "plus functional streets, streetlights, stop lights, neon signs, cars driving around. There were all kinds of normal street activity, which meant that I could light this set more from within, just as a real city is.

"We'd looked at Chicago from atop a building at one point, and I realized that most of what we were seeing were buildings that were lit from *within*, not from the outside. There were all of these window lights, with just a few streetlights peppered in. That's where I wanted to start in lighting the set at Cardington, lighting it like I would a night exterior on a regular city street, with light sources behind the windows."

Pfister was most pleased with the lighting on the full-scale Narrows set built at Cardington. "To me," he said, "those were the shots that looked the most like a real city night exterior—and yet, we lit every inch of it from scratch, placing different colored gels on the windows and hanging lights behind them. We lit it from a lot of different angles, and put just the right amount of smoke in the background. I'm quite proud of the way the Narrows came out on film."

An extended sequence shot on the Narrows set was one in which Batman investigates a slum apartment building where a shipment of the Scarecrow's hallucinogen has been delivered. Ironically, Nolan had negated one of the major benefits of shooting inside Cardington—the protection

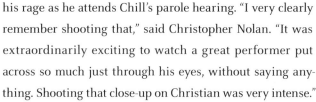

ABOVE, LEFT: The massive Cardington Shed allowed the filmmakers to create an indoor backlot.

ABOVE, RIGHT: An extended Narrows sequence required a special effects–induced deluge—and created attendant lighting and electrical problems for the crew.

from the elements it afforded—by setting the Narrows sequence in rainfall, which had to be manufactured by the special effects crew. "There were plenty of tough moments from the shoot," said Nolan, "but probably the most difficult involved shooting those rainy night exteriors inside Cardington. To make it read on camera, movie rain is much, much heavier than real rain. So we had this incredible deluge, which caused all kinds of problems with the electronics and the lights. Some of those scenes were very challenging, but, of course, I was the one who had written rain into the script, so I only had myself to blame!"

The scene includes a shot of Batman—set afire by Dr. Crane—jumping from a fifth-floor window of the apartment building into an alley below. Production captured the action with stunt double Buster Reeves attached to a descender rig—a mechanized barrel-shaped device onto which cable is wound and unwound to facilitate a controlled fall. Though descender rigs are standard stunt rigs, this one was customized to enable Reeves to perform a fall that started inside the apartment set, continued out the window, and ended at the landing point below—all in one shot, as Nolan had directed. Reeves wore a special "burn" Batsuit, as well, a collaboration between the stunt and costume departments made of a special fire-resistant silicone.

Also shot at Cardington were street-level scenes for the movie's climax, in which villainous factions attempt to spread the fear toxin by way of a "focused emitter"—a military weapon that vaporizes the city's toxin-infected water supply. Illustrating the microwave-based weapon's effect on Gotham's waterworks required that Chris Corbould's crew pump steam throughout the set using four huge steam generators, each the size of a trailer. The plumes of steam created by the generators reached a height of one hundred feet, and caused manhole covers on the set to fly upward and fire hydrants to blow. "It was total mayhem," said Corbould. "Then, after we'd done a run and all the steam had gathered in the roof, it would begin to fall like rain. We created our own mini-ecosystem!"

With each take, Christopher Nolan asked for more and more steam, until the set was obscured in a thick white fog. Nolan loved the effect, but Wally Pfister found the milky atmosphere extremely difficult to photograph and light.

When Batman is lit on fire by Dr. Crane, he jumps from a fifth-floor window into the alley below. Here, stunt double Buster Reeves takes the leap in a descender rig wearing a special Batsuit made of fire-resistant silicon.

"Light overexposed quite a bit when the steam came in," he explained, "so it washed out all the color. And, at times, we were working completely blind. It got so thick, you couldn't see the person standing next to you. Chris really liked the idea of seeing less of what was going on, but I had to tell him, 'That's all well and good, but it's kind of like filming a white card!' So we had to find a balance, a way to create the illusion that the characters couldn't see three feet in front of them, but *we* could—because we had to, in order to put it on the screen. In the end, I think we achieved the heavy fog look he was going for quite well."

From Cardington, the production moved to Chicago, which would stand in for Gotham in shots intended to give the city a greater sense of scale than what could be achieved even with the massive sets built in the hangar. Nolan's team had pegged a number of iconic Chicago structures to serve as specific Gotham locations.

The exterior of Wayne Tower, for example, was the landmark Board of Trade Building on Chicago's LaSalle Street.

The exterior of the Gotham courthouse was the Jewelers Building on East Wacker Drive, and Batman surveys the city from atop the same skyscraper later in the movie. Nolan also shot the city's bridges to depict those leading to the Narrows.

Three full weeks of the shoot in Chicago were dedicated to the five-minute-long sequence in which Batman races through Gotham in the Batmobile—with Rachel beside him, infected by the Scarecrow's hallucinogenic gas—as police give chase on the ground and in the air.

To shoot the chase, the production brought in the street-ready Batmobiles that had been built by Chris Corbould and his crew in pre-production. Filming all of the Batmobile gags had required that each car perform specific functions. One was rigged with hydraulics to raise the car's "wings" in jump shots, for example, while another featured a practical jet flame erupting from the back, fueled by six propane tanks located in the car's interior. Yet another version was employed specifically for shots of Batman entering or exiting the vehicle. Hydraulic mechanisms controlled

Basing his lighting techniques on Chicago at night, Wally Pfister lit the intricate Narrows set from inside the buildings.

Gary Oldman on the Narrows set during the filming of *Batman Begins*'s climactic
"focused emitter" sequence, wherein Gotham's toxic water supply is vaporized by way
of microwave technology. To create the fog, the special effects crew pumped steam
throughout the set—causing hydrants to erupt and manhole covers to blow.

the opening and closing of the car, which also had a small electric motor with just enough juice to move it a few feet into or out of frame.

For shots of Batman inside the car, Christian Bale sat in an oversize cockpit set—allowing room for cameras—which was mounted to a gimbal to create a sense of movement. The crew built another interior set specifically for shots of Batman engaging the vehicle's aerodynamic features. "We built a set for the mechanical stuff that happens when Batman puts the car into jump mode and the whole console changes position," said Corbould. "The driver's seat moved to the middle, and then hinged forward and down into a motorbike racing position. To get all of that motion and make it look really slick, we used a bit of everything— hydraulics, pneumatics, and electric motors."

Though Nolan intended the Batmobile chase to be dynamic and high-energy, he also, as always, wanted it to be grounded in the real world. "It's very easy to get into the mentality of wanting to do the biggest crash ever, the biggest explosion ever," noted Corbould. "But from the beginning, Chris said that he didn't want this chase to be over-the-top. He wanted it to be gritty and dirty and realistic. He wanted the audience to feel the crunch of metal on metal."

For the chase location, production had secured access to major sections of the Chicago Loop, including much of LaSalle Street and Lower Wacker Drive, the underground section of the double-decker highway bordering the Chicago River. For shots of Batman racing up the circular ramp of a parking garage, production shot at the Randolph and Wells parking garage, while the subsequent rooftop chase and other parts of the sequence were filmed on a disused section of freeway north of the city.

Wally Pfister shot the fast-paced chase action, relying on techniques he'd honed on a prior racing film, *The Italian Job*. "I knew a lot of the tricks," said Pfister, "but we never drove cars a hundred miles an hour on *The Italian Job*! We did on this movie, using an arsenal of tools."

The most indispensable tool used for the chase was the Ultimate Arm, a robotic crane arm with a gyrostabilized head—controlled by a joystick inside the vehicle— mounted atop a Mercedes ML55 camera car. "It's a very

expensive tool," said Pfister, "so we decided initially that we'd just use it for the first day of shooting, and then let Chris decide if he wanted to continue using it. It turned out to be such a fantastic tool, and it gave us such a stable, solid image of the Batmobile traveling at high speeds, we kept it on for the entire chase. We shot probably eighty percent of the sequence with the Ultimate Arm, and it allowed us to get really dynamic shots we wouldn't have been able to get any other way."

Inside the Mercedes ML55 throughout the shooting of the chase scenes were the three inventors of the Ultimate Arm—George Peters, Lev Yevstratov, and Joseph Bednar— *and* Christopher Nolan. "Generally," said Pfister, "Chris was

OPPOSITE: Batman atop the City of Gotham Courts building—in reality, the Jewelers Building in Chicago. The rich and moody influences in *Batman Begins* would be transformed into clean, modernist lines for *The Dark Knight*.

ABOVE: Christopher Nolan and Wally Pfister on location in Chicago.

in that main vehicle because he likes to get in the thick of it. He's a very visceral filmmaker, and he really likes to get in there and get his hands dirty."

"When I'm shooting," Nolan elaborated, "I like to be as close to the action as possible. For me, it's important to experience that action with all of my senses. That's a more relevant perspective for a director than sitting behind a small monitor because the film camera sees much more than you can ever see on the video hookup. So I try to use all my senses to orient myself just as the audience will be oriented in the action.

"It's also a way of knowing what the practical limitations are. If you're in the car yourself, seeing how fast they're driving and how difficult it is, then you know what is reasonable to ask for. If you're just sitting back at base camp looking at a video playback, you might as well be playing a video game."

From his seat in the tracking car, Nolan was able to communicate with stunt driver George Cottle in the Batmobile by way of an open-mic system.

"I had a set of head cans on to hear what they were saying in the tracking car," said Cottle, "so they could give

me instructions. Chris Nolan would direct me as we were shooting—'Go to the left, go to the right, speed up, slow down, don't brake.' It was great to have Chris's input as we were doing it, instead of doing a take, and then getting his instructions—'Okay, this time, do it this way'—and having to reset and do the whole thing again."

The Mercedes had its work cut out just to keep up with Cottle in the Batmobile, which clocked speeds of up to 109 miles per hour on open road, and often drove 80 miles per hour even as it was weaving between obstacles and oncoming cars. All the action had been choreographed and rehearsed exhaustively by the stunt and special effects departments. "The planning by Paul Jennings and [assistant stunt coordinator] Tom Struthers was superb," stated Chris Corbould. "And George Cottle was a master driver. We'd expected to take some hits because there was some very tight, precision driving in the sequence, and the visibility inside the car wasn't great. But George pulled it off brilliantly."

Cottle had come onto the project while the Batmobile was still in development, offering his input throughout its construction, and then testing it on a track in England.

Three weeks of the Chicago shoot were dedicated to the Tumbler's race through Gotham, a five-minute sequence shot primarily on LaSalle Street and Lower Wacker Drive.

Director Christopher Nolan relied on the Ultimate Arm—a robotic crane arm with a camera on its gyrostabilized head, mounted atop a Mercedes ML55 camera car—to shoot the complex, high-speed chase.

Rather than sitting at base camp watching video playback, Nolan called the shots from his seat in the Mercedes, communicating with Tumbler stunt driver George Cottle through an open-mic system.

"When they first told me what they wanted to do with it, I was a bit skeptical," Cottle admitted. "But then we took it out on a test track, and not only did it do everything they'd wanted, we came up with some new ideas. They told me to go out on the track and do my worst with it. [Mechanical engineer] Andy Smith actually said, 'Go out and *try* to break it.' So I did—I tried my hardest, but there was nothing I could do to break that car. Every stunt, every gag, every jump—that car just kept coming back for more."

Chase action included the Batmobile making a sixty-foot leap over an expanse, which production also captured in-camera, shooting the practical vehicle—with Cottle, again, at the wheel—as it was launched into the air on an abandoned stretch of freeway north of Chicago. "The most difficult part of the jump was that I didn't have a straight run-up to the ramp," Cottle recalled. "I had to get up to speed and then turn into the ramp—and then, suddenly, I was in the air for what seemed like a very long time. I remember looking down, and thinking, 'This is very high,' and then it landed."

"After they jumped it sixty feet, it went right around for take two," Nolan marveled. "Normally when you do a jump of that magnitude, it trashes the first car, and you need a second car to finish the scene. But our Batmobile just cruised right around and did take two. That car exceeded all of my expectations. It was an absolute beast."

Corbould and his crew weren't surprised by the car's durability. They had prepared for the gag months previously, subjecting the Batmobile to jump after jump to ensure it could withstand the impact. "We did it over and over again," said Cottle, "and I think that car made forty jumps before it ever took any damage."

ABOVE: Chase action called for the Tumbler to make a sixty-foot leap over an abandoned stretch of freeway north of Chicago.

OPPOSITE: Stunt cars were raced, flipped, and crashed throughout the sequence by *Batman Begins*'s special effects and stunt crews.

In the course of shooting the chase, George Cottle would drive all of the practical Batmobiles—but he developed a particular fondness for Batmobile Number Four. "Car Number Four was my favorite," he said. "She was always there, and she never broke down. I remember that on the last night of shooting, we had to break through a huge wall with that car. It was a breakaway wall, but it was still something like two feet thick—and I didn't want to do it! I didn't want to put the car through it. We did, and she got a few scratches, but then she was up and running again."

Christopher Nolan, too, became so enamored of the practical Batmobiles that he jettisoned a scripted scene in which the car was to be destroyed. "It had been part of the plot all the way through," recalled Emma Thomas. "And then, in the couple of weeks leading up to the moment when we were going to shoot that scene, Chris started wondering if we should really destroy the Batmobile. In the end, we couldn't bring ourselves to destroy it because it had become like a character to us."

Adding to the chase mayhem were speeding, crashing, and flipping police cars, also driven by expert stunt drivers. "We had something like sixty stuntmen out there, just driving cars," noted Paul Jennings. "On top of that, we had pedestrians on the streets, who were all stunt people, as well."

The chase also featured some spectacular aerial stunts by a "Gotham City Police" helicopter flying low and between buildings. During the shoot, there were actually two helicopters in the sky—one representing the police chopper, and another "camera ship" capturing aerial perspectives of the chase. "We did some pretty hairy tracking of the Batmobile in the camera helicopter," Wally Pfister said, "plus quite a bit of air-to-air photography, tracking the 'picture ship,' which was the police helicopter. At times we were tracking the Batmobile with the camera helicopter only about twelve or fifteen feet off the ground. It was an extraordinary, white-knuckle experience."

Hans Bjerno, Craig Hoskings, and Cliff Fleming piloted the helicopters for the sequence. "It was a fantastic aerial team that Chris and I had worked with before," said Pfister. "Hans had done five pictures with me, including the opening sequence in *Insomnia*. These are the best pilots in the

action centerpiece with the kind of visceral impact that could only be achieved by shooting real cars and stunts and special effects on real city streets.

For all intents and purposes, principal photography for *Batman Begins* wrapped with the end of the chase shoot in Chicago. All that remained was the shooting of some pick-ups and green-screen material back in England with a much smaller crew. "When we came back from Chicago," said Chuck Roven, "we worked with a reduced unit to shoot stuff that would have been done by a second unit, if not for the fact that Chris wanted to shoot everything himself."

The shoot would extend to nearly five and a half months by the time it was over, making it three times longer than any of Nolan's shoots up to that point in his career. "The length of the shoot was definitely one of the bigger challenges for us," said Emma Thomas. "We shot something like fifty-three days on *Insomnia*. On *Memento*, we shot twenty-five and a half days. So in terms of endurance and stamina, this was by far the biggest challenge of our careers. By the end, we felt like we'd run ten marathons ten times over."

"The most difficult thing about shooting *Batman Begins* was the sheer scope of it," Nolan agreed. "We tried to tell an enormous story on the grandest possible scale—because that's what Batman demands and that's what Batman deserves—and that required a lot of work from a very large group of people. But everybody pulled together marvelously and made my job a lot easier, frankly."

"As big and challenging as the movie was," added Chuck Roven, "I never worried about our ability to make it what we wanted it to be, because the team involved in putting the movie together—from acting to production design to cinematography to costume to stunts to special effects to visual effects—was very, very good. They all came to this project with a great deal of passion and professionalism. And that all started with Chris.

"I call him a 'producer-spoiler.' It's very rare that you work with a director who has a vision and then does everything to execute that vision the way he's told you he's going to. Chris always did what he said he was going to do—or killed himself *trying* to do what he said he was going to do."

world, as far as I'm concerned, and so we were able to get spectacular aerial footage of the Batmobile driving around Chicago and on the open highway."

"Those pilots were so skilled," added Paul Jennings, "one of them had actually flown a helicopter with a pencil on the runner, tracked a moving car underneath with a pencil sharpener on the roof, and put the pencil in the pencil sharpener. That's the type of talent we had in those helicopters, and it shows in the movie."

Just as he had been a passenger in the Ultimate Arm Mercedes tracking the Batmobile, Nolan was more often than not inside the camera helicopter. "I would never go in a helicopter normally," Nolan admitted, "but when I can look out and see with my own eyes what the camera is picking up, I'm very focused on that and not really thinking about the dangers. I'll often do things in filming that I would shy away from ordinarily, because I have to. Not only that, it was great fun to be in a helicopter moving sideways sixty miles an hour down a freeway with the Batmobile five feet away!"

After three exhilarating weeks on the streets of Chicago, Nolan had filmed everything he needed to assemble a fast-paced, breathtaking chase sequence—an

Special effects floor supervisor Peter Notley and stunt driver George Cottle take a break on Lower Wacker between segments. Cottle would go on to man the Tumbler throughout The Dark Knight Trilogy.

Inside the Tumbler, Batman attempts to outmaneuver the Gotham City Police helicopter.

"I want to do it bigger and better..."

After opening up Batman's world to include broad landscapes and exotic locales in *Batman Begins*, Christopher Nolan and his cowriters opted to set *The Dark Knight* almost exclusively within the confines of Gotham City. Subsequently, Nolan decided that Chicago would be Gotham's stand-in for much of the film, and months of location scouting and scheduling paved the way for the shoot.

Cast and crew gathered at the Old Chicago Post Office to shoot the film's opening bank heist—a key expository sequence, dubbed the "prologue," that would introduce the Joker—on April 18, 2007, marking the

official start of principal photography for *The Dark Knight*. Shooting the initial six minutes of the film in the first five days of the shoot was a departure from typical principal photography schedules, in which a movie's scenes are shot radically out of order, but it had been a deliberate choice, aimed at providing the Batman sequel a unique marketing opportunity. A self-contained sequence that stood on its own, separate from the rest of the film, the prologue could be released early—months before *The Dark Knight*'s opening—and thus create invaluable buzz.

Within a week, the production crew would be on its way to England, where production would continue through May, followed by a return trip to Chicago that summer, and then back to the United Kingdom again in the fall. Anticipation ran high. But on that fine spring morning, Christopher Nolan was pleased to be back in the town that had welcomed his *Batman Begins* crew so warmly three years earlier, and he looked forward to expanding the city's cinematic possibilities with *The Dark Knight*.

"Chicago is a very film-friendly city," he said. "On *Batman Begins*, they let us do all kinds of things, like raise bridges and shut down freeways. In coming into the second movie, I was determined to take the location filming even further. The real world is built on a scale you could never reproduce in the studio, and I wanted that real-world scale to broaden the scope of the sequel. I couldn't imagine a better environment for filming on location than Chicago."

Joining Nolan that day was director of photography Wally Pfister, who had earned an Academy Award nomination for *Batman Begins*, but who faced an entirely new set of challenges this time around. "With the first film having been such a great success," Pfister said, "we were cautious about becoming complacent or formulaic in approaching the second. I didn't want to fall into an easy pattern of repeating what I'd done before. And I knew, right away, that there could be a greater variety of looks in this picture, because there were many more day scenes in it than in *Batman Begins*."

PAGE 158: Heath Ledger as the Joker in Chicago on the second day of principal photography for *The Dark Knight*.

ABOVE: *The Dark Knight*'s opening prologue—shot entirely with IMAX cameras—featured an impressive zip-line slide from a fourteenth-story window by assistant stunt coordinator Tom Struthers and stunt rigger Kevin Mathews.

LEFT: Christopher Nolan on location in Chicago. With its striking, modernist architecture, the city would serve as both exterior and interior for much of *The Dark Knight*'s reimagined Gotham.

BELOW: Christian Bale returned to *The Dark Knight* as Batman, this time wearing a completely redesigned Batsuit based on a foundation of body armor.

Furthermore, Pfister and Nolan had whetted their visual appetites on their intermediary project, *The Prestige*. "Chris and I had done a couple of dusk scenes in *The Prestige* and really enjoyed that look," explained Pfister. "We wanted to incorporate that into *The Dark Knight*—keeping some of the orange-rust look from *Batman Begins*, but adding a cobalt blue dusk look. The first film was seeped in that one warm tone, while *The Dark Knight* had a number of different colors and textures."

Freed from the dark moodiness of *Batman Begins*, Pfister would be able to focus more on composition and other traditional aspects of photography, and expend less effort dealing with the idiosyncrasies of filming in near-blackness. He would, however, be forced to

deal with a new and exponentially more challenging aspect of shooting *The Dark Knight*: Looking to expand the scope of the story he'd started to tell in *Batman Begins* and to create a grand canvas for Batman's face-off against the Joker, Nolan had decided that he would shoot a full forty minutes of the film with IMAX film cameras, using the high-resolution 15/70 motion picture film format traditionally reserved for IMAX documentaries revealing the epic wonders of the natural world.

"The decision to shoot *The Dark Knight* in IMAX came out of our desire to make this film even bigger than the last one," noted Emma Thomas. "I think we expanded the story significantly, and just by shooting it on location as opposed to onstage really helped with the scope; but the one thing

ABOVE: Heath Ledger in Joker costume—but without makeup—gets ready to set the prologue in motion in Chicago.

OPPOSITE: Within the first few minutes of the film, *The Dark Knight* had declared its departure from the darker Gotham of *Batman Begins* through architecture and lighting.

that Chris had always wanted to do since he was a kid was to shoot with IMAX cameras."

Though Nolan respected the notorious challenges of shooting in the format—which included handling very large and cumbersome cameras—he felt certain that filming his dynamic action sequences with IMAX cameras would be feasible. Previous IMAX movies, after all, had been shot by astronauts in space, and by climbers carrying the cameras up Mount Everest. "Chris said that if they can do that," said Thomas, "then surely we could shoot on the streets of Chicago. So we decided to give it a try."

Because Nolan had long considered using the 65mm film stock, as used in IMAX film cameras, within the context of traditional narrative filmmaking, he was particularly intrigued when the visual effects supervisor for *Batman Begins*, Janek Sirrs, had insisted on getting some IMAX shots of Chicago for later use as CGI background plates. Sirrs preferred both the high-resolution image quality and the flexibility the unique format provided—the larger frame would give his visual effects team the option of reframing effects shots, as needed.

Even though he'd shot all but those visual effects plates in traditional 35mm anamorphic film, the viability of the IMAX process confirmed Nolan's hunch that the format could be effectively implemented, and he decided to issue eighty release prints of *Batman Begins* in IMAX theatres, enlarging 35mm footage to produce 70mm prints. "We were really surprised at how well the film handled the

blow-up," commented Wally Pfister, "and how stunning the image quality was. Later, as we went into tests for *The Prestige*, Chris decided he wanted to do a visual effect for that movie just to get an idea of how IMAX worked. About that time, he broke it to me: 'While we're doing this, I want you to keep in mind that it is kind of a test. I've got this notion of shooting a little bit of IMAX on the next Batman movie.' That was the seed for all the IMAX scenes we did for *The Dark Knight*."

To prepare, Pfister began learning the basics of shooting with IMAX cameras in January 2007, a full three months prior to the start of principal photography. "I had to crack it," he said, "so by the time we got to production, I was the one who knew how to use it. Chris had been reading up on it, but I needed to know that it was going to work—and I needed to convince the production that it was going to work—because at that point, Chris had not yet won approval from the studio to shoot in IMAX."

At four times the price of regular 35mm stock and processing, the prospect of shooting with IMAX cameras gave Warner Bros. executives good cause for worry. "They were petrified about the costs of the film," said Pfister. "So I gathered the numbers and did a lot of homework. I sent two of my camera assistants and a camera operator to Toronto to learn the system, and we had a lot of conversations and meetings about it. By the time Chris went to the studio, we had all our ducks in a row. He was able to say: 'Here's what we want to do. Here's how we're going to do it.'"

And with that, Warner Bros. was convinced.

Among the scenes in *The Dark Knight* that Nolan envisioned shooting in the larger format was the prologue. By opening the film with the visual and visceral impact of the IMAX sequence, Nolan would immediately establish the new rules of the game: Though *The Dark Knight* was a sequel to *Batman Begins*, audiences could expect it to be as unique and fresh a Batman tale as the origin story had been.

Director of photography Wally Pfister mans the IMAX camera on set in Chicago, with Heath Ledger's Joker behind the scrim.

ABOVE: The Joker manhandles the manager of Gotham First National Bank (William Fichtner) as a getaway school bus explodes through the front door. The stunt, rigged by special effects supervisor Chris Corbould and crew, required a false wall to be built within the Old Chicago Post Office, which served as the bank's interior.

LEFT: Christopher Nolan confers with Heath Ledger during the bank heist shoot.

TOP: Wally Pfister lines up a shot under the direction of Christopher Nolan on the Bat-Bunker set, built on stage at Cardington. The redesigned Batsuit was displayed via a modular storage system, which, in the film, could be lowered into the floor of the bunker.

BOTTOM: The Bat-Bunker gave Christopher Nolan a full 360 degrees of shooting possibilities—and gave Wally Pfister the perfect anamorphic aspect ratio for framing shots.

"In keeping with the Chris Nolan philosophy of, 'Let's just jump in and get it done,' we all went to Chicago to shoot the bank heist sequence," said Pfister. "It was an opportunity for me and my crew to see what we were getting into with IMAX. And Chris scheduled it in a very smart way. If we fell on our faces—if the IMAX turned out to be a complete disaster—there was enough time to reshoot it in 35 millimeter."

That week of shooting became "IMAX School" for the filmmakers. "We really learned how to deal with the weight and operation of the cameras," said Pfister, "and what we could and could not accomplish." They also learned patience, as the large-format film required special processing at a lab in Burbank, which meant a four-day turnaround before they could see dailies.

The IMAX cameras rolled as Nolan shot all of the action for the prologue bank heist, including the ending in which a school bus explodes through the wall of the bank to facilitate the Joker's getaway. To avoid doing any damage to the

old post office building—listed on the National Register of Historic Places—Chris Corbould and his crew built a false wall inside the structure, and pulled the bus through it by way of a pneumatic rig. "We hammered straight through that wall on cue," recalled Corbould. Getting the bus inside the building, on the other side of the false wall, had proven to be the most labor-intensive part of the stunt, as it was too big to fit through the building's double doors. Corbould's crew had to take it apart piece by piece, carry the pieces inside, and then reassemble it.

After five intense days in Chicago, the production decamped to the United Kingdom, where a base of operations had been established at Pinewood Studios near London. Sets were finalized onstage at the Cardington Shed and Pinewood, while other interiors, such as Gotham City's police station, were painstakingly erected again at the historic Farmiloe Building in London. Though much of *The Dark Knight* would be captured in real-world

At the historic Farmiloe Building in London, Heath Ledger and Christian Bale gear up for the scene in which Batman interrogates the Joker. The site was used for Gotham City police station interiors throughout The Dark Knight Trilogy, in addition to various other sets.

locations, these sets allowed the filmmakers to connect the dots between interiors and exteriors and make the transition from the Gotham of *Batman Begins* to Nathan Crowley's modernist vision for *The Dark Knight.*

The U.K. shoot began with a couple of days in London. At Westminster University, the filmmakers shot the *Gotham Tonight* sequence—hosted by Anthony Michael Hall's Mike Engel—then moved on to a stop at the Criterion, a swanky restaurant used for the scene in which Bruce Wayne and his Russian ballerina girlfriend (Beatrice Rosen) pull up a table and crash Rachel and Harvey's date. Then, it was back to the Cardington Shed for key interiors of the Bat-Bunker.

The Bat-Bunker interior was built on the existing concrete floor of the hangar, with concrete walls added to create a long, rectangular, boxlike shape. With the hangar ceiling 160 feet above the set, however, the challenge wasn't erecting walls, but rather mounting a bunker ceiling and lighting grid low enough overhead to suggest an enclosed space. "The rig above the set was incredibly complicated for

such a relatively simple design," said Nathan Crowley, "so it took us a while. Normally, you'd just suspend it from a concrete ceiling and hang fluorescents—but, in this case, we couldn't do that because the hangar ceiling was too high. Batman needed some light—and we got it to work. So he went from a dark cave in *Batman Begins* to a well-lit box in *The Dark Knight.*"

Wally Pfister embraced the Bat-Bunker concept wholeheartedly. "It was cold and sterile compared to the Batcave," he said, "but it gave us a complete departure, visually, from what we had done before. What I really loved about the space was its dimensions. At two hundred feet long, but with an eight-foot-high ceiling, it immediately made for a fantastic anamorphic aspect ratio. We could shoot a full 360 degrees on that set, and we could shoot very quickly, which Chris loves to do."

With the Bat-Bunker interiors captured, the filmmakers moved to Battersea Power Station near London, where scenes in which Rachel Dawes is tied up and held hostage

by the Joker were filmed. Production would return to the location a few months later for more interior and exterior shots, culminating with an explosion carefully rigged to protect the cherished historical site.

In the interim, the filmmakers spent the better part of two weeks at the Farmiloe Building where Crowley's crews had constructed interiors of the Gotham City police station, just as they had for *Batman Begins.*

By the first week in June, production was back in Chicago where crews would spend the next two months pulling every visual possibility out of the streets and buildings they'd begun to think of as Gotham.

Groundwork for their cinematic deployment had been laid many months in advance by supervising production manager James R. McAllister, who paved the way with city fathers and Chicago citizenry alike. "I had the task of going to property owners and saying, 'Hey, we'd like to have a stuntman connected to a helicopter jump off your roof,'" McAllister said, "or sitting down with city agencies to tell them, 'You know, we're going to flip a forty-foot articulated truck down LaSalle Street.' It got to the point where I'd be saying it and not even realize how unbelievable it sounded to others."

Among the locations McAllister secured was the lobby of One Illinois Center—part of a complex of five office buildings, two hotels, and a hundred shops—which served as Bruce Wayne's main residence, a posh penthouse with opulent views of Gotham. Scenes within his spacious bedroom were shot on the thirty-ninth floor of Hotel 71 on East Wacker Drive.

The art department dressed and reconfigured the interior of the Center's Building Two for the scene in which the Joker crashes Wayne's fund-raiser for Harvey Dent and pushes Rachel off the penthouse balcony—although Nolan had filmed stunt performers on descender rigs dropping one hundred feet on a partial set at Cardington for Rachel's actual fall and Batman's swooping down to rescue her. The set at Cardington had been surrounded by green screen so visual effects artists could insert CGI views of skyscrapers whooshing past the falling characters in post-production.

Wayne's ultramodern penthouse was the antithesis of his stately manor, and—to Wally Pfister's mind—exactly where a bachelor of Bruce Wayne's wealth and status would retreat. "By having Bruce Wayne live in this penthouse," Pfister remarked, "it, again, gave us an opportunity to do something different than what we'd done on *Batman Begins.*"

The location facilitated Sir Michael Caine's introduction to Heath Ledger as the Joker. At a rehearsal for the fund-raiser scene, Ledger entered, on cue, from an elevator and took the veteran actor completely by surprise. "The lift door opened, and there he was," recalled Caine. "I actually jumped. He looked very scary. His was a very different take on the character than Jack Nicholson's. Instead of a naughty clown, Heath played him as a maniacal psychopath, a murderer."

The filming of the fund-raiser scene had been much anticipated by the entire cast and crew, as it occasioned a long-awaited encounter between Ledger's Joker and Bale's Batman. "When we started shooting," said Emma Thomas, "there was quite a bit of time before we actually got to the scenes where they appeared together. Everyone waited for those moments—and they were really something to see. It was amazing to watch Heath and Christian work together."

The Wayne Enterprises boardroom was shot at the IBM Building, a Chicago skyscraper designed by architect Mies van der Rohe, which also stood in for the offices of Harvey Dent, Gotham Mayor Anthony Garcia (played by Nestor Carbonell), and Police Commissioner Gillian B. Loeb (played by Colin McFarlane). For the boardroom, the filmmakers appropriated the thirteenth floor of the structure, which had large picture windows and a panoramic view of Chicago. Wally Pfister enhanced the natural light by adding rows of reflective bulbs overhead and a highly reflective, eighty-foot glass table.

"It gave us an interesting graphic image," Pfister noted. "So much of our photography there was based on the composition and balance of what was happening in the room. It was a fun environment to shoot in." Building exteriors were captured at the Richard J. Daley Center on Washington Street.

The Joker holds Rachel Dawes at gunpoint during the Harvey Dent fundraiser sequence. Interiors of Bruce Wayne's ultramodern penthouse were shot in June 2007 at Chicago's One Illinois Center. The building's ground floor windows were draped with green screen for the post-production insertion of CGI views of Gotham.

TOP: This highly reflective eighty-foot glass table provided the filmmakers with a striking graphic image for the Wayne Enterprises boardroom set, which was built on the thirteenth floor of the IBM Building, a Chicago skyscraper designed by architect Mies van der Rohe.

BOTTOM, LEFT: The boardroom for *The Dark Knight*—with a wooden table, prior to its replacement by the glass-topped version—provided a marked visual contrast to the design of *Batman Begins*, as evidenced by the boardroom from the first film (bottom right).

The parking garage that had been used for portions of the Tumbler's rooftop chase in *Batman Begins* also worked for a scene toward the beginning of *The Dark Knight,* in which Batman apprehends the Scarecrow and his associates, along with a trio of faux Batmen.

The sequence included a confrontation with Chechen gangsters, who respond by releasing their dogs. "Chris Nolan was keen to have Rottweilers do the scene," noted Paul Jennings. "But apparently, Rottweilers are quite difficult to work with in a group—they can end up attacking each other. It was hard finding a handler who could provide several dogs that could work together, but we did."

Another Chicago locale, Navy Pier, would prove an effective stand-in for Gotham Harbor. Located along the edge of Lake Michigan, the former naval facility had been built in 1916, fallen into disuse over the years, and then reemerged with dining pavilions and a dance hall in the '30s, and again as an exhibition venue in the '70s. It received its final transformation into a convention center and tourist attraction in the '90s, and by the time *The Dark Knight* crew arrived on the scene in 2007, it was firmly established as a Chicago treasure. As a bonus, it also included a fully decked IMAX theatre, which the production used to screen dailies.

The Navy Pier waterfront served the film's climactic ferry scenes, but the ferries themselves proved much harder to come by. Production scouts had spent more than a month seeking vessels that were large enough, but to no avail. Eventually, the filmmakers arrived at the time-honored cinematic solution of building the sets themselves. Construction coordinator Joe Ondrejko and his crew erected the

The Scarecrow, his henchmen, and a trio of "faux" Batmen are captured by the real Batman after an encounter in a parking garage. The same garage was used for the Tumbler rooftop chase in *Batman Begins*.

ferries atop a couple of barges and parked them along the north side of Navy Pier, using the brick facade of the old dance hall as the ferry terminal.

The entire ferry sequence was shot over the course of a single day in June and employed eight hundred extras, whom assistant directors efficiently and systematically moved through hair, makeup, and wardrobe in shifts. "We worked out a plan to get everyone ready and onto the bus that brought them to the Pier using a choreographed time-table," explained James R. McAllister. "That way, they didn't arrive on the set all at once. People showed up in their street clothes, and within an hour and a half we had hundreds of National Guardsmen and prisoners."

Lake Michigan also doubled as the Caribbean for the scene in which Bruce Wayne jumps off his yacht to board a private seaplane bound for Hong Kong. "Lake Michigan looks exactly like what it is: a large body of water," said McAllister. "But depending on the day, it can be brown, murky, or glassy; it can also be choppy. It had been raining for several days leading up to the shoot, but, fortunately, we ended up with beautiful weather. We shot the scene looking up into the wide, open lake, with twenty miles of old steel mills *behind* us. It worked well as the Caribbean." True to form, Christian Bale himself performed the elegant dive off the boat and into the chilly waters of the Great Lake.

As they had with *Batman Begins*, the filmmakers sched-uled major action sequences in *The Dark Knight* on Wacker Drive. Much of the street has two decks, with the upper level used chiefly for local traffic, and the lower level for thru-traffic and service trucks. Considered a forerunner of the modern freeway, Wacker Drive provided the ideal loca-tion for capturing both the Batmobile and the Bat-Pod as they raced through Gotham streets.

It was also the logical choice for the elaborate chase-and-crash sequence that ensues when Harvey Dent, who has falsely confessed to being Batman, is transported via armored car to Central Holding—until the Joker introduces mayhem into the mix.

Returning to the familiar location, however, had ini-tially struck the wrong chord in Wally Pfister. "When Chris wanted to do the sequence in Lower Wacker again, I was immediately concerned that it would be too similar to the

ABOVE: Chicago's historic Navy Pier served as a stand-in for Gotham Harbor, where climactic ferry scenes were filmed. The location also provided an IMAX theatre, which production used to screen dailies.

RIGHT: Lake Michigan doubled as the Caribbean for the scene in which Bruce Wayne dives off his yacht to board a seaplane bound for Hong Kong. Here, Wally Pfister (with the camera) and Christopher Nolan (far right) line up a shot.

first film," Pfister recalled. "I actually said to him, 'Why would you want to do an action sequence in the same place we did a car chase last time?' And he said, 'Well, I want to do it bigger and better.' So that's what we did."

In part, "bigger and better" meant filming it entirely with IMAX film cameras—but Nolan also had a few other embellishments in mind. *The Dark Knight*'s chase sequence would include a SWAT van smashing through concrete barricades and into the river, an armored truck crashing into a garbage truck, the Batmobile exploding and transforming into the Bat-Pod, and an eighteen-wheel tractor-trailer flipping end over end—a stunt Nolan intended to capture entirely in-camera.

"Because he'd shot on Lower Wacker for the first film, Chris knew the environment extremely well," commented Kevin De La Noy, who served as executive producer for *The Dark Knight*, "and the City of Chicago was great. We closed sections of the street every night for three weeks to do the chase. It started off calmly enough—'Harvey Dent's in an armored car. What could go wrong?' But then it built up to something the audience wouldn't see coming."

Nolan knew exactly what the elaborate sequence needed in terms of dramatic beats, and planned to shoot it almost entirely in chronological order. The production would work its way down Lower Wacker and then back up again, eventually arriving at LaSalle Street for the climactic truck flip.

Although the SWAT van getting pushed into Gotham River kick-starts the action, it was a latecomer in terms of prep. "Chris Nolan dreamed that one up on the spot," offered special effects supervisor Chris Corbould. "It wasn't something we had planned to do. It turned out to be quite an intricate shot because it involved the camera helicopter going up the river. It was quite a tight fit, but we got it. In the end, we were just glad we didn't have to do it again."

Some of the Lower Wacker footage would ultimately be interlaced with segments shot at Cardington—the Joker launching a rocket-propelled grenade toward the Batmobile, for instance, and the Batmobile's subsequent demise—but the filmmakers continued to push the bulk of the complicated chase-and-crash sequence forward throughout July, getting everything they could on the streets of Chicago.

ABOVE, LEFT: Just inside the door of the Joker's commandeered carnival van, Wally Pfister checks light levels, backed by Heath Ledger. The Ultimate Arm is mounted atop the Mercedes ML55 camera car in the foreground.

ABOVE, RIGHT: Camera crew members film Heath Ledger as he prepares to confront Christian Bale's Batman.

For shots of Batman intercepting the Joker's grenade, propelling the Batmobile between the eighteen-wheeler and the armored car, Corbould's crew launched the full-size vehicle off a ramp—which was later removed from the shot via visual effects—on Lower Wacker and detonated explosions that blew off the vehicle's back wheels. The ensuing crash was shot separately on a full-scale section of Lower Wacker that had been reproduced at Cardington.

The rocket-launched grenade assault made for a dramatic end to the Batmobile, which had been spared a similar fate in *Batman Begins.* "I think we all wanted the car to have a really spectacular ending," said Chris Corbould, "and in the film, it does."

The segment ends with Batman pressing a button and the Batmobile transforming into the Bat-Pod. Nolan had always hoped to achieve the ejection sequence that gives birth to the Bat-Pod in-camera, and Chris Corbould and crew had risen mightily to the challenge, engineering a practical rig that moved the Batmobile's wheels into Bat-Pod configuration. In the end, they were unable to create

enough momentum to make it look like the new vehicle was actually exploding out of the old, and visual effects artists used computer graphics to create the effect.

For shots of the Joker's men using steel cables to ensnare a low-flying police helicopter, causing it to spin out of control and crash, skillful stunt pilots maneuvered a helicopter down an eighty-foot stretch of LaSalle Street, well below roof level, while visual effects crews created a computer-generated helicopter for the final crash and explosion.

The armored car chase ends with Batman ensnaring the eighteen-wheeler in cables, causing it to flip end over end, and finally stopping the Joker's maniacal wild ride. The truck-flip shot naturally called for an IMAX sequence, which meant strategically—and discreetly—placing five of the enormous cameras on the street, with another mounted on the truck itself. "Again, we used the Ultimate Arm," said Wally Pfister, "but with the IMAX camera, it looked a little like an alien because it was so long. That made it difficult to operate because we were fighting inertia a little—you'd tilt it down and the camera took you with it."

As a part of an elemental story point, stunt pilots maneuvered a helicopter well below roof level down the eighty-foot breadth of LaSalle Street in Chicago.

Another concern for Pfister was lighting the stunt, given that the enormous IMAX frame would pick up top-to-bottom as much as the more standard side-to-side view. "We knew that when we framed the truck flipping forty or fifty feet in the air, IMAX was going to pick up the top of some of the buildings in the background," he explained, "which made it a very difficult lighting situation. I wanted to keep it dark and moody, yet it was very difficult to hide any backlight there. It was a real challenge, and we spent a lot of time figuring it out."

For the next few weeks, production made the most of Chicago, picking up less heart-stopping scenes, while also shooting the Bat-Pod in motion with stunt rider Jean-Pierre Goy.

Finding a stunt rider who could successfully maneuver the unwieldy beast had been a major challenge. "We were nearly desperate to find a rider," recalled Chris Corbould, "and then, Jean-Pierre Goy showed up. No one else could ride it, but the first time Jean-Pierre got on, he rode it all around, up and down pavements—and even stood up on the seat at the end! When he got off the bike, he said: 'Riding the Bat-Pod is not the same as riding a motorbike. It is its own animal. But I can make it work.'"

Goy trained on the Bat-Pod for several months, honing his skills to its singular—and often counterintuitive—demands. "He was brilliant at it," said Corbould. "During the shoot, Jean-Pierre would scream down the road and go into a fifteen-yard skid on the back wheel. We went through tires like they were going out of style."

Wally Pfister photographed the Bat-Pod action with an IMAX camera, keeping the camera wide enough to balance the vehicle's length within the vertically oriented format. "It was stunning," noted Pfister. "The Bat-Pod was a really sexy, powerful machine, and Jean-Pierre looked great riding it. We were able to get some amazing footage of it, mostly using the Ultimate Arm."

Throughout, Goy wore the protective armor of the newly designed Batsuit. To provide additional protection—and conceal his face—Goy also wore a crash helmet with a built-in Batman mask.

Batman's cape was the most pressing safety concern. With no mudguard over the back wheel of the Bat-Pod, Chris Corbould feared that the billowing fabric would get caught up in the wheel, tearing the cape and interfering with the Bat-Pod's performance, or worse, yanking Goy off the bike and injuring him. To solve the problem, Lindy Hemming and her crew had gone to great lengths to develop a prototype backpack, into which the cape would fold, electronically.

Corbould finally suggested that they do a test run with Goy on the Bat-Pod, wearing the full cape, just to see what would happen. "I warned Chris to beware, though," said Corbould, "because I was sure it was going to be a disaster." To mitigate that potential disaster, the crew made a cape with soft-tear releases so that if it did get caught up in the wheel, it wouldn't drag Goy off the bike.

To Corbould's relief, the cape flowed out beautifully—and safely—over the wheel on the first test run. "It looked phenomenal," he said, "almost like a Grim Reaper figure on this motorbike with his cape billowing out behind him. It was such an iconic view we just had to do it in the end. I went back to Chris and said: 'I made a mistake. It looks fantastic. We've got to go with this.'"

With cape billowing out behind him, Goy pushed the Bat-Pod to real-life speeds of sixty to eighty miles an hour and executed some impressive turns—despite the Bat-Pod's limited maneuverability and the awkward position of the rider mandated by its design.

"Amazingly, Jean-Pierre only fell off once while filming, and that was coming out of an alleyway," marveled Paul Jennings. "He was turning a very hard left as an explosion went off in front of him. As he came out, the bike caught a wheel and flipped. You can see it in the film. Luckily, he just skidded and stopped. To fall off that bike only once in the whole film was pretty incredible. Jean-Pierre got a hell of a lot out of that bike in the end."

Not surprisingly, Christian Bale longed to take the Bat-Pod out for a spin himself. "Jean-Pierre was the only one who could master it," Bale admitted. "Everybody else just fell off instantly. I got dragged behind cars on it at sixty

The final stages of the semi-truck flip, executed as a practical, all-in-one gag on LaSalle Street.

177

miles an hour and had a great time, but I was never actually able to get on the Bat-Pod and be in complete control of it."

Although he never mastered the Bat-Pod, Bale more than proved his mettle in a night scene filmed at the Sears Tower, the tallest building in America. To get a shot of Batman standing atop the skyscraper, looking out over the city, the actor famously stood on a ledge 110 stories above the street. "Christian is a very brave individual," commented Christopher Nolan. "He likes to challenge himself as an actor—and he likes to challenge himself physically. We didn't put him in any actual physical danger on top of the Sears Tower, but it required guts to stand there and get over his fear. I

certainly wouldn't want to do it. But it made a beautiful shot for us, him standing there on the ledge while we drove a helicopter at him very fast. Luckily, he has the nerve for that kind of thing."

Originally, the actor's stunt double, Buster Reeves, had been tapped to climb out on the ledge. Reeves was on his way up to the tower to perform the scene when Bale got wind of it, and immediately set about persuading first Reeves—and then Nolan—that he was up to the task. "It was important for me to do that shot," Bale explained, "because I wanted to be able to say I did it. How often do you get to stand on the corner of the Sears Tower looking out

ABOVE: Stunt rider Jean-Pierre Goy steered the unwieldy Bat-Pod through the streets of Chicago at speeds that, at times, approached eighty miles an hour.

OPPOSITE: Batman tears through Gotham City on the Bat-Pod in *The Dark Knight*.

over all of Chicago? At the time, it had nothing to do with me thinking it would be a better shot. I just wanted to do it."

Heath Ledger showed similar nerve at the end of August when the filmmakers shot the explosion that brings down Gotham General Hospital. Rather than create the effect through miniatures or computer graphics, Nolan—true to character—had insisted on shooting a real building collapse, and had set his crew to finding a building that was slated for demolition. After much effort, location managers found the soon-to-be-destroyed Brach's candy factory, and Chris Corbould's crew worked with demolition experts to bring it down.

For Corbould, the anxiety of collapsing the building as cameras rolled had been ratcheted up by its proximity to a Union Pacific and METRA commuter rail line. Freight service and transit schedules afforded the filmmakers only a two-hour window in which to execute the demolition. "That was a bit nerve-wracking," said Corbould, "but we rehearsed it, we set the explosions off in time, and we got it. The firemen started putting out fires just as the train came through in the background. Five minutes later and we would have blown the whole thing."

The hospital demolition made for an unusually big day on a production *known* for big days, and most of the crew

OVERLEAF: Lindy Hemming designed a "Batpack" in the hopes of keeping the Batcape from becoming entangled in the Bat-Pod's rear wheel. Although a billowing, breakaway cape was used instead, the Batpack came in handy during Batman's visit to Hong Kong in pursuit of the mob accountant, Lau.

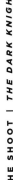
gathered around to witness the event, including editor Lee Smith. "It was quite a rush," recalled Smith. "Heath walked out of the building, and then the whole thing collapsed upon itself in the most spectacular fashion. Heath never even looked back, which was just incredible. It was all timed out by the special effects guys, and they had a load of fail-safe mechanisms in place, but still—if someone asked me to walk out of a building that was about to fall down, I'm not sure I'd do it."

The power of the explosion was such that, even standing a good five hundred yards away, Smith and the rest of the onlookers felt the heat of the blast on their faces. "It was an insanely hot day," Smith said, "but the temperature must have risen twenty degrees for a few seconds, and there was a tremendous force wave."

Nolan and crew spent the next few days filming scenes leading up to the hospital explosion. In one, Bruce Wayne jumps into his Lamborghini and speeds across town, shadowing newly appointed Commissioner James Gordon as Gotham's hospitals begin emergency evacuation procedures.

Ultimately, Wayne inserts himself—and his sports car—between an oncoming pickup truck and the SUV carrying Gordon, thus saving Gordon's life. "The Lamborghini crash all came down to our stunt driver, George Cottle," said Corbould. "We put in safety parts to make sure he had a fair amount of protection, but the stunt was between him and the driver who crashed into him. We just stood back and clapped when they were finished."

"When George got in the car," added Paul Jennings, "he put on his nice, new helmet, which he'd just bought the day before. When Chris Nolan called action, off he went. The truck nailed the Lamborghini perfectly, completely wrecked it—and broke George's new helmet. That was all he worried about, his broken helmet. The production bought him a new one and gave it to him the next day."

The intense, action-packed Chicago shoot wrapped on the first of September, and a week and a half later, production resumed at Pinewood Studios, where interiors of the prisoner and commuter ferries had been built for the

As a showcase, in-camera special effect, the old Brach's candy factory—serving as Gotham General Hospital—was demolished on cue as Heath Ledger walked away from the building.

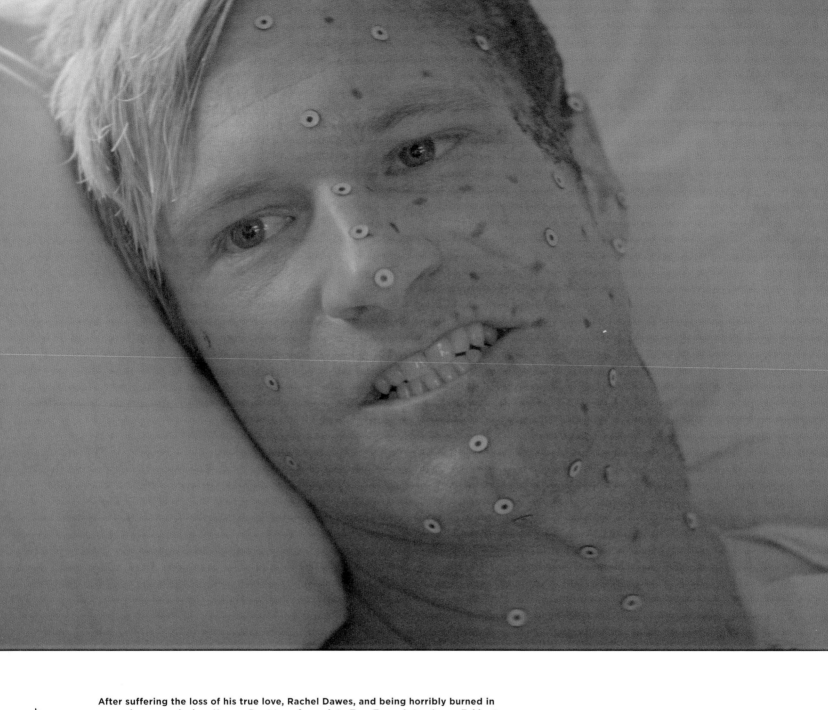

After suffering the loss of his true love, Rachel Dawes, and being horribly burned in a warehouse explosion, Harvey Dent transforms into Two-Face. Actor Aaron Eckhart wore a half-bald cap and black and white markers, which were later used for digitally tracking shots of Two-Face created by visual effects artists at Framestore.

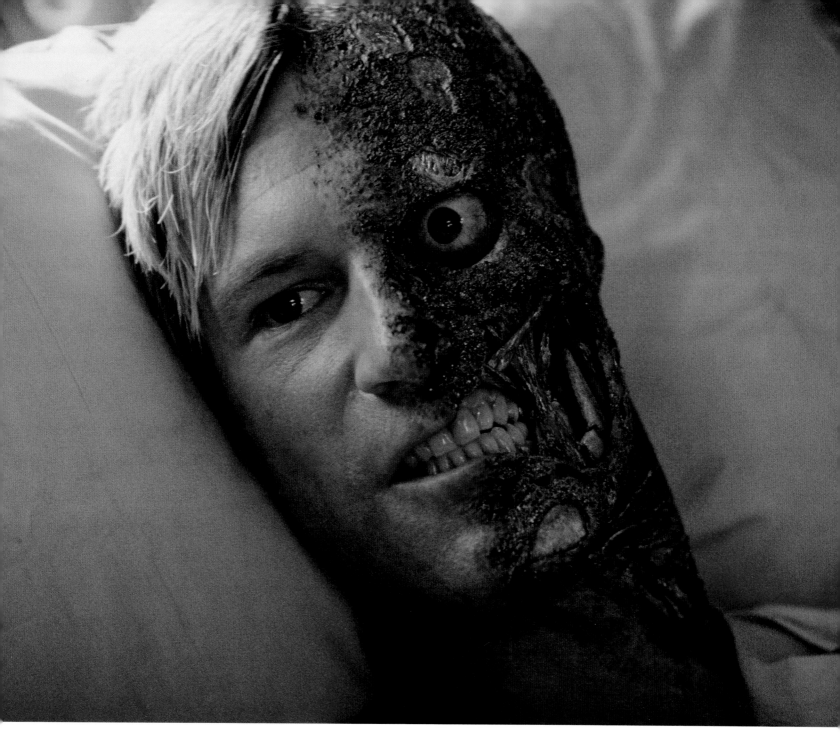

Joker-engineered confrontation between the good citizens of Gotham and a boatload of dangerous felons.

Interiors of Gotham General Hospital were also constructed at Pinewood for the reveal of Harvey Dent as Two-Face and for the exchange between Dent and the Joker, disguised as a nurse, immediately prior to the hospital demolition.

To achieve the gruesome burnt look of Two-Face, Christopher Nolan—usually no big fan of digital effects—had decided to rely on computer-generated imagery, rather than shackle Aaron Eckhart to a makeup chair for hours each day. Not only would a daily application of prosthetics have been tedious for the actor, Nolan feared that covering half his face in latex or silicone pieces would have restricted his ability to perform—and prosthetics, no matter how beautifully designed and applied, wouldn't produce the skeletal look Nolan envisioned for Two-Face. "We can *add* to an actor's features with prosthetics," explained prosthetics makeup supervisor Conor O'Sullivan, "but, in this case, Aaron's features had to be taken away to reveal his muscles, teeth, and tongue movement. That's not something we can do with prosthetics. It had to be done with CGI."

TOP: Aaron Eckhart and Christopher Nolan on location at the Battersea Power Station in South London. Wanting to avoid a separate—and possibly illogical—Two-Face costume, costume designer Lindy Hemming incorporated a red lining into Harvey Dent's classic gray suit to dramatize the character's descent into madness.

BOTTOM: The master composite of the finalized Two-Face effect, which Eckhart didn't see until long after his on-set characterization had wrapped.

On set, Eckhart wore a pattern of black-and-white markers on the left side of his face, which the visual effects team at Framestore would later use to track the CGI Two-Face effect to the actor. Eckhart also wore a customized, half-bald skullcap—also marked with tracking dots—that concealed his own very healthy head of hair.

The skullcap was based on a clay form sculpted by Julian Murray, who used a three-dimensional maquette of Eckhart's head to create a core, over which molds were then made. The makeup crew "baked" fresh skullcap pieces within those molds for each day of filming the Two-Face scenes. "It only took an hour to apply the piece," O'Sullivan said, "half an hour to deal with the hair, and then another half hour to apply general makeup and put on the tracking markers."

The process was not only fast, it also allowed Eckhart complete freedom in his performance as Two-Face. "Every day they slicked back my hair and glued on that beautiful bald cap," Eckhart said, "but I never knew it was there. I ate lunch in it, slept in it—and felt very lucky that we were doing Batman in 2007, instead of in the '90s. Conor made the whole process seem effortless." Because the Two-Face effects wouldn't be finalized until well after the shoot, however, Eckhart was unaware of what his character actually looked like even as he performed his scenes on set. "I had to have a good imagination in the meantime."

To highlight the transformation, Wally Pfister took pains to light Two-Face differently than he had Harvey Dent. "Harvey's known as the White Knight of Gotham," explained Pfister, "and Chris really wanted to emphasize that, so a lot of his early scenes took place in the daytime—which was a nice contrast with Batman, who only comes out at night. But when Harvey transforms into Two-Face, I made the lighting more moody."

Mood was not so much the issue as were practical considerations when Pfister had to light the next major sequence on the production schedule: the final confrontation between Batman and the Joker inside a half-built skyscraper, Gotham City's Prewitt Building. Interiors of the Prewitt were shot at a ten-story office building—located near the hangars at Cardington—which had been dressed to match the then under-construction Trump Tower in Chicago, where Prewitt exteriors were shot.

The challenge in lighting the action sequence, which Nolan planned to shoot with IMAX equipment, was that, once again, the larger IMAX frame left no place for Pfister to hide his lighting instruments. "With IMAX you can see everything, floor to ceiling, and out windows," he explained. "So there was literally no place to conceal the lights. To get around that, I wound up lighting the whole scene with 500-watt tungsten work lights affixed to posts. It was a pretty successful scene—and it was the first time anyone had ever shot an action sequence running through a building carrying an IMAX camera on a Steadicam."

The second week in October, production set up at London's Battersea Power Station, a long-deserted structure on the south bank of the Thames. Among other Gotham locales, the site provided both interior and exterior settings for the warehouse where Rachel Dawes is held captive and ultimately killed in an explosion contrived by the Joker—orchestrated by the special effects crew to be as low-key an explosion as possible, so as not to damage the historical site or disturb nearby London residents.

Still, the effect proved to be alarmingly convincing. On the night of the explosion, many local residents held balcony parties to watch the staged event, while some of their neighbors—who had somehow not received the production's advance notice—believed a terrorist attack was in progress and flooded emergency services with frantic calls.

The U.K. shoot finished up at Cardington the last week in October with an assortment of green-screen shots and inserts to complete the Wacker Drive chase sequence, as well as some closer shots of Rachel Dawes being tossed out the window of Bruce Wayne's penthouse by the Joker, and then being rescued by Batman, who catches and then deposits her safely to the street below.

Though nearly complete, production still had one more stop to make before it wrapped. In November, a scaled-down crew headed to Hong Kong to capture aerial helicopter footage, scenic IMAX plates shot from atop the International Finance Centre, and a shot of Batman diving from one skyscraper to gain entrance to another. "The

dive off the building was interesting," commented Kevin De La Noy, "and we looked at a number of ways of doing it. We'd done a lot of prep and rehearsal in Chicago, including some extraordinary tests of slinging a three-hundred-foot line underneath a helicopter and jumping from the forty-third story of the McClurg Building. For that, Buster Reeves jumped off with one-, two-, and three-hundred-foot-long lines and swung through the air as we recorded it. We spent a lot of time asking ourselves, 'When Batman jumps off the building in Hong Kong, how would he fly?'"

The answer involved marrying the practical effect of Reeves leaping off the building in a safety harness with additional green-screen work shot at Cardington and a computer-animated Batman created in post-production.

As he had with the Sears Tower, Bale set up the sequence by standing atop the tallest building in Hong Kong, IFC2. "There I was again, standing on the edge," said Bale. "It was a real rush. I was surprised by how soon I was able to just move around on the lip, looking straight down. I started purposely bending right out over the top of the building. No one else could be out there with me—they were all stuck inside—so the helicopter with the camera couldn't see everybody jumping every time I did it. It's a funny—and probably quite dangerous—thing how quickly I felt very, very at home out there."

A final dialogue scene between Bale and Morgan Freeman, shot at ground level in Hong Kong, drew scores of admiring locals who turned out to witness

ABOVE: As he had with the Sears Tower stunt, Christian Bale insisted upon standing on the ledge of Hong Kong's tallest building, IFC2.

OPPOSITE: Actor Morgan Freeman on location in Hong Kong with producer Chuck Roven, November 2007.

the high-profile filmmaking in action. "In all the days I've spent in movies," recalled Wally Pfister, "I've never seen so many people out to see movie stars on the street. Thousands of people came to see us shoot that scene, and Christian and Morgan got mobbed just trying to walk to the set. But all in all, it was a simple way to wind down a long and complicated film."

The 127-day shoot wrapped on November 15, in plenty of time for Thanksgiving and a well-earned holiday hiatus. Christopher Nolan had brought *The Dark Knight* in on time and under budget—and had more than cleared the bar he'd set for the production during those early conversations in the garage.

In meeting his own high standards for *The Dark Knight*'s production, Nolan also had inspired department heads and each member of the crew to achieve his or her personal best.

"Chris Nolan has this ability to drain every bit of creative energy out of every one of his cast and crew," offered Chris Corbould. "And he's very clever about the way he does it. Of course, there were times when I wanted to strangle him, but by the end of the film, we all came away knowing that he'd poured every last drop out of *himself*, as well."

With *The Dark Knight*, Christopher Nolan had successfully continued Batman's journey, while pushing himself ever forward as a filmmaker. "Each stage of making an enormous film like this presented its own challenges," Nolan reflected toward the end of the production, "but it had its own rewards, too. We wound up traveling the world and zooming around in helicopters and racing the Batmobile through real streets and creating all kinds of ridiculous explosions. It's the kind of job that if you knew you were going to be doing it when you were twelve years old, you wouldn't believe your luck."

"Everyone said to us: 'You're going to Pittsburgh in August? What are you *thinking*?'..."

Principal photography on *The Dark Knight Rises*—which would take the filmmakers to three continents and eleven major cities—commenced in May 2011, in Jaipur, Rajasthan, a rural area of India near the Pakistan border. There, the filmmakers shot the scene in which Bruce Wayne emerges from an underground prison and begins his trek home to Gotham, where he will stage an epic final showdown with Bane.

Christopher Nolan and the producers had purposely chosen the schedule's most remote and difficult location for the start of principal photography—just as they had initiated the *Batman Begins* shoot at the glacier location in Iceland. "I try and schedule according to rhythms that have

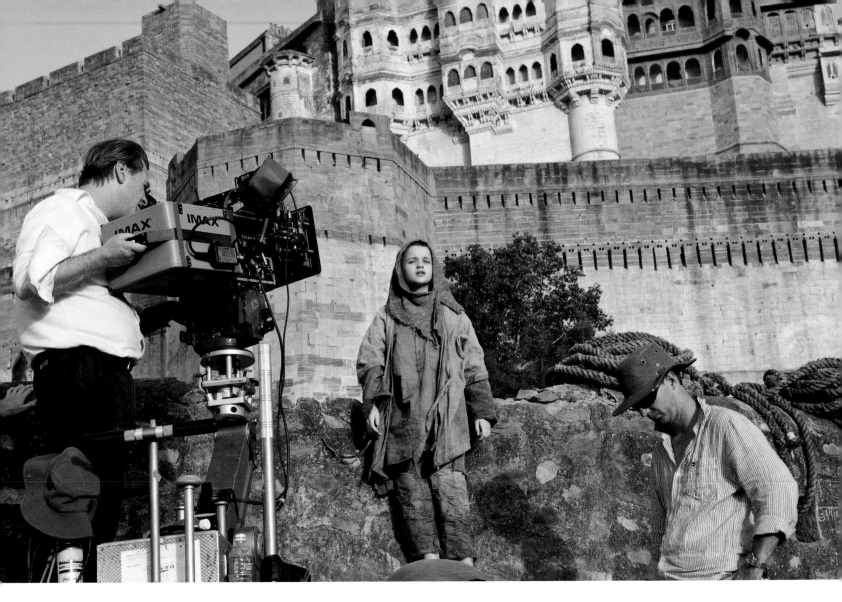

worked in the past," Nolan commented. "Knowing what we had ahead of us, I wanted to get something done early and get it under our belts so we wouldn't have to worry about it later in the schedule. Remote locations have huge question marks around them having to do with travel logistics and weather and so forth, and we wanted to limit the damage that could do later in the schedule if something went horribly wrong. I also thought that it would be quite inspiring to go to a place like Jaipur, a place that was so different and exotic and remote."

Nolan and Nathan Crowley had scouted the location earlier in the year and determined that it would provide one of the epic landscapes they had wanted to incorporate into the film from the start. "We needed a landscape that would be completely unfamiliar to both Bruce Wayne and the audience," said Crowley. "We wanted a place that would create the feeling of, 'Oh, my God, where am I?'—and we had to go a long way to find that place."

"There was a great contrast to the metropolis of Gotham at this location," added Kevin De La Noy, who returned to *The Dark Knight Rises* as an executive producer, "and it gave us that element of journey and exile we needed within the film."

For reasons of both budget and logistics, the filmmakers took as small a crew as possible to India, paring it down to essential personnel and asking that each crewmember do double or triple duty. "For example, instead of taking a dresser for all of the actors, plus a costume supervisor and the costume designer, we just took our costume supervisor—and he dressed people as well as doing his normal job," explained Emma Thomas. "Doing a small, stripped-down shoot where you only have the people who absolutely have to be there was a really nice way to kick off the movie."

Among the challenges of shooting at the location was navigating the country's notoriously bloated bureaucracy to acquire the necessary permits. The bureaucratic difficulties

PAGE 190: Filming the Bat—The Dark Knight Trilogy's third-generation Bat-vehicle—on location in Los Angeles during production of *The Dark Knight Rises*.

ABOVE: Using an IMAX camera, director Christopher Nolan frames a shot in Jaipur, Rajasthan—a remote location in India near the Pakistani border—for the scene in which Bruce Wayne emerges from the pit prison. (Photo by Emma Thomas.)

only mounted when, two days prior to the shoot, American military forces killed al-Qaeda leader Osama bin Laden at his compound in Pakistan, raising tensions across the entire region. "The location was near an air base," Thomas said, "and we'd already had a lot of wrangling over permission to fly helicopters, which we'd wanted to use to shoot a big, aerial establishing shot of that fantastic terrain. But after Osama bin Laden was killed and the whole world was suddenly on high alert, we were denied that permission. There were a lot of headaches there, but it was all well worth it for the production value that we got."

The two-day shoot itself went smoothly, and Nolan was even able to get his establishing shot, using a large crane rather than a helicopter. The speed and success of the India shoot exemplified Nolan's efficiency as a filmmaker, which often brought his films in early and under budget.

The Dark Knight Rises would be no exception. "During the shoot in India," noted Kevin De La Noy, "he was

very specific as to what was required. He is a director who clearly knows what he wants, knows when he's got it, and knows when to move on. So, in India, he achieved what was required, and then we moved on to the U.K. where our sets were being lit and dressed and readied for shooting."

A full crew awaited the filmmakers in London, where the production would shoot a number of locations that had served the previous two films, such as the Farmiloe Building. "It has done multiple things for us in the past," said Emma Thomas, "and we used it a lot for this film, too, shooting Selina Kyle's apartment and the dive bar there."

One location to which the crew wouldn't be returning was Mentmore Towers, which had served as Wayne Manor in *Batman Begins*. With Mentmore unavailable for *The Dark Knight Rises*, the crew had tapped Wollaton Hall, in Nottingham, as the new Wayne Manor, justifying the slightly altered look of the estate by the fact that, in the story, Bruce

On location in Rajasthan, India. As they had with both *Batman Begins* and *The Dark Knight*, the filmmakers deliberately launched the production of *The Dark Knight Rises* by tackling the most difficult and remote location first. (Photo by Emma Thomas.)

Wayne has rebuilt the manor after its fiery destruction at the end of *Batman Begins.*

Among scenes shot at Wollaton Hall was a gala party where con artist and burglar Selina Kyle, disguised as a member of the waitstaff, attempts to steal a set of pearls that had belonged to Bruce Wayne's mother—the pearls she was wearing the night of her murder. The attempted theft is so egregious an act that it brings the reclusive Bruce Wayne out of his self-imposed seclusion within the manor. "Selina is caught by him," noted Anne Hathaway, "and then has to escape from him. And I think Bruce Wayne owes her a big thank-you, because he was leading a pretty sad-sack life at that point. She comes in and gets his blood pumping again and reminds him that there are fun people in the world that he can play with."

An early scene shot at the Nottingham location was one in which now-commissioner James Gordon makes a speech in honor of Harvey Dent. In the film, Gordon initially intends to deliver a very different speech—one that will finally expose the lie about Dent's heroism. "It's eight years on when this story starts," said Gary Oldman, "and we know that the people of Gotham have been fed a lie about who Dent was—and Gordon is the main facilitator of that lie, which goes against everything he believes in. I think this secret has eaten away at him, and he's ready to come clean when the movie starts. But it's one thing to want that in theory, and another when you're really out there, facing the people. He realizes that it isn't the time or the place, that maybe the people aren't ready for the truth, and so he folds the speech away and puts it in his pocket."

Production crews next returned to the refurbished Cardington hangar that had been their "home" ever since Nathan Crowley and his team had first built full-size Gotham sets there for *Batman Begins*. This time, the art department supervised the building of Bane's lair and the interiors of the underground prison at Cardington. "Cardington really worked for the way we shoot," noted Emma Thomas. "It's so big, we were able to build multiple sets within that one space; and so, if we got ahead, we were able to move on to the next one. Or, if we had a problem with

ABOVE: Christopher Nolan scopes out Nottingham's Wollaton Hall, which replaced Mentmore Towers as Wayne Manor.
OPPOSITE, TOP: Director of photography Wally Pfister films Anne Hathaway at Selina Kyle's dressing table.
OPPOSITE, BOTTOM: Bruce Wayne (Christian Bale) and Miranda Tate (Marion Cotillard) share a romantic moment at Wayne Manor, which has been rebuilt in the years following its fiery destruction at the end of *Batman Begins*.

ABOVE: In part to accommodate scheduling, and in part to record it for posterity, the Cardington Shed that had served as home to The Dark Knight Trilogy's production since *Batman Begins* was used for a scene that takes place at an eastern European airstrip, as part of a set built just outside the hangar. Here, the shed stands in the background as the crew readies the fuselage set that was assembled for aerial prologue scenes in which a CIA plane is hijacked by a larger plane manned by Bane's mercenaries.

LEFT: The massive set for Bane's underground lair, at Cardington.

one set, we could use another. We were able to be very flexible in the way we scheduled and shot, which was fantastic."

"It was like having our own studio," added Kevin De La Noy. "It functioned like five stages, but it was all in one building." On any given day, Nolan, Wally Pfister, and first assistant director Nilo Otero could shoot one set while a second was being readied, and then shoot the second set while a third was being readied—and so on, throughout the day.

A pivotal scene shot in Cardington was the one in which Gordon stumbles, unknowingly, into Bane's underground lair and is attacked by mercenaries. "The way we're introduced to the underground world of Bane and the mercenaries is one of those Chris Nolan twists," said Gary Oldman. "It happens just perchance, with Gordon accidentally stumbling upon it. And then, when he is recovering from the beating, he talks about a masked man in the sewers, but everyone thinks he is just hallucinating."

The lair set was also the setting for the first fight between Batman and Bane. Choreographed by stunt coordinator Tom Struthers, the lair fight would display the full force of Bane's brutality and strength. "They wanted to show that Batman was struggling as he fought Bane," Tom Hardy noted. "I love doing fight choreography in films

because you get to look really tough, but it's not real and it doesn't really hurt! Well…it hurts sometimes. When you hit somebody in a Batsuit made of rubber and plastic, it hurts your fists. But it looks really good. You just do what you can, and whatever you can't do, the stuntmen do."

For the first time in the eight years Nolan and the Batman crew had been shooting at Cardington, they shot *outside* the hangar, as well, capturing the film's opening scene, in which the nuclear physicist, Dr. Leonid Pavel (Alon Aboutboul), is delivered into the hands of a CIA agent (Aiden Gillen).

"You actually see the exterior of the Cardington Shed in that scene," Emma Thomas said, "which is set at an airstrip in eastern Europe. We looked for airstrips around the Cardington area for that—it wasn't a full day's work, and so it had to be close to something else that we were shooting. And eventually we thought, 'Let's just do it outside Cardington.' Since this was the last film we'd probably ever be making there, we thought we should record it on film for posterity's sake."

Crews also shot prologue plane interiors outside Cardington, on a fuselage rig mechanized to tilt downward, enabling Nolan to shoot actors tumbling and falling as the CIA

transport plane is winched to another plane and lifted by its tail. "Chris Nolan's thing is always, 'When in doubt, do it practically,'" observed coproducer Jordan Goldberg. "So we built and shot this plane interior that would go from zero degrees to ninety degrees on the flip of a dime. It was a very cool set."

Though the filmmakers had hoped to shoot all of the Cardington-slated scenes in one continuous stretch, production demands dictated that they leave Cardington for other locations and return to the hanger later in the schedule. "We moved around a lot," recalled Kevin De La Noy. "On one of the most radical travel days, we started the morning in Greenwich, out in East London, to film the Italian Plaza and Café; that afternoon, we shot a waterfall in South Wales, four and a half hours away. It looked ludicrous on paper, but when we scouted it, we'd found that it was a remarkably short trip if we traveled in fast vehicles. And it was in June, so the daylight hours were really long. So that's how we scheduled it: We were in the Italian Plaza in the morning, and then at a Wales waterfall in the afternoon. To compound that, the next morning we took a small jet to Scotland, arriving at nine A.M.; and by ten thirty A.M., Chris was in the air shooting the prologue."

The producers had slated the filming of the aerial prologue early in the schedule for the same reason they'd shot the bank heist prologue for *The Dark Knight* the first week of that film's principal photography—the prologue from *The*

Dark Knight Rises, like its predecessor, would be screened in select IMAX theatres starting in December 2011, six months prior to the film's release. "By shooting this very complex sequence early in our schedule," said De La Noy, "Chris and the editors and all the other departments would be able to complete it early so it could come out in December."

Nolan shot the majority of the prologue aerial sequence in the skies over Inverness, in the Scottish Highlands. The location had appealed to him largely because it had never before been used for a cinematic aerial sequence—and with good reason. "You'd be mad to shoot this kind of sequence there," Nolan admitted, "because it rains all the time! That's why you haven't seen it in this kind of sequence before. I had assumed we'd have to shoot it in New Mexico, where these types of sequences are usually shot because the weather's good, and there's a large expanse of empty land. So we'd planned on New Mexico, but when we were in the budgeting stage, it became apparent that if we could move the sequence to the U.K., that would benefit us financially."

As it happened, Kevin De La Noy had worked in Inverness as a location manager on *Braveheart*, and he suggested that it might be a scenic, and less costly, alternative to New Mexico. "Kevin showed me pictures of the areas he'd shot there," recalled Nolan, "and I thought it would make a unique backdrop for this type of aerial sequence, since no one had ever done it before."

ABOVE AND OPPOSITE: Some of the plane exteriors and interiors for *The Dark Knight Rises*'s prologue were shot on the fuselage set at Cardington—which was engineered by Chris Corbould and his crew to tilt down at a 90-degree angle—while others were captured on and in real planes, in the skies over Scotland.

OVERLEAF: A larger-scale pit set was also constructed at Cardington, revealing the Indian stepwell influence that had been production designer Nathan Crowley's inspiration for the setting.

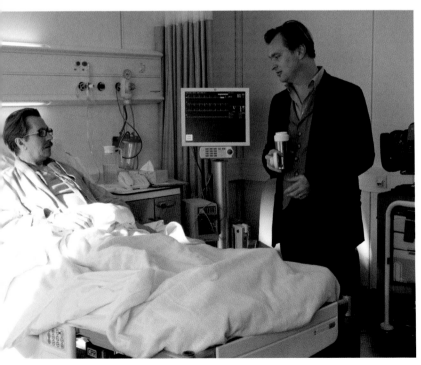

Production manager Thomas Hayslip spent months attending to every detail to ensure that the ambitious and potentially dangerous aerial shoot would go smoothly and safely. "He looked at sourcing planes, the legalities, the FAA, Civil Aviation, all the different rules as to what we could and could not do," recalled Kevin De La Noy. "We wanted this stuff to *look* dangerous, but there were very serious safety margins to consider."

In prepping the sequence, the filmmakers also reduced the number of aerial stunt shots to the bare minimum, which would enable them to do the bulk of the work in just two shooting days. "There were weeks and months of planning and rehearsals and so forth," said Nolan, "but the actual shooting was incredibly quick—and it had to be. When you've got guys hanging from a helicopter, you have to get up there, do it, and get back down safely as quickly as possible."

Arriving at the location, Nolan and the aerial stunt team and pilots were relieved to note that the weather was exceptionally mild for the area, and it would remain so throughout the two days they were shooting. Overall, the aerial shoot went off without a major hitch. "It was an extraordinary run of precision flying, great camera work, stunts, and special effects," said Kevin De La Noy. "It involved all of these intricate rigs dropping plane fuselages over land that had been cleared of all wildlife and people. Planes and helicopters had to take off and meet at just the right point in space. All of it was shot in IMAX, too, which was another component. It was complex stuff, but it was done very calmly, very efficiently, and very safely. Everything went bang, bang, bang, and worked perfectly. It was a tour de force by the entire company."

After nine weeks in the United Kingdom, production moved to Pittsburgh, where Nolan would shoot Gotham City exteriors, including some of the film's large-scale street scenes. Having shot Gotham exteriors in Chicago for the first two films, the filmmakers felt that they had exhausted that city's most interesting architectural features, and they looked for another major American urban area that would offer new cityscapes and locations. Pittsburgh fit that bill.

TOP: Christian Bale and Tom Hardy in character and ready for "action" immediately prior to a scene in Bruce Wayne's pit prison cell, one of several prison sets built at Cardington.

MIDDLE: Christopher Nolan makes an adjustment between shots as Christian Bale waits.

BOTTOM: Actor Gary Oldman rejoined the cast of The Dark Knight Trilogy for his third turn as Jim Gordon, now police commissioner of Gotham City. Here, Oldman and Christopher Nolan on the Gotham General Hospital set.

"Pittsburgh was a terrific stand-in for a larger American city," said Nolan. "It is actually quite a small, intimate town, but because of the architecture there, it photographed quite big."

The people of Pittsburgh, too, would play a major role during the production's tenure there, turning out in the thousands to stand in as citizens of Gotham in epic street scenes. "There are a *lot* more people—actual bodies on screen—in this film than in the previous two," Nolan said. "I wanted the audience to be constantly reminded of the population of Gotham, and the danger of the mob mentality. That's how I wanted to achieve scale in this film."

Historically, shooting large numbers of extras as film crowds had been standard filmmaking practice ever since Cecil B. DeMille made his biblical spectaculars, but over the past twenty years, as the cost of CGI decreased in comparison to the cost of hiring extras, it became more common for productions to hire small numbers of extras, then fill out massive crowd scenes through computer graphics.

Not surprisingly, however, Nolan still preferred to get his crowds "in camera." "I didn't think doing it with CG crowd replacements was going to impress anybody," he said. "I wanted to get out there and really put a lot of people on screen, and that's what we did."

The biggest days of the Pittsburgh shoot, in terms of numbers of extras, were those spent filming the scene at the Gotham football stadium, where fans of the Gotham Rogues watch as the field collapses and Bane emerges to announce that he has set a plan in motion that will unravel Gotham society.

To shoot the sequence at Pittsburgh's Heinz Field, production filled the bleachers with nearly twelve thousand extras. "A scene like that is a really big job," noted co-producer Jordan Goldberg. "I didn't realize how big until I got involved in this. The AD [assistant director] staff had a tremendous responsibility to keep all of those people wrangled, and the coordination of that team was amazing."

One of the typical problems in "extra wrangling" is getting them to stick around for an entire shooting day. "Especially in Los Angeles, they tend to come and go," Goldberg said. "It's not uncommon to have five hundred extras at the start of the day, and have only two hundred by the middle

TOP: Wally Pfister and Anne Hathaway between takes at Wollaton Hall, where the Wayne Manor gala was shot.

MIDDLE: Christopher Nolan and Emma Thomas in a quiet moment backstage at Cardington.

BOTTOM: Producer Jordan Goldberg and Christian Bale on location during the filming of the police chase in *The Dark Knight Rises*.

TOP: *The Dark Knight Rises*'s production team spent three hot summer days shooting at Pittsburgh's Heinz Field, but returned the field to mint condition in plenty of time for football season that fall.

BOTTOM: Pittsburgh Steelers wide receiver Hines Ward atop a military-style Tumbler. To entertain the overheated extras between setups, the filmmakers raffled off prizes and brought Tumblers onto the field in a Batman-style car rally.

OPPOSITE: An impressive sequence shot at Heinz Field—dressed as Gotham Stadium—required the cooperation of twelve thousand extras and the Pittsburgh Steelers, costumed in Gotham Rogues uniforms. The special effects department set off explosions and rigged the field's collapse as stunt players disappeared into holes—and Hines Ward ran for a touchdown.

of the day. People just don't like sitting around all day. The job seems exciting in concept, but when they get there, it's a totally different thing.

"For this scene in Pittsburgh, we needed more than *ten thousand* extras, and if a half or a third of them left by midday, we would have been in real trouble, because we were in a football stadium and everyone was going to be in view. But it was a tough order to expect thousands of people to stick around for a whole long day of shooting."

To make matters worse, the extras in the football stadium would have to bundle up in scarves and heavy coats—in the hundred-plus-degree heat of a Pittsburgh summer—to sell the scene's chilly late fall setting.

As incentives to keep the extras in their seats throughout the day, the filmmakers raffled off prizes such as iPads and a car. During downtime between setups, they provided entertainment, bringing Tumblers out onto the field, even though the vehicles didn't figure into the scene.

There was plenty of spectacle to keep the crowd entertained when cameras were rolling, as well, with special effects explosions going off, signaling the field's imminent collapse, and Pittsburgh Steelers players—dressed as Gotham Rogues—playing football alongside stuntmen.

Among them was wide receiver Hines Ward, who ran down the field as his Rogues team members disappeared into holes created to simulate the field's collapse.

"It worked really well," said stunt coordinator Tom Struthers. "The stunt players disappeared into these holes as Hines was running down the field, and then he stopped and looked around, and half the team's gone! He was just great. It was very hot and miserable out there, but he ran

his heart out. Before we shot it, he'd told the stunt guys not to tackle him because he was in 'preseason' fitness—but no one could catch him anyway! He was too fast. If that was his 'preseason' fitness, I'd like to see him when he's in shape!"

In the end, none of it—not the Steelers, nor the special effects show, nor the raffle prizes—seemed to be required to maintain crowd enthusiasm: The people of Pittsburgh expressed a Batman love the likes of which the filmmakers had never seen.

"It was one of the best crowds I've ever worked with," Kevin De La Noy said. "They were fantastic, and very responsive, even though a lot of what was supposedly happening in front of them was going to be visual effects, which meant they had to imagine it." Production spent a total of three days shooting at Heinz Field, after which the field was returned to mint condition in preparation for the Steelers season that fall.

Large numbers of extras also figured in fight and chase scenes shot in Pittsburgh's streets. To create a wintry ambience in the street scenes, the special effects department provided simulated snow, and the costume department enhanced the illusion by dressing actors and extras in appropriate cold-weather gear.

All of the on-camera performers suffered in the Pittsburgh summer heat, but none more so than Tom Hardy, wearing the face-hugging mask, armor, and extraheavy coat. "It was a challenge for everyone on the movie," sympathized costume supervisor Dan Grace. "As part of the crew, we were able to stand around in T-shirts and shorts, but everybody on camera had to wear winter attire, even in 120-degree heat."

ABOVE, LEFT: John Blake (Joseph Gordon-Levitt) bundles up against the Gotham winter. In reality, the scene was shot in stifling, summertime Pittsburgh with simulated snow courtesy of the special effects department.

ABOVE, RIGHT: In temperatures that reached well over one hundred degrees, no one suffered more than Tom Hardy, whose Bane costume included armor, a heavy leather coat, and a face-hugging mask.

ABOVE: In a radical departure from *Batman Begins* operating procedure, several *The Dark Knight Rises* fight scenes were shot in brilliant sunlight, a testament to the authenticity of the redesigned Batsuit.

LEFT: In contrast, the original Batsuit required meticulous lighting to conceal its neoprene fabrication and was nearly always filmed in dark settings.

At the center of the chaos is a fight between Bane and Batman, one of several sequences in *The Dark Knight Rises* during which the nocturnal Batman would be on display in full sunlight. "We shot much more of Batman in the daytime in this movie," said Jordan Goldberg, "which was interesting because we'd almost never seen Batman fully illuminated before. In *Batman Begins*, there are a couple of shots of him fighting in the train when he's in harsh light, and there are a couple of brightly lit shots of him in *The Dark Knight*. But in both of those movies, you mostly saw Batman in the shadows and in darkness. To see so much of him in daylight this time is going to be somewhat shocking to the audience, I think. But the suit held up tremendously well in those daylight scenes. In fact, you can't really appreciate that suit and see it in its full glory unless you see it out in the open, in sunlight."

Among the shots captured in Pittsburgh were those of the Bat flying low through the city as part of a climactic chase sequence, achieved by mounting a practical, full-scale Bat atop a heavy-duty tow truck that drove through the city streets. "The vehicle held the Bat up in the air on a giant arm so we could do flying chases with it," said Nathan Crowley. "And then visual effects would take out the vehicle and the arm. We also had to use CGI to create the Bat's blades and some of the other moving parts that would make it come to life. But it was still very important to have the practical Bat there on location. It had a cockpit that Batman could sit in, and we could move it through city streets at forty-five miles per hour." In some cases, the Bat would be flown through locations suspended from cables or, if more elevation was needed, hanging from a helicopter.

Flying Bat shots that couldn't be achieved in-camera fell to the visual effects crew, which recreated the aircraft as a computer-generated model. "It was inevitable that there would be CG shots of the Bat," said Christopher Nolan. "But we shot a lot more in-camera than people normally do with something like that, and the practical Bat gave the visual effects team a great basis for the computer graphics version of it."

ABOVE: As part of the climactic chase sequence, the Bat was mounted on a truck and driven through the streets of Pittsburgh.

The filmmakers shot the Bat chase in downtown Pittsburgh, mostly on weekends when the area was relatively empty. "We shifted our production schedule and shot from Wednesday through Sunday," said Goldberg, "doing the biggest stuff in the metropolitan area on the weekends so that we'd affect the lives of Pittsburgh's people as little as possible. On Saturdays and Sundays, that portion of Pittsburgh essentially became like a studio backlot, and so we were free to run cars up and down the streets, blow things up, and fly the Bat through the area."

Driving the massive truck-mounted Bat—which measured seventeen feet wide and twenty-seven feet long—around the compact urban center was no easy feat, however. "Those sequences were pretty hairy," said Chris Corbould, "because some of those streets were quite narrow. In one case, we clipped a lamppost with a wing and took half the wing out. Fortunately, we had a lot of spare components for the Bat, just in case something got damaged."

Hairy as it was, shooting the real Bat in the streets—as opposed to shooting empty streets and inserting a CGI Bat in post-production—gave the chase sequences a dynamic energy and realism, and also gave the actors something to which they could react. "So many movies today are just cartoons, basically," commented Joseph Gordon-Levitt. "It's much more exciting when they build something for real. And it is certainly more exciting as an actor to be looking up at an actual, huge badass machine. No matter how good the actor is, you can tell when he's just looking at an X and making believe he's seeing something. It's done with great success sometimes, but I love that Chris doesn't do that. I love that he actually built the Bat."

With all of its logistical problems, shooting on the city's streets lent the film the gritty look Nolan sought, and created an energy often lacking on a soundstage set. "We were out on the streets a lot more for this movie than we have been in the past," said Emma Thomas, "and we prefer to shoot there. The crew works in a completely different way on a practical location than they do on a stage. On a stage, the energy diminishes immediately when you walk in, whereas, on a practical location, people have to be on their toes a bit more."

There was one major disadvantage, however: Shooting out in the open, on public streets, meant the production and its secrets were vulnerable to any passerby with a cell phone. "You're very much exposed," Thomas admitted. "And technology has changed a lot since we started making these Batman films. Everyone now has a camera in their pocket that they can just pull out, and so everyone who walks past our set on the street is seeing stuff and sharing it with their friends. So it's not just the people who are there who are seeing everything, it's everyone they know, as well."

"Due to the immediacy of Facebook and Twitter," Jordan Goldberg elaborated, "the *moment* someone takes a picture, that picture is online. That was something new. That didn't even happen on *Inception*, which wasn't that long ago. On

TOP: Though filming in Pittsburgh gave Gotham the realistic, gritty look Nolan had sought throughout the trilogy, the Internet Age made the sharing of production "secrets" instantaneous as local fans snapped pictures and posted them online.

BOTTOM: For the New York shoot, the Bat was attached to cables and "flown" through a skyscraper canyon.

209

the one hand, you're glad that people are excited enough about it to film that stuff, but, on the other hand, it ruins the illusion, like someone filming a magician backstage. We don't want people coming to the movie, and thinking, 'Uh, I saw the Bat online—there was a truck driving it around.' So it sucks in that way, but there's really nothing you can do to stop it."

To a crewmember, *The Dark Knight Rises*'s production team thoroughly enjoyed its three and a half weeks shooting in Pittsburgh, and many would cite the day shooting at Heinz Field as the single best day of their careers on movie sets. "Everyone said to us: 'You're going to Pittsburgh in August? What are you *thinking*?'" Emma Thomas recalled. "But it was fantastic! The people were incredibly welcoming, and the city looks amazing on film. And beyond that, just personally, we had a great time staying there."

Production spent the next nine weeks in Los Angeles, again shooting mostly exterior street scenes. Included on the Los Angeles production schedule was the chase sequence that has Selina aboard the Bat-Pod.

Since stunt rider Jean-Pierre Goy had seemed uniquely capable of handling the bike, the filmmakers initially considered having him double for Anne Hathaway on the Bat-Pod, as well—especially since the sequence in *The Dark Knight Rises* included Bat-Pod stunts even more daring than those in *The Dark Knight*. "One of the arguments was that it took so much physical strength to ride the Bat-Pod," said stunt coordinator Tom Struthers, "but I was against the idea. There's a big difference between the look of a male on a motorbike and a female on a motorbike—and even more so on this Bat-Pod. There was no way that a male would ride it like a female."

That proved true when production hired motocross champion Jolene Van Vugt to ride the Bat-Pod as Hathaway's double. "Jolene was very strong," Struthers said, "but she also had more finesse on the Bat-Pod. Jean-Pierre looked more physical and aggressive on it, almost as if he was *dragging* the bike to where he wanted it to go. It was just a totally different look. If Catwoman was riding it, I wanted a lady riding it—and we found the right lady in Jolene. She did a fantastic job."

Anne Hathaway had been introduced to the Bat-Pod during a screen test in which she'd had to mount and dismount the bike with some style, while wearing the catsuit.

Later, during production, Hathaway sat beside Van Vugt on a coffee table and mimicked her moves as the stunt driver modeled the correct Bat-Pod body postures. "Jolene showed me how to throw my body into it and how to do all the turns," recalled Hathaway, "just sitting with me at opposite ends of a coffee table! I was really grateful for that, because all of my instincts had been completely wrong."

Hathaway also learned fight choreography from the stunt crew for scenes such as a rooftop fight—shot in downtown Los Angeles—in which she engages in combat alongside Batman.

"The rooftop back-to-back fight that Catwoman and Batman do together was really fun," Hathaway said. Working with her stunt double, Hathaway rehearsed the fight over an intense ten-day period—although she'd been working much longer on the specific kicks she'd have to perform. "We just worked it hour after hour, rehearsal after rehearsal. And then we shot it in two chunks—one on the first night and the second on the second night. I felt so proud at the end of it, because I knew that we had filmed something that was really cool, and that I had been part of something that girls don't often get a chance to do in movies. I was really excited to show a skill I hadn't had a few months before, a skill I had been working really hard on."

Though principal photography was in its fourth month, Joseph Gordon-Levitt had his first scene with Christian Bale as Batman during the Los Angeles shoot. It was a memorable day onset for the young actor. "It was no joke," Gordon-Levitt said. "I walked up to my mark, and here came Christian in his full Batman regalia, talking as Batman.

OPPOSITE: Anne Hathaway on the Bat-Pod.

ABOVE, LEFT: Anne Hathaway receives a small costume adjustment as she and Christian Bale wait for their next scene.

ABOVE, RIGHT: Christian Bale and Joseph Gordon-Levitt on location in Los Angeles. Although they were four months into the shoot at this point, the occasion marked Gordon-Levitt's first—and most memorable—encounter with Bale's Batman.

ABOVE: Court scenes from *The Dark Knight Rises*. Left, actor Cillian Murphy makes his third appearance as Dr. Jonathan Crane.

OPPOSITE: Production returned to the Farmiloe Building in London for interior shots of a violent encounter between the Gotham SWAT team and Bane's mercenaries at the bar. As John Blake, Joseph Gordon-Levitt takes aim (opposite, bottom).

To walk up to him and start doing this scene felt very real. It was *him*, the character that I recognized from *Batman Begins* and *The Dark Knight*. I was really talking to Batman. That was definitely one of the moments I took away from this movie."

Exteriors for a shootout between the Gotham SWAT team and Bane's mercenaries at a bar were also filmed in Los Angeles, on a backstreet in the city's downtown area. "It was a big firefight that went down the street, and culminated with them turning a corner," said Chris Corbould. "The baddies go down a manhole cover in the road, and as they do, there is an explosion below, and so we had to do a big ball of flame coming out of that manhole cover." The interiors for the scene had been shot previously, at Farmiloe in London.

The only stage-set shot in Los Angeles was the new Batcave, which construction crews had built on a large soundstage at Sony Studios. Rather than build a partial set, the crew constructed the Batcave as a full 360-degree set, affording Nolan complete freedom in his choice of camera angles. Among the set's spectacular features was the Bat-Bunker–inspired cube that rose out of a giant pool of water in the floor and a running waterfall at the cave's entrance.

Among those in attendance for the Batcave shoot at Sony was visual effects supervisor Paul Franklin, there to take measurements and photographs that would aid his crew as they created visual effects shots required in some of the Batcave scenes. Though he was there in a professional capacity, Franklin—like virtually everyone on the crew—couldn't help but feel a childlike thrill as he stood on the Batcave set. "I was standing there, thinking: 'Wow! We're in the Batcave!'" Franklin admitted. "It was thrilling, just because of the scope and scale of the set, and the fact that it was this iconic Batman setting. I got a kick from it every time I walked onto that set."

Production's last stop was New York—a fitting place to wrap the shoot and the trilogy, as New York had always been the model for Gotham, not only in the minds of Nathan Crowley and Christopher Nolan but since the inception of DC Comics's *Batman*. "The relationship between

Gotham and New York is a very particular one," Nolan observed. "Gotham is New York on steroids, a kind of exaggerated Expressionist idea of New York. And so it was the obvious place to shoot."

The logistics of shooting in New York were so complicated, however, that the producers and production and location managers spent eight full months preparing for the twelve-day shoot, which would cover Wall Street, the Brooklyn Bridge, and other city locations, and would extend out to Newark, New Jersey, as well. "It was a very daunting thing," said Nolan, "but it actually went very smoothly. We found the authorities in New York to be extremely helpful, and we worked in a very efficient and reasonable way. Rather than try to do too much of New York, we just did those things that we felt would really benefit the scale of the movie. I'm very happy with what we were able to get there."

As they had for part of their time in Pittsburgh, the filmmakers scheduled a Wednesday through Sunday workweek in New York, shooting the biggest and most logistically complicated sequences on the weekend, when they would be less disruptive to local businesses. Among the most large-scale of the scenes shot in New York was a climactic clash on Wall Street that featured more than one thousand extras, as well as all manner of Bat-gear, camera equipment, and special effects rigs, requiring that the streets be closed to normal vehicle and pedestrian traffic.

"It was out-and-out mayhem," said Chris Corbould, "and a very exciting end piece. The idea was to mix and match what Chris shot there with what he had shot in Pittsburgh, earlier. The closer action was Pittsburgh, but when he pulled back wide, he wanted to see New York."

The clash on Wall Street includes a violent, hand-to-hand battle between Bane and Batman. "It was a very confusing scene to shoot," recalled Tom Hardy. "Bane is looking for Batman, and then comes down the stairs, has six or seven contacts with police officers, and faces off with Batman to beat him up. And Batman is whaling through the mercenaries to get to Bane and beat *him* up. When we shot it the first time, there were so many police officers in the scene that I didn't know which

TOP: Crews prepare the fusion reactor during the Los Angeles shoot.

CENTER: The fusion reactor is loaded onto a truck by Bane's mercenaries in *The Dark Knight Rises.*

BOTTOM: Miranda Tate (Marion Cotillard) and Bruce Wayne (Christian Bale) have a meaningful exchange at Wayne Enterprises' discontinued fusion energy facility as Lucius Fox (Morgan Freeman) looks on.

Batman and Catwoman march through the streets of Gotham, ready for their
showdown with Bane.

ABOVE: Exteriors of Bane's assault on the Gotham Stock Exchange were shot at a real, but retired, stock exchange building in New York, while interiors (shown here) were captured onstage in Los Angeles.

LEFT: Christopher Nolan and Christian Bale on location in New York.

OPPOSITE: Special effects supervisor Chris Corbould works out the logistics for the finale of *The Dark Knight Rises.*

seven I was supposed to hit! So I was just hitting anybody. And then, I was down in the crowd looking for Batman, and I couldn't see him anywhere; he was twenty feet over to my right, and he couldn't see me either. It was like, 'Hey, Batman, I'm over here!' 'Oh, okay.' So we had to reshoot that a few times."

Production also shot the Bat in New York, this time suspended from cables, flying through a skyscraper canyon—a spectacle to gawking New Yorkers and tourists alike. "I think we had fifteen or twenty tour buses go by before we were able to get a cover on the Bat," recalled Kevin De La Noy. "I'm sure that made their day. People love seeing that kind of thing. Even the New York police had fun when they escorted the Bat to set that day."

One of the more logistically challenging sequences shot in New York called for the full-scale Bat to sit atop a New York skyscraper, which required Chris Corbould's team to disassemble the massive rig so that it could be transported, piece by piece, to the high-rise's roof by way of interior elevators. "We considered lifting it to the top of the skyscraper in one piece, by crane, on the outside of the building," Corbould said, "but we found that it was going to be prohibitively expensive. So we went for the cheaper option, and just cut it up into small bits and sent it up in the elevator. And then we bolted it all back together once we had it up there."

Production shot exteriors for a major assault on the Gotham Stock Exchange at a real but retired stock exchange facility in New York; interiors for the scene had been shot previously, on a very detailed and realistic stock-exchange-floor set that Nathan Crowley's team had built within a pre-existing location in Los Angeles.

Nolan wrapped *The Dark Knight Rises*'s shoot in New York on November 14, 2011, 118 days from the date of its launch in May—eleven fewer days than it had taken to shoot *Batman Begins*, and nine fewer than *The Dark Knight*.

Given the significantly increased scale and complexity of the third film, it was an impressive feat.

"A lot of it had to do with the fact that everybody really knew their stuff by then," noted Emma Thomas. "They'd done it all before. We'd made two movies before with the Batmobile, for example, so everyone knew what was involved in that. There were some new things added to it, but so much of it just *worked* by the time we got to this movie."

To a large degree, though, it was Christopher Nolan's singular approach to making movies—an approach honed in his days as an independent filmmaker, when schedules were short and budgets were small—that accounted for the well-oiled quality of *The Dark Knight Rises*'s production machine.

"Chris wears multiple hats at every stage of the game," explained Jordan Goldberg, who has observed Nolan at work ever since *Batman Begins*. "When he's writing, he's also got his director's hat on, and so he makes sure that there is no fluff in the script, that he can shoot what he writes. Then, when he's directing, he's also wearing his producer's hat, making sure that his film is done efficiently and economically. And, at the same time, he's wearing his editor's hat, only shooting what he really needs.

"His ability to do that is partly what makes him such an economical filmmaker. And part of it is just sheer tenacity. There are very few people who say they're going to achieve something and then go out and achieve it. And it's especially impressive when the thing they say they're going to do sounds *insane*. That takes real vision—and that's what Chris has."

LEFT: A stunt rider flies through the air in an elaborate stunt staged in Los Angeles for an action shot that was captured by a camera mounted on the Ultimate Arm.

OVERLEAF: Batman (Christian Bale) throws a powerful blow at Bane (Tom Hardy) during principal photography in Pittsburgh.

"Let's do it for real..."

CHAPTER 8

Present throughout the shoots of all three movies was special effects supervisor Chris Corbould. A veteran effects man with nearly fifty films to his credit, including several in the James Bond series, Corbould faced some of the biggest challenges of his career in the course of his work on The Dark Knight Trilogy.

Not the least of those challenges was building the practical, functional Batmobiles, Bat-Pods, and Bats that enabled Nolan to capture the majority of his high-octane chase sequences in-camera.

PAGE 222, TOP: Batman mourns the death of his lifelong friend and love, Rachel Dawes, killed in a warehouse explosion orchestrated by the Joker in *The Dark Knight*. To stage the effect, special effects crews built a false wall along the front of the Battersea Power Station, near London, and carefully rigged an explosion that left the building, a protected landmark, intact.

PAGE 222, BOTTOM: Special effects and stunt crews staged—and steered—the action sequences throughout The Dark Knight Trilogy. Shown here, the elaborate car chase through Chicago's Lower Wacker from *Batman Begins*.

Epic chase sequences, which were collaborations between the stunt and special effects teams, figured prominently in all three films. Nolan had set a high standard for in-camera chase action with the *Batman Begins* melee featuring the Batmobile and what looked to be the entire Gotham City police force, but he raised the stakes considerably in *The Dark Knight,* conceiving an even more spectacular chase in which Batman pursues an eighteen-wheeler that has been commandeered by the Joker, culminating with the speeding truck doing an end-over-end flip when Batman entangles it in cables. This last gag was one of the crowning achievements of the special effects team's work on The Dark Knight Trilogy.

Nolan had been determined to shoot the unprecedented truck flip from the moment he'd first conceived it, but it took a little persuasion before everyone else embraced the notion. Early on, Chris Corbould had tried to talk him into flipping a smaller vehicle, such as a SWAT van, as opposed to a fully articulated semi, but Nolan couldn't let go of the visual image of an eighteen-wheeler flipping end over end on the streets of Chicago. "I said, 'Chris, I'm sure you can find a way to do this,'" recalled Nolan of his conversation with Corbould, "'because that's who you are and what you do.' And he sort of shrugged his shoulders, and said, 'Okay, fine'—and found a way to do it."

"I had strong reservations about the truck flip," admitted Corbould, "and so I kept niggling at Chris about how he could compromise to make it more achievable—but he wasn't having any of that. In the end, I said: 'Look, I'm going to do a test and try this once. If it looks like we're anywhere *near* getting that truck to flip over, I'll go for it. If not, we will have to do it as a model or CGI.' And at that point, we got our guys together and built the biggest piston I've ever seen in my life."

Corbould's crew fitted the piston to the back of an eighteen-wheeler test truck, reinforced the driver's cabin with steel, and brought the stunt crew and video cameras to the test site. "We did the run up, pressed the button, and it just sailed over," he said. The test crew was amazed. "Every one of us thought, 'My God, I can't believe it's done that!' It was good in one way, but bad in another, because while we did the test in a big, wide-open space, Chris Nolan planned

OPPOSITE: In addition to constructing a fleet of vehicles throughout the trilogy, the special effects team rigged—as an in-camera special effect—an unprecedented eighteen-wheeler flip for *The Dark Knight*. Shown here, storyboards for the sequence

ABOVE: Veteran stunt driver Jim Wilkey drove the fully articulated semi down the LaSalle Street Canyon in the heart of Chicago's financial district, hitting a button inside the cab on cue to initiate a giant piston that caused the entire vehicle to flip end over end.

to do it right in the middle of Chicago's banking district. If it deviated ten degrees off the straight line, it would go right through the front of a bank."

Nolan had scoped out a stretch of Chicago's financial district known as the LaSalle Street Canyon for the stunt. With its tall buildings and rich architecture, the location offered visual interest, but it raised the stakes for Corbould and crew. "We got an independent survey company involved, and when I looked at their plans I noticed all these manhole covers in the road," he explained. "I said to the surveyor, 'What are these?' He said, 'Well, they're for utilities and underground vaults for the banks.' As it turned out, there were only two spots along this quarter-mile stretch of road with the sixty feet of solid ground needed to actually do the gag."

Veteran stunt driver Jim Wilkey drove the eighteen-wheeler down the Canyon wearing complete Joker makeup. "The stunt guys built a heck of a cage for me," Wilkey said. "Under the costume, I wore a fire suit and helmet, and had a five-point seat belt. Special effects had prepared everything, and so all I had to do was get my mind right so I could drive to the spot, and then reach over and hit that big red button at the right moment. They almost made it seem easy."

On the night of the shoot, already taut nerves were strained further as weather forecasts started calling for rain. "As we got into the shoot, the clouds started getting darker and darker," recalled Corbould, "but it hadn't yet started to rain. And so they turned the cameras on and we sent the truck on its way. Rather than watch, I stepped into a side street and listened, knowing that if I heard the sound of breaking glass I was in a lot of trouble. As I listened, I heard the piston go, followed by silence and a big crash. Then a cheer went up and I knew we'd got it right."

Jim Wilkey returned to the trilogy to drive a five-axle, fifty-five-thousand-pound truck that figures in *The Dark Knight Rises*'s climactic chase, during which Batman in the Bat and Catwoman on the Bat-Pod tangle with Bane's mercenaries in the Tumblers, while in pursuit of a massive tractor-trailer with explosive cargo. Nolan shot the chase on the streets of Pittsburgh over the course of several days that would prove to be a wonder of large-scale organization and production logistics.

Explosions, large and small, were also on the special effects crews' agendas throughout the trilogy. For *Batman Begins*, the team blew up an interior monastery set at Shepperton Studios. For *The Dark Knight*, the crew rigged the explosion that leaves Harvey Dent badly burned in a gasoline fire, as well as the explosion that kills Rachel Dawes. The latter required the crew to construct a false wall along the front of the Battersea Power Station structure, using lightweight materials that would disintegrate when laced with less-powerful explosives—thus leaving the historical building intact.

Though an emotionally compelling moment—ending as it did the life of Bruce Wayne's oldest and dearest friend—the Battersea explosion looked modest in comparison to the hospital demolition orchestrated by the Joker in a ruthless act of one-upmanship against Batman.

Months of frustrating location scouting had gone into finding the right site for the gag before the abandoned Brach's factory came to the filmmakers' attention. The factory had a four-story redbrick facade and banks of windows that would stand in beautifully for Gotham's aging hospital; even better, the building was already scheduled for demolition.

"When I told Chris Nolan I fancied demolishing it for real, he got quite excited and actually wrote it into the script," said Chris Corbould. "But he didn't want it to simply come down. He said, 'If you're going to demolish the building, I'd like to see something different.'"

Corbould arranged a meeting with explosives expert Doug Loizeaux to plan how they might execute that "something different." The pyrotechnicians ultimately designed an explosion that would look as if the structure was being bombed *out*, as opposed to imploding, starting the event at one corner, and then bringing down the building in a wave of successive explosions.

Production hired American Demolition to affix explosives to the factory's key supporting columns, as well as set special charges to break out the windows. As a further embellishment, the demolition team set up rigs to knock out columns on the vertical plane and send the building into free fall, while allowing a portion of the structure to remain standing. Once initiated, the series of explosions

Special effects supervisor Chris Corbould worked with demolitions expert Doug Loizeaux to bring down the Brach's candy factory in Chicago—which served as Gotham General Hospital—as a full-scale explosion, captured entirely as an in-camera effect.

227

and demolition rigs cut through the building like a knife through butter. Crews also strategically placed fire bars and debris mortars around the site to add the visual impact of shooting flames and exploding rubble. "We all felt quite the adrenaline rush as we watched that building come down," Chris Corbould recalled.

Large-scale explosions and structural collapses would be cause for adrenaline rushes—for crewmembers on the set and audiences at their local theaters—in *The Dark Knight Rises*, as well. Over the course of five months, Nolan shot scenes of epic destruction and mayhem on the streets of Pittsburgh, Los Angeles, and New York, as well as on massive sets built at the Cardington hangar.

Among the destruction sequences shot on a Cardington set was the partial collapse of Bane's underground lair. The special effects team had plumbed Nathan Crowley's lair set with running water—much as it had the Batcave set in *Batman Begins*—to enhance the illusion of a sewer system and serve scenes such as the one in which a badly beaten Commissioner Gordon falls and is swept away in the current.

Water would add dynamics to the collapse of Bane's lair, which Crowley's construction crews had built as a large, cylindrical column. Initial shots of the lair collapsing were in-camera effects orchestrated by Chris Corbould. "We put a charge in a portion of the set to make the ceiling collapse,"

he said. "We also dropped one of the Tumblers eighty feet into the set, because Bane's lair is under Applied Sciences. So we rigged one of the real Tumblers on an electric release, blew the ceiling, and then dropped it right into the middle of the lair."

Other shots of the underground tunnels collapsing were filmed on separate, stand-alone sets or at real underground subway stations, where Corbould's crew engineered very controlled explosions and rigged false tunnel support structures to fall on cue.

After months of collapsing tunnels and setting off explosions in football fields and hanging Bats from helicopters and flying them through real city streets, Chris Corbould completed his work for The Dark Knight Trilogy in New York, wrapping up an eight-year adventure within the world of Christopher Nolan's Batman.

"It's been fun watching Chris grow as a filmmaker from the first movie to the second to this one," Corbould said of the experience. "When we started *Batman Begins*, he was a fairly rookie action director, and so he was just learning what was achievable. Then, for *The Dark Knight*, he took it to the next level, with big events like the semi-truck flip and the hospital demolition.

"On this last one, *The Dark Knight Rises*, it was just full-on effects and action, all the way through. He really went

ABOVE: Massive fight sequences—such as this one from *The Dark Knight Rises*, shot on location in Pittsburgh—required large-scale planning, choreography, and rehearsal prior to filming.

OPPOSITE: Christian Bale rehearses the monastery fight for *Batman Begins*.

for it on this movie! And he's no rookie anymore—he's a real master of it. What makes a great action director is being a good storyteller, because action in movies can get very boring if you don't have a really gripping story line—and that's where Chris excels. He makes sure that the action is always character-driven, and that makes all the difference."

Just as the same special effects crew worked on all three movies in The Dark Knight Trilogy, so too did the stunt team remain more or less intact, with only a few changes in supervisory positions.

Central to the stunt work were the films' many fight sequences, each of which required months of choreography and training. All of the fights in *Batman Begins*—overseen by stunt coordinator Paul Jennings and fight arranger David Forman—were based on the Keysi Fighting Method, which was developed in Spain in the '50s. Part defense, part offense, Keysi draws from every major martial arts discipline, as well as from street-fighting techniques.

Christian Bale's stunt double, Buster Reeves—a jujitsu world champion—had first suggested Keysi as a possible fighting style for Batman. "We'd wanted to come up with a new, different style for Batman's fighting," said Paul Jennings. "We wanted it to be visual, but we didn't want

him doing kicks and leaps just because they looked good, either. Every move had to have a purpose." Keysi was ideal for Batman's purposeful, utilitarian fighting style, as it is based on the principle of using whatever is on hand in a given situation. "In Keysi, you use what your opponent uses and what you have available to fight with. It's very much about being mentally aware of the environment and the actions and reactions of the person you're fighting—and that seemed perfect for Batman."

The hard-hitting, gritty fighting style influenced all of the Bruce Wayne and Batman fights—although it required some modification to ensure it would read on camera. "Kicks and leaps work best in movie fights because they are big and visual," explained David Forman. "But Keysi is very tight, with a lot of small moves. It is also such a fast art, you can do four moves in a second. To make it work for the movie, I had to adapt it to make the moves bigger—otherwise, they would have been too small and too quick for the audience to even catch them."

Specific choreography was different for each fight, depending on the environment. For the fight between Henri Ducard and Bruce Wayne on the frozen lake, for example, the fight choreographers incorporated moves that would take full advantage of the lake's slippery, icy surface. "We gave that fight some sliding movements," said Jennings,

Along with wirework and car chases, the stunt team was responsible for staging numerous fights for all of Christopher Nolan's Batman films. The Keysi Fighting Method—a gritty, utilitarian style of street fighting—was introduced in *Batman Begins* and also used in *The Dark Knight*.

"just to give it a slightly different look. We went to an ice rink to design the fight, and then filmed it and showed it to Chris Nolan to make sure he was happy with it. Then we brought in the actors to get their take on it. After that, it was just a matter of rehearsing it over and over again so that by the time we shot it, everything was locked down."

Christian Bale began his Keysi training prior to the start of principal photography, and immediately understood why the style so suited Batman. "It's based on natural instinct," Bale said, "on pure animal rage. I always adopted an animalistic attitude for Batman, and the Keysi just flowed from that."

Once in training, Bale proved to be an especially quick study. By the time he got to the set, he had learned all of the fighting moves so thoroughly, he was able to concentrate on performance, rather than fight choreography. "Once I had the moves down," said Bale, "it was instinctive, so I felt natural going into them. There's a great difference between really acting the fighting scenes and just fighting in them."

"Fighting is still very much performance and very expressive of what's going on with the character," Christopher Nolan added, "and so I found it to be a great privilege to have actors willing to do so much of the fighting themselves. It was a great advantage to have actors like Christian and Liam who were willing to just dive in and express the character's physicality, even in the most extreme situations."

For both Bale and Neeson, the dual responsibility of acting while also performing tightly choreographed fight moves was most tested in the final fight between Batman and Rā's al Ghūl aboard the monorail train. The actors performed the fight beginning to end for the cameras, and then stunt performers repeated it, giving Nolan the optimum number of options when assembling the sequence.

"The final monorail fight was Keysi against Keysi," said David Forman, "punch for punch, kick for kick—and that's what made it so intense and dynamic. It was a real battle, like two bulls going at it, and I think the actors really enjoyed doing it. When Liam and Christian finished, you could just see the gleam in their faces."

Keysi remained the foundation for the fights in *The Dark Knight,* which included two major engagements between Batman and the Joker: one at the Harvey Dent fund-raiser,

and another within the Prewitt Building near the film's end. The second proved significantly more complex than the first. "The Prewitt sequence was difficult because there were so many components," explained Paul Jennings, who again served as stunt coordinator. "We had doctors and nurses dressed like clowns who are actually goodies. We had the Joker's men dressed like doctors and nurses who are actually baddies—and we had SWAT men we *think* are baddies but who are actually good. We had floors blowing up and SWATs falling and smashing through windows. And, of course, we had the Joker and Batman fighting it out. In the end, Chris Nolan found a way to make it work. He always knows in his head exactly what he's going to do."

Nolan's intention for all the fights in *The Dark Knight* was to showcase Batman's fighting abilities to a degree far beyond what he'd been able to do in *Batman Begins.* "We used the Keysi Fighting Method in the first film," Nolan said, "but it was obscured by the way in which we chose to present the character, which was from the criminal's point of view. That meant we could only catch glimpses of Batman. It wasn't until *The Dark Knight* that we got to see the way he moved. That's when this unique fighting style really started to pay off. Also, thanks to the new Batsuit, he could move his arms and neck—which are a big part of Keysi—much more effectively. Christian was able to show what he could do far more than on the first film."

"That suit really worked in motion," Bale agreed, "and it certainly made a difference in the fight sequences." For Bale, there was also a psychological component to the suit. "You can't help but feel different in the Batsuit. You're so protected you feel that you could easily beat the crap out of anybody who messed with you. In a way, it makes you feel more aggressive."

For each of Batman's fights in *The Dark Knight,* stunt double Buster Reeves first blocked out the moves and rehearsed camera positions, and then he would teach the fight to Christian Bale, once all the specifics had been established. "Christian could come into the rehearsal room and learn it in half a day," said Jennings. "The next day, we'd video him doing it, and he would go slowly through the moves until he knew the fight absolutely, one hundred percent—and then he'd do it at full speed, straightaway."

TOP: At the under-construction Prewitt Building set, Christopher Nolan and Christian Bale go over details for *The Dark Knight*'s final battle between Batman and the Joker.

BOTTOM: Fight coordinator Richard R. Ryan and Christian Bale discuss fight choreography between takes. The new Batsuit provided both physical protection and a psychological advantage during fight scenes, while allowing Bale greater range of motion.

OPPOSITE: Though Bale's fighting approach was methodical, Ledger's was more improvisational, in keeping with his chaotic character.

While Bale's approach to the fights was methodical, Heath Ledger's was more improvisational, befitting the Joker's more chaotic character. "Heath let his emotions drive the fighting," noted Jennings. "He would deliver kicks and blows wherever he wanted, as opposed to being told, 'You need to be in this position at this time.' What he did was repeatable, though. We knew exactly what he was going to do when the time came to shoot it. In a straight fight, Batman would beat the Joker every time, but the Joker is a clever, erratic, quirky fighter who uses his street knowledge to give himself a fighting chance. And he loves a knife."

Batman would face an even more daunting opponent in *The Dark Knight Rises*, engaging in two major fights with Bane, a villain who would prove his equal both physically and mentally.

Tom Struthers, who had served as assistant stunt coordinator on *Batman Begins* and co–stunt coordinator, with Jennings, on *The Dark Knight,* returned as stunt coordinator for the third film, reassembling the core stunt crew that had been with the trilogy from the beginning. As part of his duties, Struthers oversaw *The Dark Knight Rises*'s epic fights between Bane and Batman and other characters in the film.

"There was a lot more emphasis on fights in this movie," Struthers commented, "and especially the fights between Bane and the Dark Knight himself. We brought a few added elements to the fighting this time, too, building on what we'd done before and taking it one step further. The fights in this film definitely surpassed the other two."

Bane's fighting style, in particular, would be more violent and aggressive than that of his villain predecessors, harking back to the League of Shadows ninjas in *Batman Begins*. "The League of Shadows is a brutal community," said Struthers, "just because of the extreme environment they live in, and the skills that they need to survive and to be the 'guns for hire' that they are. With Bane, especially, we went back to that idea of extreme brutality. You see some of it in Batman, too, but Bane has a *mental* brutality that Bruce Wayne doesn't have—and that's what makes him so unique. When they are fighting, you've got one guy who's trying to save the world, and another guy who's trying to destroy it, but they are very evenly matched.

For *The Dark Knight Rises*, new fighting elements were brought into the fray, thus enhancing Bane's brutality while recalling a League of Shadows ninja influence from *Batman Begins*.

That works well in the two long fights between them in this movie."

One of the pivotal Batman–Bane fights is set in Bane's underground lair. The fight comes to a shocking end with Bane breaking Batman's back—an event chronicled in the '90s-era comics.

"It's very difficult to come across with something that has been depicted in comic books," said Struthers, "to bring it to the screen with real characters and actors. It's difficult to get that kind of violence on screen without getting into *undue* violence. It had to read well on screen, without making the audience disgusted by it—and I think we achieved that. It's pretty gruesome, but I don't think it will completely turn off the audience."

For her role as Selina/Catwoman, Anne Hathaway also engaged in intense physical training, sitting down with Struthers twelve weeks before she was scheduled to shoot her first fight scene. "I told Tom that I was going to work really hard," Hathaway recalled of the meeting, "and that I was really excited because we had twelve whole weeks to prepare for it. And he took one look at me, and said: 'Yeah. I wish we'd started a week ago.' And I was like: 'Oh… well, I'll just work *harder*, then! More sit-ups! More push-ups!' "

The pressure was on for the actress, as Christopher Nolan had impressed upon her that he expected her to perform all of Catwoman's fights herself, without relying on a stunt double. "He wanted to make sure that in addition to learning the fights, I would be strong enough to do them for hours or days on end," Hathaway stated. "So that was an opportunity to push myself in a way that I never had before. I worked out with my stuntwoman, Maxine Whittaker, and she couldn't have been more supportive."

In choreographing Catwoman's fights, the stunt team deviated from the whip-cracking, sexually tinged, feline-inspired style of the '90s-era Batman films. This Catwoman, rather, would be an aggressive street fighter—albeit in four-inch heels. Those heels worried Struthers more than anything else as he watched Hathaway perform the fight choreography: One wrong move or an ill-placed kick could have resulted in the actress suffering an ankle sprain or break.

even more than vanity, I was motivated by the fact that this was a once-in-a-lifetime opportunity. Any actress would give anything to play this part, and I didn't want to take that for granted. It was great to audition for this role and to earn it, but once I got it, I had to make sure that I continued to earn it. I really just wanted to impress Chris every day. I think the world of him, and so just to try and get a compliment out of him was great motivation."

Joseph Gordon-Levitt had learned the "Nolan drill" when he'd worked with the director on *Inception.* For a major fight sequence in that film, Nolan had told the actor essentially what he said to Hathaway—that he'd be expected to perform the fight himself, and that he'd have to be in good enough shape to do it repeatedly, over the course of days.

Gordon-Levitt came through with flying colors on *Inception,* and he would do the same for John Blake's fight sequences in *The Dark Knight Rises,* training with the same stunt team with which he'd trained previously. "Tom and all of those guys knew me from *Inception,*" said Gordon-Levitt, "and so they trusted me. They knew that I could do it and make it look good. That was really nice because you always have to establish that trust between actors and the stunt team. They knew that I wanted to do this stuff, and that I didn't mind getting a little bruised up. I was like, 'Put me in the game!' They knew that I'd play."

"That always concerned me," Struthers said, "but Anne did great. She wasn't afraid of getting in there with the big boys, even though she'd never done this kind of thing before."

Hathaway impressed everyone by continuing to put in long and intense hours of training throughout the entire shoot. "A lot of people in this business just show up," Struthers said. "But that doesn't work on a Chris Nolan film, and I think he chooses people, including actors, whom he knows will work hard. I think part of the reason he chose Anne for this was because he knew she'd put everything she had into it—and she did. Anne worked exceptionally hard, and she continued to train and work hard until the very last day of filming."

"Part of that was vanity," Hathaway admitted. "If you had to wear a catsuit in front of the entire world, you'd get your ass to the gym, too! It was a really good motivator. But

In addition to fight sequences, the stunt crew was responsible for the significant number of high-wire setups required for shots of Batman flying from one Gotham rooftop to another, or swooping down onto unsuspecting criminals in the streets. In *Batman Begins,* shots of Batman in flight were achieved mostly at Cardington, which afforded Nolan the opportunity to shoot an aerial Batman against real, full-size Gotham sets—rather than resort to the more common technique of shooting a wire-rigged performer against green screen or blue screen, and then compositing him into live-action background plates.

Nolan also wanted to shoot the flights using a handheld camera tracking along with Buster Reeves—as Batman—in the wire rig. He suggested to Wally Pfister that he hand-operate his camera while in a harness, flying on a wire rig

ABOVE: Bane's most ruthless encounter with Batman was first chronicled in *Batman* no. 497, written by Doug Moench and illustrated by Jim Aparo. Shown here, page 21 of that issue. Published by DC Comics, 1993.

OPPOSITE: Batman's first encounter with Bane in *The Dark Knight Rises.*

Christian Bale on the ledge of IFC2, Hong Kong's tallest building.

in front of, to the side of, or behind Reeves. "In the end," Pfister said, "it was neither safe nor really the most effective way to do it, but that was the spirit that Chris was always going for—get in there, handheld, and fly along with the flying Batman! He just wanted to grab the camera and capture the action. Once I understood that, I was able to capture the spirit of it, even if it meant having to use some technology to film the flights, rather than getting up there myself."

Specifically, the technology used to film the high-wire stunts was a gyrostabilized camera head that traveled along the wire rig and filmed Buster Reeves as he flew across the Gotham cityscape. "It was a very big deal to set that up," recalled Pfister, "but once we had it going, it gave us amazing shots of Batman flying across the city, all without visual effects. It encapsulated Chris's philosophy of filmmaking, which is 'Let's do it for real.'"

To avoid having to re-rig wires and reset lights, Nolan shot the majority of Batman's flights on the same eight-hundred-foot-long stretch of the Cardington set, redressed with neon signage and other set pieces to make it look like different areas of the city. The crew also created variety in the flights by shooting the run in opposite directions or with different camera lenses.

Early on, the filmmakers had considered shooting Christian Bale on the wire rig, as well, but they ultimately rejected the idea as too risky. "It was a shame," said Bale, "because I was eager to try it." Bale would get his chance at the very end of the schedule, on the last day of shooting descents and ascents in front of a green screen for the few shots that hadn't been filmed "live" on the Gotham set. "I'm sure they were thinking, 'We have the film in the can now, so if he lands on his face and splits it, it doesn't really matter!'

"After that one day of doing it, though, I was glad I hadn't had to go up on those wires a lot. Hanging in the harness is not comfortable at all in certain places. I was meant to be speaking in a deep voice as Batman—but it was difficult not to sound like a choirboy!"

Among the most memorable flight shots in *Batman Begins* is the one in which Batman swoops down the grand stairway at Arkham Asylum, his cape spread in its glider configuration. "Chris had a very clear idea of how he wanted Batman to appear in that scene," recalled Paul Jennings. "Once they'd found the location, we went there with the special effects guys and our stunt riggers to figure out how to make it work. We found that it was very narrow between the stairs where we were going to bring him down. What made it worse was that we also had to have all

the safety gear in that narrow space. We had crash mats all the way down the stairway, plus stuntmen standing there to protect the performer if he didn't fall exactly as he was supposed to. We also had an emergency stop, so we could stop the descent immediately if something went wrong."

Not all of the wire rigs set up by the stunt and special effects teams were for shots of Batman in flight. The team engineered an entire system of cables and pulleys for the scene in *Batman Begins* in which Henri Ducard and Bruce Wayne, escaping from the burning monastery in Bhutan, slide down an icy slope, the former going off a cliff at the bottom and dangling over a two-hundred-foot drop, spared the final plunge when Bruce catches him with one hand.

The stunt crew first rehearsed the ice slide at Shepperton Studios, with stuntmen attached to cables sliding down a set piece that simulated the icy slope. "We built a ramp that was forty feet tall and forty feet wide," said Jennings, "and then had our guys slide down on little skateboards since we had no ice on the stage."

The stunt crew then went to Iceland—where the stunt would be executed—in advance of the production crew to oversee the building of a similar slide, boarded on two sides and covered with snow and ice, on the mountainside. The same unseasonably warm weather that would plague the

entire shoot in Iceland melted the ice on the slide, requiring the special effects department to replenish it over and over again. "It was really a labor of love keeping that ice slide intact," recalled Chris Corbould. "There was a local Icelandic effects guy who was up there every night, spraying it down with water and packing in truckloads of snow we'd brought in from the top of the glacier."

Wearing safety harnesses and attached to cables, Christian Bale and Liam Neeson performed the first part of the long slide themselves, while stuntmen executed the final few feet that ended at the real cliff on location. "On the day," said Paul Jennings, "we actually talked about putting Christian at the edge of the cliff. Christian wanted to do it, Chris [Nolan] wanted to do it, and I wanted to do it. Everyone was up for it, but we just ran out of time. So we ended up shooting the close-ups of Christian at the edge of the cliff on a set piece back at the studio."

More technically challenging than the ice slide was a scene near the end of *Batman Begins*, in which Batman, on a street in the Narrows, shoots a cable from his grappling gun to attach himself to the monorail train as it speeds by on an elevated track. To violently and quickly jerk Batman into the air, crews employed jerk rams—hydraulic rams attached to a nitrogen energy source. "You just

Christian Bale and Liam Neeson performed the first part of the *Batman Begins* ice slide on location in Iceland, with stunt performers finishing it off at the edge of the cliff. True to form, Christian Bale had wanted to perform the entire stunt from beginning to end, but time constraints prohibited it.

push a button and this ram fires the person into the air or backward—whichever direction you want," explained Jennings. "We had to make it quite powerful and fast because he was supposedly being snatched up by this speeding monorail overhead."

The stunt team rehearsed the gag, first pulling a stunt double into the air slowly, and then ramping up the speed with each subsequent test. Watching the rehearsals, Christian Bale suggested that Batman get ahold of a Narrows bystander as he flew into the air. "To do that," Jennings explained, "we just attached a second ram to a second performer and had them work in parallel, so it looked like they were stuck together. Then, we had one quick release so that the second performer would drop away as Batman carried on."

For following shots of Batman dangling beneath the moving train, crews hooked Buster Reeves to a three-hundred-foot-long, computer-controlled traveling rig and filmed the action with a remote-controlled camera suspended from cables. "Hanging Batman underneath the monorail train was probably the hairiest thing we did on the show," commented Chris Corbould. "The winches we used on the traveling rig have a top speed of about twenty-five feet per second, but when we tested this stunt at that speed, it wasn't fast enough. In fact, it had to be *twice* as fast to look right."

Corbould's crew devised a way to double-gear the winch, which doubled its speed. "It was so fast," said Corbould, "it was actually frightening. He was traveling fifty feet a second on this thing, hanging onto the end of a wire, just missing cars and crashing through a walkway, which we fabricated as a breakaway piece so that it wouldn't break every bone in his body. When you've got somebody on wires moving at that great a speed, you have to be very vigilant in testing everything, making sure the pulleys are all free-running—because a simple thing like a pulley seizing up could have been very dangerous at that speed."

Christopher Nolan upped the ante on the wire gags for *The Dark Knight*, conceiving even more intricate and breathtaking stunts. These included the climactic Prewitt Building battle in which Batman clips SWAT team members to a rappelling rope and throws the team leader out an

For a shot of Batman being jerked violently into the air by the speeding monorail near the end of *Batman Begins*, a stunt performer was harnessed to a ram and yanked quickly aloft.

upper-story window, sending the SWATs out the window, one by one, and leaving them dangling out the side of the building like a "string of sausages," which is what production dubbed the stunt.

Though production had shot most of the Prewitt Building exteriors at Chicago's Trump Tower, Trump authorities refused permission to execute the string-of-sausages stunt there, requiring the filmmakers to tap a second skyscraper as the site for the gag. At the fortieth floor of the structure, Corbould's crew built a sliding steel rig connected to hydraulic accelerators and decelerators, on which five stuntmen lay, tied together, end to end. When the slide was activated, the men went over the side of the building as Nolan captured the action from a helicopter hovering overhead. "We heard, 'Standby...action!'" recalled Corbould, "and we started to see them going over the edge of the building: one, two, three, four, five. Then we waited until we heard 'Cut!' It was nerve-wracking, but everybody was all right. The stunt guys really earned their money that night."

The Prewitt Building melee culminates with the Joker being thrown off the building and Batman firing a cable to pull him up again. Heath Ledger performed the stunt, falling from a height of 110 feet. Stunt crews attached the actor by wire to a descender rig and initiated a fall that was rapid at the beginning, and then slowed and stopped 75 feet into the 100-foot drop.

"Heath insisted on doing it himself," said Paul Jennings. "He and Christian wanted to do everything themselves, and they would keep at it until it was the best they thought it could be. It was never, 'Oh, let's just get this done and get out of here.' It was always, 'What can we do here that's going to be great?'"

Nolan and his cowriters scripted another major wire stunt to appear in the first few minutes of *The Dark Knight*. In the bank heist prologue, the Joker's clown-masked thugs gain entry to the bank's rooftop by shooting a zip line through the fourteenth floor window of a building across the street.

In Chicago, production shot the gag from a helicopter, filming the action as Tom Struthers and stunt rigger Kevin Mathews, attached to cables, jumped from one building and made the long slide to the roof of the Old Chicago Post

Framed by a Prewitt Building backdrop, Batman shoots a cable and ensnares the Joker in mid-fall in *The Dark Knight*.

Office across the street that served as the bank location. "In England," said Paul Jennings, "we call it the 'death slide.' We were about four hundred feet up, going from one building to another. It was the first thing we did, stunt-wise, on the movie, and it looked fantastic."

For sheer audacity, none of the stunts in *Batman Begins* or *The Dark Knight* could match the aerial prologue sequence that opens *The Dark Knight Rises*. Tom Struthers, an aerial-stunt specialist, was particularly enthusiastic about executing the complex and challenging prologue action, most of which would be shot in the skies over rural Scotland, with aerialists and real planes.

"A lot of organization went into that sequence," said Struthers. "It was all about the prep—many discussions around the table with Chris and Wally Pfister and Nilo Otero, the production designers and the producers, talking about where and how to do it. And then it took us nearly three months to get approvals from the FAA and the United Kingdom CAA, allowing us to hang people out the back of a plane or have them stand on the side of an aircraft turboprop. We had to show them that we could do it in a safe manner and what emergency procedures we'd have in place."

In the sequence, Bane's mercenaries hijack the CIA plane in which he is being transported by making a midair plane-to-plane transfer on cables and then walking on the outside of the fuselage to gain entrance to the aircraft. "We had parachutists wing-walking on the plane," said Struthers, "and we shot it from a helicopter overhead. We also had four aerialists on lines, flying behind the C-130 Hercules. We did a lot of rigging tests with dummies and bags for that, throwing them out the back of the C-130 with single lines, two lines, three lines, four lines. I think the military has had one or two people on a line out the back of a C-130, but to my knowledge, this was the first time there were ever four people on individual lines, flying behind that aircraft."

The filmmakers had allowed eight days to shoot the complex air-to-air sequence over Scotland—but, remarkably, Christopher Nolan captured the action in less than three. "It was totally unheard of," said Struthers, "but we got all of the footage that Chris needed in those two and a half days."

After retrieving Bane and Dr. Pavel, mercenaries in the larger transport plane attach a cable to the tail of the CIA aircraft, lift it ninety degrees so it is nose-down, and then release it to make the long fall to the ground. For segments of the action that couldn't be filmed with real planes in the air, Nolan shot hydraulically controlled fuselage rigs built outside the Cardington hangar and engineered by Chris Corbould's team to tilt from a horizontal to a vertical position. Miniatures built and shot at New Deal Studios in Los Angeles completed the sequence.

Throughout production of *The Dark Knight Rises*, Tom Struthers would be called upon to orchestrate bold, daring,

and inventive stunt sequences—none so harrowing, perhaps, as the aerial sequence, but all requiring a very high level of trust between his team, the special effects team, Christopher Nolan, and the actors.

"To me," Struthers said, "the key to all of the action in these movies is that the actors did the majority of it. The actors achieved maybe 85 percent of the stunts themselves, and I'm very proud of that. It is a big leap of faith to jump over a ledge with a thirty foot drop, wearing only a line that's been set up by our rigging team. Having actors do that kind of thing with so much enthusiasm shows the trust and the confidence that they had in my team."

The Dark Knight Rises featured a midair sequence over rural Scotland with aerialists and real planes. This hydraulically controlled fuselage rig was built outside the Cardington hangar by Chris Corbould's team to accommodate shots at ground level.

"It went from cool to rockin'..."

Throughout pre-production and production on *Batman Begins*, the film's code title—used to prevent leaks—was *The Intimidation Game*, a title that sounded like a typical Hollywood thriller, and that suggested no ties to Batman.

In post-production—during which time Nolan and his collaborators attended to editing, sound-mixing, and scoring the film—*Batman Begins*'s code title changed to *Flora's Wedding*. "We wanted it to sound like a romantic comedy," Emma Thomas explained, "and so we came up with *Flora's Wedding*. Flora is our daughter's name, but fortunately, nobody caught on to that."

Within a week or so of the end of principal photography, Smith had assembled the entire film—albeit a version that ran far longer than its final two hours and twenty minutes. At that point, Nolan joined Smith at the Avid, and together the two men went through the film scene by scene, tightening and refining it.

The film's action sequences presented a unique set of challenges. "There are several factors involved in editing an action sequence," said Smith. "Primarily, you want the audience to follow what is going on, but it also has to be exciting, and to my mind, it has to have a point. It has to move the narrative forward; otherwise, it is just meaningless action, and that gets boring real quick."

As he started to assemble the first major action sequence for *Batman Begins*, Smith was surprised when Christopher Nolan requested that he do so without using temporary music. "In all the films I've worked on with Chris," he observed, "we haven't cut with music—not until we got to our tech mix. The reason is that music is a great cover. You can put music on a really sloppy piece of work, and all of a sudden, it looks like poetry. You've let the composer bring all of the emotion and energy to it, when it wasn't there on its own.

"So, if you can struggle on without music for as long as possible, you can create an action sequence that is much better than it would have been if you'd relied on the crutch of music. Of course, it is very hard, and it was especially difficult on *Batman Begins*, because Chris was the first director who'd ever asked me to do the assembly without music. I thought it was an interesting idea, but it sure made me work harder. I remember looking at some of the sequences and thinking, 'If only I could throw in some pounding music here, this would be so much better!' I just had to keep working at it. And then, when the music did come in, it made it so much better. It went from cool to rockin'."

After the first edit had been refined, the pair worked on cutting the film for time. Due to Smith's aggressive editing style, and the fact that Nolan had done a great deal of self-editing as he wrote and shot the film, even the first cut of *Batman Begins* was unusually tight. "I'd written many drafts of the screenplay," said Nolan, "and so, as the director, I went out and shot the script I'd written.

As is common protocol for an editor, Smith joined the *Batman Begins* production just a couple of days before the start of principal photography, and commenced assembling scenes on his Avid editing system as soon as footage began to roll in. "I started to assemble the film from day one," said Smith, "and I continued to cut and edit all the way through the shoot. That way, if there was a shot missing or we needed more coverage somewhere, we could solve that before moving forward." Generally, however, Smith's goal was to keep up with the camera as he assembled the movie. "The idea was to keep apace with the shoot and get a sense of how the film was going to look by the time we got to the end. Of course, how it looked at that point was a long way from where we were when we released the movie."

PAGE 244: Following Christopher Nolan's protocol of *not* editing major action sequences to music, editor Lee Smith cut each film in The Dark Knight Trilogy into a tight, visual narrative, as demonstrated by this chase sequence from *Batman Begins.*

ABOVE: Editor Lee Smith was on board for the entire Batman trilogy. (Photos by Jordan Goldberg.)

EDITING, MUSIC & SOUND

What we were doing in the editing suite was trying to establish the pace and the tone of the piece, while fitting this massive story within a two-hour-and-twenty-minute framework. That was the timing I had decided on very early on, and that was what the script was written to, but we'd shot such a massive amount of material, we had to make some hard choices and be quite ruthless in terms of condensing the story."

With the film cut to near final-release length, Nolan began screening it for select people, which led to more refinements. "We screened the movie for an audience once we'd laid in all the music and sound effects," said Lee Smith. "After we got feedback from audiences and got the studio approval, we did the final mix and recorded the music."

The editing process was much the same on *The Dark Knight*—except that Smith came onto the project earlier than usual, due to Nolan's decision to shoot about a fifth of the film with IMAX cameras.

Nolan had first spoken to Smith about using IMAX equipment while they were still editing *Batman Begins*. "I knew IMAX would have technical challenges that we would have to surmount," Smith said, "so I started by experimenting a bit with multiformat editing. We did a lot of tests to see what it would look like as we cut from the full aspect ratio of IMAX down to the slimmer 2:4:0 format of conventional 35mm film. We needed to determine if the aspect ratio change would be a concern; and also, if the quality would be a concern—because the IMAX negative is so large, and the quality of the IMAX original negative is so spectacular, it's difficult for regular 35mm, which is an eighth of the information, to look as good. We had to make sure that wouldn't be a problem."

Of particular concern were the film's fast-paced action sequences, which would feature quick, back-to-back cuts from the 35mm format to the IMAX version. "I worried that if I was cutting between IMAX and 2:4:0, it might become like a 'pop' fest and the audience would get sick," Smith explained. Smith had reason for concern since, on the twenty-eight-inch monitor of his editing system, the changes in aspect ratio were quite evident, and also quite disruptive of the viewing experience.

Working with first assistant editor John Lee, Smith decided to test the theory on the big screen. "We took it to an extreme," he said, "producing a hybrid scene all the way through to a print, and then projected it in IMAX at an IMAX theatre. To my amazement, it became seamless in IMAX because of the scope and size. I found that you were aware that something was changing, but not in a bad way. The larger experience has a completely different rhythm than the small world of a monitor." To better simulate that IMAX experience—and thus, get a better idea of what the final result would be as he worked—Smith set up a much larger screen near his editing bay.

All of the testing and experimentation convinced Nolan and Smith that the IMAX footage would pay tremendous

dividends in the final film. "The picture quality is stunning in IMAX because of the size of the screen and the stability of the projector," said Smith. "And because we did all of that testing and prep beforehand, we went into *The Dark Knight* fairly confident that it was going to work, and it did. In fact, it ended up going exactly the way that Chris had planned from the beginning. He had a vision, and we just all had to get our brains together and work it through."

Initially, the filmmakers had planned to shoot five key sequences with IMAX cameras: the bank heist prologue, the armored car chase, the hospital demolition, the assault on the Prewitt Building, and the Batman sequence in Hong Kong. As Nolan got into production, he decided to add some IMAX footage for the Lamborghini chase, as well, but by the time he got to the editing process, he had decided to pull back and be a bit more judicious in his use of the IMAX aspect ratio.

In the Prewitt Building sequence, for example, all of which had been shot with IMAX cameras, Nolan opted to delay going to the full IMAX aspect ratio until later in the scene. "At the last minute," John Lee explained, "they realized that the earlier stuff in the Prewitt Building sequence just wasn't big enough for IMAX. The SWAT guys are gearing up to go in after the bad guys, and Batman jumps off and flies in, but for a lot of that setting up and talking, it

didn't make sense to be in IMAX. So we waited until the big music beat, and then made the switch. It was fantastic."

Two IMAX cameras rolled on the hospital demolition, which was also shot, simultaneously, by a helicopter. "That sequence also had a 'hero' camera that was focused on Heath Ledger as he walked out of the hospital," said Lee Smith, "and a couple of cameras for subordinate coverage, including the angle from inside the hospital. There was also a VistaVision camera inside the bus that the Joker climbs aboard.

"Interestingly, after reviewing all of that footage from all of those cameras, I ended up using only the two IMAX camera angles, simply because of the nature of the shot. With Heath Ledger walking out and an entire real building being demolished behind him, keeping it in the one-shot made it much more appealing than doing multiple cuts. And Heath really was in that shot. He really did get on the bus, and the hospital really did come down. So we

IMAX

Christopher Nolan's decision to shoot the first six minutes of *The Dark Knight* entirely with IMAX cameras upped the ante for Lee Smith, who came to the project earlier than usual to experiment with multiformat editing.

just elected to go the simple route and use the two IMAX camera shots."

While simplicity served the final presentation of the hospital demolition, the complex armored car chase involving Harvey Dent, the Joker, and Batman was assembled from many fast cuts and multiple camera angles. "The armored car chase was the biggest single event we edited," said Smith. "It had several scenes aboveground, and then went belowground into Lower Wacker, and then came back up again for the finale. We tried to give each of those areas and parts of the sequence slightly different rhythms to keep them fresh. At times, we also slowed things down a bit so we could see what was happening. The natural tendency is to cut action films very, very quickly, but we wanted to give the audience a chance to see more on this one. The action sequences in this film were a little more lovingly held, because the shots were so stunning."

The semi truck flip that occurs at the climax of the armored car chase had been covered by seven cameras, but

Nolan and Smith opted to reveal it from only two angles—again, as with the shot of Heath Ledger in front of the collapsing hospital, to dispel any notion that the stunt was a "cheat" assembled from multiple camera setups and takes, rather than the incredible, all-in-one feat it was.

"Back in the day," Smith commented, "when you had multiple camera angles on stunts, you would double-cut and try to stretch the event. But now, that kind of thing looks dated, and it also lets the audience know that they're watching something that isn't *really* in real time. So when the truck flipped, we used only two angles, even though I probably had five that would have worked. It is, after all, a semi-trailer flipping in reality on a street. And if you saw something like that for real, you wouldn't turn away while you were watching it, or run across the road to have another look from another angle. You'd just stand there and stare at it."

The film's climactic scenes were, not surprisingly, among the most complex in terms of editing, interweaving

ABOVE: Intercutting the full IMAX aspect ratio with the slimmer—and wider—2:4:0 format (shown above) was of particular concern to Smith, but in the end, the IMAX footage richly enhanced *The Dark Knight*—and was featured for an impressive 28 minutes of the film's 155-minute final cut.

OVERLEAF: Batman puts the Bat-Pod through its paces in *The Dark Knight*.

as they did the attack on the Prewitt Building with the ferry hostage story line. "Because there was a lot of parallel action happening," said Smith, "we spent a lot of time working that sequence out: Where should we be? Should we be on the boats? With the Joker? With Batman? The sequences where you've got a lot of story lines coming together are always more work because you've got to keep everything balanced. Of course, Chris is the master of writing scripts where you've got five different story lines going, all converging on one another! Those become fun in post-production, though, because you can swap events around and start playing with what you reveal at what point."

When it came to creating parallel and converging story lines, Nolan outdid himself on *The Dark Knight Rises*. The film's finale, especially, would follow multiple characters and narratives—all of them culminating in an explosive, epic climax that did full justice to a three-film story arc to which filmgoers would have devoted more than seven hours of screening time from beginning to end.

Though he'd embraced the prospect of making a third film that was bigger in its scope, its themes, and its scale, Nolan resisted the temptation of making it significantly longer than its predecessors. "We assumed *The Dark Knight Rises* would be about the same length as the other two films," said Smith. "The last two were around two and a half hours, and once you get much beyond that, there are all kinds of issues. So we knew we wanted to be well under three hours. And to get there in our edit, we looked for anything that was repetitious. The action sequences were particularly long in the first assembly, because they had shot a *ton* of material, and we tried to put everything in at first— even though we knew we couldn't have everything in the end. Every moment of the film was squeezed a bit to cut it down for time."

Nolan also rejected the notion of embellishing the film with significantly more IMAX footage: *The Dark Knight* had featured twenty-eight minutes, and *The Dark Knight Rises* would boast an additional forty-three minutes or so of the large-format film, again concentrated in its big action

Christian Bale and Christopher Nolan prepare for a scene atop the upper pit prison set at Cardington. The hefty IMAX cameras were maneuvered up and down the well-like set, the base of which was later enhanced with CGI.

sequences. "Because we didn't want to jump in and out of IMAX," said Smith, "there were cases where Chris shot even a smaller moment in the format, if that smaller moment was part of the larger IMAX section. But, generally, we used it in those places where they were looking for the really big visual experience—the stuff shot in India, for example, when Bruce Wayne gets out of the underground prison. All of that large, spectacular vista footage was shot in IMAX."

In editing the film's climactic action sequence—which has the entire city of Gotham disintegrating into chaos—Smith and Nolan again had to contend with multiple narrative threads, cutting back and forth from one action story line to another, maintaining both clarity and pace throughout. "I started off just following the script precisely in editing that sequence," said Smith. "And then we started shuffling scenes around, seeing what scenes could move forward or backward. The joy of the second pass is all of that shuffling and refining that you get to do."

By the time Lee Smith concluded his work on *The Dark Knight Rises*, he had committed a good part of seven years to The Dark Knight Trilogy. "Each film was its own beast," he reflected. "Even though these were three films with an obvious commonality, each film was different and was its own experience. Fortunately, we worked on other films in between. If I'd worked on all three, one right after the other, I would have been passed out on the ground by the end. But doing other films in between kept it fresh for me, and kept me from getting Batman fatigue."

The trilogy's scores would be among the last elements to be integrated into the films—and also among the most critical. The score for *Batman Begins* was a first-ever collaboration between two celebrated movie score composers: Hans Zimmer, who had scored *Gladiator*, *Pearl Harbor*, *Black Hawk Down*, and *The Last Samurai*, among dozens of other films, and James Newton Howard, whose credits included *The Sixth Sense*, *Waterworld*, *The Fugitive*, and the television series *ER*.

Longtime friends, the two men had been looking for an opportunity to work together on a project for ten years

before *Batman Begins* came to their attention. "We'd talked for a long time about similar ideas we had," said Zimmer, "and this project seemed like a good opportunity to try out some of those ideas. It helped having a director who encouraged experimentation and naughty behavior."

Much of the appeal of collaborating was just that promise of experimentation, as both composers—after twenty-five-plus years in the movie business—were eager to shake things up and stimulate their creative energies. "We'd both written so many things so many times," observed Howard. "How many ways can you approach a car chase? By doing this, we wouldn't be on as sure a footing as we normally would be—and that's what we were looking for."

The experimental nature of the endeavor was apparent from the start. Rather than hand over the edited film to the composers and have them write music to the specific beats of the picture—as is the typical process—Christopher Nolan asked that the composers begin by writing musical notions connected to the story. Only later would Nolan take those bits and pieces of music into the editing suite and fit them to the picture.

It was a unique approach, one aimed at letting *story* drive the musical composition rather than the moment-by-moment musical needs of the movie. "That way," explained Nolan, "they would be free to write whatever occurred to

them based on the themes of the story, rather than worrying about hitting specific cuts or action beats in the film. Hans and James were very accommodating in working this way, and it was a very productive process for us."

Among the ideas Zimmer and Howard had discussed over the years—and which they wanted to explore with *Batman Begins*—was moving away from a traditional orchestral sound. "I didn't want to do another big, orchestral score," admitted Howard. "I told Chris that I wanted to do something more out of left field, to do something electronically."

Zimmer agreed. "We wanted to push it a bit," he said, "just as Bruce Wayne pushes his human capabilities." Toward that end, the men composed music as they would for electronic instruments, and then recorded it with a live orchestra, using modern technology to enhance certain notes and motifs.

It wasn't until late in post-production that the composers began refining their compositions to fit specific beats in the movie. By then, the men—long accustomed to working independently—had developed a methodology for composing as a unit. "It was a fascinating thing to watch," said Nolan. "For example, one of the key musical themes in the film originated as two thematic treatments that Hans and James had composed separately. I was more or less being

ABOVE: **Hans Zimmer and Christopher Nolan with James Newton Howard at the keyboard.**

OPPOSITE: **Christopher Nolan listens to a work in progress with score contributor Lorne Balfe. (Photos by Peter "Oso" Snell.)**

asked to choose between the two, and it kept bothering me because the two pieces seemed very related. In the end, they literally put them on top of each other, and worked the music as a point-counterpoint.

"That was representative of the genuine nature of their collaboration. They really found the sound and feel of the music together—even though they have very different styles. James is a technical perfectionist, whereas I think Hans takes a slightly more experimental view—he sort of throws it against the wall and sees what sticks. Having those two very different composers brought something new to the mix, and it supported the duality of Bruce Wayne's character in *Batman Begins*."

In the end, Zimmer and Howard found their experiment in collaboration to be tremendously rewarding. "It's a lonely thing, composing," Zimmer commented. "It's just one guy against the forces of the whole screen, the sound effects, and the dialogue. The great advantage of collaborating was having James there to ask: 'What do you think of these notes? Am I going to make a complete idiot of myself if I do this?'"

"It was like having two safety nets," Howard agreed. "When I did something terribly wrong for the movie, Hans's sensibilities were there. And I think I was there for him in the same way. *Batman Begins* was perfect for this experiment because it supported a wide swath of musical ranges.

It gave us both room to exert tremendous influence on each other, and to overlap stylistically without ending up with something that felt as if it had been compartmentalized between two composers."

So successful was their collaboration on *Batman Begins* that Zimmer and Howard agreed to cowrite the score for *The Dark Knight*. Nolan's brief to the composers was that he wanted them to bridge the musical narrative between the first film and the second. "The music for *Batman Begins* was a very successful part of that film," Nolan commented, "so I felt very strongly that we should continue with what we started there. I wanted the sounds, the themes, the musical ideas to carry through—and then introduce fresh elements as needed."

Once again, Nolan withheld the film from the composers, and instead encouraged them to write music that was inspired by the story and the characters, rather than write to specific beats of the film. "That way," he said, "they were free to do whatever they wanted. Then, when they gave us that music in the edit suite, the editors and I would see what went where and what worked. We would then offer that back to the composers, and ask, 'What do you think of this?'

"That is a very gratifying process for me. I can't imagine working with composers who would just score a film and have you turn up after it was finished to hear it for the first time. I think that would be very unsettling. Instead, they let me be privy to their creative process and I really enjoyed watching that develop. I learned the music very well this way, and understood exactly how it was going to come together. It was very exciting to be part of that."

As Howard and Zimmer approached *The Dark Knight,* they revisited the idea of dividing up the composition task—much as they had at the inception of their *Batman Begins* collaboration.

But given the duality of the two central characters introduced in *The Dark Knight*—Harvey Dent and the Joker—separating the score by character seemed more appropriate. "James took on Harvey Dent as the particularly American kind of heroic figure that's at the heart of the film," explained Nolan, "whereas a lot of what Hans did had to do with the Joker, who is the complete antithesis of that. And then there was an interesting meeting of those elements toward the end of the film."

With his emphasis on the Joker, Zimmer started by writing music for the film's prologue. "I try to deconstruct everything," he explained. "And so, for the prologue, I threw out everything that had gone on before and started from scratch. For scenes later in the movie, I went back and pulled in some of the old stuff, but the prologue was all new."

Zimmer's original instinct for the Joker's musical theme was to compose it around a single note. "Imagine one note that starts off slightly agitated and then goes to serious aggravation and finally rips your head off at the end," he said. "It didn't quite work out, and I had to use two notes at the end of the day. But they're still not two notes you'd want to go home and play for your mom."

Zimmer continued his Joker-themed improvisations in the recording studio, encouraging the musicians to start on a single note and, over three excruciating minutes, gradually move to the second note. "It was almost imperceptible," commented James Newton Howard, "but it was horribly off-putting. For the musicians to have to sit there and abandon everything they'd ever learned about their instruments was incredibly hard for them."

"It was important to get performances out of people that would instantly put the audience into 'alert mode,'" Zimmer explained. "But it's not easy to lead your musicians down a path where they are actually uncomfortable, and have to show a side they usually keep hidden."

The free-form explorations continued with Zimmer inventing new sounds. "I spent forever just plugging in old synthesizers and making crazy noises and recording musicians—just as experiments. That went on for months and months, while I really should have been writing cues. But I think that time was well spent. I wanted to have a sort of punk aesthetic without resorting to the cop-out of using a punk track. There was a great vibrancy to the performance."

The abandon with which Zimmer dove into writing musical themes for the Joker came to an abrupt halt with the sudden, tragic death of Heath Ledger in January of that year. Privately, Zimmer wondered if he should back off the "punk" vibe and reconsider a more traditional approach. "There was a split second of doubt in my mind," he recalled. "But then I realized that the only way to really honor the performance was to carry on with what we started—and make *that* really good."

Ultimately, Zimmer composed the Joker Suite—ten thousand bars of music that, to his mind, was a musical representation of the long-form idea of the character. Nolan downloaded the four-hundred-track piece onto his iPod and listened to it on the long flight to Hong Kong for location shooting. "I was a very different person by the time the plane landed," Nolan laughed, "but there were incredible ideas in there."

Not surprisingly, James Newton Howard approached the music for the all-American Harvey Dent as the antithesis of Zimmer's punk aesthetic. "This guy represented hope," explained Howard, "but it doesn't work out for him." To create the arc of Harvey Dent's tragic story, Hans Zimmer suggested that Howard compose a Harvey Dent Suite—just as he had composed the Joker Suite. "I sat down and wrote a ten- or eleven-minute suite, and from that piece of music, we derived most of the material for Harvey."

Orchestral sessions for *The Dark Knight* were recorded at Air Studios in London, and the result was a musical score that would go on to win the Grammy for Best Score

Soundtrack Album for Motion Picture, Television, or Other Visual Media in 2008.

Scheduling conflicts three years later thwarted a third collaboration between Howard and Zimmer for *The Dark Knight Rises*, and—for the first time—Hans Zimmer composed an entire Batman score alone. The process, however, was the same, with Zimmer first delving into musical explorations fueled by the story and characters. "The huge advantage you get with someone like Christopher Nolan," Zimmer commented, "is that he's a writer-director, and so when he told me the story for *The Dark Knight Rises*, I knew that what he told me would actually be there on the screen.

"As soon as we talked about the story, I started getting some ideas. I turned the tables on him this time, in fact—I started composing and throwing ideas at him long before he started shooting. I tried to be well ahead of him because I believe a composer has the duty to inspire his director— not just vice versa. The more toys I could give him to play with at an early stage, the better it would be for him. These wouldn't be pieces of music that were plastered onto the movie afterwards—they would be part of the fabric of the movie even as the movie was being made."

An intriguing idea that occurred to Zimmer at the earliest stages of his musical explorations was to incorporate a chant into Bane's theme. Based on the Moroccan Arabic dialect, the chant—phonetically, 'dey-shay bah sah rah'—translated to "he rises." "I wanted to suggest a

distant, isolated culture," Zimmer explained, "something we couldn't quite identify. So I had this idea of a very tribal, rhythmic chant that would be chanted by thousands of people. I wanted the sound of a rabble. I wanted a hundred thousand people making a terrifying noise!"

Zimmer started more modestly, first recording eleven people chanting in his studio in Los Angeles. Sound artists then "aged" the recording electronically, as if—as Christopher Nolan had suggested—it had been recorded on an old cassette tape found in a jungle, its origins unknown. "It sounded very interesting," Zimmer recalled, "but, of course, it was still a hundred thousand or so people short. Where was I going to get a hundred thousand people doing this chant? And then, I had the thought that we could let the fans be a part of the movie. So we did this call to arms and figured out a way that people from all over the world could contribute to this chant. We set up a website people could go to, which talked them through how to do the chant, record it, and send it to us."

Prompts on Twitter and word-of-mouth Internet chatter yielded somewhere in the neighborhood of 180,000 recorded chants—a response so overwhelming, it crashed the system in the first week. "We thought that the servers could handle the traffic," said Zimmer. "But thousands of people *per second* went to this site, and the whole thing melted down that first week. The technology guys were working around the clock trying to figure out how to

ABOVE: Composer Hans Zimmer in his Los Angeles studio—which he dubbed the Batcave— two months before the premiere of *The Dark Knight Rises*. (Photo by Daniel Pinder.)

OVERLEAF: The chaotic essence of the Joker, a self-described "dog chasing cars," was reflected in Zimmer's "punk aesthetic" for the character.

handle it, and eventually, they did. Once we had all of these thousands of voices chanting, my recording engineers layered them together and created the chant out of this tapestry of people from around the world. I don't think anybody had done that before."

The chant led Zimmer to compose music that was similarly tribal and primitive, music that would suggest something *beneath* the veneer of western civilization. To Zimmer's mind, a symphony orchestra represented the very pinnacle of that civilization. "I had the thought: What if I turned what we so treasure as a symbol of our western civilization, the symphony orchestra, into an expression of ancient tribalism—like a drum circle, essentially? So, at the end of June—just about the time Chris got back from shooting in India—I went to London with this piece of music I'd written and spent a day turning the orchestra into this weird, tribal ensemble. It became a real talking point for those players. A few months later, I ran into some of them, and they were *still* talking about that day when they made music in a way they'd never done before."

The musical elements Zimmer composed for Bruce Wayne—a broken man, both spiritually and physically, in *The Dark Knight Rises*—would make for an interesting counterpoint to the aggressive "terrifying noise" of Bane's theme. "After going on my 'Bane Rampage,' the next thing for me was figuring out how to frame Bruce Wayne in this movie," he said. "From the first moment of seeing Bruce in the movie, I wanted to create the feeling that everything was heading toward inevitable tragedy. The music is incredibly lonely and creates the sense of tremendous loss and melancholy and darkness."

Christopher Nolan had characterized *The Dark Knight Rises* as an epic struggle, and Zimmer found inspiration for scoring that struggle in images of the Russian Revolution and in scenes from *Dr. Zhivago* as he continued to compose throughout the film's production and post-production. Ultimately, the score was composed almost entirely of new, original music, but Zimmer introduced motifs from *Batman Begins* and *The Dark Knight* as well, skewing them ever so slightly—just as memories of events are often skewed. "The story of this movie takes place eight years after the previous movie," he said. "And when we remember things that

happened years ago, we don't get them exactly right. So I changed the music a bit—moving a note here and there—to make it not quite the same as it was, just as our memories are faulty, and what we remember is not really quite what happened."

Zimmer recorded the completed score in early May 2012, again returning to Air Studios' Lyndhurst Hall, his self-described "home away from home." So familiar was the great hall to Zimmer, he had become accustomed to writing specific musical elements he knew would reverberate in a particular way when played inside the structure. "That architecture has always been part of how I write the score," he noted. "For example, the two-note French horn Batman motif was written for that studio, because I knew how those notes would travel from one side of the hall to the other. I know how to get something interesting out of that space, because I know every nook and cranny of it."

The orchestra was equally familiar to Zimmer, comprising musicians with whom he had worked on the previous films in The Dark Knight Trilogy, as well as *Inception*. "One of the reasons we love recording in London is because it gives us access to players from so many great orchestras," Zimmer commented. "We get to work with players who play our Dark Knight music by day, and then go out and play symphonic music at night."

Just two months prior to the premiere of *The Dark Knight Rises*, Zimmer was still composing, happily ensconced in his studio in Los Angeles. "This is my Batcave," he laughed, "and it is all chaos right now. It is a reflection of the year and a half I've put into this movie. That's a big chunk of one's life, so even though it's 'just a movie,' I take it seriously. I peel away the layers that are always there in Chris's writing—the layers beneath what is on the surface. This movie has a lot of depth and asks a lot of philosophical questions. It is also an extremely exciting and emotional story. So, for me, this movie was a great gift. It allowed me to try out all of these ideas that I'd been thinking about for years—ever since I was a child, in fact.

"When I was a kid growing up in Germany, I had this dream of being a film composer—but of course, I never said that, because everybody would have thought it was ridiculous. How could a kid with no education, growing up in Frankfurt, end up being a film composer in Hollywood? But that was my secret dream, and I always had this sense of 'the' movie I wanted to compose for. About halfway through working on *The Dark Knight Rises*, I suddenly realized that this was the movie I'd always dreamt about as a kid."

A defining characteristic of The Dark Knight Trilogy productions was that nearly every crewmember who started with Christopher Nolan on *Batman Begins* continued with him on *The Dark Knight* and *The Dark Knight Rises*.

One of the few exceptions could be found in the sound department. On the first film, post-production was based out of London. David Evans and Stefan Henrix had served as supervising sound editors, while James Boyle had designed sound effects that were layered into the final mix.

On *The Dark Knight* and *The Dark Knight Rises*, post-production shifted to Los Angeles, and Richard King headed up the department, serving as both supervising sound editor and sound designer. Though the film's final soundtrack wouldn't be mixed until near the end of post-production, King and a crew of eight had begun gathering sound from the first day of the shoot, recording dialogue as spoken by the actors on the set.

A veteran of *The Prestige*, King came onto *The Dark Knight* well aware of Christopher Nolan's preference for recording on-set dialogue rather than doing ADR (Automated Dialogue Replacement) in a sound studio during post-production, a common filmmaking practice. "Using the dialogue recorded on the set is a little unusual for a big-budget action film," said King, "because there's usually a lot of noise in the background, like wind machines or generators. Also, Chris likes to shoot in practical locations—streets and real buildings—so there's always a lot of background noise. Ed Novick, the production sound mixer, was our guy on the set recording the actors. He had a tough job getting good, clean sound, but that was our main focus during production."

The sound crew also recorded crowd scenes on set. "We can remake pretty much everything else later on—vehicles, weapons, Batman's devices, even punches—but it was

important to get the sound of, say, a thousand people on the street," explained King.

Beyond what was recorded on set, King built up the various elements for the soundtrack throughout production, collecting sounds from any and all sources. "No matter where they came from," King said, "the sounds had to sound as if they were recorded on the day they shot the scene. That was the trick."

King often sampled sounds and played them for Nolan when the director made a specific request pertaining to a particular weapon or vehicle. "Chris created a very tangible world for *The Dark Knight*," noted King, "and it was our job to live up to that and give him something tangible to respond to. It is very hard—and usually, meaningless—to talk about sound theoretically. He needed to actually hear it, and have a visceral reaction, or not."

Harvey Dent (Aaron Eckhart), Rachel Dawes (Maggie Gyllenhaal), and Mayor Anthony Garcia (Nestor Carbonell) walk the funeral procession for slain Police Commissioner Loeb in *The Dark Knight*. The sound department recorded on-set crowd sounds for large street scenes such as this—and the one below, from *The Dark Knight Rises*—to ensure a more realistic and spontaneous effect than what could be replicated in a sound studio.

In creating sound effects for Batman's gadgetry and weapons, King followed the "Nolan Directive" that had guided their visual design: Each had to sound like something that could actually exist. "We tried not to go too sci-fi," said King. "All of his devices had to have a high-tech, but believable sound. For example, Batman had a grapple in *The Dark Knight* that could cut through metal. It was a handheld device, but it shot a pointy object that he could use to pull himself from building to building. In a microsecond, you had to understand—just from the sound of it—how the thing worked. The sound had to tell you that it was a projectile being fired. Any sounds that detracted from that understanding by being too peculiar had to be thrown out." King's meticulous work on *The Dark Knight* won that year's Academy Award for Best Achievement in Sound Editing.

The sound designer returned for *The Dark Knight Rises*. "The sound guys came on board as Chris got further along with the director's cut of the film," noted Jordan Goldberg. "As always, the sound was a long process in itself, with Richard King figuring out the sounds for the hardware—especially the Bat."

"Creating the sound for the Bat was definitely the biggest challenge on *The Dark Knight Rises*," said King, "because that was something that doesn't and couldn't really exist; and yet, rather than go into the realm of fantasy or science fiction, it had to sound like a real thing that could fly, something that ran on fuel. It had to sound like it was of the same world as the Batmobile and the Bat-Pod."

Ultimately, King arrived at the sound through a lot of trial and error. "It was a 'feel' thing, a matter of just trying a bunch of different combinations of sounds until we found something that worked. We combined elements of recognizable flying craft, such as helicopters, but changed them to create something that was unique to the Bat."

For all of the sound effects, King drew on a library of sounds that he'd collected over the course of twenty-five years in the field, including material he'd recorded for *The Dark Knight*. But he added to that library significantly for *The Dark Knight Rises*. "We didn't want to just retread the old stuff," he explained. "So we recorded new guns and vehicles, all to create something that had never been done before. The idea was to push the envelope a bit so that we could excite the audience in a new way and live up to the rest of the movie. The script and the visuals were so striking, the sound had to live up to that. So we went out with new modern hard-drive field recorders and microphones and spent weeks and weeks recording stuff."

As part of that process, King and his sound crew set up a microphone in the middle of the biggest soundstage at Warner Bros.—which is the biggest soundstage in the Northern Hemisphere—and recorded all manner of things whooshing by. "For example, we recorded the sound of a bullroarer—an Aboriginal Australian instrument that you spin around your head," King said. "There's a piece of wood on the end that flutters and spins and makes a great roaring sound. We recorded a lot of strange stuff like that to use as elements for some of the devices in the movie.

"What we got from that were good, clean raw elements, without a lot of background noise, and so I was able to manipulate them in my software to a really high degree and make them do what I wanted. And then I combined

Sound designer Richard King created an auditory environment for both *The Dark Knight* and *The Dark Knight Rises*. (Photo by Bob Beresh.)

those raw sounds. So the Bat might be a combination of hundreds of sounds that I converted into one."

A particularly interesting sound challenge was Bane's mask, conceived as an industrial construct of tubes and motors that continually pumps medication into Bane's body. "What was recorded on the set had no sense of the sounds those mask tubes would make," said King. "There was just this muffled voice, picked up by the boom mic, and then a close sort of tinny voice picked up by the radio mic inside the mask, which was about five millimeters from his mouth. So we had to create the sound of the mask, but without getting in the way of the performance. It just had to exist there in the background, and then, every now and then, make itself felt."

As the filmmakers began screening the prologue in the winter of 2011, some audience members expressed an inability to clearly understand Bane's dialogue from behind the mask. Nolan knew that the roar of the planes' engines in the prologue exacerbated the problem, and he remained confident that in nonaerial scenes, Bane's dialogue would be clearly audible.

Ultimately, the quality and clarity of Bane's dialogue would be, to a large extent, determined by the way it was mixed into the soundtrack—and Nolan was as involved in that final mix as he was in every other aspect of making the film. "He has the best ears of anybody that I've ever met," said King. "He can hear things that most people can't hear. And I've learned the hard way that when he thinks he hears something, he's right. He will hear something in the mix that nobody else hears—and then, when we isolate the sound, we find that he was right. He's like that with everything, really.

"I remember hearing a story about when they were shooting, and he thought there was something wrong with one of the camera lenses. Everybody kept saying, 'No, no, it's fine.' But then they sent it back to the manufacturer, and the manufacturer tested it—and, sure enough, there was something wrong with that lens. He has a laser focus that he aims at every component of this huge, vast undertaking of making a movie. He doesn't let anything slide. It's very intense working with Chris because everything has to be exactly right—and what that means for me is the constant search for the perfect sound."

TOP: Rigged with tubes and motors, Bane's mask required a sound design all its own—which then had to be layered in with actor Tom Hardy's speaking voice, recorded by both a microphone inside the mask and a boom mic on set.

BOTTOM: Creating viable sounds for the various Bat-gadgets used throughout The Dark Knight Trilogy provided Richard King with some of his biggest sound design challenges.

"One day of shooting with the real bats convinced everybody that we were going to go digital with those..."

CHAPTER 10

Committed as he was to an in-camera, "Let's do it for real" philosophy throughout the making of all three films in The Dark Knight Trilogy, Christopher Nolan had recognized from the beginning that *some* visual effects would be required—evidenced by the fact that he had visual effects supervisors Janek Sirrs and Dan Glass on the *Batman Begins* set throughout the shoot. In fact, Nolan had brought Sirrs into the project at its earliest stages, meeting with him in his garage office while the screenplay was still evolving.

From that first meeting, Nolan had emphasized that he wanted to get as much of his film in-camera as possible, using visual effects only when absolutely necessary. "I understood that it was going to be more like a James Bond type of movie than a super hero movie," Sirrs recalled. "Everything was supposed to be reality-based, with the visual effects in the background, rather than front and center. Christopher Nolan didn't want the visual effects shot to draw attention to itself."

Later, Sirrs supervised a small visual effects team that joined the production in England and then traveled with the main unit to all of the major locations. "Normally," said Sirrs, "we stick pretty close to the director because you never know what might come up while he's shooting. He might suddenly decide, 'Okay, this or that is going to have to be digital'—and we have to be there to deal with that situation, to shoot plates and take our surveys and measurements, et cetera. A lot of times, you're just working by the seat of your pants. It's exciting!"

The extensive build at the Cardington hangar and the location shoots in Chicago had been integral to Nolan's in-camera approach, largely eliminating the need for visual effects extensions of sets. The execution of ambitious and large-scale stunts and special effects gags, too, had reduced the number of visual effects shots required. Rather than inserting a digital Batman dangling from the monorail train, Nolan shot a real Batman dangling from the train; rather than a visual effects fireball chasing Alfred and Bruce down the elevator shaft as Wayne Manor burned, Nolan shot a real fireball on set.

In addition to on-set effects and stunts, Nolan had engaged a miniatures unit to produce those shots that couldn't be done in full scale. The miniature photography shots wouldn't be real in the same sense that the live-action gags had been real, but they would still be in-camera events, realized with cameras rolling on tangible, practical models.

Working out of Shepperton and Leavesden Studios—the latter, another London-area facility—Robbie Scott's Cutting Edge crew built large-scale miniatures for key action sequences, and director of miniature photography Peter Talbot and miniature effects supervisor Steve Begg shot them in tandem with the main unit. Nolan was very involved with planning the model-unit shoot. "He had his hand in just about every single shot of the movie, even the

PAGE 264: Batman—surrounded by a roiling colony of digitally created bats—strides through the halls of Arkham Asylum in *Batman Begins*.

ABOVE: Cutting Edge constructed the Narrows—Gotham City's island slum and home to its criminal underbelly—as a 40-by-80-foot miniature with hundreds of buildings, including Arkham Asylum. The set was internally lit to match Wally Pfister's lighting, and shot in multiple motion-control passes—which were then composited by Double Negative and blended into production plates shot in Chicago.

model shots," recalled producer Chuck Roven. Visual effects houses then composited the miniature photography into live-action plates in some instances, and in others, blended them with computer-generated views of Gotham.

Miniature and visual effects make an early appearance in establishing shots of the monastery in Tibet. Nathan Crowley's crew had built a monastery facade for the exterior front doors and stairs of the temple in Iceland, but the wide establishing view of the structure nestled into the side of a Himalayan mountain was a composite of a monastery miniature and a background plate shot on location by the visual effects crew. "We used a computer to track the motion of the camera when we shot those backgrounds," explained Sirrs, "and then used that data to drive a computer-controlled camera and repeat the move exactly when we shot the monastery model. By matching the camera move, we could composite the model photography with the plates shot in Iceland." For shots of the monastery explosion, the crew detonated a ⅙-scale model with balsa breakaway sections as four high-speed cameras rolled.

Cutting Edge also built a ¹⁄₁₂-scale miniature for wide establishing shots of the Narrows, which comprised several

TOP: An early design model of the full-scale Batcave—with Wayne Manor foundation—was built at Shepperton Studios, near London, for *Batman Begins*.

BOTTOM: For this view of the Tumbler entering the Batcave, Chris Corbould and the special effects crew used a high-pressure nitrogen catapult to launch a full-scale, driverless version of the vehicle through a waterfall on the spacious Batcave set.

hundred buildings, including Arkham Asylum, with structures measuring up to four feet tall, all internally lit to match Wally Pfister's lighting scheme on the full-scale set. The miniatures crew shot the Narrows model in multiple motion-control passes, including some in atmospheric smoke. Double Negative then composited the separate passes, blended them into production plates shot in Chicago, and added digital embellishments such as plumes of steam, traffic, bridges, and water.

Despite the fact that the majority of the high-speed chase sequence had been captured in-camera, that sequence, too, benefited from work by the model unit. Nolan had filmed the full-size Batmobile driving to the top of a real parking garage, for example, but subsequent shots of its rocketing across adjacent rooftops fell to the miniature effects crew. "There are whole sections of the chase that were done practically," noted Janek Sirrs, "but there was no way to make that full-size car leap between rooftops, and so we had to take over from there. That was done, largely, with a miniature Batmobile that we jumped thirty or forty feet from one miniature rooftop to another."

The model team shot the radio-controlled ⅓-scale Batmobile atop a ⅓-scale rooftop set, surrounded by green screen to accommodate the compositing of Gotham City backgrounds. "One-third scale was the most believable and manageable scale at which to do this sequence," noted Steve Begg, "but that ⅓-scale Batmobile was big enough to break your leg if it hit you!" The set had breakaway pieces made of aluminum, and was dressed with miniature newspapers and other debris.

An exterior shot of the Batmobile's airborne entrance through the waterfall at the mouth of the Batcave after the chase sequence was a miniature element filmed on the back lot of Leavesden Studios.

Water is notoriously difficult to scale, and so the miniatures crew determined that ⅓-scale was as small as they could go and still create a believable waterfall. Chris Corbould's special effects team aimed air jets at the falls to break up the water droplets and thus "miniaturize" the flow of water as the crew catapulted a miniature Batmobile-shaped buck through it to create the appropriate interaction. For the subsequent view from the Batcave side of the

falls, Corbould's crew had used a high-pressure nitrogen catapult to launch a full-scale, driverless, lightweight version of the vehicle through the full-scale waterfall on the Shepperton set.

The monorail collapse onto city structures in the film's third act also was realized, in part, through miniature effects. Cutting Edge built the last four buildings of LaSalle Street at ⅙-scale, and then collaborated with a pyrotechnics team and Chris Corbould's mechanical and hydraulic engineering experts to destroy the model, rigging it to fall under its own weight as cameras captured the event at eighty frames per second. Cutting Edge also built scaled rails and girders out of malleable aluminum and plastics that would buckle easily, supporting them on steel wires and then releasing them via pyrotechnic charges to send them crashing to the ground.

The model makers built a separate miniature set for views of the destruction from an underground car park. As cameras rolled, the special effects crew pulled three breakaway aluminum train carriages through the set, propelling

ABOVE: When an experiment with real bats proved ineffective, the animation of digital bats was assigned to The Moving Picture Company.

RIGHT: Director Christopher Nolan wields the freeze-dried bat-on-a-stick that was used to obtain the on-set visual effects lighting reference that would be used during post-production.

the carriages along fifty feet of track by way of a hydraulic ram, pulleys, and steel cable at up to thirty miles an hour, hitting cars and concrete blocks before slamming into a wall.

Miniature effects also provided exterior views of the burning and collapse of Wayne Manor, built as a ⅙-scale model that was set aflame and photographed at Shepperton.

Despite the heavy reliance on in-camera effects—both full-scale and miniature—some shots in the film could be realized only through the use of computer-generated imagery. Computer-animated bats, for example, were used for scenes set in the Batcave, in the abandoned well, and inside Arkham Asylum. Nolan had considered using real bats, and had even had the effects team shoot a test with the live creatures against blue screen, with the idea of matting the footage into photography from the set.

"One day of shooting with the real bats convinced everybody that we were going to go digital with those," recalled Janek Sirrs. "The real bats didn't respond to anything, and they tended to fall to the ground from the shock of being in a studio environment. They also crapped all over the place, nonstop. So we did a few tests with digital bats, and when Christopher Nolan saw what we could do with that, he decided it was a good idea to avoid the bat guano and go this way instead."

To get lighting reference, the on-set crew had a freeze-dried bat on a stick that Christopher Nolan would often walk through a scene. "Normally," noted Sirrs, "that would be my task, but he seemed quite keen on doing that. So he walked around the set with this bat on a stick, and we recorded that to see what the bat would look like in each specific environment." The film's title sequence, in which bats form a giant cloud in the iconic shape of the Bat-Signal, also featured the computer-animated creatures.

Hallucinations suffered by victims of Crane's fear toxin were computer-generated effects, as well. Each hallucinatory vision of the Scarecrow had its own style, based on the particular phobia of the person under the influence of the fear gas.

One manifestation had the Scarecrow's face covered in animated worms, while a toxin-infected Batman sees bats appearing out of the Scarecrow's mouth and eyes.

"The idea is that what people see in the Scarecrow is their own worst nightmare," said Sirrs, "so we had to figure out what kinds of horrific things a person might see in that mask. We tried different things, always being careful to stay away from a fantasy look. Chris didn't want it to be overly grotesque or too explicit. He wanted it to be more implied, something you'd catch only a glimpse of, never sure what it was."

To create the transformations, effects artists built a digital model of Cillian Murphy's head—in the sackcloth hood—in three dimensions, and then tracked the animated hallucinations to that geometry. For shots of the

BUF Compagnie animated several of the hallucinations induced by the release of Rā's al-Ghūl's fear toxin on the Narrows, including the worms crawling out of the Scarecrow's mask.

gassed Scarecrow hallucinating Batman as a demonic man-bat, artists added digital effects to a prosthetic makeup, darkening Bale's features, painting out the whites of his eyes, and adding a black lavalike substance pouring from his mouth.

The most significant examples of computer-generated imagery in the film are its wide views of Gotham City—a metropolis so sprawling, in Nolan's mind, that even location filming in Chicago and the massive sets built at Cardington couldn't adequately portray its epic grandeur.

A 3-D digital Gotham provided that scope. Initially unsure as to whether or not a computer-generated Gotham would meet his standard for gritty realism, Nolan asked to see a test before committing to the idea. CG artists started with a low-resolution architectural model of Chicago, and then proceeded to revise it, swapping out recognizable Chicago structures for Gotham buildings. "Even though Gotham was based on Chicago," said Janek Sirrs, "it had to have its own unique buildings that didn't exist in reality. So we created certain hero buildings, as well as the monorail system. It was like Chicago-plus. We also looked at some Asian cities to see how Gotham might have developed. We threw in a bit of modern architecture, some spires, some Kuala Lumpur–style towers and that type of thing."

OVERLEAF, TOP: This aerial view of Gotham at sunrise was created by Double Negative using nearly 1,500 photographs of the actual sun rising over Chicago—and proved to Christopher Nolan that Batman's world could be expanded digitally without compromising its foundation in reality.

OVERLEAF, BOTTOM: Double Negative also created digital monorail exteriors for *Batman Begins*, which were backed by skyscraper canyons built from Chicago surface textures.

For an all-IMAX sequence in *The Dark Knight*, Framestore delivered an animated digital double of Batman swooping from atop Hong Kong's tallest building and flying through the city's skyscrapers.

Impressed with the test results, Nolan committed to a fully digital city that would be used for expansive establishing shots, such as the dawn view from the Wayne Enterprises jet when Bruce Wayne returns to Gotham. For the final shot, the effects team nestled its 3-D Gotham structures, including Wayne Tower and Wayne Station, into an aerial plate of Chicago's Wacker Street area, shot from a helicopter on a sunny afternoon in August 2004. "You see the Chicago River to the right as the camera follows the monorail train around the corner, running on an elevated track and heading toward Wayne Tower at the end of the street," said Paul Franklin, visual effects supervisor at Double Negative, the London-based effects company that created the 3-D Gotham. "We extended the plate to make it look as if the city continued into the distance." Visual effects artists also enlivened the original aerial plate, adding moving traffic, pedestrians, and other signs of bustling activity.

To ensure an ultrarealistic look in how the sun rose over the city, Franklin gathered real-world reference and photographic elements, spending a long and very chilly night atop the Sears Tower in Chicago. "I was perched on the edge of the building," Franklin said, "roped off with a safety harness so I wouldn't fall fifteen hundred feet to street level. I was sitting behind my camera, waiting for the sun to come up over Lake Michigan and illuminate the city to get the lighting we wanted for that shot." Franklin shot approximately fifteen hundred photographs of the sun rising over the city, providing ample real-world reference for Bruce Wayne's dawn view.

Likewise, the extended Gotham skyline was based on photographic material that the effects crew shot in Chicago in May 2004 as part of its preliminary visual effects work. The crew photographed buildings from LaSalle Street up to the Chicago Board of Trade building, shooting everything from the ground level to the top floors. The photography sessions resulted in more than one million exposures and netted 360 degrees of city views, from which Double Negative constructed digital matte paintings and set extensions that were used throughout the film.

Among Double Negative's other visual effects contributions were computer-animated shots of Batman swooping

into and out of shots. To create the digital Batman—which would be featured, ultimately, in only twenty shots—Paul Franklin and his crew started with reference footage of Christian Bale in full Batman costume. The crew also had access to the Batsuit, which helped the digital artists develop textures and determine how the suit would react in different lighting setups.

In addition, Franklin and his team shot video reference of Buster Reeves performing leaps off large structures at Cardington, which they captured with up to ten witness cameras to cover every angle. "We got Buster to do that about six or seven times," recalled Franklin, "and I think he was getting awfully sick of jumping off the side of a building by the time we finished." From that footage, the team determined how the cape moved during a fall,

as well as Batman's overall body language in flight. Double Negative then built its CG Batman from cyber-scans of Bale in costume.

The most effects-heavy sequence in the movie is the finale's monorail train crash. "That was a combination of a digital train and digital city and a miniature train in a miniature environment," explained Janek Sirrs. "It switched from digital to miniature when things started to blow up and there was a lot of crashing and interaction, with smoke and steam everywhere. It was easier to get that in-camera. But those weren't just straight miniature shots. They were all enhanced with digital elements."

The digital monorail train was based on Chicago's elevated trains, which were thoroughly photographed by the visual effects team. "We photographed the L trains in close

Scenes of Bruce Wayne's penthouse were shot against green screen in Chicago and digitally matted with Gotham cityscapes during post-production.

detail," said Paul Franklin, "and then painted that detail onto the surface of our train to make it look very grungy and dirty. Also, since we were going to see *inside* the train, we had to create a fully lit interior, based on digital scans of the monorail interior set built at Shepperton Studios. We captured the interior of the train right down to the individual bits of graffiti and stickers and handbills that had been stuck to the windows."

Since the train interiors had been shot on a set, with green screen in the windows, views of the city passing by had to be incorporated into the plates. Double Negative created the backgrounds as process plates, shooting 360 degree Chicago views to accommodate any angle Nolan might need to insert into the handheld camera shots captured on the interior train set.

Double Negative also created Wayne Tower and Wayne Station as digital sets for climactic shots of the monorail tower collapsing when Sergeant Gordon fires on it with the Batmobile cannons. "The station was built to an extraordinary level of detail," noted Franklin. "Every nut and bolt and supporting strut was in there. It was a very impressive piece of digital modeling."

Visual effects supervisor Nick Davis and visual effects producer Joyce Cox steered the visual effects shots in *The Dark Knight*. At seven hundred effects shots, the assignment was nearly double what it had been for *Batman Begins*, although it was still modest in comparison to other films in the super hero genre. Nolan had, again, turned to visual effects only as a last resort.

ABOVE: *The Dark Knight* culminates in a final battle between Batman and the Joker, which was intercut with scenes of two Gotham ferries transporting evacuees. Double Negative built digital ferry models based on New York's Staten Island ferries and composited them into a background shot at Navy Pier, in Chicago.

LEFT: As imagined by the visual effects team, Gotham City was an amalgamation of New York, Chicago, and Hong Kong, shown here in map formation.

OPPOSITE, TOP AND BOTTOM: Three floors of Lau's Hong Kong high-rise were built as a ¼-scale miniature by New Deal Studios and matched to the full-size set shot at Cardington. Miniature pyrotechnics were detonated to blow up the corner of the building.

THE CITY OF GOTHAM   1:15 000

The number of effects wasn't daunting, but the high resolution of *The Dark Knight*'s IMAX sequences significantly increased their difficulty. "The IMAX sequences were much bigger than what anyone had ever done before," noted editor Lee Smith, "which made all of our visual effects companies very agitated. We just pushed everyone to the limit."

The bank heist prologue, which featured visual effects shots that were fairly routine, became the testing ground, and Double Negative effectively added an animated wave of 3-D rubble and debris to the shot of the school bus exploding through the wall of Gotham National Bank.

Another U.K. effects house, Framestore, delivered shots for the all-IMAX sequence set in Hong Kong, and animated a digital double built by Double Negative for shots of Batman swooping from atop Hong Kong's tallest building and flying between the city's skyscrapers. The redesign of the Batsuit between the first film and the second mandated that the effects team rebuild the digital Batman model it had produced for *Batman Begins*.

Framestore animated digital doubles for Batman and mob accountant Lau (Han Chin) at the end of the Hong Kong sequence, when Batman fastens himself to Lau and fires his grappling gun, inflating a balloon that carries the pair up and over Hong Kong where a C-130—a real plane

filmed from a helicopter—picks them up, Skyhook style. Double Negative's Batman digital double made another brief appearance in the scene in which the Joker throws Rachel off Bruce's penthouse balcony, and Batman leaps after her, his cape electrically charged into its glider-wing configuration. Views of the 110-story skyscraper canyon and the whoosh of buildings as the pair tumbles downward were also computer-generated.

Framestore also created the film's one hundred and twenty Two-Face shots, which required digital artists to design and then track a computer-generated model of Harvey Dent's grotesquely burned and scarred visage to Eckhart's live-action performance. The seamless blend of the "good" side of Dent's face with the "bad," disfigured side required artful frame-by-frame digital paint effects.

Double Negative provided CG views of Gotham as seen from Bruce Wayne's penthouse. Production had shot the penthouse interiors on the ground-floor lobby of One Illinois Plaza, with green-screen material in the windows. Double Negative filled the green-screen matte areas with digital matte paintings representing the top-floor penthouse view.

Nolan would make judicious use of Double Negative's computer-generated Gotham throughout the film, as he had in *Batman Begins.* At the earliest stages of production, Nick

VISUAL EFFECTS

VISUAL EFFECTS

To enhance the car chase that had been filmed on Lower Wacker—with its resultant garbage truck/Tumbler encounter—New Deal built a ⅓-scale garbage truck and refurbished the original *Batman Begins* Tumbler to stage the crash in miniature.

Davis and team had determined the layout of Batman's fictitious city. "Gotham was basically an amalgamation of New York, Chicago, and a little bit of Hong Kong," Davis said. "Clearly, Chicago was the bulk of our Gotham, but to create the sheer size and scope we needed, we had to expand that."

Double Negative also provided digital embellishments to the armored car chase, 95 percent of which had been captured in-camera, on the streets of Chicago. The company's contributions to the sequence included shots of pavement erupting and lampposts ripping out of the ground when Batman ensnares the eighteen-wheeler truck, and shots of a CG helicopter crashing and exploding. For the sequence's culmination, a shot of Batman driving the Bat-Pod vertically up a wall, pivoting around on the vehicle's central axis, and then driving back down again—a move beyond even the capabilities of the crack stunt and special effects teams—Double Negative animated a digital Bat-Pod.

The company's final series of shots are featured in the film's climax, which intercuts between the ferry evacuation and Batman's battle with the Joker inside the Prewitt Building. Double Negative digitally replaced the water around the ferries, adding more dynamic wakes and undercurrents than what had been filmed on Lake Michigan. Double Negative also added expansive Gotham backdrops, stitched together from photographs shot in Chicago, and extended the lake in wide shots of the stalled ferries.

Effects artists animated two digital-double shots for Batman's dramatic swooping approach of the Prewitt Building from the top of an adjacent building and created a digital establishing shot of the skyscraper, based on photographs of Trump Tower. For Prewitt interiors—shot at a ten-story office building located at Cardington—Double Negative tracked 3-D and matte-painted Gotham views into green-screen windows. The effects team also digitally removed stunt rigs and crash mats from the in-camera "string of sausages" shot of SWAT team members dangling from the side of the building.

Miniatures also played a role in the visual effects for *The Dark Knight*, just as they had for *Batman Begins*, with New Deal Studios providing the miniature effects.

For shots of Batman blowing up a corner of the Hong Kong high rise, New Deal built and shot a ¼-scale miniature representing three floors of the skyscraper, using miniature pyrotechnics to destroy a corner of the model, which had been fitted with breakaway glass windows that matched those on the Cardington set.

Photographic elements of a ⅓-scale Batmobile were used to embellish the elaborate and largely in-camera armored car chase sequence. New Deal refurbished the Cutting Edge radio-controlled model from *Batman Begins*, changing out the lights and electronics and upgrading the steering for the 180-degree spinout that ends the scene.

For shots of the Batmobile crashing into the garbage truck commandeered by the Joker, the New Deal crew built a ⅓-scale fiberglass stunt Batmobile and shot it hitting a lightweight garbage truck miniature head-on.

The miniatures crew attached the stunt Batmobile and the truck model to steel skates and pulled them toward each other by cable from beneath a 120-foot-long miniature replica of the Lower Wacker location. Ten feet short of the miniature vehicles making contact, the crew released the garbage truck, allowing it to fly erratically forward, just as a real out-of-control vehicle might do. Double Negative cleaned up the miniature photography and augmented the partial Lower Wacker miniature with a 3-D computer model of the location.

Christopher Nolan's preference for getting as much as possible in-camera hadn't wavered by the time he came to the making of *The Dark Knight Rises*—even though CG effects had made significant strides in the eight years since he'd embarked on *Batman Begins*. "If anything, I'm *less* inclined to have CG shots now," said Nolan. "The more you work with computer graphics, the more you understand the strengths and weaknesses of it. The strengths of computer graphics are enormous when applied to plate photography, things you've actually photographed. But if you're trying to create a shot from scratch using computer graphics, it always has an unreal quality to it, no matter how well the work is done. So, on *The Dark Knight Rises*, as on the other two films, I always tried to shoot something."

Even in cases in which that "something" couldn't reasonably be filmed at full scale—such as prologue shots of the turboprop CIA plane being picked up by the C-130 Hercules

Production art reveals the Bat maneuvering through a Gotham alleyway. In reality, the Bat was made to fly through the concerted efforts of on-site special effects crewmembers and post-production visual effects artists.

and its wings blowing off—Nolan opted for shooting minia-tures, if possible, again working with the miniature effects specialists at New Deal Studios.

To prepare for the task of creating what computer-gener-ated embellishments *were* required, visual effects supervi-sor Paul Franklin was on set throughout much of the shoot in London, Pittsburgh, Los Angeles, and New York. With him was a small team from Double Negative, which would deliver all of the film's visual effects shots.

"We spent a lot of time meticulously photographing and surveying sets, locations, and all of the special effects vehi-cles and props that were created for the film," said Frank-lin. "We also recorded all the actors in their costumes, in case we needed to make digital versions of the performers. We built up this huge archive, a library of material that was almost forensic in its detail. There was so much mate-rial and detail, we could have reconstructed the film com-pletely from scratch, if we'd needed to. And that gave us a lot of flexibility in post-production, in case Chris suddenly said to us, 'I need a visual effects shot that bridges these two moments in the film.'"

The visual effects team's documentation of "all things *The Dark Knight Rises*" resulted in many terabytes of data. "We photographed this film in even more detail than we had the previous two," Franklin noted. "When we did *Batman Begins*, we generated something like a quarter of a million digital stills. On this one, we had well over five million—and they were at much higher resolution. It was an ever-increasing level of detail to get the ever-increasing level of realism that Chris was asking for."

Given Nolan's penchant for filming practical stunts and special effects as much as possible, much of the work on the visual effects team's slate involved digitally painting out safety rigs and harnesses, or supplying a missing piece that would connect one part of a filmed stunt or gag with another. Such visual effects work figures into the film's stunning aerial prologue.

Visual effects artists first made an animatic—essen-tially, a low-resolution 3-D cartoon—of the entire aerial sequence, working closely with Nolan. "I'd show Chris this animatic," said Franklin, "and he'd give me feedback, and then the animators would adjust the animatic based on that feedback."

The animatic helped the filmmakers to determine, in pre-production, which elements of the sequence could be done with real planes and stunt aerialists, which could be achieved with special effects rigs on a set, and which would have to be left to Double Negative or the miniature effects crew at New Deal Studios.

"We provided the moments that were too difficult for them to do any other way," said Franklin. "For example, there was no way for them to safely hoist a plane up by its tail, and so we built a ⅓-scale miniature of the turboprop plane, hoisted it up by the tail, and blew off its wings."

The crew shot the plane miniature at New Deal Studios over the course of a week, producing an element that visual effects combined with the real aerial footage—shot from a helicopter over the Scottish Highlands—and the foot-age shot inside and outside Chris Corbould's fuselage rigs. "We used a lot of computer graphics 'glue' to blend it all together," said Franklin. "For example, we added the cables that the wing-walkers are hanging on in the sequence—because, in reality, they weren't on cables. We also took out all of the safety harnesses. It was just a matter of add-ing the little pieces that would really tell the story—all at IMAX resolution."

Both *Batman Begins* and *The Dark Knight* had required some visual effects contribution to shots of the Batmo-bile and Bat-Pod, respectively—although Nolan had been able to get enough of those shots in-camera, largely due to the ingenuity of the special effects team, that his reli-ance on computer-generated versions of the vehicles had been minimal.

Visual effects would play a slightly bigger role in real-izing shots of the flying Bat simply because, as ingenious as they were, the special effects crewmembers hadn't been able to build a practical Bat that could fly.

"The Bat was always going to be the most challeng-ing thing for visual effects," noted Paul Franklin. "Special effects had built a fantastic practical one that did a lot of the action you see in the film, but to make it do all of the things it couldn't do—like fly—required visual effects.

"The challenge was to make it feel like it was still of a piece with the special effects work, and to make it feel very real, even though it is this extraordinary, multirole combat helicopter. It's a fantasy vehicle, but we wanted the audience to believe that it was real and that Batman could fly around in it and do the things he does." To create that sense of authenticity, the visual effects team animated the Bat to move in the complex—but recognizable, to an audience—manner of a helicopter. "Putting that kind of realistic movement onto this outlandish-looking vehicle was tricky."

The Bat makes a spectacular entrance into the Batcave at one point in the film, flying through the cave's waterfall opening—an echo of the Batmobile's entrance into the original Batcave in *Batman Begins*. To fly it through the water, the special effects team had put the Bat on a track on the massive Batcave set at Sony Studios. Franklin and his visual effects teams removed the track in the live-action plates, added the spinning blades kicking up plumes of water, and also added a computer-graphics ceiling in all up-angle shots of the Batcave to enclose the open set.

Visual effects executed similar set extensions for the pit prison that was built as a very large, hundred-foot-deep set at Cardington. "The pit is like an inverted pyramid," said Franklin, "with the widest part at the bottom of a very tall shaft that leads up to the surface. So the poor unfortunate souls who wind up there are lowered down into this shaft, and then left in this awful space at the bottom."

The art department built the shaft itself as a separate set for shots of Bruce Wayne attempting to make the climb out. Visual effects married the two separate sets together and made them look as if they were all one underground structure. The department also removed rigs and safety cables worn by performers as they climbed up and down the shaft set. "As Bruce Wayne climbs up the shaft," said Franklin, "he's assailed by a swarm of bats—which was another big visual effects moment. That was probably our biggest challenge because we see the bats in bright daylight. Making those bats look real in sunlight, and in IMAX, was quite difficult."

For shots from inside the shaft, looking down into the wider part of the set below, the visual effects team created a digital version of the primary prison set and blended it with the bottom of the physical shaft to create the point-of-view of the characters as they are being lowered down. "The script doesn't specify just how deep this pit is supposed to be," noted Franklin, "but my guess is that it was supposed to be something like five hundred feet deep—whereas the set was a hundred feet deep. So there were a couple of shots where we had to extend the set and make it look deeper—but not too many because it was a huge set, as it was, and it looked deeper than it was on film."

In addition to digitally extending sets, where needed, the visual effects artists digitally extended crowds in wide shots of street battles and for the sequence at the Rogues' football stadium. "There was a very substantial crowd in the stands at Heinz Field on the day," said Franklin, "but even that crowd of twelve thousand or so wasn't big enough to fill the whole stadium. The stadium holds something like fifty thousand people, so, if the camera pulled back wide enough, or was at a certain angle, you'd see empty seats in the original plates. We extended the crowd to fill those seats, which required a lot of careful, painstaking work to match our digital extras to the in-camera ones."

To create crowd elements that they could plug into shots where needed, Franklin and his on-set visual effects team had digitally recorded extras, one at a time, on a small green-screen set they'd built outside the stadium. "We built up the crowd from all of those individual elements. There were some challenges there, but they paled in comparison to the destruction of the stadium and the field that happens when Bane triggers all the explosives that he's buried underneath the city. We see the whole football field collapse, as if there is a tremendous earthquake happening.

"That was a big Hollywood disaster-movie moment, but we had to give it the sense of gritty reality that Chris always wants. Special effects had done some fantastic pyrotechnics on the field, so we had those real explosions, and we had the real stuntmen as football players, running and falling into specially prepared holes they'd made in the fake pitch—but pretty much all of that had to be replaced digitally so we could create the massive destruction."

The larger bottom pit set was married with the upper shaft—built separately by the art department—via green screen and post-production visual effects.

Visual effects provided more large-scale destruction for the collapse of Bane's underground lair. "There's a moment where Bane triggers his plan and blows out the roof of his lair," said Franklin, "and a Tumbler crashes to the floor—and you realize that Bane's lair is directly underneath the Applied Sciences Division of Wayne Enterprises, which allows his mercenaries to climb up and steal all the super-weapons that Lucius Fox has been developing.

"The special effects crew had done a brilliant job of dropping a real Tumbler into Bane's lair set, but there was no ceiling on that set, and so, whenever the camera pointed up, that was a shot we had to do, either as a digital extension or as a miniature." Working again with New Deal Studios, the visual effects team shot the ⅓-scale Batmobile built for *Batman Begins* and *The Dark Knight* dropping through a ⅓-scale lair set. "There's also an up-angle that reveals the Applied Sciences basement, and we did quite a bit of work to create that shot."

Most of Double Negative's work on *The Dark Knight Rises* was in the film's third act, for which the effects team created Gotham City destruction on a scale far greater than in the previous two films. So epic was that devastation that Christopher Nolan—a director committed to the live, practical, in-camera approach—had to release significant portions of it to the artistry and technical expertise of the visual effects team. But even when generating the imagery with a computer, those teams held as their standard the hardcore realism Nolan had demanded in every shot, every moment, and every frame of The Dark Knight Trilogy.

The challenge of meeting Nolan's expectations was what had moved many of the same visual effects artists to stay with Batman from the first film through the third. "To work with Christopher Nolan is a high point in anyone's career," reflected Paul Franklin. "And getting the chance to work on the Batman films—and to work on all three parts of the trilogy—was absolutely fantastic. The experience was more than any of us could have hoped for or expected. And everybody did their best to bring their A-game all the way through, from the start of pre-production to the final delivery of the visual effects."

Pittsburgh's Heinz Field—as imagined here, in this Gotham Stadium concept art—was reduced to catastrophic rubble for *The Dark Knight Rises*, with explosions rigged by special effects crews during production—and embellished with Nolan-style "grit" during post.

**"We're signaling that
something very different is
about to happen . . ."**

CHAPTER 11

MARKETING

In nearly every respect, The Dark Knight Trilogy turned the comic book

movie genre on its masked-and-hooded head.

Many of Christopher Nolan's methods and techniques, born of his years

as an independent filmmaker, were idiosyncratic and outside the norms of

big-budget Hollywood productions. The films' screenplays offered literary

thematic allusions and characters that were rich and multidimensional.

Sets had been designed and built with real-world detail and complexity.

Locations had been chosen with an eye toward epic grandeur—more suited

to a David Lean film than a super hero movie. Serious actors with serious careers and credits had been cast, not only in the films' central roles, but also in the most minor ones.

Christopher Nolan's Batman was *different*, and it sparked a very different type of marketing campaign, as well, which would roll out in full force for *The Dark Knight,* tapping into the zeitgeist in a whole new way and riding on the wave of exploding social media.

Such new-wave marketing ideas were less forthcoming for *Batman Begins*, which came out before Facebook and Twitter had entrenched themselves in the culture. Also, as the debut entry in the trilogy, *Batman Begins* didn't have the built-in, primed-and-pumped audience that the sequels would. As a very different type of super hero film, *Batman Begins* was, in fact, a bit of a gamble, and neither the filmmakers nor Warner Bros. knew if it was going to pay off.

It did. Not only did *Batman Begins* score big at the box office, but it also crossed a particularly tricky Rubicon: earning a positive reaction from the notoriously discerning devotees of DC Comics. "I was personally delighted with the response from the fans," Christopher Nolan said. "I knew it was always going to be tricky to please both the general public and fans of Batman, and I never really expected to do both. But I think the goodwill we got from the fans was very much a product of their realization that we were striving to make the best possible film—and that we took the character seriously."

The film's marketing campaign had stressed that very point. "*Batman Begins* was a unique situation because we were rebranding the franchise," explained Sue Kroll, president, worldwide marketing, Warner Bros. Pictures. "There had been a lot of other Batman films, so the most important thing was to let the world know that a very different take on Batman was coming—and, uniquely, the vision of Christopher Nolan.

"The centerpiece of that campaign was Batman himself, and reintroducing him to a new generation of moviegoers. We presented him as a very different kind of figure than audiences had been used to—more tragic, more contemplative, and much more human. We also sold the character's

origins. He was a self-made hero, but where did he come from? What was his background? What motivated him?"

Early teasers and poster designs hinted at answers to some of those questions. "One of our designers came up with this beautiful bat motif," Kroll recalled, "and that, pitched against the iconography of Batman—whether it was Batman standing on a building, or leaping off a building and creating that silhouette of the bat wingspan—really served us visually. It may have seemed a bit pedantic, the bats and Batman, but that kind of iconography pulled everything together in a way that was immediate, and yet artistic. It wasn't meant to be literal. It was much more high-minded."

Batman Begins thoroughly reenergized the studio's sagging franchise, and paved the way for a sequel that would be as highly anticipated as any in its history—and Warner Bros. wasn't going to squander that opportunity with a routine marketing campaign. The marketing department also knew that Christopher Nolan would be expecting something new and unique for *The Dark Knight*. "We challenge ourselves every time we work on a Chris Nolan film," Kroll said, "because he challenges us. The expectation is always that we're going to do something more wonderful and exciting than what we've done before. Our goal is to produce a campaign that lives up to the quality of the film and is an extension of the film."

Ideas for what would become *The Dark Knight*'s unprecedented viral marketing campaign emerged in conversations between writer Jonathan Nolan and coproducer Jordan Goldberg. "Jonah and I were trying to figure out ways to event-ize the film when it came out," recalled Goldberg. "And we knew that the Joker was going to be a big pull. In fact, I remember watching *Batman Begins* and the audience audibly gasping when that joker card was pulled out at the end. So the question was, how do we take advantage of that? At that point, the Internet was starting to become much more interactive, and Jonah and I both respected the viral campaigns that had already been done. So, we found a company that was doing those types of campaigns—42

PAGE 288: Marketing for Christopher Nolan's new take on the Batman franchise drew upon the director's unique vision for the origin story, as shown in this poster for *Batman Begins.*

OPPOSITE: Early teasers and poster designs were pitched against iconic images of the super hero, as shown in these composites—none of which ended up being used by the studio, with the exception of the larger image (upper right).

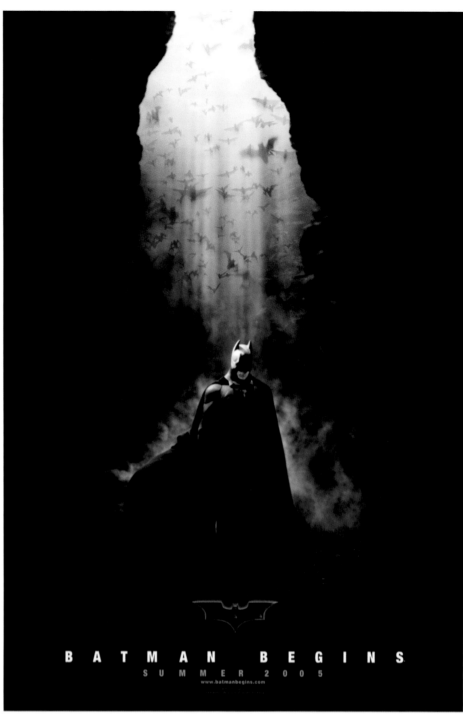

Entertainment—and we worked with them to come up with a lot of fun things to get the word out."

The timing offered some interesting possibilities: Dent's cinematic run for Gotham district attorney coincided with the 2008 presidential race. Americans were primed for politics, and Harvey Dent fit right in.

In May 2007, the viral campaign was launched with friendsofharveydent.org, a website touting the virtues of the handsome politico, which included endorsements from Gotham's finest and a slogan pulled straight from the film: "I Believe in Harvey Dent." Additional sites would follow in the months to come, including the Joker's whysoserious.

com, a *Gotham Times* website—thegothamtimes.com—and a Joker-generated rejoinder, thehahahatimes.com.

"It was fun to let the fans take part in the marketing of the film and allow them to become the soldiers and the messengers of that marketing," said Goldberg. "We are lucky enough to have a lot of fan love, and sometimes an incredible level of creativity comes with it. If you can tap into that, it's exciting."

San Diego's Comic-Con International, in July, was a key marketing event. "Comic-Con was the real beginning of our viral campaign," noted Goldberg. "In addition to the teaser trailer, we had the Joker amassing his army of Joker stars

OPPOSITE: This poster for *The Dark Knight*—with its burning bat symbol—reflected the colors, lines, and energy of Batman's new Gotham.

ABOVE: The unprecedented viral campaign built around *The Dark Knight* was based, in part, on the conflicts arising in the Harvey Dent and Joker story lines, and drew heavily on exciting new trends in social media and Internet usage, as evidenced by this page from the *Gotham Times* website, right.

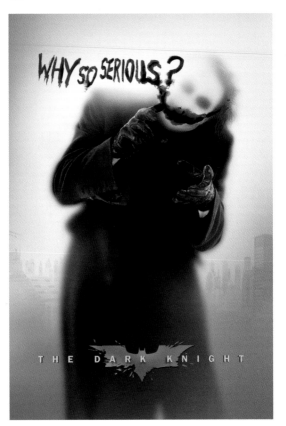

Marketing strategies for *The Dark Knight* were inspired, in large measure, by Heath Ledger's singular take on the Joker, as shown in the poster art above, but images were also developed to reflect the film's modernist design shift—and Christopher Nolan's conceptual departure from *Batman Begins*.

at Comic-Con. We gave out Joker masks, and people were running around town in them."

Intrinsic to the Comic-Con launch was the scavenger hunt that kicked off the campaign. Throughout the convention, altered one-dollar bills revealing George Washington in lipstick and with blackened eyes had been distributed to fans, which, in turn, led them to the "Why So Serious" website address—and a recruitment page for Joker henchmen. Attendees were also directed via the website to gather at a specified time and place, where—wearing full Joker makeup—they were rewarded with a phone number written in the sky that set the hunt in full motion throughout the city. Finally, after solving all clues, one lucky fan was rewarded by being "apprehended" by a Warner Bros. publicity team in place of the real Joker. "The idea of really engaging these fans in new and interesting ways was very, very important to the filmmakers," noted Kroll. "We never explicitly publicized any of the key parts of the viral campaign, but the fans were led to discover these websites and events, and it really increased their personal involvement in the marketing."

The Comic-Con launch fed into the larger campaign, which was built, to a considerable degree, around Heath Ledger's singular take on the villain. With posters bearing the Joker's scarred face and the ironic "Why So Serious?" tagline, Ledger's visage became as integral to *The Dark Knight*'s marketing campaign as it would to the film itself.

The marketing team ramped up the "I Believe in Harvey Dent" campaign, as well, which had campaign "volunteers" driving around cities throughout the United States, handing out Harvey Dent pins and T-shirts, as if the handsome Dent were actually running for public office.

"We also printed hard copies of the *Gotham Times* and put them in various locations," said Sue Kroll, "including comic book stores. All of this turned the marketing for the film into a game that brought fans in to play along with us—while investing them in the different characters and story lines. People started writing about it, and it really got into the vernacular of the culture."

The studio rolled out Christopher Nolan's much-anticipated IMAX bank heist prologue as planned—in

Maggie Gyllenhaal and Christian Bale at the Warner Bros. Pictures premiere of *The Dark Knight*. (Photos by Bryan Bedder, courtesy of Getty Images Entertainment.)

December 2007. The nearly six-minute reel declared Nolan's intentions for *The Dark Knight* and introduced Heath Ledger's Joker for the first time.

Following the December release of the Joker-centric prologue, the multilayered campaign fell into a deliberately timed lull as Kroll and the marketing department geared up for the next Harvey Dent/Joker–inspired wave.

And then, on January 22, 2008, Heath Ledger died unexpectedly, leaving his family, friends, and fans in shock and devastation. As Christopher Nolan and *The Dark Knight*'s cast and crew struggled to come to terms with Ledger's passing, Warner Bros. respectfully put its marketing decisions on hold.

"Heath's death transpired during this quiet period in the campaign," said Kroll, "which gave us some time to process his loss and think about what to do next. The first thing we did was consult with his family and walk them through our future plans. As we worked together, we concluded that it was right to proceed with the campaign as planned because Heath was such a huge part of the movie."

The marketing team reinitiated the campaign, with the blessing and cooperation of Ledger's family. "We made very few changes to the original marketing campaign," explained Kroll. "We didn't pull anything back, but we didn't add anything, either—and we were very, very careful not to put anything out there that was unplanned. By the time the campaign kicked back in, it was as it had been originally."

With his courageous interpretation of the Joker—a man hell-bent on watching the world burn—Heath Ledger had made an indelible mark on The Dark Knight Trilogy. Little more than a year after his death, the actor was posthumously honored with the 2008 Academy Award for Best Supporting Actor, accepted on his behalf by his father, mother, and sister.

The marketing campaign for *The Dark Knight Rises* started more than a year before the film's release, with Twitter feeds leading fans to a website where Bane's image was unveiled. "We wanted to have an image out there before anything leaked so we could present it in the right way," Sue Kroll explained. "That became a trending topic, number three worldwide. It was wildly successful."

An announcement trailer soon followed, screened with the final Harry Potter film, *Harry Potter and the Deathly Hallows: Part 2*. "We had a teaser image and teaser poster," said Kroll. "It was very spare, just teasing the events to come, but it was very, very exciting. And then, in December, we released our second poster on the website, an image of Bane and Batman's broken cowl with the tag: 'The Legend Ends.'

We wanted to position *The Dark Knight Rises* as the epic conclusion to the trilogy, to the legend of the Dark Knight." The film's first full-length trailer also launched in December, playing with Robert Downey Jr. and Jude Law's second Baker Street outing, *Sherlock Holmes: A Game of Shadows*.

The most significant marketing gambit of that holiday season, however, was the screening of *The Dark Knight Rises*'s aerial prologue sequence with Tom Cruise's *Mission: Impossible—Ghost Protocol* at select IMAX theatres.

"We employed the same strategy that we had for *The Dark Knight*," said Kroll, "introducing audiences to the film's main villain, Bane, through this six-minute-long prologue, shown on IMAX screens. And then we had a new, regular trailer that went out everywhere else."

The marketing campaign for *The Dark Knight Rises* gained traction throughout the winter of 2012, and interviews with Christopher Nolan and the film's cast began to appear in newspapers, magazines, and online, whetting audience appetites for what the imaginative writer-director had wrought for The Dark Knight Trilogy's denouement.

Mostly, fans were eager to see what had become of Batman in the years since the poignant final moments of *The Dark Knight*, in which—for the good of Gotham—he had taken the fall for Harvey Dent's crimes and gone from hero to villain, chased by Gotham police as he rode out into a dark night.

Graphics for *The Dark Knight Rises* drew upon the immediately familiar bat image used for the first two films—while signaling that something completely different was in store.

SUMMER 2012
IN THEATERS AND **IMAX**
WWW.**THEDARKKNIGHTRISES**.COM

CHRISTIAN **BALE** MICHAEL **CAINE** GARY **OLDMAN** ANNE **HATHAWAY** TOM **HARDY** MARION **COTILLARD** JOSEPH **GORDON-LEVITT** AND MORGAN **FREEMAN**

A FIRE WILL RISE

A FILM BY CHRISTOPHER NOLAN

THE DARK KNIGHT RISES

THE LEGEND ENDS
JULY 20
EXPERIENCE IT IN IMAX

THEDARKKNIGHTRISES.COM

"Marketing is all about creating cultural icons," Sue Kroll concluded. "And these properties, especially, have played a huge role in people's lives, beyond just going to the movies. Batman really is in the vernacular of the culture. And these campaigns feel very different. They last and they sustain. They stand up to the test of time, and are just as vivid years later as they were when they were conceived. That's important, I think—because so many campaigns for so many films are forgettable and very much of the moment.

"These campaigns aspire to do much more. Fans, obviously, are more involved and obsessed with them, but even the average moviegoer remembers them. People still talk about the Joker teaser campaign. It just sizzled into people's minds because it was so iconic and unusual—and that's what I hope happens with the marketing for *The Dark*

Knight Rises. We're signaling that something *very* different is about to happen."

Nothing dreamed up by the marketing teams, no matter how innovative and exciting, did more to promote The Dark Knight Trilogy than the films themselves, each of which generated intense audience enthusiasm and critical acclaim. "When a director delivers something unique and fresh," noted Jeff Robinov, "that gives you a *big* jump on the marketing campaign. What Chris delivers is always unique and fresh. And once he realized his vision, he was supported in how and where it was placed in the marketplace. It may sound arrogant to say, but Warner Bros. has the best marketing person in town with Sue Kroll, and the best distribution group—and because of that, the odds of success for a movie are greater at Warner Bros. than they are at any other studio."

OPPOSITE: This poster for *The Dark Knight Rises*, introduced in spring 2012, effectively incorporates the same "burning bat" imagery used throughout The Dark Knight Trilogy— while making a distinct visual impression all its own.

ABOVE: The marketing campaign for *The Dark Knight Rises* was launched more than a year before the film's release, with Twitter feeds leading fans to a website where this simple image of Bane was unveiled.

By June, *The Dark Knight Rises* was ready for distribution to thousands of screens for its release on July 20, 2012. With the completion of the movie, Christopher Nolan and his close-knit filmmaking family brought to a close a creative odyssey that had started nine years before—and there would be no going back.

While filmmakers typically leave doors ajar by adopting a never-say-never attitude toward future projects, Nolan was unequivocal in his assertion that he would not be making another Batman film. He had said what he wanted to say and done what he wanted to do in the world of Batman, and through the experience, he grew and changed as a filmmaker.

"You learn a lot on every film," Nolan reflected. "*Batman Begins* taught me a huge amount about how to express the *feeling* of an emotional story to an audience in a mainstream way—all kinds of very specific things having to do with reaction shots of characters and the way you balance the pyrotechnics and the action with the human face of whatever story it is you're telling. I was quite lucky on *Batman Begins*, really, because I didn't know those things when I shot it, but I had enough material so that when we got into the edits, which is where I really began to learn these things, I had enough to draw on to make the film work.

"By the time I got to *The Dark Knight Rises*, I was able to go into it knowing what I needed to shoot to make the story emotionally accessible to the audience. That's something that I've learned over the three films, and it's been a very valuable lesson. It's not something you can figure out just through screenwriting or through the technical side of filmmaking. It's something you can only really learn through experience."

For Nolan and all of those involved in the making of The Dark Knight Trilogy the experience gained in Batman's world had been profound—and all said their good-byes to that world with a tremendous sense of pride and accomplishment, but also with some regret.

"It's definitely a bittersweet thing," said Emma Thomas. "We've had a great experience making these movies, and I wouldn't change anything about it. I'm happy that we have finished the story that we started with the first movie, and very happy to go onto something new. But at the same time, there is a poignancy about its being over, especially given that we worked with such an amazing group of people on all three movies."

At a December 2011 Universal City event in which the completed prologue sequence was screened for members of the press, Nolan—a reserved, self-contained man—spoke to a *Los Angeles Times* reporter about his Batman adventure nearing its end. "I tend not to be too emotional on the set," Nolan said. "I find that doesn't help me do my job. But you definitely get a little lump in your throat thinking that, 'Okay, this is going to be the last time we're going to be doing this.' It was emotional as we would finish these characters and say good-bye to Alfred for the last time and say good-bye to Commissioner Gordon, and eventually with Christian, fairly close to the end, say good-bye to Batman. It was a big deal. It's been quite a journey."

Later that same month, Nolan sat with a writer at his home, just a few feet from the garage where that journey had started almost a decade earlier. As he reflected on those years, Nolan seemed, more than anything else, grateful for the experience, and even humbled by it—as if the characters and iconography of Batman's world were family treasures that had been passed to him, a mere stranger, for safekeeping... but only for a time.

It was a sentiment he'd expressed eloquently in that earlier interview for the *Los Angeles Times*:

"I'd love to be able to claim that I invented the whole thing," he said, "but I did not. I was just given a very precious thing to do my best with and look after. And that has been a great privilege."